BAAZ

Anuja Chauhan was an army brat, born in Meerut Cantonment and educated in Meerut, Delhi and Melbourne. She has worked in advertising for over seventeen years and is credited with many popular campaigns including PepsiCo's *Yeh Dil Maange More, Mera Number Kab Aayega, Oye Bubbly* and *Darr ke Aage Jeet Hai*. She is the author of four bestselling novels (*The Zoya Factor, Battle for Bittora, Those Pricey Thakur Girls, The House That BJ Built*), two of which have been optioned by major Bollywood studios and one of which has been made into a prime-time daily Hindi serial on &TV. She lives outside Bangalore with her husband, television producer Niret Alva, their three children and a varying number of dogs and cats.

D0639510

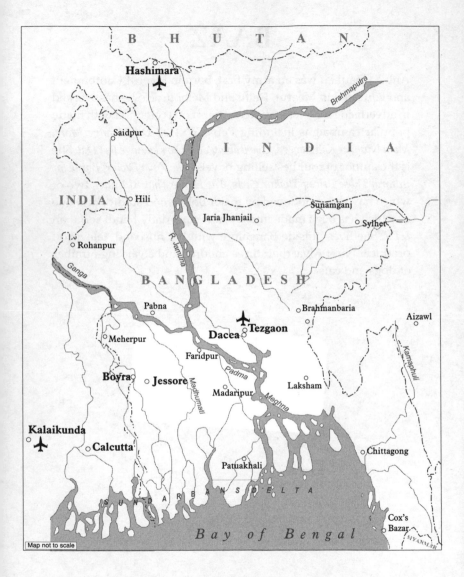

BAAZ
ANUJA CHAUHAN

HarperCollins *Publishers* India

First published in India in 2017 by
HarperCollins *Publishers* India

Copyright © Anuja Chauhan 2017

P-ISBN: 9789352644124
E-ISBN: 9789352644131

2 4 6 8 10 9 7 5 3 1

Anuja Chauhan asserts the moral right to be identified
as the author of this work.

HarperCollins *Publishers*

A-75, Sector 57, Noida, Uttar Pradesh 201301, India
1 London Bridge Street, London, SE1 9GF, United Kingdom
Hazelton Lanes, 55 Avenue Road, Suite 2900, Toronto, Ontario M5R 3L2
and 1995 Markham Road, Scarborough, Ontario M1B 5M8, Canada
25 Ryde Road, Pymble, Sydney, NSW 2073, Australia
195 Broadway, New York, NY 10007, USA

Typeset in 10/13 Palatino Linotype at
SÜRYA, New Delhi

Printed and bound at
Thomson Press (India) Ltd

Jai Jawaan
Jai Kisaan

ONE

Ishaan starts baiting the trains when he is ten. They steam past on a line about a twenty-minute walk from his stepfather's small, crumbly pista-green haveli in Chakkahera, and whenever the embittered man starts turning on his children to vent his many frustrations, the skinny boy, small for his age, backs quietly out of the aangan, slips on his too-large Bata chappals and makes for the train tracks, defiantly humming a jaunty tune.

The Republic of India is but ten years old, and Chakkahera is just a large village in Punjab province, named for its many tyre factories – smoke-spewing monstrosities that drown out the sweet rural scents of harshringaar, dung fires and mustard flowers with the aggressive smell of burning rubber.

Well accustomed to this odour, the boy emerges from a muddy lane, trots past the ancient banyan tree and the unblinking, wallowing buffaloes in the village pond, takes a sharp left at the government school and plunges into the fields of sarson.

A brisk run through the cool green fronds, heavy with ripening mustard, and he is at a rocky cliff. Looking down, he can see the vast vista of countryside below – rolling earth, white sky, blue hills – all just a pale backdrop for the main attraction, a set of gleaming, parallel steel tracks snaking across the broad bosom of India, linking Dilli to Kalkatta.

Not even a little out of breath, he picks his way down to the tracks and squats beside them, one hand on the cool steel, waiting for it to start humming. The humming begins a good ten minutes before the train arrives. It is followed by strong vibrations, a queer rushing noise and the sound of a whistle blowing, and then the train turns the corner, a pulsating iron monster, the fastest, most powerful thing in the child's universe, hurtling towards him with all it's got – huge, indestructible, unstoppable.

Ishaan leaps up to straddle the tracks, arms thrown out to keep his balance, body tense as a drawn bow, heart thudding faster and faster, pupils dilating, muscles contracting, concentration pinpointing onto just one thing – the massive iron face of the engine rushing at him.

He is standing there one afternoon, cotton shirt billowing in the wind, heart pumping like a piston, when he is jerked roughly off the steel blades and thrown onto the side of the tracks.

As the train khata-khats by at eardrum-popping speed, Ishaan looks up to see a wizened, bald figure – the wind from the rushing train has wrenched the pagdi away – staring down at him. Its gold earrings are gleaming, its eyes are red, its face slick with sweat. It is nanaji, father of his dead mother.

'Baawda hai ke, Shaanu!'

'I jump off as soon as I can read Bhaartiye Rail,' Shaanu

explains immediately, not wanting to be mistaken for some pathetic, suicidal nutcase.

The old man rolls his eyes, a scary sight.

'You've made a habit of this!'

Shaanu scrambles to his feet, shrugging.

'Sort of.'

Then he smiles. It is a heart-stoppingly beautiful smile, lighting up his curiously slate-grey eyes and scrunching up his straight, even features. 'It's fun.'

The old man stares at him for a moment, still breathing hard, then turns away to spit. After sending an impressive gob of phlegm shooting through the air in a graceful arc, he curses long and thoroughly, grabs the boy by the collar of his shirt, shakes him till his bones rattle, then lets him drop.

Bending to retrieve his pagdi, he jams it back on his head and grunts, 'Walk!'

They make their way up from the tracks to the mustard fields atop the cliff, the young boy moving lithely, the old man stumping behind him on his lathia, breathing laboriously.

'Who told you?' Shaanu asks after a while. 'About me and the trains, I mean.'

'Goatherds,' comes the old man's brusque reply. 'First they thought you were just coming out here to do your morning job, but then they realized you'd gone stark raving mad. So they came to me and said, your grandson's mad, poora baawda, pack him off to the paagal-khana in Agra.'

'I'm not mad,' Shaanu replies indignantly.

'No?' says the old man. 'Have you thought about how your brothers and sisters would feel if you got squashed by a maal gaadi like a dog tick beneath a camel's foot?'

'Dog ticks don't squash that easy,' the boy tells him

knowledgeably. 'They just pull in their legs and pretend to be dead – and once you think they're done for, they quickly crawl off again.'

This remark earns him another whack on the side of his head. He takes it stolidly, not even bothering to duck, and says, in a more placatory voice, 'Everybody would feel bad if I died, of course. They all love me best. But I won't die. I'm too fast. I whip my body sideways *just* before the train hits me – *sataaack!* like *this*—'

'*Enough!*' thunders nanaji.

And this time, the fury in his voice moves the boy to silence.

They march through the sarson for a time, then the old man asks, in a calmer, more conversational voice, 'Kyon, chhore?'

'Hmm?'

Nanaji tchs impatiently.

'Why do you do it?'

Shaanu looks up, grey eyes sparkling.

'I like the feeling of my heart going *dhookk-dhookk-dhoookk*,' he confides.

This artless revelation makes the old man lunge forward to slap him again, but the boy skips out of reach, laughing.

Nanaji grunts, stumps along silently, then asks, 'What else makes that happen?'

Shaanu frowns, thinking, sliding his thumbs into the waistband of his worn cotton pyjamas. 'Sometimes on Diwali, when I'm lighting a very big bomb?' he offers. 'That's pretty dhookk-dhookk-dhookky. Because the rich kids, they can *afford* the big bombs all right, but they don't have the guts to light them, ne? So they make me do it.'

'Rich boys, eh?' his grandfather says. 'You're rich too.

Your family owns fifty acres of very fertile land. I should know, I gifted thirty of it to your stepfather as your mother's dowry.'

'Yeah, but Chimman is so stingy.'

'Don't call your stepfather by his name!'

Shaanu shrugs disdainfully.

'*Pitaji* is so stingy, then. Anyway, I like lighting patakas. And long-jumping over the wells is fun too.'

'Long-jumping over the *wells*?'

'Yeah. Some of the big ones don't have any wall around them, ne, just a wooden cover. So you take off the cover, take a running start and *whooomp*, you long-jump over the open well!'

He gets a sharp crack across the back of his head.

'Idiot!' grunts nanaji. 'Fool! Son of a fool!'

Shaanu draws himself to his full height and squares his skinny shoulders.

'Ay nana, don't call my father a fool!'

'Nana*ji* to you, miserable rat!'

Shaanu tucks his hand placatingly into his irate grandparent's.

'The *reason* I do it,' he confesses finally, 'is because I like to be happy. And Chimman Si—*pitaji* toh, you know, he's always pulling a long face and grumbling about something. When I do these things, I can tune his voice out.'

The old man absorbs this for a while, thinking long, dark thoughts of his own.

'*Never* do dangerous things except for a very, very good reason!' he says at last. 'Do them only when there's something worthwhile at stake.'

'What's worthwhile?'

The old man tilts back his head and thinks some more.

'Eiiiii … saving some bosomy chhori's honour from bad people,' he hazards. 'Like a fillum-ka-hero, you know? But if there's no chhori, why take risks, ne?'

The boy looks at him like he's a moron. 'If I don't practise taking risks when there's no chhori, how will I be able to save the chhori when the time comes?'

'That is also true,' the old man admits.

They walk on in silence, until the drone of a plane flying past causes their eyes to turn skyward.

'You know what you should do?' nanaji says, suddenly inspired. 'You should learn to fly one of *those*! They will make your heart race like nobody's business!'

Shaanu stares up at a sky the colour of his eyes, watching the plane threading through the clouds like a flashing silver needle.

'Can *anybody* fly them?'

'Only very brave lads,' says nanaji cunningly. 'And clever ones, the ones who do well in school. And they do it not just for bloody dhookk-dhookk-dhookk, but to defend Mother India.'

'Like my father.'

'Er, yes! Like your father. Ah, there is no higher honour! You get a smart uniform – tight-fitting, city-tailored, with shiny buttons made of solid, twenty-four-carat – and you get into one of those pilanes and *vrrrroooooooom*, you're the king of the world!'

Shaanu savours this wonderful image.

'Twenty-four-carat gold?'

'Then what!'

'And *every time* you fly your heart beats superfast?'

'Every single time,' swears the old man. 'It's the fastest thudding ever. Except when you meet your real, true love, of course. *That* is even faster. The fastest.'

Shaanu's clear grey eyes turn to his. 'Do girls like pilane drivers?' he enquires.

'They're called pie-lutts,' says his grandfather. 'And girls love 'em! Can't get enough of them! They're always following them around, trying to unbutton their shirts...'

'To steal their buttons?'

'To make love to them!'

The boy is quiet for a moment.

'Even if they're not very tall?'

It is the old man's turn to fall silent now. Then he bends, a painful thing for his arthritic joints to have to do.

'Dekh, Shaanu,' he says, his voice a rough caress. 'You're only ten. I don't know yet whether you'll grow up to be tall or short...'

'I'm the shortest kid in my class.'

'Well, in that case, I'll let you in on a big secret. It's a God secret, actually – an *enjuneering* secret – one of the main geometrical principles on which human beings are designed.'

Shaanu leans in.

Nanaji whispers into his ear, at the same time moving his hand in a very specific gesture.

Shaanu's eyes grow huge. He holds up his hand and repeats the gesture several times, his grey eyes sparkling brighter with every repetition. Then he throws back his head and lets out a crow of laughter, a whooping, joyous sound that echoes through the rolling mustard fields and merges with the drone of the plane still flying overhead.

• • •

'Where's Shaanu?' Choudhary Chimman Singh Faujdaar demands ten years later. 'Shaanu kitt se?'

His ruddy-cheeked, round-eyed band of children stare back at him disingenuously.

'Shaanu bhaiyya?'

'Just now he was here.'

'Must be guarding the fields.'

'Or studying.'

'Or praying.'

'Chuppp karo sab ke sab!' snarls Chimman Singh, his livid face twitching with suspicion. 'I haven't seen the fellow since last night. I know he's up to something! What?'

This is met with silence and some scuffling. Finally Sneha, the eldest of the girls, shakes back her heavy plait and puts down her mending. 'Should I make you a cup of tea, pitaji?'

The Choudhary's gaze softens and he pulls on his hookah. Daughters. So much better than sons. Sweet and loving and biddable, they light up the house and make it comfortable – unlike sons, who challenge your authority, defy you and disappoint you, have a huge sense of entitlement and make you feel old.

Unfortunately, Sneha is getting married next month.

'Yes, I'll have tea,' he says politely. 'And a lice of cake.'

'Si-lice,' giggles Sulochana.

The Choudhary smiles a tolerant, toothy smile.

'Silice,' he says amiably. Then his voice grows sharp again. 'But where *is* Shaanu?'

Shaanu, as the entire Faujdaar brat-pack knows, has borrowed a cycle and pedalled off early this morning for Bengali Market – which is in New Delhi – which is eighty-five whole kilometres away. There has been no news of him since.

The five of them immediately swing into action. Sneha brings her father tea and cake, Sulo and Sari, the two little girls, start to squabble over the severed arm of a plastic doll, pulling each other's plaits. Surinder, the brains of the family, with aspirations of being a doctor, asks his father if he knows that the average human intestine is fifteen kilometres long, and Shelly, the youngest boy, turns up the volume on the leather-covered radio to the maximum.

Chimman Singh sips his tea and ruminates, not for the first time, on the unfairness of the cosmos.

It is unfair that he was forced into marriage with a skinny, pregnant widow by his bully of a father when he was barely sixteen. He'd just started frequenting the kothas then and had fantasies of travelling to the big cities, landing a big job in a mill or factory and marrying a well-endowed city mem. He'd wept bitterly on his wedding day, the kajal they'd put in his eyes running down to merge with his chapped, dark brown cheeks, but there had been no escaping the nuptials. The widow brought with her thirty acres of land to sweeten the deal, and his father, in the age-old tradition of zamindar fathers everywhere, had threatened to cut him off without a penny if he defied him, and that, of course, had been that.

It was unfair that after they had lived together in mutual discontent for several years, the widow (he'd continued to think of her as such, even though she'd come to him clad in red and borne him four children) had upped and died, leaving him to bring up a brood of pesky brats alone, when all he wanted to do was celebrate his newly single status by sleeping with as many sturdy chamari women as possible.

And the height of unfairness was that the eldest of these brats was the light-skinned, grey-eyed Ishaan (a new-fangled name the widow had chosen out of some wretched book or the other). Mother and son had shared a bond that had always made Chimman Singh feel excluded. They were both fair-complexioned, read books and laughed – all three were things he couldn't aspire to. And it didn't help that the younger children hero-worshipped Shaanu.

When Shaanu was thirteen he got behind the wheel of the family tractor and flattened half the wheat crop. When he was fourteen he helped a high-caste boy elope with an untouchable girl. At fifteen, the school masterni got obsessed with him, much to the embarrassment of her husband and teenaged children. At sixteen, when Chimman Singh was beating him with a leather belt for daring to spray himself with Chimman's much-prized bottle of scent, he wrested the belt from his stepfather's grasp with a throaty roar and glared at him with such anger that Chimman spat on the ground, cursed and walked away. They have maintained a wary distance since.

The Choudhary pulls on his hookah and works himself into a state of righteous indignation. There's the arhar standing ripe in the fields, needing constant rakhwaali, and the kanji-eyed cuckoo has left its nest and gone off gallivanting somewhere! The Choudhary's best white shirt is missing too! Hundred per cent, he thinks as he pulls at his hookah agitatedly, our fine fellow has started frequenting the kothas in Tanki Bazaar.

'Bachhaaaa paaaarty! Where are you?'

Startled, the Choudhary swallows smoke the wrong way and starts to cough, even as the double doors of the haveli are thrown open with a flourish to reveal Shaanu Faujdaar framed in the door, grey eyes blazing with excitement, every clean line of his lean muscular body radiating triumph.

'I'm in,' he says, his low, vibrant voice trembling. 'I've been selected! I took the written tests and I passed the physical and…' He pauses, looks around the courtyard and finishes in a hushed, proud whisper, 'I'm going to the Air Force Flying College in Jodhpur!'

All the children immediately set up a roar.

Sneha gets to her feet with a gasp and runs across the aangan to throw her arms around him. *'Shaanu Bhaisaab! What great news!'*

'I know,' he replies simply, receiving her full weight upon his breast without staggering even a little. 'It's my dream come true.'

She laughs and places a smacking kiss on his cheek. Shaanu twinkles.

'Learn to kiss properly, Sneha behenji,' he tells her gravely. 'If you make such a loud, dehati *puuchh!* sound your husband will disown you!'

'They didn't mind about your height, then?' Sari wants to know.

'No, Sari behenji!' Shaanu's cocky grin blooms. 'They said it didn't matter, that I'd fit into the fighter planes better!'

'They'll pay for everything then, Shaanu bau?' Surinder asks excitedly. 'Your fees, the uniform, food – sab kuch?'

Shaanu nods. 'Everything, Surinder bau!' he says proudly. 'They said not to worry about anything, you're a sarkar-ka-damad now – a pampered son-in-law of Bharat Mata!'

Shelly cackles gleefully and leaps onto a moodha.

'Bhaaaarat Mataaaa kiiii…'

'Jai!' chorus the others as they rush to hug Shaanu. He buckles a little under their collective weight, but manages to stay standing, laughing, and dashing the sudden wetness from his eyes.

'Bharat Mata kiiii…'

'Jai!'

Surrounded by his siblings, Ishaan looks towards his stepfather, a question and hope burning bright in his eyes, but the older man just mutters something incoherent and looks away, knocking the ash out of his earthenware pipe. The bright hope dims, then dies.

'*Bharat Mata kiiii...*' chorus the kids.

'*Jai!*' says Ishaan, just a little resignedly.

• • •

'First, you stuff your nose down, Baaz-ke-maaphik! Then you swoop down, Baaz-ke-maaphik! Then you pull back and open the throttle wide, all the way till you're on your back, if you have the guts, Baaz-ke-maaphik!' Instructor Hosannah Carvalho pauses, panting, his black eyes glittering like manic torches in his dark face. '*Unnurstand?*'

The newly recruited class of the Air Force Flying College Jodhpur nods back at him, hypnotized.

With a satisfied grunt, the basic flying manoeuvres instructor wheels around to the board and continues his graphic, fast-paced and extremely bloodthirsty lecture.

'Aggression and awareness are the keywords to being a good Fighter. *Never* let your guard down! Baaz-ke-maaphik, you shoot up, up, up! Baaz-ke-maaphik, you keenly take stock of your surroundings. Baaz-ke-maaphik, you plan your route home...'

'Raka, my man,' Madan Subbiah drawls cautiously out of the corner of his mouth. 'What is Baazky-Maafee?'

'Like-a-Baaz,' Rakesh Aggarwal provides in a muted mutter.

'And a Baaz is...?' Madan wants to know.

'A hawk, Maddy. Or maybe a falcon. A murderous bird, basically.'

'A *bird?*' Maddy looks confused. 'Why the hell do we call it a dogfight, then?'

Pacing like an undernourished hound in the front of the room, Carvalho holds forth for a good forty-five minutes, then pulls to an abrupt halt at ten a.m. sharp.

'Dismissed,' he roars. 'Practicals by the poolside in twenty minutes.'

Saying which, he heads out of the room like a bullet, clearly thirsting for his ten o'clock mug of over-boiled, extra-sweet tea.

The boys pack up their books and make their way to the sprawling, sunlit grounds outside. These are early days for the class of '68; friendships, factions and pecking orders are still being worked out, but certainly, the cadets who've made it here after spending three years at the National Defence Academy, Khadakwasla, have an edge over the lads who have qualified through the direct entrance exam after graduating from 'civilian' colleges.

Maddy and Raka are part of the elite NDA corps. Both over six feet tall, athletic and good-natured, they seem poised to be crowned the coolest cadets in the batch.

The title would not be altogether undeserved. A lanky brown twenty-one-year-old with a charming smile and dark dreamy eyes, Madan Subbiah is a third-generation Forces kid with three retired generals in his family, who has had tales of valour read to him like fairy tales every night. Most of the instructors here know his father or grandfather. He comes from old money, is very anglicized and is a gifted musician. He loves to party and is happy to pay for everybody. Unlike Rakesh Aggarwal. Fair, curly moustachioed and apple-cheeked, Raka is fast with figures and physics but tight-fisted with money. His devout, vegetarian Baniya family owns a chain of mithai shops spread all over Delhi. Though Maddy would have preferred to wear his hair in a tousled mop to enhance his resemblance to Pat Boone and Raka to strut around in a slick Elvis puff, they both sport the regulation crew-cut, like everyone else.

Sauntering along at the rear of the scrum, as befitting their hip personas, the two friends head for the swimming baths behind the tree-lined parade ground. Today their mood is decidedly ambivalent. While swimming is a sport they both enjoy, their seniors spent all of last evening psyching them about what is to happen in class today.

'It's the leap of death, kiddos. Kiss your girlfriends goodbye and tell ammi you love her.'

'Scarier than skydiving, because there's no parachute.'

'That pool is tiny. There was this guy back in '59 who actually landed on the tiles and splattered like an omelette. The IAF hushed it up.'

The sound of water slapping against tiled walls comes to them now, along with the sharp reek of chlorine. They turn the corner, and there it is, an Olympic-sized pool and, squatting above it like a fantastic iron spider, a maze of metal stairs zig-zagging up to four diving boards – three feet high, ten feet high, twenty feet high and, finally, forty feet high.

'Mummy,' whispers Maddy.

'Jai Mata di,' mutters Raka.

'The steps are designed for climbing up, not coming down,' their seniors have told them. 'You'll trip if you try to walk back down. Once you're there, you've just gotta jump.'

As they line up along the pool, Carvalho makes his reappearance, clearly invigorated by his tea break.

'Volunteers!' he roars.

Raka and Maddy, their expressions wooden, carefully avert their gaze from Carvalho's bulging orbs to stare fixedly at a spot behind his head. So does the rest of the batch.

Carvalho smirks and starts to pace up and down the line, sniffing (Maddy thinks fancifully) for fear.

He stops a few times and stares at particular cadets,

only to move on again. Finally, he places his hand on one uniformed shoulder, caressing it tenderly.

'You,' he purrs. 'You're the volunteer.'

A palpable sigh of relief ripples through the line of cadets even as all eyeballs swivel surreptitiously to check out the chosen bakra.

A smaller lad, this, than most of the others, but lean and well proportioned. As he raises his chin, his expression calm, he is seen to have clean-cut fair features, a square jaw, spiky, shiny black hair and unusual grey eyes. He seems serene, cocky even, practically grinning back at Carvalho.

'What's your name, cadet?' Carvalho barks.

The 'volunteer' snaps to attention.

'Ishaan Faujdaar, *sir*!'

'Where're you from?'

'Chakkahera, *sir*!'

Carvalho smirks.

'Where?'

The cadet bellows even louder.

'Chakkahera, sir!'

'Has *anybody* here heard of this ... Chakka-hera?' He stretches the name out mockingly.

'*No, sir!*' the class shouts back.

The volunteer's face flushes.

'It's in Haryana, sir! The new state just created out of Punjab, sir!'

Carvalho's voice drops to a whisper.

'I am well aware of Haryana. Only a fool would take me for a fool. Are you a fool, cadet?'

'No, sir! I'm a Jat, sir!'

Laughter, hastily smothered, from the rest of the class. Carvalho's gaze grows baleful.

'Do they have beaches in Chakkahera, cadet?'

'No, sir!'

'Or rivers?'

'No, sir!'

'Learnt to swim in a buffalo pond, did you?'

Stifled giggles from the crowd. The Jat boy's fair features flush slightly, but his expression remains unchanged.

'Sir!'

Carvalho's hound-like eyes gleam. He cracks a dark grin. 'The purpose of today's class,' he roars, 'is for you to face your fear of heights.'

'Every time he's about to shout, he breathes in so hard his pants get sucked into his ass,' whispers Maddy. 'Look. He'll give himself a bloody heart attack if he isn't careful.'

'You may *think* you have no fear of heights,' Carvalho continues, 'but when you're diving downwards, the sight of the ground rushing up at you can be paralyzing. Even scarier if you have to bail out at, say, 40,000 feet!'

He lays a hand on the volunteer's shoulder. 'Strip down to your trunks, cadet,' he purrs. 'Or no, on second thoughts, keep your clothes on. Then climb up to the highest board, take a running start and jump.'

'Into the water,' Raka clarifies with a snicker, in a louder aside than he'd intended. 'You've got to explain things out clearly to Jats.'

Carvalho's gaze grows malevolent.

'Yes, into the water – and as you're being so helpful, Aggarwal, you can go before him and show him how it's done. You too, Subbiah. You've both been talking so much today, a long jump will cool you off. Aggarwal first, then Subbiah, and you – Jat from Chakkahera – you go last.'

'*Great*,' Maddy mutters.

'Reach the top in three minutes!' Carvalho bellows. 'Or patti parades all around! And jump on my whistle. Move, move, *move!*'

And so the three young men make their way up the long zig-zagging metal ladder to the top of the diving board. As their batchmates grow smaller and smaller below them and the pool shrinks to the size of a twelve-by-twenty-four-inch bathroom tile, Raka says aggrievedly to the Chakkahera boy at the end of their little line, 'Stop pushing, shorty, what's your rush? Can't wait to hurl yourself from the top and end it all?'

'The name's Shaanu,' says the Jat good-naturedly. His English is halting, and his voice, now that he's not shouting back responses to the manic Carvalho, is pleasant and curiously vibrant. 'Shaanu Faujdaar.'

'So now we know what to write in your obituary,' comes Raka's disgruntled reply. 'My name's Aggarwal.'

'Yeah, I heard.' Faujdaar pats him on the back sympathetically. 'Don't be ashamed of being afraid. Baniyas aren't bred to be brave.'

'What the hell!' Raka splutters.

'And what are you?' Shaanu addresses Maddy.

'I'm Maddy.'

Shaanu nods amiably. 'Caste, I mean.'

'Why're you so obsessed with caste, buster?' Maddy asks mildly. 'The caste system's been abolished by the government of free India. Or hasn't that news reached your unelectrified village yet?'

'Relax, brother.' The Jat chuckles. 'Don't take it so hard. I just haven't heard that surname before.'

'He's Coorgi,' Raka explains. 'They're a race of martial fighters from Karnataka. General Thimayya is Coorgi – General Cariappa too.'

'We, uh, prefer being called Coorg, not Coorgi,' Maddy puts in.

From the Jat's blank expression, it is clear that these illustrious names have rung no bells. But he puts out his hand readily enough.

'Pleased-to-meet-you!'

He rattles it off like he has learnt it as a phrase and doesn't know where one word stops and the next begins. But he has a pleasant voice, Maddy has to admit. A smiling voice.

'What say we splash Carvalho really thoroughly when we hit the water?' the Jat suggests, grey eyes sparkling.

But this is far too cocky a suggestion for the NDA boys' tastes.

'You won't make much of a splash, shorty,' Raka says reprovingly. 'And don't be cheeky about our instructor. An officer and a gentleman respects his teachers.'

Faujdaar bursts out laughing. 'Oh, you can make fun of him, but I can't? What two-faced fellows! Or snobs – which is worse.'

They continue their climb in silence. Then Maddy says stiffly, 'Ever since he was a cadet, folks have been calling him Kuch Bhi Carvalho. The man's game for anything. *Anything*. Which is why you've gotta respect him.'

'Wah.' The Jat ducks his head appreciatively. 'Of course. That I can respect.'

They cross the final zag in a more companionable silence, then suck in their breath in unison.

They've reached the top – a little platform, eyrie-like and serene. There's a smell of woodsmoke and a grand view of the rose-hued hills and scrubby dunes beyond the campus.

'Have you ever done anything like this before?' Maddy asks the direct recruit curiously.

The Jat looks around.

'No,' he says simply, drinking in the view. 'I've never been this high up in my life, I think. Except when I climbed to the top of the Qutub Minar with my grandfather, perhaps. But I was little then.'

'And look at you now,' Raka mutters. But the snideness is half-hearted. His eyes are on the diving board.

It juts out from the end of their little platform like the protruding tongue of the iron monster. It has no railing and seems to be sloping slightly downward. And it's narrow, no more than twenty inches wide. The wind is strong here, whistling around their ears, making them cling to the railing. Far below them, their batchmates look like a colony of blue and grey ants.

The two friends peer over the edge to the sickening drop below. As Carvalho's whistle sounds, Maddy can feel his stomach lurch.

'Ugh,' he says. 'Well, Geronimo then, Raka. Go for it!'

Raka has turned rather green. 'You go first.'

Maddy pales. 'But Carvalho said you first. He'll get mad if I go before you.'

'He can't tell us apart,' Raka replies.

Pause.

'You're chubbier,' Maddy says.

Pause.

'But fairer,' Raka replies.

'Oh, I'm clearly the fairest here,' says the Jat breezily from behind them. 'Should I go first?'

They ignore him.

'I'd rather you went first, yaar Raka,' Maddy says finally. 'This isn't really my cup of Brooke Bond.'

They stare at each other, while the whistle sounds again below them. Sharper, more peremptory.

'You people have a problem with heights, clearly.' Shaanu Faujdaar leans comfortably against the railing. 'First you had a problem with my height, now you have a problem with the height of the diving board.'

'Shut *up*, shorty!'

Maddy's voice is raw, the fear palpable. He edges forward, takes a few uncertain steps, teetering a little on the narrow, springy board, then abruptly makes as if to turn back.

'I can't,' he says hoarsely. 'My head – I think I'm gonna…'

Raka, at the safe end of the board, finds that his feet are frozen. He can't do anything to help Maddy.

'Think of all those Coorgi generals,' Shaanu says helpfully. 'Thin-amma and Curry-appa.'

'Everything's spinning,' Maddy continues. '*Spinning and spinning and spinning…*'

He looks around at the bright blue earth above and the cemented sky below, heaving up at him, sucking him down…

'Careful!' The village boy's voice is sharp. 'Don't jump off there, you'll hit the cement! Walk back to us!'

But Maddy can't. His face pales, his hands stretch out wildly, his body starts to tilt…

Then a steady, firm forearm locks around his stomach.

'Gotcha,' says the Jat.

'I made it back.' Maddy opens his eyes in disbelief.

'No, actually, I walked out to you,' comes the cool reply. '*Now* we'll walk back.'

Calmly he walks Maddy back along the narrow board till they're holding onto the railing again.

'You go first,' he pants out to Raka. 'That *was* the order.'

'Jai Mata di,' Raka mutters, his chubby face grim, and walks forward slowly to the end of the board.

'Good!' shouts Shaanu. 'Now jump!'

But Raka shakes his head. 'Like I *told* you, shorty!' he yells, voice ragged with fear and frustration. 'I *can't*.'

A fraught little pause follows. Nobody knows quite what to do. The wind whistles around their ears.

The Jat grins. 'Seriously? NDA waalon ki phat gayee?'

The other two ignore this, their faces sick and resentful.

Far below, Carvalho's whistle sounds again, shrill and commanding.

Shaanu straightens himself, his young face intent. Bouncing a little on the balls of his feet, he asks, 'Wanna see something my grandfather taught me?'

The responses come at him fast and fervent.

'Never mind your stupid Jat grandfather!'

'Whyn't you *scared*, you short fucker?'

Faujdaar grins, his light eyes sparklingly alive, then holds up his left hand, forefinger pointing skyward, thumb jutting out at a right angle to it. 'Big guy, small cock,' he shouts, waggling the thumb. He flips his hand so that his thumb is now pointing skyward while the forefinger is jutting out at right angles to it. He waggles the forefinger. 'Small guy, big cock.'

And as Raka and Maddy stare at him, torn between outrage, vertigo and laughter, Shaanu Faujdaar places a hand in the small of Maddy's back and runs full-tilt ahead, propelling him forward, till they collide with Raka, frozen at the end of the diving board. And then they're in the air together, whooping and kicking and flailing wildly as they drop safely, straight as stones, into the tiny patch of azure far below.

• • •

'*Baaaaaaz ... tard*!' Raka declares with proprietary pride. 'How pretty you look! Prettier than Sharmila Tagore!'

The new batch from the Flying College is very drunk. They've taken over the only pub in Jodhpur and are swinging on the dance floor, eyeing the cantonment girls and knocking back large quantities of rum. The adrenalin from the jump is still very much with them, coupled with the excitement of being let loose after a week of rigorous training. There are corduroy pants on display, flared denims and mightily collared shirts and bright, Chinese-collared kurtas. But the peacock of the parade is definitely Shaanu Faujdaar, sitting between his two new best friends at the bar, dressed in charcoal-grey drainpipe pants, an extremely sharp turquoise blue shirt and a thin maroon tie.

'Prettier than Audrey Hepburn!' agrees Maddy, thumping his new pal on the back.

Faujdaar has been giving the modest, taciturn ones, but at this his grey eyes narrow.

'Who's ordinary hip burn?'

Maddy sighs and ignores this.

'You don't talk much. Why?'

'I'd like to,' Faujdaar admits. 'But my English is little bit basic.'

Much drunken laughter all round.

Raka leans in closer.

'But you should've told us, Shaanu, meri jaan – in Hindi, in sign language or in *something* – that you don't know how to swim!'

Because once they'd hit the water (splashing Carvalho most satisfyingly with their collective impact), Faujdaar had started to flail and sink. It had taken the others a while to realize what was happening, by which time he was already in trouble. They had to swim back, hoist him up by an underarm each, tow him to the side and pump out his stomach. It took him three minutes to cough and sit up, red-faced and spluttering. Three very long minutes, Maddy thinks now.

'Nobody asked,' Shaanu replies. 'They said jump, I jumped. I figured the Air Force would get me out before I drowned.'

There is silence as the others digest this philosophic remark.

'*Baaaaz … tard!*' Raka says feelingly. It seems to be his favourite drunken exclamation, uttered in trademark, rhythmic style. He thumps Ishaan on the back affectionately. 'More drinks for my brother here! My other brother's paying!'

Everybody downs their drinks with gusto.

Maddy straightens his tie. 'Let's head for the girls, what say? The one in the middle has a certain *je ne sais quoi*.'

'Chup, saale qwa qwa.' Raka yanks him back. 'You think *all* girls are pretty. You have no standard.'

'All girls *are* pretty,' says Maddy doggedly and makes to rise, but Shaanu puts a hand on his arm.

'Wait. All in good time.'

'But those civilians are stealing a march on us!'

Shaanu's grey eyes sweep the room.

'We're easily the coolest cats here.'

Raka and Maddy turn to stare at him in disbelief.

He grins.

They burst out laughing.

'Cocky little bugger, aren't you?' Maddy says, settling back in his seat. 'So, was that shirt really stitched by a Chakkahera yokel?'

'Then what.' Faujdaar pats his taut abdomen complacently. 'My sister chose the cloth. And the cut. She says this shade – it's called firoza blue – works really well for me.'

Maddy and Raka, studying the glove-like fit of the shirt, have to agree that it does.

'I wish *I* had some sisters,' Maddy says gloomily. 'All I have in my family are men. Each one a fucking hero with a mantelpiece full of shiny trophies.'

Faujdaar puts down his glass, concerned. 'Who's a mental piece, yaar?'

'Never mind.' Maddy knocks his drink back. 'I'll just never be as good as my uncles and brothers and father, you know? At NDA everybody thought I had an advantage because the instructors knew my family – but it's *not* an advantage, it's a bloody golden shackle.'

Raka pats his arm.

'That's why when I got the Air Force I grabbed it,' Maddy continues. 'All the army men at home were so impressed, because they're all too dumb to handle the math and the science required. But … I'm not in love with heights.'

A sympathetic silence reigns.

'I have problems too,' Raka says finally, letting out a sigh so gusty the collars of Ishaan's shirt flutter in its blast. 'I've been in love with Juhi Gupta for four years now. Haiii … Juuuhiiii Gupta. Tell Shaanu how beautiful Juhi Gupta is, Maddy.'

'Oh, *beautiful*,' Maddy agrees obligingly. 'A living doll.'

'*Too* right!' Raka rocks back in his bucket stool and sips his drink, gratified.

'But Maddy thinks all girls are pretty,' Shaanu can't resist pointing out.

'Chup, chutiye.' Raka frowns. 'Juhi Gupta is something *else*.'

'Have you known her long?' Shaanu asks.

The pride of the NDA shifts uncomfortably in his seat.

'Four years.'

'Kuch setting ki hai? Told her you like her? Or only far far away se?'

Raka sits up with great dignity. 'We're good friends.'

Shaanu chuckles. 'Loser.'

Raka looks indignant. 'Baaztard, we have an understanding! And we're *meant to be*. Otherwise why would her father get a transfer to Jodhpur this year only, huh?'

Shaanu sits up.

'She lives *here*? Why didn't you call her here tonight?'

'I can't just *call* her!' Raka says, horrified. 'What will she *think*? I mean…' As Shaanu's pitying grin grows broader he recovers himself. 'She's studying for her MA na, that's why she can't come. She wants to be a teacher.'

'But you said you have an understanding,' Shaanu points out.

Maddy chuckles. 'He's her rakhi brother.'

'No!' Shaanu swivels to look at Raka, appalled.

Raka sighs, looking part-miserable, part-coy.

'At least I get to see her this way.'

'Pathetic.' Maddy sips his beer. 'And incestuous.'

'Besides, her father doesn't like the IAF. The moment I picked it, he made a glum face and told her, *Bade risk waala job hai, beta! They fly such small, undependable planes, not even pressurized properly. His ears will burst, his lungs will rot, he'll be dead before he's thirty.*'

'What crap.'

'We'll live till we're hundred.'

Raka gulps down his drink and continues. 'He's sat in a sarkari office and pushed files his whole life, the coward. Typical babu mentality. He has no cuncept of patriotism, of protecting our nation from the bloody Muslims—'

'Pakistanis,' Maddy corrects him.

'Same thing. *And* he has no cuncept of striving to be the best that you can be – or courage or daring. He says a man's job is to earn money. I *despise* the bastard.'

Faujdaar drums his hands on the bar counter, studying his downcast friends. Then,

'I *am* a bastard,' he says lightly.

Maddy and Raka sit up, their woes forgotten.

'Shut *up*, bastard.'

'That *can't* be.'

'Yes, it can,' Faujdaar insists, his grey eyes glittering strangely. He pauses and adds with a savage smile. 'Well, that's my stepfather's theory, anyway. He's told me about a million times that my mother wasn't married to my father. That she didn't even know his name.'

The other two stare at him.

'He's a liar,' Raka declares finally.

'Of course he's a liar!' Maddy agrees stoutly.

'Did you *hear* that, guys?'

The trio turns around. A group of civilian boys who were trying to chat up the girls has just returned to the bar counter, rebuffed.

'The pretty Jat doesn't know who his father is!'

Raka and Maddy look at each other, not sure what to do.

But Shaanu Faujdaar's having no such problems. He puts down his glass and gets to his feet, legs planted wide, arms folded across his chest.

'Bad mood mein ho?' he enquires kindly. 'Girls didn't give you any patta, ne?'

'No,' the self-designated boss of this group admits, rocking back on his heels cockily, mimicking Ishaan's accent. 'Because they weren't your mother, ne.'

'Stop him, Maddy!' Raka shouts. But it is too late. Before they can restrain him, Shaanu Faujdaar has lunged forward and punched the smirking boy right in the face, drawing blood from his nose and a howl of outrage from his lips.

Faujdaar silences the howl by hitting the boy again, straight in the mouth. He grunts and crumples, and his friends leap to take his place.

'Aajao kameeno!' roars Shaanu Faujdaar, dancing from foot to foot, fists raised. 'Who's next?'

Raka and Maddy exchange glances, shrug, and roll up their sleeves to defend their new friend. Raka picks up a barstool and swirls it about over his head. Maddy lets out a blood-curdling yell.

'*Doggggfightttt!*'

And the scuffle blooms into a full-blown melee.

• • •

Two hours later, a beautiful buxom girl, creamy-complexioned, dark-haired and clad in a tight kurta-churidaar, stalks into the Ghantaghar police thaana in Jodhpur, her face thunderous.

She leaves ten minutes later, a trio of ruffians trailing in her disgusted, magnificent wake.

'Thanks, Juhi,' says the first of these thugs humbly, the ends of his lopsided handlebar moustache pointing one to the glowing moon above and one to the dusty road below. 'Sorry for disturbing your studies.'

She tosses her bounteous waves of hair and sniffs, ignoring him.

'Yeah, thanks Juhi,' says the second rowdy, modestly trying to hold together his gaping shirt, which is missing several buttons.

'Don't mention it,' she snaps.

'Pleased-to-meet-you,' says the third obsequiously, producing a charming smile, which would have been more charming if his eyes weren't so puffy and blackened.

'Hullo.' Juhi's voice is distinctly discouraging.

There is an awkward pause. They stand around an ancient green Morris Minor parked on the side of the road. Raka puts out his hand hesitantly.

'Do you want me to drive?'

'I got here without a problem, didn't I?' she replies curtly. 'Get in the back.'

They shuffle into the back and discover a weedy, chinless lad in the driver's seat. As he takes in their ruffianish appearance, his Adam's apple starts to bob up and down agitatedly.

'Didi,' he croaks, his eyes darting about. 'You never told me that this was a police ka chakkar ... if Tauji finds out—'

'He won't, Kusum bhaiyya.' Juhi's voice is sweetly persuasive as she gets into the front passenger seat. 'Besides, these are decent boys – aren't you decent, boys?'

They all nod vigorously.

'Oh yes!'

'We're decent!'

Raka leans forward and claps him on the back. 'Now be a good support and drop us to the Flying College, Kusum bhaiyya!'

Juhi's cousin obliges, still looking worried. The Morris Minor rattles down the dark street.

Juhi stares out through the windshield, her beautiful face inscrutable.

In the back seat, Shaanu stares out of the window, his expression pensive, even as Maddy's head droops onto his shoulder drowsily.

Raka clears his throat.

'Getting into fights is a very bad thing,' he ventures. 'Of *course* it's a very bad thing! But sometimes you have to take a *stand*.'

He can't be certain, sitting where he is, but it seems to him that Juhi's figure has stiffened in the front seat.

He delivers a sharp kick to Maddy's ankle.

'They were saying really objectionable things, yaar Juhi,' Maddy wakes up to say dutifully. 'Mother-sister things. That's not done.'

'Yeah,' Raka chimes in. 'We *couldn't* have kept silent.'

Juhi turns to face them, her expression slightly softened, a question on her lips, but before she can get it out, Shaanu raises a hand in protest.

'*No*,' he says emphatically. 'This particular thing, it *isn't* important. It was stupid of me to get into a fight about it.'

The other two murmur in protest.

'Because...' Ishaan continues, his voice low and searching, 'this is the Indian Air Force, right? We've got brand new uniforms and brand new haircuts and all the old shit's been wiped clean. We've made a new beginning. We could be anything! That's what Carvalho keeps saying.'

He looks at his friends for confirmation, his puffy, black-rimmed eyes painfully intense.

'You're right,' Maddy says strongly. 'We could! We will! You show your stepfather how worthy you are!'

'And you out-hero every damn Subbiah ever born!' Shaanu replies. 'And you, Raka, you stay alive and ask Juhi to—'

'*Baaaaz*...' Raka starts to hiss, then checks himself. 'Just shushh, okay?'

'Let him talk, Raka,' Maddy says.

Raka whirls around and glares at Maddy.

'*You* keep quiet!'

'But why can't we talk about this?' Ishaan demands. 'Juhi has a right to know.'

'*Baaaaaz…*' Raka begins imploringly, then checks himself again. 'Just keep *quiet*.'

'No, let him talk.' Juhi fixes her beautiful eyes on Shaanu and says kindly, 'What were you saying, Baaz?'

He begins again, without any hesitation. 'Just that he's been in love with y—'

'*Shut up!*' protests Raka, agonized.

'Continue,' Juhi says calmly.

'He's been in love with you for four years and is too darponk to admit it,' Shaanu finishes calmly. Also, he burnt that rakhi you tied to him, and flushed its ashes down the toilet. And said gandi-gandi gaalis while he did so.'

There is stunned silence. Even the weedy cousin senses that something monumental is unfolding and eases the car over a speed breaker with utmost gentleness.

Juhi smiles, turns around and looks ahead at the road.

'I know.'

And the sweetness in her voice is such that Maddy and Shaanu let out a whoop while Raka tugs at his moustache and looks idiotically pleased.

Kusum bhaiyya's high-pitched, croaking voice joins the conversation unexpectedly.

'That's why she tied you the rakhi in the first place. She thought you'd object, or say something! But you didn't. She came home and cried for hours. What a useless fellow you are!'

Scorn from such a source renders Raka speechless.

His friends chuckle.

'Clarity at last.' Maddy beams.

'Thanks to Baaz.' Juhi tosses her hair. 'No thanks to a phisaddi like you – or Raka.'

'Why do you keep calling him Baaz?' Raka demands, blushing coyly even as he strives valiantly for normalcy.

'Because *you* keep calling him Baaz.' She blinks, confused. 'I thought that was his name.'

Raka stares at her, perplexed, while Maddy's face splits into a delighted grin.

'It wasn't.' He chuckles. 'But now it is. And it fits. Saala, how he swooped down and did your setting for you, ekdum Baaz-ke-maaphik!'

'Not just mine,' says Raka. 'The girls at the club *specifically mentioned* that they'd be there again next Saturday.' He changes his voice to a lilting falsetto. '*We'll save a dance for your friends and you!*'

'No need,' Juhi tells him sternly.

He smiles at her fatuously. 'Okay, baby.'

But Maddy is thrilled at this update.

'Wow, they *like* us!' He turns to Shaanu, impressed. 'That was fast work, Baaz!'

'Then what.' Shaanu's grey eyes sparkle cockily in their bruised, blackened sockets. 'I *told* you we were the coolest cats in the place.'

TWO

'She's the coolest cat in the place,' a starry-eyed first-year science undergraduate whispers to her friend as Tehmina Dadyseth strides past them, her vibrant red miniskirt swinging, a plate of samosas in her hand, clearly late for her first class of the day. 'I wish I were her.'

'You wish you were a crack, you mean,' sniffs the friend. 'All these rich arts girls are crack, but she's the crackest. Look what she's doing now!'

Because Tehmina, having reached Room 33, has dropped dramatically to her knees in the open doorway, and is holding out the samosas like a tribute to the professor, pleading to be let in. The unseen professor relents and the briber rushes in gratefully, still on her knees, dropping her register in her eagerness and scurrying back out a moment later to retrieve it.

'Clumsy too! *And* a show off, maaroing that fake American accent!'

'Arrey, she lived in America till she was ten, and it's very slight – besides, her Hindi is so good!'

Her friend isn't convinced. 'Do you know she organized an antim sanskar with an actual funeral pyre and last rites for three of her friends who are getting married this month? She has no respect for religion – must be because she's Parsi.'

'That was a bonfire party.' The starry-eyed first-year defends her heroine stoutly. 'Anyway, I think it's a shame that girls come here – to the best women's college in India, for heaven's sake – to get quality education and then get married off without even completing their degree! Tinka's protesting against that in a symbolic sort of way – what's wrong with that?'

'It's against our traditions.' Her friend shakes her head. 'And I don't think she's pretty, she's so frowny and browny – there are at least ten girls in MH more fair-complexioned than her!'

These accusations are not entirely invalid. As Tinka Dadyseth officially enters our narrative, seated within the gracious, red-bricked walls of Miranda House, University of Delhi, furiously scribbling on a chart paper with a black crayon, it must be admitted that she is not conventionally pretty. She is wheatish and unfashionably thin, with slender, tennis-player limbs, unusual in a time when most girls aspire to voluptuous curves. Eschewing the floral prints in vogue, Tinka dresses in skirts of red, orange or emerald-green, teamed with white tops in the summer, and black polonecks in the winter. In an establishment as conventionally fashionable as Miranda House, this is indeed brave. Her hair is black and wavy, her large eyes combative, her nose straight, her mouth generous, her opinions decisive. Her face is long, ending in a pointy chin, and when she smiles, two tiny dimples flash in her cheeks. 'You look like an imp,' Jimmy used to say, chucking her under the chin. 'A young imp – an implet. An implet with dimplets.'

But we mustn't talk about Jimmy. Nobody in Tinka's family does.

Now she gives a satisfied little grunt and leans back from the chart paper banner she has been working on.

HANG US! screams the banner in psychedelic colours. Underneath, in smaller handwriting: *Quality photo prints from around the world!*

It is the eighteenth Republic Day of independent India and Miranda House is celebrating with a mela on the front lawn. There are several stalls selling tea and chaat and jewellery and kolhapuri chappals, as well as the standard hoopla and lucky dip. Usually a fiercely guarded all-girls bastion, Miranda House has opened its gates to the general public today, as the proceeds of the mela will go to soldiers' widows and orphans. Students from other colleges have been allowed in, and the crowd is peppered with carefully groomed hopeful young men.

Principal Vidya Surendran makes a short speech, the choir performs a rousing version of '*Kadam kadam badhaye ja*', a second-year botany student renders a particularly lachrymose rendition of '*Aye mere vatan ke logo*' and the mela is declared open.

The photo prints stall does brisk business through the day, some of which might have to do with how animatedly Tinka makes her sales pitch. The other girls in the stall are all extremely charming, but none of them light up like Tinka does while talking about the merchandise.

'This is the Rann of Kutch,' she tells a group of smitten boys, her eyes glowing with passion. 'A moonscape – literally a moonscape – doesn't the sand look like waves in the sea?'

With a wriggle of excitement, she turns to an elderly professor. 'Oh, you like the dupatta market? Yes, the colours are so hectic! This was shot in a chunni bazaar in Lahore. The rangrez there can make the most amazing patterns!'

And with a scornful curl of the lips, to a gaggle of girls: 'I'm sorry, I cannot reduce the price a little. The photographer sat in the branches for days to capture that shot! It's a tigress and two cubs, she was very fierce, he risked his life.'

Whether at the prompting of this last group or just organically, a rowdy group of boys swaggers over to the photo prints stall later in the afternoon, when the crowd has dwindled to a trickle.

One of them, clearly the leader, slams a meaty palm down on Tinka's table and demands, 'You are selling Pakistani goods?'

She leans back, crossing her arms over her chest. 'Of courrrse not,' she replies, her New England twang getting stronger, like it always does when she's angry. 'I'm selling photo prints, some of which were shot in Pakistan. Would you like to buy some?'

'Haw ji!' exclaims the leader. 'Shame on you! Selling the enemy's goods, that too on Independence Day!'

'It's Republic Day, actually,' Tinka tells him. 'Also, it isn't illegal to sell these and Pakistan isn't our enemy.'

The thug, clearly not used to being spoken to so dismissively by a girl, shouts, 'How dare you! Our soldiers are dying at the border and you—'

Her eyes blaze with anger. 'Watch your mouth. My brother was a soldier at the border, and he died too.'

This gives him pause. 'Huh?'

'Huh yourself, duffer.' Her voice rings with scorn. 'Now back off, you're soiling my prints.'

But this is too much for the rabble-rouser. Humiliated and desperate to regain prestige, he lunges forward and upturns Tinka's table. Her girlfriends scream. Passers-by gasp.

And Tinka Dadyseth picks up a large bell from the Moradabad brass stall next to her own and whacks him hard across the head with it. He crumples immediately, the expression on his face one of intense surprise.

'*Go Tinkkaaaaaa!*' comes a scream mixed with delight and horror from the scrum of spectators.

Tinka grins. The rabble-rouser's underlings pick up their leader and bear him away, swearing revenge, even as the MH back-gate guards come stumping up, hissing and cursing and shooing all the boys out.

Fifteen minutes later, Tinka is sullenly dunking biscuits into tea in Principal Vidya Surendran's office.

'Don't do that, Tehmina, it's a disgusting habit.'

'Sorry, ma'am.'

'I would have thought an intelligent girl like you would know better than to resort to crude violence.'

Tinka flushes. 'You're right. I'm sorry.'

'You mustn't engage with these people, my dear, it isn't safe. Suppose they make a target of you?'

Tinka throws up her hands.

'Well, *somebody* has to engage with them!'

'Does it always have to be you?'

'I guess not,' the girl admits, blowing on her tea moodily. 'But honestly, ma'am, they come around picking on me. And don't say it's because I'm pretty. There are tons of prettier girls around.'

'Ah, but they aren't Amerrrican,' says the principal, deliberately rolling her r's.

Tinka colours. 'I was born in the US, sure, but I live and study in Delhi. I think that makes me more patriotic than Indians who'd love to leave but can't.'

'But you're influenced by American ideas,' Principal Surendran points out. 'You've been all praise for their anti-war movement, and I've seen you singing *"Where have all the flowers gone"* in a peasant smock with flowers in your hair. You looked very fetching.'

'Thank you,' Tinka mutters, wondering if she's being reprimanded for being shallow. She is guiltily aware that her love for the American peaceniks might have a little to do with how nicely their funky fashions match her personal style.

The principal arches her brow. 'I hope it hasn't gone any further than that?' she asks meaningfully.

Tinka's biscuit drops into her tea with a plop. 'Oh, Professor Surendran, of course not. I'm not into free love. Or drugs.'

'Good. So tell me, what exactly got you so heated up today?'

Tinka knits her strong brows, looking undeniably frowny and browny.

'Everything! No, actually – d'you know, ma'am, all cantonments have a big flower and garden show every year?'

'How nice,' the principal replies. 'We have that here at Delhi University too. Miranda House wins every year. Our salvias and sweetpeas showing is the best in the city. What's your point?'

Tinka leans in.

'In the Army flower and garden shows, they always have a flower-arranging contest. The Army wives read up all these Ikebana booklets and make fancy flower-arrangements and compete for a prize; and *every single* year somebody stands a bunch of menacing-looking dark thorns in a big fat bowl, places one small, perfect white rose in the middle of the thorny jungle, calls the damn thing "War Widow" and wins!'

'Don't swear, Tehmina.'

'Sorry, ma'am. It's the most hackneyed idea possible! But *such* a holy cow that nobody dares to make fun of it or challenge it!'

'There's nothing funny about being a war widow, my girl.'

Tinka nods her head passionately.

'Exactly! I just think hyper-patriotism is a disease. It's narrow, manipulative and exploitative. Look at the havoc it's wrecked all over the world. And in India, patriotism virtually means hating Pakistanis – who, till twenty years ago, were our own countrymen!'

'Patriotism cannot be our final spiritual shelter,' murmurs her principal. 'Humanity stands higher. Do not buy glass for the price of diamonds, my countrymen! And…'

'… never allow patriotism to triumph over humanity as long as you live!' Tinka finishes delightedly, eyes glowing. 'Tagore said that! Yes, ma'am, I know.'

Principal Surendran studies her bright young face.

'What are your further plans, Tehmina? I've heard you're not too keen on marriage?'

The girl nods. 'I want to study photography and human rights.'

'An unusual combination – but one that you will excel in.'

Tinka glows. 'Thank you.'

The principal smiles and inclines her grey head.

'Go, child. And for heaven's sake, try to stay out of trouble.'

After the reassured girl has strode happily out of the room, Principal Vidya Surendran sighs and pens a troubled

note to Tinka's widowed father, Major General Ardisher
Dadyseth (retd):

*Tehmina's passion and outspokenness, though praiseworthy,
could get her in trouble with the patriarchal elements at Delhi
University. More and more, I worry for her safety on this campus.
Perhaps, after the exams (in which she is sure to do well) you could
consider sending her to the USA for further studies.*

*I also suspect that her brother's death has affected her deeply. I
would strongly urge you to speak to her about this at the soonest.
Of course, as a teacher, I can only make suggestions. The final
decision rests with you...*

General Ardisher Dadyseth reads this missive and
decides that he needs to find a nice Parsi boy for Tehmina
and get her married and off his hands as soon as possible.

• • •

'She has a certain *je ne sais quoi*,' declares Maddy dreamily,
chin in his hands. 'I could like her.'

'Abbe, don't start that qwa qwa again,' Raka groans.
'You'll fall in love with anything in a skirt!'

'Focus!' Shaanu frowns. 'She could have disguised
herself, worn a burqa or something. We'll have to be sharp.'

The three friends are sitting on a bench at the Jodhpur
Junction Railway Station, sipping hot, sweet tea and
examining a black-and-white photograph. It has been
handed to them by the wife of their Chief Instructor, Mrs
Poncha, and features a slim, vivacious young woman in a
polka-dotted cocktail dress. At the back the Chief Instructor
himself has written, in his small cramped handwriting:
Tehmina Dadyseth.

This Tehmina has run away from Delhi and, clearly being
an enterprising girl, has bought two tickets from New Delhi
Railway Station. One for a bus to Udaipur and one for a

train to Bombay. Mrs Poncha and three hatta-katta nurses from the Military Hospital are waiting to apprehend her at the bus stop, while Maddy, Raka and Shaanu have been instructed to stake out the railway station. They have to find her and bear her back (quietly, with minimum fuss) to Chief Instructor Poncha's residence, and he will ensure she gets sent back home, to be married off to the good Parsi boy with the big shipping business her rich father has found for her.

She is the daughter of Poncha's first cousin, Mrs Poncha has told the boys. He is a retired general, very well-respected, settled in Delhi.

'All this is Maddy's fault,' Raka grumbles now. 'Mrs Poncha's nuts about him – because he's a rich Coorgi murgi. All Parsis are like this only.'

'It's Coorg, not Coorgi,' Maddy replies.

'Well, I think it's all a bit high-handed frankly,' Raka declares. 'The girl's an adult, if she doesn't want to marry this boy, she shouldn't have to! I mean, she could be my Juhi!'

'Why is she going to Bombay?' Maddy wants to know. 'It's not a safe city for young girls to run away to. The papers are full of horror stories about girls who run away to Bombay.'

'You all are thinking too much,' Shaanu says. 'Let's just uthao her, bundle her into the Jonga and drop her off at the WingCo's.'

'This isn't Chakkahera.' Maddy frowns. 'We don't treat girls that way.'

Shaanu throws out his hands. 'But he's her *uncle*.'

'*And* he has the deciding vote on the Sword of Honour,' Raka says slyly. 'Is that why you want to keep him happy, Baaz?'

Shaanu grins. Old Kuch Bhi Carvalho has already sought him out and briefed him on this. 'Just keep your nose clean through this final week, Chakkahera,' he advised him in an aside during parade drill. 'And the Sword of Honour will ride home with you to your dusty village in your battered tin trunk.'

'That sword's got my name on it, brother,' says Shaanu confidently. 'I don't need to keep anyone happy!'

'Dream on, brother,' Raka smirks.

'Look, how are we supposed to get her off the train without creating a commotion?' Maddy demands. 'Suppose she refuses to come? We're in our Flying College uniforms, we aren't even proper officers! We can't just—oh shit, here comes the train.'

The Desert Queen has just steamed onto the platform, puffing self-importantly and creating quite a stir.

'I'll check bogies 1, 4 and 7,' Shaanu says, springing to his feet. 'Maddy, you take 2, 5 and 8. And—'

'I'll take 3, 6 and 9,' Raka finishes. 'It's a five-minute halt. Let's go, boys!'

They board their designated bogies even before the Desert Queen comes to a full halt, moving smoothly down the central aisle, scanning every face. The innards of the train are a warm, humming space smelling comfortably of puri-aloo, Odomos and overripe oranges. Under the dim glow of the blue night lights, mothers rock their babies to sleep, fathers move about importantly, listening to the radio or brushing their teeth. In the doorways, there is the usual hubbub of passengers getting off and on, hailing coolies, humping suitcases or barking out instructions.

The three cadets move rapidly through the bogies with no success. Shaanu is just starting to think that Mrs Poncha's information was incorrect when suddenly, sandwiched between a lugubrious-looking villager in a turban and a snazzy city slicker in a yellow bush shirt, he spots the girl in the photograph.

She is bundled in a long dark coat, a far cry from the cocktail dress in the photograph, but it's her all right. She is fast asleep, her head tilted back against the bench. Her eyes are shut tight, the lashes dark, almost fanlike against her cheeks. Her fingers are curled loosely around a fancy purse and her mouth is slightly open. She looks limp, exhausted and absolutely defenceless.

Shaanu looks at the smudgy shadows under her eyes.

She sleeps on.

The two men seated on either side of her stare back at him with undisguised hostility. Shaanu recognizes the self-important, slightly self-conscious look of self-appointed protectors. With a quick, confident movement, he flashes his Flying College ID at them.

'Indian Air Force,' he says in a low, business-like voice, motioning to the one in the aisle seat to move. 'On national security business. Out of my way, please!'

The man gets to his feet without demur. So far so good, thinks Shaanu. He bends, slides a muscular arm under the sleeping girl's knees and another behind her neck, and lifts her up bodily.

He is striding down the aisle to the door when several things happen at once. The girl's eyes fly open, her body tenses and she lets out a scream piercing enough to make his back teeth rattle. Then she starts to struggle.

Simultaneously her two protectors spring to their feet, protesting hoarsely. 'Hain? Aise kaise? Hullo! IAF! You are kidnapping and raping! Shame shame! Stop him, somebody!'

At the same time, Raka and Maddy appear on the

platform and let out a roar. 'You've found her! Oh, well done! Shabaash, Baaz, shabaash!'

And the train starts to move.

Ishaan Faujdaar gives a laugh of pure reckless enjoyment, tightens his grip on the struggling girl, runs to the door and leaps off the train.

• • •

'*Whooofff!*'

Pain explodes like fireworks inside Shaanu's head. He winces, shakes his head vigorously, then opens slightly glazed eyes.

'*Oww*, ma'am, easy,' he says, still doubled up in pain. 'I want to have children one day.'

The Air Force Jonga is rattling along at a terrific pace. Raka's at the driving wheel, Maddy beside him, while Shaanu is slumped in the back, facing Tinka Dadyseth, who is sitting with her back to the stepney, an expression of grim satisfaction on her face.

'Yes, do calm down, Tehmina,' Maddy drawls reassuringly from the front. 'We're decent folk. Please.'

She remains crouched in her corner, knees pressed together, hands balled into fists, but her eyes narrow to slits.

'Where'd'you find out my name?'

She has a slight American accent. Under her half-open coat, she is dressed in a black poloneck and a gathered, gaily printed, red miniskirt. The kind of skirt, Shaanu thinks through a haze of pain, that female performing monkeys wear when they come around with their madaris and put up little shows on the roadside in Chakkahera. A bandariya skirt. She has slender brown thighs and shoes of a kind Shaanu has never seen before on a girl – boys' shoes made of buttery leather, with laces and a design picked out with little holes in the front.

He decides she is a snob.

'We didn't uthao you just like that, you know,' he tells her, still doubled up, elbows on his thighs. 'We're not a bunch of tharkis. We're officers.'

Her lips curl in scorn.

'You're too young to be officers.'

Definitely a snob.

Shaanu reddens and draws himself up.

'Well, cadets then.'

She tosses her head and sniffs.

'I despise armymen.'

'So do we.' He grins. 'We are IAF. Which is fifty times better than being Army. And we're Fighters. Which is fifty times better than being just IAF. Well, at least two of us are Fighters,' he clarifies. '*He's* in transport.'

She stares at him blankly.

'What are you *talking* about?'

Shaanu goes a little red. Why is he babbling?

'I mean-to-say,' he fumbles over the English phrase, 'that we're only following orders.'

The girl bridles. 'Whose orders?'

The Jonga hits a pothole and they're all jolted hard. Shaanu lets out a groan and doesn't reply.

'Your uncle's,' says Raka from the driver's seat. 'Wing Commander Poncha. He is our Chief Instructor. We're taking you to him.'

'*Shit*.' All the fight seems to go out of the girl. She wilts visibly. 'Popo uncle! I should've known.'

'*Popo* uncle!' The boys exchange delighted grins.

Tinka dashes her bony knuckles to her eyes angrily. 'God, I'm such a pathetic little *idiot*!'

She throws herself back against the stepney in disgust.

'Hey.' Shaanu sits up straighter. 'Careful, ma'am. You'll hurt yourself.'

'I'm not made out of glass,' she snarls. She adds in a resentful voice, 'Chauvinist!'

Hain? Shaw-one what? His stint at the Flying College has bolstered Shaanu's halting English, but he doesn't recognize this particular word. Is it a swear word? He looks towards Maddy for help, but Maddy hasn't heard.

Shaanu shrugs and falls silent. The Jonga bumps along, and soon blue and grey walls loom up on either side of them, and they cross the barrier into the Air Force area.

In the front seat, Raka's conscience has been troubling him. He turns around and addresses Tinka earnestly, 'We're only following orders, you know, ma'am. On a personal level, we also feel that if you don't desire this arranged marriage, you shouldn't be forced into it.'

'Shut up, Raks,' Shaanu growls.

Raka ignores him.

'Can't your boyfriend just speak to your family?'

Tinka looks blank. 'I don't have a boyfriend.'

This stumps Raka. He turns around and sits back, saluting the sentry as the Jonga drives through the main gate of the college.

'I am *not* going to get out of this vehicle without a fight,' Tinka says in a tight voice as they pull up outside the Chief Instructor's residence. 'I'll make a scene if you force me to. I'll scream and shout, I'm warning you.'

The boys look at each other uneasily. There are several VIP cars parked outside Poncha's residence. Clearly, some high-powered meeting is going on.

'Mrs Poncha said to keep this quiet,' Raka says doubtfully. 'Should we just...'

'Baaz, you stay here with, uh, with the lady.' Maddy decides. 'We'll go in and inform Popo uncle that she's been found, safe and sound.'

'Yeah, you probably still can't walk, anyway,' Raka says, the solicitousness in his voice patently fake. Shaanu throws him a dirty look but doesn't disagree.

They slam out of the Jonga and stride away, leaving Shaanu and Tinka alone. They glance warily at each other, then quickly look away.

Is she pretty? Shaanu wonders as he gazes out of the Jonga window. Not really, she's too brown, much browner than him. And yet ... He steals another look at her. There is something nice about the clean, athletic lines of her body. Her eyes are huge, the lashes crazy long and spiky with tears. And her mouth looks so soft! There is also something else, something he'd felt when he was carrying her out of the train. A curious kind of ... connection. There had been a moment, he could swear, when she'd just woken up and stared directly into his eyes, her own drowsy with sleep, and she had smiled, her longish face scrunching up in happy recognition, two tiny dimples flashing, and cuddled closer into his chest, sighing trustingly.

He had breathed in the scent of flower borders in the springtime and felt like all those bench presses he'd been doing all his life had been leading up to exactly *that* moment.

But then she had realized where she was and started to scream.

And kicked him squarely in the crotch.

He winces again at the memory, then realizes she is talking to him.

'Look, I'm sorry I hurt you,' she is saying. 'It was nothing personal. I'm against violence as a solution to anything, as a matter of fact.'

She speaks English so fast! He has trouble understanding all of it, but he sort-of gets the gist.

He grins, the grey eyes sparkling.

'Well, you kick like a camel,' he says lightly, then tries out a phrase his boxing instructor always uses. 'Employing both strength and science.'

Tinka looks gratified. 'My brother taught me,' she says with a faint trace of pride.

'Oh, really?' Shaanu is interested. 'Fauji?'

She gives a terse little nod.

'Which Corps?'

'He's dead,' she says baldly.

He extends a hand in sympathy.

'I'm sorry, ma'am.'

She gives an awkward shrug. He notices the dark circles under her eyes.

'Stop calling me ma'am,' she says tersely. 'It sounds ridiculous. Officers only call married ladies ma'am. Not girls my age.'

Shaanu flushes, feeling like a bumpkin. Clearly the general's daughter has her cantonment etiquette down pat.

'I thought ki maybe you *were* married,' he says in retaliation.

She rears up. 'I am *not* that old!'

He grins. 'Okay, okay,' he says peaceably. 'But didn't your brother teach you not to fall asleep when you're travelling alone? You could miss your station. Or get kidnapped.'

She dashes angry tears from her eyes. 'I was tired,' she admits. 'Plus I was relaxed. I'd planned this for so long, and I thought I had *finally* got away with it!'

Shaanu moves in closer.

'There's *really* no boyfriend? You can trust me. I won't tell.'

She throws up her hands violently.

'*No!*'

'Then why you are running away?'

No reply.

'C'mon, tell no,' he urges, then grins. '*Tell*-me-na, Dadyseth!'

She blows her nose hard on her grubby shirt.

'Because.'

It is a small despairing whisper that goes straight to Shaanu's heart.

'Because what?' he asks gently.

She looks up at him, her eyes huge in the dark.

'Do you believe in God?' she asks.

Shaanu blinks. This seems a major leap in topic. 'Uh, I don't know.' He scratches his head. 'I suppose so? My sisters do, at any rate. I'm more a live-in-the-moment kind of chap, really.'

Tinka sits up and hugs her knees.

'Well, my dad believes in Country,' she says gloomily. 'Country is his god. But I think it's a bullshit, fake, artificial god. And I can't say that at home, can I, because that would mean Jimmy died for nothing – and if Pa has to face that he'll go mad.' She rolls her eyes. 'Not that he isn't half-mad already.'

Shaanu's young face grows stern. 'So you think your brother and all of us here at the academy and my father, who was a freedom fighter, are all a bunch of fools protecting some nakli god?'

Her eyes flash.

'You don't know anything about my brother,' she

retorts. 'He joined the Army, not because he was patriotic, but because my dad made him. Dad was *obsessed* with the Army! We had a tank-shaped birthday cake on every single one of Jimmy's birthdays! Ugly green thing with six Swiss rolls for wheels and a long cream wafer sticking out of it as a cannon barrel! What kind of sick man orders a cake like that on a small child's birthday?'

At least he ordered a cake, Shaanu thinks privately. We've never had a bakery ka birthday cake in our life! And we found out about birthday parties only from that filmi song where Jeetendra wears a tux and sings '*Happy Birthday to Sunita*' to a white-frock-wearing Babita on the piano. This rich girl is clearly spoilt.

'And most of Jimmy's batchmates weren't patriotic either. They were poor boys from small towns who got lured in by the promise of a glamorous upper-class lifestyle and a Defence Services alcohol quota.'

But this is too much for Shaanu. This girl is rude and she's making all sorts of assumptions.

'My family is rich,' he hears himself say. 'We talk only English in the house and nobody in our family touches alcohol.'

He wonders why he, who is always so open about his background, is feeling pressured into lying about it to this girl. Who the hell is she, anyway?

She shrugs.

'Well, then you must be a thrill freak,' she says dismissively. 'The kind who's in it for the kicks. That's the worst sort.'

'I'm patriotic,' Shaanu says loftily, suppressing with a guilty twinge the memory of the glee he feels every time he flies.

Tinka looks unimpressed. 'Whatever. Anyway, the point is that there's nothing noble about war. Wars are fought for greed, not patriotism, and soldiers are mere pawns.'

Myerpons? Shaanu is stumped again. This girl uses words nobody else does.

'To be used and sacrificed, just like that!'

As she snaps her fingers, his brow clears.

He folds his arms across his chest and sets his handsome young jaw.

'I'm nobody's myerpon,' he says grimly.

Tinka stares at him for a moment, and then laughs – a laugh that is too old for her twenty years.

'Okay.'

Silence reigns for a while.

'If you don't like living with your father, why not just marry this rich boy he's found for you?' Shaanu suggests. 'Is he so ugly?'

Tinka curls her lip. 'He's pretty enough. But he only wants to marry me because I have a Green Card.'

Shaanu absorbs this information, feeling rather intimidated. So she's a Green Card, how very hep! She's lived in foreign, she's eaten hotdogs and hamburgers and can go there any time she wants!

Out loud, he says lightly, 'That's not very patriotic of you. How did your father allow it?'

She shrugs. 'My mum's family was settled in America. She came to India after marriage. My brother was born here, in Dehradun, but by the time I came along, she'd figured Dad was a nutcase, scooped up Jimmy and fled. I was born in the USA. Then she died and we had to come back to live with my dad.'

Poor little rich girl, Shaanu thinks. Her name should've been Richa Rich.

'So who's the real God then?' he asks roughly. 'What do *you* believe in?'

This shuts her up. She sits quiet for a while, before spreading out her hands helplessly. 'In ... in people, I guess. Human beings living in mutual respect of each other.'

He knits his brows. 'That doesn't sound like a proper religion.'

'It's not.' Then she adds, rather randomly, 'I want to study photography.'

'They *teach* that?' he asks cautiously.

She nods, her eyes brightening. 'Yes, in Bombay. It's a post-grad course at a really good institute. I was lucky to get in. Well,' she gives a modest shrug, 'I *did* go to Miranda House – which, you know, is the female version of St. Stephen's College,' she adds, noting his blank expression.

Shaanu's vaguely heard of this safety pin college. It's in Delhi or something. But the girl's got her facts wrong – the best college in India is the National Defence Academy, where Raka and Maddy have studied. Everybody knows that.

'And maybe after that, I could spend a year in New York specializing.'

'Oh, really?' He struggles to sound casual. New York is too far removed from his sphere. His big achievement has been to make it to Jodhpur. 'I'll probably go on a lot of international trips too, to buy planes and missiles and all and fly them back. Or as part of a peace-keeping force. Few years back, some Canberra crews went to Congo.'

She smiles politely.

'And then do what?' he asks, piqued.

She blinks. 'What?'

'Like, when I finish Flying College, I'll defend my country. When you finish studying photography, what will *you* do?'

'I'll put an end to war,' she says confidently.

Shaanu, elder brother to three sisters, is sensitive enough not to laugh.

'Put me out of business, you mean,' he says lightly.

He must have sounded patronizing anyway, because she stares at him resentfully for a while.

'The one thing I won't do is get married,' she says finally.

Shaanu is suddenly struck by the similarity between their two situations.

'Chimman Singh didn't want me to join the Air Force,' he tells her. 'I had to sneak off, just like you.'

'Who's Chimman Singh?'

'My mother's husband.'

She gurgles appreciatively. 'Nice. I think I'm going to start calling my father by his first name too.'

'Go for it,' he advises her. 'Such a peaceful, powerful feeling it gives you, matlab ki, I can't explain! Anyway, I cycled 85 kilometres to the admission test venue. And when I cycled back, after getting *selected*, mind you—'

Her eyes widen. 'Where do you *live*?'

'In a vill—' He stops, then continues carefully, 'In a large town. In Haryana. We're zamindars. Anyway, I told Chimman Singh the good news, thinking he'd be so proud and all, but he just ignored me.'

His tone is light as he recounts the incident, but his eyes are bitter.

'*Why?*' she says, indignant.

Shaanu gives a short laugh. 'Because some nilgai got into the fields I was supposed to be watching that day and ate up half the arhar.'

Now it is Tinka's turn to look blank.

'Oh,' she says doubtfully. 'So maybe Chimman had some justification?'

Shaanu snorts. 'Naaah, it was a doomed crop anyway. He'd burnt it all up by putting in too much fertilizer. He's not too smart with dosages.'

'*Dog,*' she says, not understanding much but getting the gist.

'So, in a way, I helped him save face. I think he just wanted me to live under his heel and be bossed around all my life.'

This she understands completely.

'What a *dog,*' she says warmly.

Shaanu looks at her with more approval now. Maybe this girl isn't that bad, after all. Sure she's strange, more boy than girl – whoever's heard of a girl risking her reputation and running away from home, not to marry a boyfriend or become an actress but to put an end to war! But all Parsis are strange, people say. Clearly, however, she can tell good from bad.

Suddenly, she ducks behind the stepney.

'Wha—?' Shaanu turns around.

A flurry of activity animates the driveway of the Chief Instructor's house. Drivers are moving back to their parked cars and starting up the engines. The gate is being opened.

Popo's meeting seems to be over.

Shaanu looks at Tinka as she crouches low and watches the gate, biting down on her knuckles and swearing hard.

Listening to the string of seriously impressive swear words emerging from those sweet, full lips, he comes to a decision.

'Dadyseth.'

She is too focussed on the gate to hear him.

'Oye, Tell-me-na.'

'Huh?' She turns around.

'If anybody on the train tries to get over-funny with you, you'll kick them with that camel kick, right in the crotch, won't you?'

She stares at him uncomprehendingly, then slowly, a gleam of hope dawns in her eyes.

'Yes,' she says breathlessly.

'And you'll go seedha to Bombay?'

She nods eagerly. 'To Altamont Road. My aunt's house, my fui.'

Shaanu holds up one hand. 'And you'll be safe at Ultimate Road.'

'It's not Ultimat—yes!'

'And you have money?'

'Oh, I do.' She nods fervently.

Shaanu grins, his grey eyes warm and curiously alight.

'Then run. Jump out of the Jonga and *go*. You'll get a rickshaw at the barrier, and you'll be back at the station in twenty minutes. Buy an unreserved ticket on the next Bombay train. One leaves in two hours, I think so.'

She stares at him. 'But what about you? You'll get into trouble…'

Shaanu throws his arms out. 'Arrey nahi, I'm on a good wicket here. Everybody loves me!'

She looks hesitant. 'Why … why would you do this?'

He leans forward and smiles. 'I know what it's like to have an asshole for father. Also, you kick well.'

She gives an oddly tremulous, excited laugh. 'Tell him I asked for the bathroom and crawled out through the window while you were waiting outside.'

'Good suggestion. I'll take it.'

She hugs him and he feels strong slim arms around his neck, a pointy chin digging into his shoulder. Again he breathes in the faint fragrance of spring.

'I'll never forget you,' she vows. '*Thank* you.'

She pulls back but he holds her fast.

'Your brother didn't die for nothing,' he says steadily. 'What we fight for, it's *worth* fighting for, ne?'

But she just shakes her head and pulls away, averting her gaze.

Shaanu lets her go.

'Thanks,' she says again, squeezing his hands fervently. And then she is gone, scurrying towards the barrier with her fancy purse over her arm.

Shaanu watches her go, a strange leaping exultation in his heart and an equally strange sense of loss twisting his insides.

She wheels around when she is about a hundred metres away, her dark coat whirling around with her, and slaps a hand to her forehead.

'What's your name?' she calls.

Shaanu leans out of the Jonga and cups his hands around his mouth.

'Ishaan!' he shouts back. 'Ishaan Faujdaar!'

But a three-ton Shaktiman truck crosses the road right then. And by the time it rumbles out of the way, the road is clear and she has gone.

THREE

It is a beautiful morning in October, crisp and fragrant. Sunshine pours down like a benediction through white candyfloss clouds, its slanting golden beams against the blue sky reminiscent of the bhavishyavanis depicted in the Amar Chitra Katha comics that have just taken the young nation by storm.

Below this glorious dome, the Air Force base at Palam is all decked out to celebrate India's 38th Air Force Day. Freshly drawn white lines mark the perimeters of the airfield, while multicoloured flags flutter bravely above. The mood is proudly patriotic. Cantonment kids have missed school to be here – to eat crunchy-on-the-outside, gooey-on-the-inside boondi ka laddoos, to watch their beloved Tiranga dance in the crisp breeze and to shout lusty *Jai Hinds* in response to the perfectly synchronized marching. Sunshine sparkles on their neatly oiled hair and on the red-and-grey school uniforms their principal is so fond of describing as 'blood and iron'. Behind them sit the who's who of New Delhi, capital of the Republic of India. Smartly uniformed officers, shoes and epaulettes agleam with Cherry Blossom and Brasso, and floral chiffon-wrapped ladies smelling sweetly of Revlon's *Charlie*. Journalists both Indian and international. The defence minister, a rotund, twinkly eyed, gulabjamun of a man and, next to him, the Chief of Air Force Staff. But all eyes are on the sky, where, with a deafening roar of engines and an intoxicating whiff of aviation fuel, a formation of fighter jets has just come streaking in like a spray of silver bullets.

'And now ladies and gentlemen, we come to the climax of the show!' The plummy, BBC-accented voice of the old commentator echoes through the airfield. 'After the de Havilland-made transport carrier Caribou and the Canberra Bombers, here comes the IAF's pride and joy! India's fighting squads – the faithful Hawker Hunters, the gallant HAL-built Gnats, the hero of the '65 war, the spanking new MiG 21s and the electrifying Sukhoi-7s! This up-to-date, absolutely first-class fleet is what keeps us safe in the skies from the enemies of Hindustan!'

Everybody cheers. The defence minister – a respected freedom fighter and Congress stalwart – gets to his feet and applauds.

The commentator starts to rattle off statistics.

'The Gnats are powered with a Bristol Orpheus turbo jet engine which can attain a maximum speed of 695 kilometres per hour! They have a range of 805 kilometres and can carry two cannons, two 500-pound bombs or eight rockets each!'

'Kya plane hai, saab!' says the defence minister admiringly. 'So small that it's invisible till it's almost on top of you! Aur design aisa gajab ki you don't know if it's coming or going! Confuse kar ditta Pakistaniyon ko!'

'Our new Russian acquisitions are superb too, sir,' counters the Air Chief. 'The MiGs, the Sukhois...'

'Arrey, hamaare Gnats are known as Sabre Slayers,' says the the old Congressi, who has done his homework. 'Pakistan's F-86 Sabres shake at their very name!' He winces. 'Uff! What a noise they all make but, to be sure!'

'The formation is led by Flying officer Ishaan "Baaz" Faujdaar, flying his HAL-built Gnat,' proclaims the commentator as the jets dip their silvery wings, raise their snouts and spiral up into the air in a tight formation. All different shapes and sizes, they sport the same roundel on their flanks: a green dot inside a white circle inside a saffron circle. Their fin flash is a vertical rendition of the Indian tricolour – saffron, white and green. Five of them bloom outwards and away like the petals of a fantastic flower, leaving three in the middle to shoot up through the clouds and perform a series of complicated loops, making the ladies gasp in fear and the children whoop in delight.

'These young guns from Air Force Station Kalaiganga will demonstrate the manoeuvrability and climbing and diving abilities of their jets. Hold on to your hearts, ladies and gentlemen!'

The three jets shoot downwards, freefalling like diving hawks. Two of them slew smoothly to either side while the Gnat in the middle shoots straight up into the air, whirling and buckling like a silver fish hooked at the end of an invisible line. Its movements get faster and faster, until it is spinning. Finally, as the crowd gives a collective gasp, it swoops down to rejoin the rest of the formation.

The spectators breathe again and exchange sheepish looks, some reaching for bottles of water, some wiping their sweat. Even the commentator's voice, booming through the speakers, is shaken.

'And that was Baaz Faujdaar, ladies and gentlemen! The pride of his squadron, the Air Force and the nation!'

The original formation of five, led by the cocky little Gnat, swoops low over the crowd in a neat line, tilts first one cheeky wing and then another to the fluttering Tiranga and roars away towards the sun.

• • •

'Baaz, were those final aerobatics part of the planned programme?' Raka asks Shaanu a couple of hours later.

'Of course not,' responds Maddy lazily. 'He added 'em to show off to the missus of the defence minister.'

They have just taken off from Palam in the bulbous Caribou. They're headed for Kalaiganga, a large Air Force station of the Eastern Air Command, outside Calcutta, which houses a division of MiGs, Gnats and Caribous.

'You were too low,' Raka says seriously. 'It was dangerous – you could've lost control, broken your stupid neck and killed a bunch of spectators.'

'Of course they were part of the planned programme,' Shaanu protests with a laugh as he lounges near the window, tearing the wrapper off a kebab-and-rumali-roti roll. 'Wing Commander Carvalho and I felt the crowd deserved to see something *good*, yaar! Poor things had been watching pineapple-shaped jhaankis and Bharatnatyam dances all morning.'

His voice trails off towards the end of this little speech, as though he feels his explanation is not quite adequate. He takes a bite of his roll, leans back and gazes out of the Caribou's window.

Dazzling sunshine filters in from the round opening, lighting up his grey eyes and bronzed features. He has grown wider around the shoulders since the Flying College. They all have. Their jaws are stronger, their hair longer. Now they really *are* cool cats, handsome young men in their prime, their awkwardness and rough edges smoothed away.

'The sarson's ready to be harvested,' he says after a while. 'See, the fields are bright yellow.'

'You bloody farmer,' Raka says exasperatedly. 'You just wanted to upstage my MiG. And the Sukhoi.'

'The Gnats are the best,' Shaanu maintains.

'*What*?' Raka chokes in outrage at the obvious illogic of this statement. '*Why*?'

''Coz they're small.' Maddy grins. 'Like Baaz.'

Shaanu cracks a reluctant grin in response. 'Shut up. You know what my grandfat—'

'Yes yes, we all know,' Maddy interrupts him hastily. 'Don't start waggling your thumb about, for heaven's sake.'

After they had been commissioned and streamed, Shaanu had hoped to be assigned to the gleaming black metal MiGs, like every other star-struck young Fighter. But the Air Force, in its wisdom, had sorted him into 'The Streaks' – the Gnats of 34 Squadron. He had been bitterly disappointed then, but the very first time he clambered up the Gnat's flank and dropped into the leather seat in the cockpit and inhaled what, over the next four years, was to become a much-loved scent, he had felt like some vital search had come to an end.

Home.

The Gnat's cockpit was a tiny, bubble-shaped space. The perspex canopy was just ten inches above his head, the walls a foot from his face. The AC kicked in only after take-off, so the first time he climbed into it, the Gnat had been as hot as hell. The G-suit had been tight and clammy around the lower half of his body, and he had begun to perspire. But he had locked down the canopy, strapped up, popped a stick of A1 chewing gum into his mouth and reached for the controls. And as the Gnat lifted off the ground, that old familiar dhookk-dhookk-dhookking had kicked in again.

Shaanu loved how small and light it was. Old Kuch Bhi Carvalho, who tended to get mystic-romantic when very drunk, had once told him that fighter pilots don't strap themselves into their planes, they strap their planes onto themselves, like soldiers in the old days used to strap their armour onto their bodies. The Gnat is an extension of *you*, he had told Shaanu, his dark eyes gleaming manically. Its sides are your sides, its belly, your belly. Together, you are Baaz.

Not everyone understood this mystic connection, though.

When his stepfather visited him, curious to see what sort of jet the bastard was flying, his face had fallen ludicrously when he saw the squat little Gnat, barely twenty-two feet from wingtip to wingtip and no more than five feet off the ground, canopy and all.

'Hain? So small! Tu proper pilot naa, ke?'

Then the old man had pointed to a massive transport carrier parked behind the gleaming row of Gnats. 'When you will fly that *big* plane, huh?' he had asked belligerently.

Shaanu had tried to explain that the transport plane was an inferior aircraft, flown by lesser pilots, but the Choudhary hadn't looked too convinced. He had slyly produced a battered-looking second-hand camera and hissed to Shaanu to stand in front of the fifty-foot-high transport carrier for a picture. To send for marriage proposals, he had said wheedlingly. 'If you stand in front of that dinky plane, nobody will marry you.' Shaanu had indignantly refused, the conversation had ended in a bitter argument and the Choudhary had left the station in a huff.

It's not like Ishaan needs help attracting female attention, anyway.

Nowadays he spends most evenings at the Sarhind Club, in charcoal gabardine trousers paired with brightly coloured, snugly tailored shirts painstakingly ironed by his room bearer. Sarhind is a colonial-era club at the edge of AFS Kalaiganga, very exclusive but open to officers from the Armed Forces. Under the gleaming chandeliers, Ishaan plays billiards with other young Fighters, relishing the click of ball striking ball, the muted clinking of sparkling glasses on the trays of the uniformed bearers and the sound of gramophone music drifting in from the atrium. When he steps in through the heavy teak doors, marked MEMBERS ONLY, inhales the privileged blend of crisp air-conditioning, beer and perfume, looks around at the rich mahogany panelling, the deep-green walls and the thick, red velvet curtains, he can scarcely believe that he, Shaanu Faujdaar, of village Chakkahera, from the newly carved state of Haryana, is here, blending, belonging, even shining.

Because shining he is. His name crops up virtually every week on All India Radio's *Forces Request*, the hugely popular Western music show through which young ladies send out messages and song requests to their military sweethearts posted away from home. *'You ... are ... my theme for a dream'* has been belted out for Flying Officer Ishaan Faujdaar more than seventeen times on *Forces Request* so far, prompting disgruntled Raka and Maddy to accuse Shaanu of mailing the request postcards to the radio station himself.

Ladies are drawn to his frank friendly spirit, that good-natured way he has of both talking and listening like he's genuinely interested. There is innocence in Baaz Faujdaar, he doesn't lech or clam up or flatter but (perhaps because he has three sisters) speaks to women easily and naturally. Admitted, he is cocky and swaggers shamelessly, but he isn't snooty, even though Fighters are the most revered breed on the base.

The fact that he is a divine dancer helps, of course. But the others dance well too – Rakesh Aggarwal, for one, has all the Shammi Kapoor moves down pat, *and* he flies a MiG, which everybody knows is much cooler than a Gnat. And Maddy Subbiah, though he's only in the transport division, is wealthy and from a famous fauji family, and can play the piano and sing, and bears more than a passing resemblance to Pat Boone.

Of course it is possible the ladies may have heard the story of how a bunch of older officers once took Baaz Faujdaar to an infamous red-light area and made him recite the bawdy 'Code of the Fornicator', a parody of the solemn 'Code of the Warrior' taught to all cadets at the National Defence Academy.

He'd done this good-naturedly enough, apparently, standing atop a chair, butt-naked and beautiful, enunciating every word clearly.

I am a sex fiend, fornicating is my Dharma,
I will train my mind, body and spirit to fornicate,
I will excel in all devices and weapons of fuckery,
present and future,
I will always use protection,
I will be truthful to bluntness,
I will be humane, cultured and compassionate,
I will fornicate and embrace the consequences,
God, keep me erect, I ask nothing else of you!

But when it came to going into a suite with one of the resident beauties, he pulled on his pants and ran all the way home – a distance of a good twenty-five kilometres – because his brother officers, as part of their evil bid to deflower him, had confiscated his motorcycle.

That pimply young MiGGie Dilsher Singh had put out

this story hoping to shame Ishaan, but it seems to have made the ladies like him even more.

Or perhaps the real ace Ishaan Faujdaar holds over the other Fighters is simply the aesthetically pleasing sight he makes as he leans over the billiards table to score a shot, his dark grey trousers faithfully outlining the shape of his taut, muscular butt.

Little groups of giggly girls are always coming into the billiards room to stand behind him and watch him play.

'Hai, Baaz Faujdaar is just so *cute*, yaar!'

'You ought to see him in his flight overalls, then,' says a ribald auntyji. 'The way that G-suit locks around his waist and thighs but leaves all the vital bits uncovered ... uff tabaahi!'

Even married ladies are not immune to his charm.

'Why weren't you born twenty years ago, or me twenty years later?' one of them sighs coquettishly as he tangoes her bulk across the well-sprung wooden floor.

'Because you and sir are made for each other,' is Faujdaar's reproachful reply.

She laughs. 'You're blushing! Your cheeks are pink. Ah, you're such a pure boy, Baaz!'

But he isn't that pure. He has held some hands under starry skies, stolen kisses behind pillars, scored more than food and fresh air at scenic picnic spots in the nearby countryside. But much to the disgust and disappointment of his brother officers, Baaz Faujdaar, their best and brightest, refuses to take things to the next natural level.

Now he turns to Raka apologetically.

'I didn't mean to upstage anybody. I just wanted to have fun – I should have told you, I'm sorry.'

'He told *me*,' Maddy says smugly. 'Because I'm his best buddy. His buddyroo. His buddy-o number one.'

'Because you live in my armpit!' Shaanu clarifies quickly as Raka starts to look stormy. 'And Raka, saale, you don't talk. You're too busy slurping gobi-paneer biryani from Juhi's beautiful hands to bother with the friends who helped you elope.'

This is true. Raka is newly, blissfully married and does not spend as much time with his friends as he used to. This has especially upset Maddy, who has been Raka's closest buddy since they both met at the NDA. He's been grousing about it regularly to Shaanu.

Raka chooses to ignore this jibe.

'If Baaz confided in you, Maddy, you should've told him it was stupid,' he says roundly. 'You're too scared to do those stunts yourself so you're living vicariously through him. It's pathetic.'

'Jeez, that's low!' Maddy protests. 'And when *you* tag along and avidly watch us chat up the ladies at Anchor Bar, what is *that*, Mr Married Man? And stop hogging so much biryani, you're getting fat.'

Raka responds with great dignity, 'If it's biryani you buggers are after, don't worry, Yahya Khan will soon be feeding home-cooked biryani to all of us! He's gonna arrest Mujib and that will mean war.'

'Who's Mujib?' Maddy asks.

'Seriously?' Raka looks disgusted. 'Mujib ur Rahman, the chap who just got elected Prime Minister of Pakistan.'

'Good for him,' is Shaanu's laconic reply.

'*Bad* for him, actually – 'coz President Yahya Khan isn't letting him rule, because he hails from lallu-panju East Pakistan, not cool cat West Pakistan.'

'*All* of Pakistan is lallu-panju, man,' Maddy drawls. 'It has *no* cool cat areas.'

'It won't be a war, anyway, it'll be a *civil* war,' Shaanu says. 'East versus West. Not our problem.'

'Don't talk like idiots, guys,' Raka says soberly. 'Refugees escaping the violence will clog our borders. We'll get drawn into it for sure.'

'Where d'you get all this info, brother?' Maddy asks wickedly. 'Have you started reading the papers? Wait, does Juhi give you a cup of fragrant handmade tea in the morning, while you read at the head of the table like the man of the house? How cosy and domestic. Hai!'

'Haiiiii!' moans Shaanu, with a hand on his heart.

Raka clicks his tongue.

'Don't you guys ever read the papers?'

'No,' Shaanu admits sunnily. 'I just follow orders. And waise bhi, I wouldn't mind a bit of war. We'll get to use real missiles then, not dummies. *Dhishoooom!*'

'Maybe it'll blow over,' Raka says, not with much hope.

'And maybe it won't,' Shaanu concludes, sounding quite happy at the prospect.

• • •

The newly married Mrs Aggarwal has settled down nicely at AFS Kalaiganga. Pretty, outgoing and intelligent, Juhi makes friends quickly and admirers even quicker. With Raka gone for flight training every day, she spends her time decorating their cosy 'married officers' quarters', keeping up with her studies and experimenting with new recipes. She teaches the airmen's wives how to crochet pretty lace along the edges of their cotton shameez, learns croquet and mah-jong and creates a minor sensation at the May Queen Ball with her daring 'contrast' halter choli in the latest cut.

She joins the Air Force Wives Welfare Association, where, being the youngest member, she quickly becomes everybody's pet. Mrs Pomfret (wife of the Air Officer Commanding, a.k.a. Pomfret, who is both pompous and fretful, besides looking like a fish) is a stringy, battered battle-horse of a lady, without much enthusiasm for 'doing things', but jolly Mrs Carvalho, mother of six, is always up for anything and is an encyclopaedia on all things fauji.

'Your husband, my dear, flies the most elite of all fighter jets,' she tells Juhi, her bone-china mah-jong tiles clicking as she arranges them on her stand. 'The MiG 21s, they're the most expensive jets we have! Well, apart from the Sukhois – but Sukhois are too new for anybody to have a verdict on.'

Juhi glows. 'What can a MiG 21 do?'

'Most things,' says jolly Mrs Carvalho knowledgeably. 'It pounces and dogfights and intercepts and airdrops bombs too. Hosannah says there's something wrong with the placement of its fuel tanks, though. As the fuel gets used up, the centre of gravity shifts and the engine can shut down mid-flight.'

Juhi pales.

'But your Raka is a fine pilot,' Mrs Carvalho reassures her. 'The only pilot who can give him competition is Baaz Faujdaar, Hosannah says.'

'So how come Baaz doesn't fly MiGs then?' Juhi wants to know.

Mrs Carvalho sighs gustily, sets aside the mah-jong stand, draws Juhi to her bosom and starts to whisper confidences. When she finishes, gentle Juhi's eyes are flashing with anger.

'That is so unfair!' she exclaims. 'Can't we do anything about it?'

'No,' says Mrs Carvalho in the flat tone of one who has tried and failed. 'Let's talk about something else, shall we?'

All in all, Juhi's life is blissful. Spring ripens into summer in a happy haze of Easter balls and Holi parties, the Lady Wellesley Swimming Bath reopens and everybody agrees that Mrs Raka looks amazingly fetching in her new ashes-of-rose swimsuit. Raka and she spend three glorious days in Darjeeling. But then her sunny world starts to smoulder and curl around the edges.

It begins with the news of the arrest of that intellectual-looking, pipe-smoking Bengali politician Mujib ur Rahman by the West Pakistani Army, swiftly followed by a crackdown on Bengali intellectuals. Scores of thinkers, journalists and student activists are brutally killed on the night of 25 March, the papers report, when the military enters Dacca University's predominantly Hindu Jagannath Hall and indulges in an orgy of arson and murder.

Then, when Juhi and the other Air Force Wives go into Calcutta to shop for saris and gold jewellery, eat puchkas and maybe pick up a dragon carpet from Chinatown, they come face to face with a more concrete face of the madness in the East.

There are thousands of refugees everywhere, stoic and emaciated, streaming in from across the border with terrible tales of atrocities – rape and death and the murder of babies. Calcutta is groaning with the sicknesses they have bought with them. Cholera, malaria, conjunctivitis and, most dangerously, a simmering intolerance. Juhi comes back to Kalaiganga feeling thoroughly unsettled.

Next, the Army gets busy at the border and Baaz and the other Gnatties are called in to provide CAS. Juhi isn't very clear about what exactly they're doing, but she knows that CAS means Close Air Support. And one evening she sees Baaz's squadron flying back in a rag-tag formation, one jet lagging behind, leaking fuel and streaming smoke.

And then Raka gets busy perfecting some strange new manoeuvre in his MiG 21.

It is called steep-glide dive bombing and the technical whizzes have come up with it specifically to bomb airfields. It's more dangerous than the old way, because it leaves the pilots exposed for a much longer time to the anti-aircraft guns on the ground. But it is much more accurate, apparently.

Juhi knows all this in full technical detail because she's made Raka explain it to her again and again, late in the night when they're both lying under the olive-green Army-issued mosquito netting on the double bed his parents have gifted them. Raka held out initially, telling her that his work was confidential, but she wormed it out of him with a mixture of weepy interrogation and steamy seduction. Now she wishes she hadn't. She has nightmares – sometimes of Baaz, sometimes of Maddy, but mostly of Raka, wounded, groaning or dead in some muddy paddy field, white-faced and blood-smeared, burning like a rick.

Raka, of course, thinks the whole thing is a big fat joke. In fact, he's been using his steep-glide dive attacks as unfair leverage in the bedroom.

'Here's your husband, safe and sound, after risking his life for his country!' he warbles as he emerges from the bathroom every evening just as she likes him – fragrant, freshly shaved, with only a towel around his trim waist. 'Show him you're happy he's home, madame wife!'

And Juhi does. But after he falls asleep, she lies awake and looks at his face, at those lips that curve upwards even as he sleeps, the rounded cheeks, the brave curl of moustache, and she worries and worries and worries.

Theirs is a runaway marriage – Baaz and Maddy had

spirited her away from the back gate of her house while Raka created a distraction by letting her father beat him up in the front garden – and her family still hasn't accepted it. If anything happens to Raka – her stomach roils at the very thought – where will she go, what will she do?

She has panic attacks in the afternoon, and tears fall fast upon the hem of the black dress she is shortening to wear to the next ball at the Sarhind Club. She spends hours praying for an overcast monsoon, which will ground all aircraft, and is ecstatic when Kalaiganga is rocked by thunderstorms in June and July and flight training gets cancelled. She quickly learns to expect the summons, brought to her quarters by a grinning airman, that Raka sir and the others are free for the day and request her presence at the airfield.

Life becomes a whirl of impromptu parties, full of music and dancing, laughter and banter, lovely food and drink. But the knot at the pit of her stomach never eases away entirely.

Diwali is early this year, and for some reason Juhi is convinced that once it is over things will get worse – much worse. She pushes this dark premonition to the back of her mind and focuses on keeping her Navratra fast devoutly, planting chrysanthemums in her little garden and taking Raka to the best tailor in Kalaiganga to be measured for a brand new dinner jacket for the festive season.

'I'm getting a fancy jacket too,' Raka tells Shaanu one day, when Juhi takes pity on the bachelor officers and invites them over for a home-cooked feast the day after Karva Chauth. 'Watch out for me at the Winter Fete, brother!'

Shaanu, chewing busily, flashes him a pitying grin.

'Nobody's going to be looking at you at the fete, Raka,' he says, swallowing. 'All eyes will be on Juhi.'

Having said that, he heads for the kitchenette in search

of more piping-hot puris, leaving Maddy and Raka to suffer a long soliloquy from their frog-faced commanding officer, Wing Commander Mohindar Dheengra, a middle-aged bachelor fondly known as Deengu because of his tendency to spin tall tales of bombs and bravery and beautiful female spies whenever his tissues have been well-irrigated.

Deengu leans one hip comfortably against the Aggarwals' prized turntable, pins Maddy and Raka into place with his jewel-like, long-lashed eyes and holds forth hoarsely.

'Look lads, you have to be mentally prepared for any eventuality! In '65, I flew my Vampire in a silk Pathan suit instead of my IAF dungarees, with Pakistani currency jingling in my pockets. I had it all planned! If I got shot down over enemy territory, I was going to open a paan-ki-dukaan, find a beautiful begum to grind my qimam and father half-a-dozen infidel brats. Imagine my joy, when, after bailing out at 31,000 feet, I landed unhurt in a sugarcane field, to find a voluptuous beauty, bosom heaving, kneeling next to me...'

In the kitchen, Shaanu finds Juhi flushed pink from the heat of the kadhai, a cheesecloth apron tied around her waist. He hoiks himself up to sit on the countertop next to her stove, thus establishing a monopoly on all the hot puris emerging from the kadhai.

Sopping up spicy sabzi with a large chunk of puri, he tells her teasingly, 'How pretty you look, Mrs Aggarwal! Any good news?'

She blushes rosily and rolls her eyes. 'Don't do nonsense talk.'

Shaanu grins and bolts down three puris with slurps of contentment while Juhi concentrates on frying up a new batch, her eyes wistful.

As he springs down from the countertop to wash his

plate, she says, 'Baaz, do you think there is going to be a war?'

Shaanu stops for a moment, then walks up to her and puts an arm around her neat waist.

'Of course,' he replies lightly. 'Raka's going to stride into the kitchen any minute now and accuse me of flirting with you. I will fight him off, because how dare he doubt your faithfulness? There's gonna be blood on the kitchen floor, for sure.'

'There will be blood on the kitchen floor *before* that, you bundal Baaz, if you give such stupid evasive answers,' she retorts, waving a mehendi-decorated palm in his face. 'You know exactly what I mean!'

He gives a vibrant, reassuring laugh and turns to the sink. 'Sorry! And sorry to disappoint you, but there isn't going to be a war. This is real life, not a Hindi film.'

'But Raks says—'

'Raks just wants to look more romantic in your eyes,' Shaanu says firmly. 'The poor fool.'

She looks deep into his eyes, letting the water run in the empty sink, even though his plate has been washed, dried and put away. 'Swear?'

Shaanu nods.

'Swear,' he says steadily.

And then he turns off the tap and leads her back to her husband, profoundly thankful that he has no girl in his life, as such. Because of course there's going to be a war.

• • •

'Uh, there's just been one small change, Yo Hi sir.'

The Chief Creative Officer of India's largest advertising agency pushes back the bush of grey hair from his lean, raddled face and pinions the weedy account executive with a vulpine eye.

'Eh?' he growls.

He's sitting in the best seat at Regal movie hall, bang in the middle of the first row of balcony seats. An ancient rickety fan circles above his head, ruffling his grey curls. The account executive edges closer to him obsequiously.

'Uh, Yo Hi sir, you remember the script from the Freesia presentation, don't you?'

Yo Hi, whose nickname, an abbreviation of Your Highness, was created only half in jest, deigns to remove the cigar from his mouth.

'Of course,' he says gruffly. 'Come alive with the freshness of Freesia. The bikini-clad babe under the waterfall. What about it?'

The account exec licks his lips and launches into a clearly rehearsed speech. 'Well, sir, as you know, LevarBaths loved the idea. They wanted us to shoot the film immediately. We contacted the best model coordination agencies, and you personally picked out a ravishing international model...'

'Well-stacked,' nods Yo Hi wisely. 'Fair, with a mole on the upper lip. Yeah, I remember.' He waggles his cigar impatiently. 'Now play the damn ad. Let's see how it turned out.'

Tharki old man, thinks the weedy account exec, smoothing his clammy palms along his pants.

'Yeah well, turns out she was a bit of a washout.' He giggles nervously. 'Heh heh ... no pun intended.'

'Whaddyou mean washout?' growls the CCO. 'Those titties weren't padding. I can always tell.'

'Oh no, they weren't padding.' The account executive gives another nervous giggle. 'I can vouch for that personally! It's just that...' He gulps and wilts with relief. 'Oh, here's my writer! Let *him* tell you!'

He gladly hands over the reins to a chubby youth who has just stuck his head into the EXIT door. This smug fellow steps onto the balcony, smiling a little too brightly, and takes up the narrative.

'To cut a long story short, sir, our ravishing heroine donned the emerald-green bikini and got into the waterfall readily enough,' he begins glibly, 'but then all hell broke loose. She kept slipping on the rocks, and when she got under the waterfall, the water pressure was too strong. She clutched at the rocks, but they crumbled away. So we got out a rope and tied it around her so she wouldn't fall, and then the water-guys – who were locals and spoke only whatever freakin' language they speak in the wilds of Kodaikanal – got a bit enthusiastic and tied it too tight so she got welts around her stomach. So then we had to wait an hour for the welts to fade. And then the sun went behind a cloud, so we had to wait some more. And *then* somebody thought it would be a good idea to give her a stiff drink, but it wasn't, because the moment she got back under the waterfall she started shrinking against the rocks, alternately whimpering and snarling that the water was too cold, that the rope was chafing, that there were hairy black crabs crawling about in the rocks. And then these two jolly little snakes came wriggling up in the water – a big green one and a small brown one – and flickered their tongues at her, and she fainted.'

He pauses, risking a glance at Yo Hi to see how he's taking this.

'Snakes, eh?' muses the CCO, steepling his fingers. 'Why didn't we think of snakes before? Snakes are sexy.'

'Freesia is a clean, wholesome brand,' puts in the weedy account exec hastily. 'Snakes don't fit—'

'By then, of course, it was the middle of the afternoon and the DOP was getting gloomier and gloomier and muttering about losing light.'

'And of course we had attracted a crowd,' says the AE, rolling his eyes. 'A bunch of toothless old women and horny young men plonked themselves on the ground behind the security cordons and began heckling our crew.'

'Their first suggestion was to give her a drink to warm her up, which of course we were dumb enough to take,' says the writer. 'Next, they suggested *I* play the bathing beauty. They coarsely told me to take off my shorts and show 'em what I've got.'

Yo Hi gives a short laugh.

The writer clears his throat and continues with careful casualness.

'Anyway, we'd taken along this still photographer chick to shoot some pics we could use for posters and hoardings – and someone from the crowd shouted out that we should try her only under the waterfall. So, with the supermodel fainting away and the DOP and client in hysterics, we did.' He takes a deep breath. 'The film's ready, editing and music all done – d'you wanna take a look?'

There is a rather terrible silence.

'It's ... not that bad,' the AE ventures finally, timidly. 'She has dimples.'

'Small ones,' adds the writer with scrupulous honesty.

Yo Hi's eyes narrow.

'And breasts.'

'Small ones.'

Yo Hi's eyes are mere slits now.

The AE guy reveals the final, most damning bit of news. 'And she's slightly, um, wheatish, sir.'

The silence now is absolutely dreadful.

'But she was born in America!' the AE continues heartily, like this can somehow compensate for the sin of wheatishness. 'She's really artsy. Shoots women in red-light areas and street kids and old people and cows and all that. She took on the Freesia assignment because she went broke buying this really fancy camera.'

'And she wasn't at all afraid of the cold or the snakes,' puts in the writer. 'Just went for it!'

The CCO leans back in his chair and jiggles one leg restlessly.

'Show me,' he says.

Gulping and breathing heavily, they gesture to the unseen technician in the projection room, then stand back to watch Yo Hi's face, as narrowly as he's watching the ad.

There are three cuts of the ad. As he watches the first cut, Yo Hi slowly raises his eyebrows and purses his lips.

'Nice jingle,' he says when it is over.

During the second viewing, he leans in closer to the screen, his elbows on his knees.

And through the third cut, he sprawls back in his seat and strokes his beard, barely looking at the screen at all.

When the screen goes dark, he gets to his feet, hitching his pants up by his jaunty red suspenders.

The two-man team looks up at him, their eyes agonized.

'You dumb fucks,' Yo Hi says mildly.

They quiver and quaver.

'Sorry sir, sorry sir,' they mumble, cringing. 'We can reshoot, what's there?'

Yo Hi throws out his arms.

'You've stumbled upon an absolute *star*!'

'You like her?' They gulp in relief, collapsing against the backs of the rickety seats. 'Really?'

'Don't you?' he demands.

They sit up straighter. 'Oh, ya ya,' they say with belated cocksureness. 'We knew, we had this gut feel that she was going to be good!'

'Good!' snorts the old man, who has launched a hundred advertising stars. 'She's *great*. Let's run this!'

• • •

At Air Force Station Kalaiganga, which falls under the vital Eastern Air Command, the lengthening days and short hot nights are often enlivened with talk of war. Both the MiG 21 squadron and the HAL Gnat squadrons are eager for first blood, but at the moment all the action seems to be limited to the transport and heli-borne divisions, which are often called in to airlift refugees from the border areas. Still, all valuable aircraft have been put into blast pens and Combat Air Patrols are often mounted over the base, the buzzing of the constantly circling Gnats as irritating as the insect they're named after. Army vehicles now move about with shrouded headlights at night, and war siren drills are held on a regular basis.

Needless to say, Shaanu is thriving in this thickened atmosphere. When he strides onto the tarmac at dawn for his morning briefing with his Wing Commander, good old Hosannah 'Kuch Bhi' Carvalho, he is a man who is where he wants to be, doing what he loves. The roar of the jet engines is music to his ears, the smell of aviation fuel intoxicating. In his flying overalls, helmet under his arm, his Flying College strut developed into a full-blown swagger, he looks (as his doting sisters tell him whenever he sends them a photograph) like a hero from a particularly heroic war movie. But alas, there is no heroine in the movie of his life.

'Maybe he *has* a girlfriend. Somebody special, who has

sworn him to secrecy,' speculates Juhi as she slips on her earrings at her dressing table one evening.

Raka, who's putting on his shoes, immediately looks up, extremely offended.

'He wouldn't keep secrets from *us*.'

'Yes, because *your* lips are always sealed,' says his wife, bouncing up to kiss him on his open mouth. 'I know what you all do once you're up in the air, connected by the R/T, on the supposedly flying missions. Chatter chatter chatter.'

'Are you making fun of this lean mean fighting machine?' Raka grabs her and spins her onto his lap.

'Yes!' she gasps, laughing. 'Ow ow ow, *stop it*!'

He stops it, pulling her closer and placing a smacking kiss on her rosy cheek.

'Maybe he's in love with you,' he says whimsically. 'The poor bastard.'

'That they all are,' she says complacently and starts counting her admirers on her fingers. 'Baaz, Deengu, Maddy...'

'Maddy falls in love with every girl he meets.' Her husband chuckles, rubbing his cheek against hers. 'And Bundal Baaz, none.'

'He's a one-woman man,' says Juhi wisely. 'Wait and see. When he falls in love, he'll fall hard. Maybe it's got something to do with him being, you know...'

She gives him a meaningful look.

Raka looks blank.

'Short?'

'Uff!' Juhi tosses her head in disgust and gets off his lap. 'Illegitimate!'

That evening, when they go to see a film in Calcutta, Raka brings up the subject with Shaanu.

'What the hell were you doing all those years in bloody Chakkahera, man?' he demands. 'Why didn't you lure some hot chamari into the ganna fields when you were fifteen?'

'We don't grow sugarcane,' is Shaanu's entirely pragmatic reply. 'Only mustard and channa. And channa grows only about one foot high – if you go in there to have sex, people can *see* you.'

'He's just playing hard to get,' Maddy says. 'Building up this dark, romantique mystique…'

'I'm fairer than you, fucker,' Shaanu interjects.

But Maddy is on a roll.

'Because what is gettable is … forgettable!' He flicks his fingers dismissively, then pauses, impressed with his own rhyming skills. 'Arrey wah! Say wah wah, you guys.'

'You know what I think?' Raka muses. 'I think you're sexually frustrated. That's why you feel the need to do suicidal stunts in the sky. It's like a release for you. That's it! Baaz, your over-choosy, pent-up penis is going to get you killed.'

'I'm *not* over-choosy.' Shaanu's grey eyes shine with conviction. 'Just choosy. I mean, the girl should be special … and the first time should *mean* something. Aise hi thodi? Like gajar mooli?'

There is silence. Then,

'Baaz's penis … is waiting for Venus!' Maddy says sagely.

Raka guffaws.

Juhi and Ishaan regard the two of them in disgust.

'Animals,' Juhi says. 'Don't let them corrupt you, Baaz. Here, have a sandwich.'

She smiles at him approvingly, opens her capacious handbag and produces a large plastic tiffin box, brimming with goodies.

Raka stops laughing instantly.

'Juhi!' he hisses. 'You can't smuggle food into the movie hall like this! Outside food isn't allowed!'

But Juhi just sniffs. 'Arrey aise kaise? Why should I pay so much money for their baasi popcorn and oily salty chips? These sandwiches are ekdum fresh. Take Maddy, take Shaanu – cheese, lettyoose and cucumber.'

'Yeah, shut up, Raka,' say his buddies, cramming sandwiches into their mouths gratefully.

'I want cheese,' Raka capitulates, grabbing one before they're all gone. 'Achcha, Baaz, what about Afsana Sidnani? She's lovely. You helped her run her stall at the fete. Why don't you try your luck with her, huh?'

Shaanu puts down his sandwich. 'What the hell, man?' he demands, hassled. 'What is this try your luck, try your luck? A lucky dip or what? I like Afsana, she's a nice lady, but not like that, yaar.'

But both his friends are already spluttering into their sandwiches. 'Lucky dip!' they guffaw. 'Ha ha, Baaz, *lucky dip*! Maybe if you're *lucky* she'll let you *dip*.'

'Hawji!' Juhi gasps, swatting at them with the tiffin box lid. 'Dogs! Pigs! Chhee!'

'Tum dono kutte ho,' Shaanu gives his verdict as he sits back with folded arms in the rickety folding seat. 'Sick, perverted dogs. I have three sisters, I don't like all thi—'

But right then, the screen, which had been showing the standard black-and-white Films Division News Reel, flickers and displays an image of green mountains and a pristine waterfall. An insistent drumbeat kicks in and a guitar begins to strum.

They turn their attention to the screen.

'Hey, what's this?'

'Must be the new Freesia soap ad.' Raka sits up excitedly, so excitedly that his seat snaps shut and spits him out. He gets up and sits down again, his eyes glued to the screen. 'The first-ever bikini ad of Bharatvarsh! Dilsher from my squadron saw it last weekend – he said the girl is too good, ya!'

'*You* close your eyes,' his wife says grimly. 'What will you do watching a Freesia soap ad? You bathe with Lifebuoy.'

But they all keep their eyes wide open. Expensive, frivolous ads are a rarity in strictly socialist India.

A breathy female voice croons *la … la-la-la-la … la-la-la-la …* and the hall comes alive with wolf whistles. A pair of slim bare legs flash on the screen and click playfully at the ankles, sending a spray of water droplets onto the screen.

And then, as Shaanu, Raka, Juhi and Maddy watch open-mouthed, sandwiches forgotten, a slender golden-brown girl in an emerald-green bikini prances joyfully under the waterfall, black hair mantling her shoulders, skin aglow. Her teeth do chatter slightly under the cascading water in the close-ups, but she still manages to convey innocence, energy and a great sense of fun.

The boys approve of her, immediately and whole-heartedly, but hold back from vocalizing this, very aware of Juhi sitting between them.

'No shame,' Juhi declares finally.

'C'mon, Juhi, she's charming,' Maddy protests.

'I think she has a certain jaa ne say qwa.' Raka grins, mispronouncing atrociously.

'Because she's got *qwater* of her clothes on,' is Juhi's tart response. 'Quarter ka bhi quarter!'

'I like her.' Maddy sticks to his guns. 'She doesn't simper.'

'Well, she *should*,' Juhi says hotly. 'She has no business

being itna comfortable while exposing so much! And she's so kaali! *Baaz* is fairer than her.'

Shaanu looks like he hasn't heard a word anybody has said. 'I like her,' he says slowly. 'Very much!'

It isn't till the end of the ad, though, when the girl flashes a grin in a particularly impish close-up, revealing two little dimples in her cheeks, that he sits up abruptly, his feet slamming down hard on the linoleum tiles.

'Oooooohhh teeeeri!'

The other three ignore this Haryanvi exclamation, their eyes riveted to the screen.

Somehow, Maddy and Raks don't seem to have made the same discovery he has, making Shaanu wonder if he's imagining things. But the other two had been sitting in the front of the Jonga, he recalls. And they'd spent much less time with the runaway than he had.

By the time a photo of Freesia soap slaps onto the screen and a deep voice declaims *Come alive with the freshness of Freesia*, Shaanu is sure of it.

The girl under the waterfall is the girl from the train.

The one with the red bandariya skirt, the slender brown thighs, the dead brother, the bossy father and the put-an-end-to-war agenda.

And suddenly (maybe all it took was the sight of her in her emerald-green bikini?) Shaanu is sure that she's filter and he's tobacco, and they're perfectly matched. Not that he smokes or anything.

Tehmina Dadyseth.

What the hell has she been doing with her life?

FOUR

The Howrah Mail is an iconic train, sixteen bogeys long, travelling from Dilli to Kalkatta over a period of one night and two days. It slices across the Gangetic Plain, the rocking rhythm of its wheels conspiring to create a cosy intimacy in which passengers share innumerable cups of tea, food from every corner of independent India and the occasional tube of toothpaste. Rishtas have been fixed on the Howrah Mail, lifelong friendships established, the nation's politics discussed threadbare and the nasty nature of many a mother-in-law lamented over.

Today, the topic in the second-class bogey is the civil war in Pakistan. As the train khata-khats its way briskly across rural Haryana, the occupant of 27C holds centre stage. He is a paunchy, hairy character, poured into a straining sando-cut vest with several small holes sprayed delicately across the front, rather like a sprig of daisies.

'Bhaisaab, all this problem started at the time of independence only!' he declares. 'The British carved up the subcontinent in such a foolish way! One long, big India in the middle with one small-sa Pakistan hanging to the right of it and one small-sa Pakistan hanging to the left of it...'

'Like a pennis with two balls,' remarks 30A from behind a newspaper.

The men gathered in the bottom berths guffaw loudly.

'Mind your tongue, bhaisaab!' admonishes a voice from an upper berth. 'Ladies and children are present!'

'Sorry, behenji,' 30A says placatingly. 'No bad this-thing intended! Point is ki these two pieces of Pakistan have nothing to unite them – one speaks Punjabi, another speaks Bengali, their culture vagehra is also ekdum different, even their Islam is not the same type.' He pauses to shudder. 'Not that I claim to understand Islam. And they are separated by 1,600 kilometres of Indian territory. Naturally, they are fighting! And then saying ki *we* are the ones who are causing the fight! Batao!'

There is a murmur of general agreement.

After a quick look around the bogey to establish that it is safe to speak, the clerkish-looking fellow in 28B leans forward and says in a lowered voice, 'Ji, it's all because of eating non-veg. Cow and goat and what not! It makes them violent. That's why they are killing each other.'

'There is a kahawat, na,' says a thin, elegant old man in starched kurta pyjama, 'ki let sleeping dogs sleep. To that I add today a kahawat of my own. Let fighting dogs fight!'

There is a hearty chorus of hear-hear followed by a companionable, munching silence. Then a slender girl with short tousled hair gets to her feet. Pulling a scarf from her bag, she wraps it around her head, covering her hair, neck and ears. Then she kneels down in the aisle, holds up her hands and begins to pray.

A hush falls in the bogey. 28B sits back, consternation writ large on his face, and even 27C looks shamefaced.

'Haw,' gasps a young matron surrounded by three sleeping children. 'She's Mohammedan!'

The praying girl smiles, tiny dimples blooming in her cheeks. She opens one bright eye, then the other.

'No, I'm not,' she says calmly. 'But supposing I was? All of you would have been pretty embarrassed, na?'

The young matron looks confused for a moment before letting out an appreciative peal of laughter. The rest of the bogey stare at the speaker with uncertain, hostile eyes.

'Oversmart.'

'Trying to show us down.'

'I'm sure she is Muslim only, pulling a double bluff.'

'I'm Parsi, actually,' the girl says amiably to the group at large as she scrambles back up to sit in her place. 'Tehmina Dadyseth.' She removes the scarf from around her head and stuffs it into her bag. 'Namaste!'

The gathering isn't mollified.

'What were you trying to prove, waise?' 27C says belligerently. 'That you are a very great secular?'

Tinka, for it is she, rumples her short hair thoughtfully. 'I don't know,' she admits. 'I just thought that if somebody sitting in this bogey was a Muslim, they'd feel so upset but be too intimidated to admit it and would have to sit silently while all of you said ill-informed, bigoted things about their religion and their way of life.'

This is met with a tense silence.

'You are too young, beta,' the lady from the upper berth says finally, with maddening condescension. 'You have not seen what we have seen, suffered what we have suffered...'

'Oh, please don't start off about the Partition again!' Tinka entreats. 'If Muslims did terrible things then, so did Hindus.'

But this is too much for her audience. They start to whisper to each other, their mood swinging firmly back to hostile again.

'All these minorities are the same.'

'Parsi, eh? They're all mad.'

'I think she's an actress or something. I've seen her somewhere. Acting people have no morals.'

'Is she travelling alone? Where's her husband? No brother-father?'

As Tinka's eyebrows start to rise in comic alarm, the young matron speaks up in a sweet voice. 'I think Tehmina has a point. We're all human beings first, nahi?'

The bogey seems ready to argue this point, but just then the sleeping children begin to stir, the muscular toddler sending up a deep-throated wail. People draw away, turning back to their food, their newspapers and their card games.

'Hello!' Tinka bends to address the cranky child cheerfully. 'What's your name?'

He hides his face but the two young girls with him rub their eyes and sit up, eyeing her with interest.

'Is that a boy-cut?'

Tinka rumples her hair ruefully. How she misses her long mass of hair. But there had been no other solution. After the Freesia ad came out, people started recognizing her everywhere. At the kirana store, on Marine Drive, once even at a funeral. Men whistled the *la ... la-la-la* tune whenever she walked by, while women whispered and pointed. After being blown a particularly lascivious kiss by a grandfather from a BEST bus, she'd walked down to the beauty parlour in Colaba and got what the girls there described as an 'Audrey Hepburn *Roman Holiday* pageboy bob, which will really set off your ingénue features, madam'.

'I guess so,' she says. 'It's new. I'm not sure I like it … do you?'

'No.' The younger of the two girls speaks up first. She looks about ten years old, round and fair, dressed in a green-striped sweater over a salwar-kameez, her eyes lined fearsomely with kajal. 'You look like a boy.'

The other girl, thinner and taller but equally kohl-eyed, shakes her head at her sister. 'I think it's nice. We have an LP of an Amaarikan lady singer, and on the cover her hair is short too. Where did you get it cut?'

'In Bombay,' Tinka replies. 'What are your names?'

She smiles as she asks this question, and the three children smile back – Tinka's smile has that sort of quality. She's dressed in a tight black poloneck, emerald-green cord pants and scuffed leather brogues. There is a complicated-looking camera slung around her neck, which she now removes and places carefully in a leather case. To their young eyes, she seems incredibly exotic.

'I'm Sulochana Faujdaar,' says the elder one. 'She is Sarita Faujdaar. And *this*' – she pats the gap-toothed toddler who has stopped wailing and is staring at Tinka with his fingers in his mouth – 'is our nephew Jaideep Singh. He's Sneha didi's baby. We're going to visit our Shaanu Bhaisaab.'

Tinka doesn't know it just yet, but this last name is one she is destined to hear many many times tonight. It is always pronounced with capital letters clearly implied, as if one were speaking of royalty.

'Shaanu Bhaisaab's a very big pie-lutt in the Air Force,' Sulochana continues, clambering to the upper berth and dangling her sandalled feet right in front of the nose of the elegant gentleman who wants to let fighting dogs fight. 'Posted at Kalaiganga. He's a *fighter* pie-lutt. They're the *best*.'

'How nice,' Tinka responds politely.

'Shaanu Bhaisaab has a two-room sweet with balcony and attached bathroom in the Afsars Mess!' Sulo continues, swinging her legs. 'And his own personal room bearer to do all his jobs – ironing, washing, shoe-polishing, all!'

'Good for him!' Tinka replies.

'He's my Mercury,' Sulo confides.

'Your what?' Tinka is confused.

Sulo rolls her eyes in the face of such stupidity.

'My *Mercury*! And Sneha behenji is my Venus and Jaideep Singh is my Earth and Sari is my Mars. And Surinder bhaisaab and Shelly bhaisaab are my two Jupiters. And Pitaji I think-so is my Pluto. I don't like him very much, you know, but one should love their parents. Or maybe he could be my utmosphere or something!'

Comprehension dawns on Tinka. 'Oh, I see! This is your own personal solar system! You're the sun, and these are the people – sorry planets – who are closest to you! Why isn't your mummy your Mercury?'

'Because she's dead,' Sari tells her. 'Who's *your* Mercury?'

Good question, Tinka thinks wryly.

In the sixteen hours it takes to get from Delhi to Kalaiganga, she becomes well acquainted with the Faujdaar brood. Refreshed by their nap and by the puri-aloo Sneha doles out from a huge red mithai-ka-dabba, the children proceed to get extremely boisterous. The other passengers retreat, put off as much by their volume as by Tinka's and Sneha's sinister Muslim sympathies.

Tinka and the Faujdaars play games of Donkey and Cat's Cradle. They giggle at the paunchy-man-with-the-holey-vest's lusty snores and watch the nasal-voiced lady's elaborate cleansing, toning and moisturizing routine with open curiosity. As the passing landscape darkens and the cosy blue night light comes on inside, the girls get Tinka to French braid their hair. Jaideep Singh develops a solid crush on this strange new female and spends the night with her on the lower berth, snoring lightly, his red cheeks puffing up every time he inhales.

Sneha can't get over the fact that Tinka is travelling alone.

'Aise kaise, how can your family let you go?' she asks over their morning tea, as the rest of the bogey listens in while pretending not to. 'Without any gents?'

Tinka's expression grows airy. 'Why would I bring my family along on a work trip?'

Sneha's eyes widen. 'You *work?*' There is wistful awe in her voice. 'I'd like to work – I could teach, maybe classes four and five, maybe even seven.'

Tinka suppresses a twinge of guilt. Actually, this is stretching the facts a little. She *has* had a chat with the New York head of WWS, the World Wire Service, and they've agreed to look at the pictures she sends – but she isn't a full-time employee. They've issued her a press card, though.

'You work too,' she replies evasively. 'You work *very* hard, actually. I've been watching.'

It is Sneha's turn to laugh.

'And *you're* travelling without any men as well!' Tinka continues.

'Oh, pitaji hain na.' Sneha gestures vaguely in the direction of the next bogey. Apparently pitaji is too mighty a personage to travel with women and children and has booked himself a separate first-class berth. Clearly, just his presence on the train is enough to provide protection to his family.

'Besides, Shaanu Bhaisaab will be there to pick us up,'

Sneha says, her eyes lighting up. 'Oh, such fun it'll be. I've got some *very* exciting news for him!'

She looks like she expects Tinka to ask what this exciting news is.

'What is it?' she asks dutifully.

But Sneha just gives a mysterious wriggle and shakes her head.

'What do you do? Matlab, why are you going to Kalaiganga?'

'Calcutta,' Tinka corrects her. The Faujdaars seem to think everybody on board the train is headed not for the big metropolis but for the small town that houses the Air Force Base where Fabulous Shaanu Bhaisaab is stationed. 'To photograph the refugee camps on the outskirts and do some volunteer work with the Missionaries of Charity.'

Sneha looks at her with stars in her eyes.

'Missionaries of Charity! Mother Teresa!' she breathes reverentially. 'You must be such a good person!'

Tinka suppresses another pang of guilt. Because she *isn't* such a good person. She's staying at the luxurious Sarhind Club, for one, and she's planning to get in a fair bit of shopping too.

'No no,' she says weakly.

'What all photos have you taken that have been published?' Sneha asks interestedly.

'Well, I took this one picture of the Taj Mahal that came out in last week's issue of WWS,' Tinka replies. 'With the big dome all bundled up in gunny bags and bamboo scaffolding. It's been camouflaged because our government is worried it may be bombed.' She grins at the kids. 'It used to shine like a big white rasgulla at night, apparently.'

'Kalaiganga may get bombed.' Jaideep Singh sounds quite excited at the prospect.

'Kalaiganga is not the Taj Mahal,' replies his harassed mother.

'But it is such a big Air Force 'tation!' Jaideep Singh looks offended at the insinuation that his uncle's base isn't important enough to be bombed.

'That's true,' Tinka says placatingly.

The train stops at Jamshedpur and disgorges most of the occupants of their bogey, including Nasal Voice and Holey Vest. As if lightened of this sour baggage, it starts to practically sing its way down to Kalaiganga.

Khata-khat, khata-khat, go the wheels of the Howrah Mail briskly. *Phata-phat, phata-phat.*

The children go ballistic as the track curves, and for about a minute the whole train is visible from their window, a black-headed, bright red wriggly caterpillar in a bed of green. The engine chugs harder, the whistle blows and smoke blows past their ecstatic faces. As the train shoots past several level crossings, they lurch to the bathroom with mugs filled with toothpaste, toothbrush, Lifebuoy soap and cold cream. When they stagger back, all wet hair and flushed cheeks, Sneha rubs coconut oil into their hair and combs it out ruthlessly. Bright frocks and shiny shoes are pulled on. Rubber bands are produced, braids are tied, kajal is reapplied. Finally, one black dot is carefully placed on Jaideep Singh's left cheek.

'Shaanu Bhaisaab, Shaanu Bhaisaab!' Sulochana jumps up and down as the train pulls into the station.

Sarita, older and more dignified, just wriggles delightedly in the window seat.

Sneha, composed but bright-eyed, puts on her bindi in the mirror.

Tinka feels strangely forlorn in the face of this familial

excitement. Swallowing the stupid lump in her throat, she stands up to get a book out of her rucksack.

The train comes to a halt. Sulochana utters a piercing scream, presumably at sighting Shaanu Bhaisaab. Footsteps tread quickly up the stairs and then a smiling, vibrant voice rings out cheerfully:

'Bacchhccha paaaarty?'

On her knees, wrestling with her rucksack, Tinka hears one loud thud and then another as the two girls hurl themselves upon the new entrant, shrieking joyfully. Feeling decidedly unwanted, she stays where she is, pushing the rucksack back slower than she needs to.

By the time she straightens up and turns around, the aisle is empty. Oddly deflated, Tinka finger-combs her mop of hair and stretches out on the vacated berth, using her rucksack like a pillow.

Through the large train windows, she can see the Faujdaars bunched together in a noisy, colourful huddle. They have been joined by a thin-shanked, crusty old gent in a dirty-white dhoti and pagdi. Pitaji, presumably. Famous Shaanu Bhaisaab has his back to Tinka. He has lifted up Sulochana and is swinging her about like an aeroplane, making whooping noises. He presents a rather good rear view, Tinka has to admit. Or maybe it's those Oxford blue Air Force dungarees that can make even saggy-paunched unclejis look hot.

Then he turns around, laughing, and Tinka is immediately transported to another train station, and to a feeling she'd last felt four years ago.

The cadet from Jodhpur Flying College.

With the smiling grey eyes that are exactly the same colour as the Kota stone floors of her darling Kung fui's ancestral kothi in Kathiawar.

Now with longer hair, leaner, more tan and much more polished-looking.

He sees her staring at him through the bars and raises a questioning eyebrow.

'That's Tinka didi,' Sulo supplies, her arms around his neck. 'She's our friend. We played Donkey on the train. She got Do and Don and Donk.'

The cadet – an officer now, her eyes flicker to his stripes, a Flying Officer, no less – steps up to the window, still holding his little sister, his face creasing automatically into a polite smile.

'Hullo, ma—'

One hand rising self-consciously to adjust her hair, Tinka smiles back.

He checks himself abruptly.

Tinka's eyes twinkle, her smile widens, scrunching up her face, turning her into an implet with dimplets.

He scans her face, his gaze growing keener as he takes in her hair, the camera around her neck. An answering grin spreads across his face.

A genuinely welcoming grin. Like he's thought about her over the years too, the way she has of him, at odd hours, on odd days and even on even days sometimes.

'Tell-me-na Dadyseth,' he drawls deliberately, the Kota-grey eyes sparkling with pleasure as he extends one sinewy hand at her through the bars. 'How have you *been*?'

• • •

'Arrey bhai, can we go?' the Choudhary demands testily, shaking his stick about. 'All this standing around, chatting can happen at home also. I am so tired!'

Tinka's head immediately snaps away from Shaanu to Sneha, indignant that the old man is complaining about being exhausted when he's snored peacefully in first-class comfort the whole way, leaving Sneha to handle the children in the second-class bogey.

Sneha's eyes gleam in acknowledgement, but all she says, looking with interest from Shaanu to Tinka, is,

'You two know each other.'

'Slightly.'

'Very well.'

Their answers come simultaneously, as their hands grasp each other.

His grip is cool and firm and somehow familiar. Hers, she is sure, is all warm and clammy from the train.

Silence. Well, if one doesn't count the Choudhary haggling loudly with the coolies in the background.

'Can I get you anything?' Shaanu enquires finally, still holding her hand fast. 'Water? Biscuits?'

'I'm fine, thanks,' Tinka assures him. 'Calcutta is just two stations away.'

Shaanu nods and lets go of her hand. As he steps back, Tinka notices that the tips of his ears have gone slightly red. Or perhaps it is only the sun behind him.

'What are you doing in Calcutta?' he asks.

'She's volunteering at the Missionaries of Charity!' Sulochana provides the answer, her sweet voice hoarse with exhaustion. 'She's come to work in the refugee camps and take photos with that special camera. Isn't that great?'

Tinka goes red and endeavours to look great.

Shaanu's eyebrow shoots up.

'They have Indian-style WCs there,' he says, looking her up and down quizzically. 'And string beds and erratic electricity. Tough going for a lady. Can you handle it?'

'Yes,' Tinka replies loftily.

He looks sceptical but also impressed.

Feeling a bit of a hypocrite, she quickly admits, 'I'm, uh, staying at Sarhind Club, actually.'

'*Aha.*' The grey eyes sparkle. Then he adds briskly, 'I'll come to meet you there. Tomorrow night, seven o'clock at the Anchor Bar. It's in the club itself. Does that work?'

She looks at him, taken aback.

'Huh?'

'Does that work?' he repeats suavely. She doesn't remember him being suave before. It's something he's picked up recently.

She hesitates. Why does he want to meet her? They've already said their how-nice-it-was-to-see-you-again piece. What more is there to talk about?

'Can we *go?*' calls a cantankerous voice from behind them. 'I have to do peshaab.'

Tinka's eyes widen.

'Is that Chimman?' she whispers. 'Chimman Singh?'

Shaanu's eyes light up in surprise that she remembers.

'Yeah.' He gives her a wry grin.

Well, maybe there *is* more to talk about.

'C'mon, Dadyseth,' he presses, just as the Howrah Mail blows its whistle and lurches back to life. 'Let's meet someplace that isn't a railway station.'

Tinka laughs, but shakes her head.

'It'll be *very* proper,' he assures her, walking along with the train, holding the window bars. 'I'll bring my friends. One of them is married and very boring, and the other is just very boring. Say yes!'

He's joking, of course, but his eyes are not. There's something compelling about that direct grey gaze – a potent mixture of genuine concern, you-owe-me and something more intimate. She's not sure what, but whatever it is, it's making her heart beat faster.

Right in tempo with the train.

Shaanu is running lightly now, still holding onto the bar of her window. He is tremendously fit and looks like he could run for miles, but he is in dire danger of running out of platform.

'The name's Ishaan,' he calls. 'Ishaan Faujdaar!'

She hears him this time. She smiles through the bars and nods.

'Okay!'

• • •

Sarhind Club is exactly as Tinka expected it to be. Sprawling, opulent, deliciously colonial. Thanks to the Freesia ad money, she has been able to splurge on a suite. As she smiles at the bearer who's carrying her rucksack to her room, she notices that he is looking at her a little oddly. Oh God, please let him not recognize her!

The bearer comes to a halt outside a door labelled MAPLE SUITE and opens it with a welcoming flourish.

'*There* you are.'

The husky matter-of-fact voice causes Tinka to shriek, slam to a dead halt and swear colourfully. The bearer, entering the room at her heels, bumps right into her. She stumbles and so does he, apologizing profusely. They detangle themselves, even as a tall, haggard lady with jewel-like hooded eyes and a fabulous purple dahlia in her greying upswept bun, watches them serenely from her seat at the three-mirrored dressing table.

'What vulgar language, bachche,' she says, flicking back the pallu of her floral chiffon sari. 'Why must you always be so dramatic?'

'*I'm* being dramatic?' Tinka demands. 'You're the one who's lurking in my room like a James Bond villain! What are you doing here, Kung fui?'

Kainaz Dadyseth tries a tinkling little laugh.

'Aren't you thrilled to see me?'

'No,' says Tinka, still confused and rapidly getting upset. 'I'm working. You're old. You have high-blood pressure. What's the deal?'

Her aunt kicks off her high-heeled sandals and sighs.

'I want to work with the refugees too.'

Tinka's jaw sags.

'You do *not*!'

'Oh, I do,' Kainaz assures her earnestly. 'I lie awake at night, my heart aching for all of them! And when I fall asleep, they haunt my dreams, endless, emaciated lines of bhookha Bengalis...'

'Don't call them bhookha Bengalis!'

'... straggling into the country through the border from Mysore.'

'Jessore.'

Kainaz's lips form a moue.

'Don't quibble, darling. Besides, it's very fashionable, you know. Everybody at Altamont Road is into it. But so far they've only held charity shows or collection drives. I've just raised the game to a whole new level!' Her face brightens. 'Achcha, you have that very expensive camera – take some nice pictures of me holding some thin but photogenic children, hmmm? I want to make a nice album. I bought lots of blue-and-white saris.'

Tinka tries to make sense of all this.

'Why blue-and-white saris?'

Kung fui stares at her like she's mentally deficient.

'Because Mother Teresa's nuns wear blue-and-white saris! I only packed silks – some peacock, some aqua, some Feroza, some navy. And my most discreet jewellery – nothing thopa-thopu or vulgar like gold – just diamonds, *so* subtle and khandaani.'

'Stop talking about clothes!'

Kainaz's hooded, glittering eyes grow even huger.

'Who's talking about clothes? I've come to do my bit for the liberation of Bangladesh!'

Tinka throws up her hands. 'When did you start caring about the liberation of Bangladesh?'

'Ever since I read the reports on the Muktis,' says her aggravating aunt. 'They're a rebel guerrilla army, fighting the West Pakistani oppressors—'

'I know what the Mukti Bahini is!'

'And they sound so dashing and romantic, like the VietCong or Che Guevara, only more intellectual, because they're Bengali, na.'

Tinka stares at her, not wholly convinced. Kainaz Dadyseth, now fifty, had been only thirty years old when her husband, a brilliant young Indian Foreign Service Officer, dropped dead of a heart attack at the Indian consulate in Cairo. Some (unkind) people blamed her for this, and it must be admitted that she had often got him into trouble because of her candid utterances. Her short, turbulent career as an IFS spouse had included confiding to the Russian attaché that she'd invited him over for lunch because she had 'so many leftovers from the party we had for the American attaché last night!', and asking wide-eyed in front of a room full of press people 'But wasn't he always?' when her husband gravely announced that the East African President had just been blackballed.

After her husband died, she reverted to her maiden name and sought solace within the pages of Margaret Mitchell, Lucy Walker and Barbara Cartland. She also surprised everybody by doing a remarkably fine job of reviving her family's many businesses (including a cloth mill, a dockyard and a canned foods factory).

'Kainaz fui, why are you really here?'

The older woman squares her shoulders and looks deep into her niece's eyes.

'I'm worried about you.'

'Uff!' Tinka throws herself down on an armchair in disgust. 'I *knew* it!'

There is silence in the opulent suite.

Finally, Tinka speaks again, her voice gentler. 'Fui, go back to Altamont Road. I'm twenty-three years old. You can't follow me around pretending to care about refugees. It doesn't suit your image.'

Kainaz lifts her chin combatively.

'Oho, and it suits yours? You're only a brainless bimbo who dances nanga under waterfalls!'

'Ouch. I deserved that, I guess.'

'No, you didn't,' her aunt says with swift contrition. 'You're a very talented photographer and you genuinely want to help, but bachche, understand, you're on TV eight times a day, your hoardings are up in all four metros, and the *India Post* has called you namkeen, as if you were a sort of cornflakes chevdo. You need a bodyguard.'

'Ya well, you're too frail to be it!'

'Uff, you don't need a mushtanda.' Kainaz shudders delicately. 'You need a person of foxy intelligence who can tell you what's what. Also, Tinka, have you spoken to your father?'

'Ardisher? No.'

Kainaz looks distressed.

'Don't call him Ardisher, Tehmina.'

'Don't call me Tehmina.'

'You did the ad just to annoy him.'

Tinka rolls her eyes.

'I did it to earn money, Kung fui!'

'But I have money!'

'Don't show off,' Tinka tells her severely. 'My *own* money.'

'Well, now that Jimmy's dead, all my money will go to you.' Kainaz's voice wobbles. 'Who else will I leave it to?'

Tinka sighs, her expression softening.

Even though Kung fui can't abide her brother – 'Such a wet sock, poor Ardisher, buried in Defence Colony, knee-deep in Punjabis' – she has always loved his children and supported them in every way. She was totally broken when Jimmy died.

There's not much point in arguing, Tinka realizes with a sigh. Her aunt has already settled in, commandeering the 'better side of the bed' (closer to the window, to flick ash out of) and eighty per cent of the dressing table. Tinka resigns herself to the inevitable. Kissing her aunt on the cheek, she enters the white marble bathroom, gets under the steaming hot shower and proceeds to wash the grime of the train off her body.

I'll scout out the best developing studio tomorrow, she thinks as she soaps herself. Make friends with the technicians there. Maybe even drop into Mother House and check out the refugee camp. Basically, not let Kung fui throw me off my stride.

Resolutions made, she slips into the cosy white bed,

shivering slightly, slathers her body with Afghan Snow and falls into a sound sleep.

But then, most aggravatingly, Fabulous Shaanu Bhaisaab shows up in her dreams.

Lightly browned, like the best crunchy cookies. Walking that prowly, tomcat walk, the kind Alistair MacLean novel heroes walk in movies, when they saunter away casually from mega explosions. Dressed in his Oxford-blue dungarees, sleeves rolled up to show off his sinewy forearms. His Kota-grey eyes sparkling and his lips twisted into that cocky but somehow sympathetic grin, like he knows what deep shit she's got herself into and is here to help her get out of it.

I don't need your help, she tells this dangerous Dream Shaanu. I've managed to dig myself out of deep shit *myself*, thank you very much. And you only look good because the IAF uniform is so hot. If you weren't wearing it, you'd look entirely ordinary.

But then the Dream Ishaan starts to pull off his overalls, and it turns out that it wasn't his uniform that was making him look so hot, after all...

Tinka wakes up from the dream smiling and flushed and appalled.

It's stupid and shallow to build up some man in your head like this, she tells herself sternly as she brushes her teeth. You don't know him at all. Stop attributing qualities to him he may not possess and imagining a made-for-each-other vibe that doesn't exist!

Which is why (she is now having a full-blown dialogue with herself, never a sign of an ordered mind) the sensible thing to do is to meet him again, so you can prove to yourself that he is not really what you think he is, and thus get him out of your system forever!

She rinses, dries her face and walks out to the attached balcony where her aunt is already sipping tea.

'Good morning!' says Kainaz Dadyseth brightly. 'Isn't this lovely?'

She gestures to the silver tea tray, the crunchy toast-butter-jam and the grounds of the club stretching out green and lush before them.

'Yes,' Tinka agrees. 'Er, Kung fui, I have to go out.'

Tinka spends the day at Park Street, shopping for film rolls and taking in the sights. There is a larger-than-life hoarding of her at a major crossroad, clutching a Freesia soap and smiling as a deluge of water pours over her head. Though she sees several young men ogling it and a man on a scooter actually careening into a cow because he's looking at it so raptly, nobody notices any likeness between it and her.

When she returns in the evening, Kainaz Dadyseth is settled in the armchair in their room, nursing a whiskey-paani. She is dressed in a grey Chantilly lace sari, and there is a fresh hot pink dahlia in her hair. She demands to be entertained.

'But I don't know anybody in Calcutta!' Tinka protests.

'I know some people. There are the Periwals – they're maardus, you know, from Kutch, but they've lived here for years. And the Lodhas from Colaba. And the Khambata family—'

'Kung fui, stop,' Tinka says hastily. 'Please, I don't want to hang out with a bunch of expat Bombayites. Actually,' she continues, perhaps a little too offhandedly, 'I'm meeting some officers from the station for drinks this evening.'

Kainaz Dadyseth puts down her glass.

'*Really*,' she drawls, jewel-like eyes gleaming. 'And what officers are these?'

Tinka shrugs. 'I met them at the train station.'

Kung fui jiggles the ice in her glass vigorously. 'Bachche, you can't go around picking up strange young men at train stations. It's so unbecoming. And Air Force officers are a very mixed bunch. They used to be exclusive, but with all these wars, they've started recruiting them straight out of the sugarcane fields. Some of them are wealthy ex-royals, certainly, but many of them are country bumpkins.'

'Fui, don't talk like Ardisher, please!' Tinka rolls her eyes as she wriggles out of her slacks and heads for the shower. 'This boy is nice – he's the one who helped me run away to you that night.'

Kainaz sniffs, her hooked Parsi nose well up in the air as she enquires, 'What is he?'

This sounds both vague and rhetorical, but Tinka understands exactly what her aunt wants to know.

She leans against the bathroom door.

'He's a Jat,' she replies.

'A jhat?' Kainaz raises delicately arched brows. 'You mean a pubic hair? Chhee, don't be crude, darling.'

'You know exactly what a Jat is, Kung fui. Don't be a snob.'

Her aunt sips her whiskey-paani.

'Darling, have some pity.'

'What do you mean?'

'I mean, haven't you rubbed your father's nose in the mud enough? First you ran away from the wedding, leaving him red-faced at the Agiyari practically! Then you did that ad. Now you're getting all dolled up to go canoodle with some impoverished Jat.'

'He's not impoverished. At least, I don't think so. There was some talk of a haveli.'

'My dear, not one of those rundown, so-called havelis!' Her aunt shudders. 'It'll turn out to be just a hovel, I bet. A hoveli.'

'*Besides*,' Tinka continues, ignoring this crack, 'this is *not* a romantic outing!'

Kainaz fui responds to this statement with a cackle of such disbelief that Tinka is goaded into slamming the bathroom door shut in her face and standing under the shower for a good twenty minutes.

When she emerges she finds that a clingy, sleeveless maxi of flame-coloured georgette, which she believed to be hanging in her wardrobe in Bombay, has been laid out on the bed for her. Matching strappy sandals are on the floor while a pair of dangly diamond earrings glitter inside a velvet box on the dressing table next to a vanity case loaded with expensive cosmetics.

Tinka raises an eyebrow.

'I was thinking of wearing just a sweater and slacks.'

'Rubbish!' declares her aunt. 'All that is okay for the refugee camps, this is Sarhind Club, people we know may actually be there – don't go down dressed like some middle-class frump who has to do ads for money.'

Tinka sucks in her breath, exasperated.

'Oh, for heaven's sake, fui!'

Kainaz's tone grows wheedling.

'Darling, *dress* up ... it soothes my old eyes to see you look beautiful.'

Tinka relents. Besides, the thought of appearing before Ishaan in these clothes is somehow very appealing.

'Are you planning to scare the Jat off?' she asks as she drops the maxi over her head. 'Because I don't think he's the type to be intimidated by wealth.'

Kainaz Dadyseth tugs the maxi lower, making Tinka's head disappear.

'What Jat, darling? I've forgotten about him already.'

Tinka's head emerges from the dress.

'It does feel good to wear stuff like this again,' she admits, grinning a little breathlessly.

Kainaz smiles in satisfaction. The flaming orange sets off Tinka's glowing brown limbs and tousled cap of dark hair perfectly.

Tinka slips on her sandals and walks to the mirror.

'I'm too brown,' she says with vague dissatisfaction.

She must really like this boy, Kainaz thinks, surprised. She never worries about her complexion.

'This obsession with fairness is very lower class, darling,' she says firmly. 'Draupadi was as dark as Dabur Chyawanprash, remember, but that didn't stop her from snaring five husbands. All for the price of one mother-in-law too.'

'I meant my *lipstick*,' Tinka says exasperated. 'I needed a brighter shade. Ah, here it is.'

'These Haryanvi peasant types are very highly sexed, waise,' Kainaz says knowledgeably as she watches Tinka apply the bright pink lipper. 'I hope…' She pauses, sips her drink, then continues delicately, 'Has he recognized you from your ad, by any chance?'

Tinka's eyes narrow in the glass. 'What are you trying to say?'

'I'm trying to say that maybe he thinks you're a *modern* khayalat ki ladki.' Her aunt emphasizes the word like it's dirty. 'In other words, easy.'

'Understood,' Tinka replies tightly. 'Now that you've got that off your chest, should we go downstairs?'

'I don't want to tag along,' says her aunt in a prim voice that isn't at all convincing.

'Oh, please.' Tinka rolls her eyes. 'All this finery cannot go to waste.'

Kainaz preens.

'True.'

Tinka laughs, leans over and hugs her fiercely. 'I'm glad you came,' she confesses. 'You're my *Mercury.*'

• • •

'Gentlemen, action has picked up at the border. This is Garibpur village, located in the northwest part of what we now call Bangladesh but what most of the world *and* the United Nations still persist in calling East Pakistan. Within Garibpur lies the Boyra salient – vital for us, as it includes a highway that links India to the major Bangladeshi city of Jessore. The West Pakistani forces are intent on wresting it from our grasp, but our 14th Punjab Battalion and the Mukti Bahini are in position, hanging on to it tight.'

'Sir!'

Ishaan is having an eventful day. He had reported to the base in the morning expecting to fly his routine training sortie, but then Hosannah Carvalho had bounded into the briefing room and started doing his best impoverished panther impersonation, pacing up and down, his eyes agleam with battle-lust. There is a chance for the 34 Gnat Squadron to prove its mettle today, and everybody is leaning in, keenly absorbing the briefing.

'Basically, a snarl of men, machinery and tanks are slugging it out in foggy conditions. The West Pakistanis have numerical superiority and, logically, are in a position to decimate our intrusion, but the 14th Punjab has dug in its heels and is acting recalcitrant. The West Pakistanis have

Close Air Support from a posse of F-86 Sabres, powered with front guns and air-to-air Sidewinder missiles, which are strafing our people brutally. There have been over thirty casualties. You need to sit tight, maintaining Stand By Fire readiness level, and as soon as I give the order to scramble, get cracking and knock those Sabres out of the sky.'

'Yes, sir!'

This rousing briefing is followed by a complete anti-climax. Shaanu and his fellow Gnatties – Janardhan, Gonsalves and Mansoor (nicknamed Jana-Gana-Mana for obvious reasons) – spend the morning in the ops room, chafing in their G-suits, passing time by playing Scrabble, waiting for the order to scramble.

By lunchtime, they're starting to get claustrophobic.

'MUZJIK, behenchod, what the fuck is a MUZJIK? You're just making up shit now,' says Jana, scowling over the Scrabble board, shuffling his O and A tiles.

'It's a sort of Russian peasant,' replies Gana loftily. 'Look up the dictionary if you don't believe me.'

But the dictionary has been confiscated, because the last time the Gnatties played, somebody had hit somebody else over the head with it.

'You can't use Russian words!'

'I make ZA,' says Shaanu calmly, putting down a single tile.

'Hain? What's a Za? There's no word called Za.'

'It's Russian for king. I thought you knew Russian.'

'That's *czar*, Chakkahera. C-Z-A-R!'

'Superb, I have C and R too. Thanks, brother, that's 160 points!' Shaanu says, delighted.

'Hello, wait, there's no space for an R! Where you gonna put your R?'

Shaanu is just telling Mana, in the choicest Air Force language, exactly where he plans to put his R, when the scramble order sounds.

'Streaks to scramble. Streaks to scramble, *now*!'

Very excited, they storm out through the door, race onto the field, buckling on their Gs, clamber into the waiting Gnats and drop into the cockpits.

'Vector to Garibpur!' barks Carvalho on the radio from the main briefing room. 'Baaz is middle finger. Go go go!'

The four Gnats rise, stubby steel bullets in the afternoon sky, in a formation that resembles the tips of the four fingers of a human right hand, and, with Shaanu in the lead position, start pelting for the border.

Seven minutes later, they are circling over the salient, triumphant and breathless.

'We're here, we're here, we're here!'

Radio silence.

Then the Forward Air Controller's voice sounds over the R/T, bleak and crackly. 'You're late, boys. They're gone.'

'What!'

The Gnats scan the skies. Nothing.

Just flat grey sky and, below, through the gloom of fog, the humped shapes of tanks, some friendly, some not.

As the enemy ack-acks start to fire, they wheel around and head home, thoroughly out of temper.

'ZA *isn't* a word,' says Mana in a subdued voice as they circle over Dum Dum to land.

'Shut up, piss finger,' Shaanu growls. 'Two one *za* two, two two *za* four. Of course it's a word.'

And everybody is too disheartened to even snark back.

Three hours later, right after they've polished off a heavy conti lunch of shepherd's pie and apple crumble, they have to scramble again.

'What the...?'

'You think the Muktis are just having fun with us?'

'I wouldn't put it past them. They're Pakistanis, after all. East or West, Pakistanis are a pest...'

'C'mon c'mon c'mon!'

They race out to the jets again, Carvalho comes roaring out, shouts the same instructions and they zoom back to Garibpur. They make it in six minutes flat this time, but when they circle over the salient, the voice of the FAC crackles through the milky fog like déjà vu.

'Late again, ladies,' he says grumpily. 'I told you not to bother putting on make-up and sexy lingerie. We find you fuckable anyway.'

'They've gone?' Shaanu can't believe it.

'Long gone, Gnattie,' says the FAC. 'Strafed us good too. We lost ten good men just now.'

'Shit!'

'So traipse off back to base and leave me to defend the ruddy IAF to these bloody landlubbers, while being feasted on by mosquitoes.'

'Sorry, brother,' Shaanu says soberly. 'Let's just circle around for a bit, lads. Eyes peeled.'

But the Sabres have melted away.

As the enemy anti-aircraft guns start to spurt again, Shaanu gives his formation the order to head home and the Gnats fly back to base against the setting sun, too deflated to wisecrack, and wearily call it a day.

FIVE

Kainaz Dadyseth practically purrs with pleasure when she descends the staircase and sets eyes on Shaanu and his friends, waiting in the foyer for Tinka.

'What a delish batch of Brylcreem Boys!' she murmurs. 'Which one is yours, darling?'

'The one in the middle,' Tinka replies, then hastily clarifies, 'He's not *mine*.'

Her aunt ignores this disclaimer, already scanning Shaanu with a critical, experienced eye.

'Very decorative,' she decrees finally. 'But beware, my dear, fair boys are vain. Their mothers tell them they're handsome about a hundred times a day so they grow up absolutely insufferable.'

'His mother's dead.'

'Ah, good,' Kainaz replies, her glittering eyes now taking in Shaanu's companions. 'Who are those others with him? The tall boy is handsome now, but he'll age badly – fat will pack onto those high cheekbones and he'll end up looking like a chipmunk. And Chubby Cheeks will only get chubbier.

Anyway, he's taken. See how proprietarily that plump piece of nonsense is clinging to his arm.'

'*Behave* yourself, Kung fui,' Tinka hisses. 'Those are his friends, and I think they were there that night at Popo uncle's orders. They helped me get away. Be nice!'

'Popo!' Kainaz snorts. 'Popo's a fool. And peeing in a bedpan now, I believe! Poor fellow,' she adds in a conscientious afterthought. Then, as Shaanu approaches them, she inclines her head regally. 'Hullo, hullo, Ehsaan and party. How nice to meet you...'

'It's Ishaan,' Shaanu corrects her, his smile wavering. He has had to rush back and shower, then round up his friends, none of whom had been feeling particularly enthusiastic, and then make the long bike ride to Calcutta, all in order to spend a little quality time with Tinka. And she repays him by bowling this total googly – this formidable lady with the disdainful nose and the throaty smoker's voice, oozing rich Parsi khandaniyat from the tip of her arrogant silver head to the straps of her glittering silver stilettos.

He looks at Tinka, his eyes communicating comical consternation, and falters again. Because she too looks so ... rich tonight. More than just rich – alien. Like a glamorous being from another world, sparkling with diamonds and clad in a long flame-coloured dress of unusual cut that Juhi is staring at with open envy. Not at all like the red-skirted bandariya from Jodhpur or the blithe sprite under the waterfall.

'Meet my aunt,' says this intimidating new Tinka. 'Kainaz Dadyseth. And Kung fui, this is Flying Officer Faujdaar.'

Shaanu steps forward, suddenly convinced that his dinner jacket is too bright, his carefully tailored camel-coloured jodhpurs too clichéd, his hair too sleeked back, and that if he opens his mouth, all that will emerge is chaste Haryanvi.

'Hullo, ma'am.'

His English sounds stilted to his ears, his sophistication superficial, the cover of his IAF fighter status paper-thin. He has never felt more inadequate in his life.

'Charmed, I'm sure,' sniffs the old lady. 'What a pretty jacket. I have fluffy bedroom slippers in that exact same shade.'

Clearly the Dadyseth women specialize in camel-kicking men in the nuts on the first meeting, Shaanu thinks as he reels from this blow. His disheartened, doubt-filled eyes meet Tinka's and her face scrunches up into a grin, and suddenly, she's a familiar implet, just with expensive dangling earrings, and everything becomes all right again.

'Well, don't you two look familiar!' Tinka addresses Maddy and Raka gaily.

They immediately push forward, grinning, introducing Juhi and claiming old acquaintance with Tinka. Then the smiling doormen open the big double doors and the group enters the Anchor Bar.

The bar is unusually full tonight, lined wall to wall with elegant people sipping elegant drinks. When this happens, the club management opens the double doors to the pillared terrace outside and sets out little tables with candles glowing inside glass holders. Plump, resplendent bearers move at a stately pace through the crush, like benign red-and-gold bumblebees. There is a live band, and several couples are on the dance floor, circling to

'Weeeeeee ... 'll drink a drink a drink
to Lily the pink the pink the pink
the saviour of ... the human ra-a-ace...'

'Where's the family?' Tinka asks Shaanu as naturally as she can. She's finding it hard to look at him, suddenly consumed by this illogical fear that if they make eye contact he'll know about the stupid dreams she had last night.

Besides, he's so intensely ... *there*. Walking beside her, beckoning to the waiter with a crooked finger. All in a relaxed way of course, but there's something about his sauntering that suggests incredible energy, carefully contained.

He likes her, Juhi is thinking meanwhile. This ajeeb, snooty general-ki-beti from Bombay. Hey Bhagwan, he tried to pull out a chair for her and missed! His hand just clawed the air and fell away! He is so nervous! Hamara Baaz!

'Sneha's sleeping it off,' Shaanu says as he successfully draws out a chair for Tinka on the second attempt. 'I got her and Pitaji a suite at the Mess. The brats are in my rooms, swinging from my boxing bag. I had to empty out half the sawdust so nobody would get hurt.' He picks up the laminated menu card and offers it to Tinka. 'What'll you have?'

Tinka immediately has a vision of him all sweaty and shirtless punching the crap out of his punching bag. She blinks.

'What fun,' she says. 'Uh, a shandy please. Beer and Fanta.'

She sits back and tunes in to Raka, who is in full flow, recounting their first meeting at Jodhpur Station. Kainaz Dadyseth is listening, enthralled.

'He *picked you up and carried you* off the train? Tinka!'

'I kicked him where it hurt,' Tinka assures her aunt.

'Good!'

'So there was Baaz all doubled up and too much of a gentleman-cadet to swear! And when he had recovered enough to speak, all he said was...' Raka drops his voice to a soft, soulful entreaty. 'Ma'am, be gentle, I hope to have children someday!'

Everybody bursts out laughing.

'Oh, *poor* Baaz!' says Juhi, shooting a reproachful look at Tinka. Tinka gets the distinct feeling Juhi doesn't like her.

'Hey, I didn't kick him *that* hard,' Tinka protests, turning pink. 'You're exaggerating!'

But Raka sticks to his guns, laughing.

'No no, you *did!*' He turns back to Kung fui. 'So we left him with her, the poor injured soul, and went in to tell WingCo Poncha the mission had been accomplished. But when he came hurtling out, relieved and happy, we found that Tinka here had somehow persuaded Baaz to let her go!'

'*How?*' Juhi asks Tinka, her tone rather hostile. 'What did you *say?*'

Everybody turns to look at Tinka. She hesitates, risking a glance at Shaanu. He is sipping his drink and smiling and looking at her – well, everybody is – but there's something in his eyes that makes her heart sort of … trip. Like when you're running down the stairs and you miss a step. Which is silly because hearts don't run down stairs.

'Nothing, actually,' she confesses. 'I was surprised myself. He just suddenly said, run! Go!'

There is general protest at this.

'No! There's got to be more!'

'You kicked him again, didn't you? Or bribed him?'

'Duped him!'

'Smooched him!'

'I did *none* of those things!' Tinka retorts with spirit. Then she turns to Shaanu. 'Why *did* you let me go?'

They all turn to look at him. Silence falls over the table.

'Because…' His eyes rise to meet hers like she is the only person at the table, that curious, glowing light back in their Kota-grey depths. 'Because in your own mixed-up way, you were the bravest person I'd ever met.'

'Balls!' Maddy and Raka blurt out in one voice and then have to apologize furiously to the ladies, their faces bright red with embarrassment. Then, indignantly, they put forth their own bravery credentials, but Shaanu just ignores them, continuing to look at Tinka until she looks away, her pulse quickened.

He looks away too, sipping his drink, and good-naturedly tells his mates to pipe down.

'Did you get into a lot of trouble when they found me gone?' she asks him a few minutes later.

A peculiar expression slides across his face for a moment before he shakes his head. 'Of course not.'

Tinka frowns, ready to take this further, but just then somebody stumbles up to their table and addresses her in a breathless voice:

'Ma'am, uh, hello ma'am! Raka sir, please could I get an introduction?'

Tinka looks up to a see a gangling young sardar with a beard too straggly to cover his many pimples gazing down at her with bashful lust.

Raka looks slightly exasperated, then shrugs.

'Miss Tehmina Dadyseth. Flying Officer Dilsher Singh, the baby of our battalion.'

'CouldIpleasehaveadance?' the young sardar says determinedly.

'She's having a *drink*, Dilsher,' Raka starts to say, but Juhi puts a hand on his arm.

'Bichara Dillu! Raks, don't break his heart.'

'Yes, ma'am!' says the sardar, his eyes fixed avidly on Tinka. '*Please*, ma'am!'

She really hates me, Tinka thinks, as she smiles and gets to her feet. I wonder why.

Dilsher Singh's hands are clammy, just as she expects them to be. Holding her too tightly, he gallops her to the dance floor and starts jumping awkwardly to the beat, grinning at her enthusiastically. Tinka endeavours to match his 'steps'.

'Poor Tink-a-tink-a-tink,' Kainaz murmurs, watching from the table. 'Ah well, at least it's not a waltz. One must be grateful for small mercies.'

She turns to Maddy.

'Are you the coffee plantation Subbiahs?' she demands and when he nods, continues unimpressed, 'I've had your coffee, it's muddy. The Robusta isn't very robust and the Arabica isn't very...'

'Arabic?' Maddy hazards.

'Aromatic!' She frowns. 'Don't you know *anything* about coffee?'

'No,' he admits sheepishly. 'We have managers on the estate. They do all that.'

'It's about six hundred acres, isn't it?'

Maddy is looking embarrassed now.

'I think so,' he says vaguely.

'And you're an only son?'

'Er, yes.'

'So you're loaded!' Kainaz looks at him with such open approval that he starts to squirm. 'Go get Tinka off the dance floor!'

Ishaan's eyes smoulder at this, over the brim of his glass, but he doesn't say anything.

Maddy shakes his head hastily.

'Ma'am, I'm too much of a funk to tackle the fire-breathing Dilsher! For that you have to wheel out the big guns, like my friend Baaz here!'

He claps Ishaan, rather frenziedly, on the back.

Ishaan puts down his glass and locks eyes with the older woman.

'Permission to proceed, ma'am?'

The challenge in his gaze is unmistakable.

Kainaz tucks the hot pink dahlia into her hair more securely and sniffs.

'You hardly look the type who requires *permission.*'

Maddy laughs nervously. Raka and Juhi join in.

Ishaan continues to look at Kainaz enquiringly.

'Oh go, go!' she says crossly, waving him away.

Shaanu smiles, nods and gets to his feet.

On the dance floor, the music has changed to the slower, swingier *'Oh, you can kiss me on a Monday a Monday a Monday'.* Tinka is getting reacquainted with Dilsher Singh's moist hands. His notion of the foxtrot is to take two enthusiastic steps forward, then two enthusiastic steps backward, all the while staring at her hungrily like she's a juicy pineapple pastry.

'I'm a MiG Fighter,' he informs her for the third time as they lurch together, back and forth. 'MiG Fighters are *Number One.'*

'That's great,' she responds.

'We have split-second reflexes,' he assures her. *'Split second.* We move like greased lightning across the sky!'

But not across the dance floor, she thinks privately as he hauls her back and then forward again, like a piece of furniture he's trying to manoeuvre around a tight corner.

'Wow!' she says dutifully.

'The gourmint of India trusts me to fly a machine that costs eleven lakh rupees. Eleven!'

'How nice.'

He looks down at her, nettled by these tepid responses.

'That's the Mukti Bahini major over there,' he nods. 'Macho da.'

He gets a reaction now. Tinka chokes.

'*Excuse* me?'

Dilsher gives her a naughty, wannabe-dangerous grin.

'Haha. Sounds dirty but there's a squeaky-clean explanation.'

'*Really?*'

Dilsher Singh nods confidently. 'Ya. See, the West Pakistanis have this notion – not *totally* wrong, because being Punjabi myself, I know where they're coming from – that Punjabi Pathans are a macho, hatta-katta, mardaana martial race. They look down on the East Pakistanis for being sissies, all Ravindar sangeet and rasgullas. But the Muktis insist ki they are as brave and as macho as the Pathans. So now, though his official name is Maqhtoom da, we call him—'

'Macho da,' Shaanu says curtly, appearing out of nowhere. 'Yeah, that was for *you*. Run along, half-pant. This dance is mine.'

For a moment, Dilsher looks like he wants to argue, but then he releases Tinka from his clammy hold.

'I suppose that on the *dance floor*, at least, Gnats can score over MiGs. But *not*,' he holds up one dramatic finger, 'in the sky.'

'Kat le.' Shaanu smiles, his grey eyes glinting dangerously.

Dilsher Singh turns to Tinka and flashes her a cocky smile.

'Later,' he says meaningfully, reducing her to uncontrollable giggles, and swaggers away, seeking whom he may devour.

Shaanu watches his retreat with grim satisfaction, one arm coming up to circle Tinka's waist.

'Cocky little bugger. Pitega ek din. What's so funny?'

She shakes her head, convulsed with laughter.

'They say it's your own faults that you dislike the most in other people.'

One dark eyebrow flies up at this.

'What's that supposed to mean?'

'Oh!' She tries for nonchalance, fighting the inexplicable confusion she's feeling at being in his lean, muscular arms (not that she can *see* his muscles, per se, he's covered adequately by his dinner jacket, but she can sense them below, lurking) and says as naturally as possible, 'Just that, you must've been like him once. In your pimply phase.'

'I never had a pimply phase.' He looks mock-outraged. 'My sisters used to put multani mitti on my face, so I never got any.'

Tinka finds this confession rather charming. No man she has met till date has ever confessed to using beautification products. And he took half the sawdust out of his boxing bag so his kid sisters wouldn't get hurt, she remembers. Jimmy would never have done that.

Ishaan continues to protest. 'Hey, you *met* me back then, you know I wasn't that cocky!'

'That's true.' She nods, suddenly serious. 'You were nice. Thank you *so* much for all your help. I don't exaggerate when I say you saved my life.'

The tips of his ears turn a little red.

'It was nothing.'

They move to the music in silence for a while and Tinka discovers what all the ladies at AFS Kalaiganga know already, that Flying Officer Ishaan Faujdaar is a dreamy dancer. In her heels she is practically the same height as him, and this, she tells herself, is what is making their eye contact so disturbingly potent.

'Can you really nail a guava from forty feet?' she asks him as the silence starts to get awkward. 'Ten times out of ten, with the sun in your eyes?'

'Who says so?' he asks, eyes widening.

'Your family. They regaled me with tales of your bravery on the train.'

'Ah, my family!' Shaanu looks rueful.

'Yes.'

He ducks his head uncertainly. 'Uh, I have some memory of telling you, back in '68, that my family speaks only English at home…'

'I don't remember,' Tinka says promptly, embarrassed for him.

But Shaanu perseveres.

'And that we're very rich and nobody drinks. Well, that's all untrue. We're not very rich, we speak Haryanvi and Chimman Singh really appreciates the booze quota.'

His eyes had slipped away from hers while he was speaking, but towards the end of this little speech they come back, raking hers painfully to see how this revelation has affected her.

'So what?' she says bluntly. 'My father speaks perfect English, and he's nuts.'

His fingers grip hers harder.

'Really?'

Tinka gurgles.

'Oh, yes, he's really nuts!'

'That's not what I meant!' he says seriously.

'I know,' she replies, sobering. 'I mean, speaking English isn't proof of anything. And your sisters are great.'

'Yes.' His eyes glow with pride. 'They *are*. I'm sending the little ones to a good convent school now. I want them all to have careers.'

'Sneha wants to teach, she told me.'

'Yes. I'm not a...' his eyes study her face again as he pronounces the word with careful pride, 'chauvinist.'

'That's so good to hear!' Tinka says approvingly. 'Do you know, most men don't even know the meaning of that word? They have to look it up in a dictionary.'

'Asses,' Shaanu says lightly and, then, as the music changes to a happy, reggae beat, whirls her away from him, then spins her back deftly, his eyes sparkling with enjoyment. 'This song reminds me of you.'

'Daddy is a doctor,
Mother is a debutante,
Pillars of society,
Living in a mansion,
Somewhere in the country
And another in Chelsea.'

Tinka gives a peal of laughter that carries above the music and causes several people to turn around and smile.

'I've never heard you laugh!' He has to raise his voice above the music. 'It's nice.'

'You've met me only once!' she shouts back. 'And God knows I didn't feel like laughing that day.'

'Twice,' he corrects her as he jerks her close, her back against his chest, as they rock to the beat together.

'Freedom is a rich girl,
Daddy's little sweet girl,
Freedom is a sunny day,
Freedom what would you do, if I said I loved you.
Freedom, would you run away?'

'But somehow,' his lips brush her ear, his voice low, 'I feel like we know each other really well.'

He spins her away, and when she turns, his hand is there to grasp hers, and so are the intense grey eyes, stabbing hers, seeking confirmation.

'Don't we?'

Freedom come,
Freedom go,
Tells me yes, and then she tells me no,
Freedom never stay long,
Freedom moving a-long.'

Now it is Tinka who forgets to dance. She stands still, thinking back to him sitting opposite her in that Jonga, wincing from her crippling kick, listening to her rant, laughing with her and finally letting her go. She thinks of last night's dream.

Then she colours, shakes her head and looks away, pointing and smiling.

'Look, everybody's on the floor!'

Too soon, Shaanu thinks with savage regret even as he acknowledges Raka and Juhi's arrival on the dance floor with a cheerful wave. Much too soon. What the hell is wrong with him? What kind of prize idiot trots out a cheesy line like that to a girl he's just met? He's not even sure he means it.

Maybe the two dud missions to Garibpur-Boyra have got me all wound up, he rationalizes. I want to make up for that anti-climax by planting a jhanda *somewhere* today. Shit, maybe Raka and Maddy are right, maybe I'm too primed and too pent-up and I should just lure somebody, anybody, into a sugarcane field and get it over with...

The music kicks into a higher gear, the dancing gets faster and talking becomes impossible. Fifteen minutes later, very out of breath, they all head for the bar for refreshments, where they find Old Kuch Bhi Carvalho lurking on a bucket stool, chowing down pork chops and swilling rum, with all the air of a sociable crocodile presiding over the jungle watering hole.

'Hullo hullo!' he greets them, eyes agleam. 'What a pretty little lady! So light on her feet! And wearing a dress the colour of a well-mixed shandy! Introduce me, Chakkahera!'

Shaanu makes a brief introduction and turns to the bearer to order more snacks. Carvalho, whose keen eyes miss nothing even when he is three large pegs down, immediately takes it upon himself to issue a glowing character certificate to Ishaan.

'We call him Baaz because he's our least-worst Fighter,' he declares, clapping Ishaan on the back heartily. 'Least-worst!'

'Whoa.' Shaanu straightens his jacket. 'Um, thank you, sir.'

'That's quite a recommendation,' Tinka says smilingly and catches Juhi looking at her with that hostile look on her face again. Tinka raises an eyebrow enquiringly and Juhi flushes and looks away.

Carvalho isn't done. He points a bony finger straight at Tinka's nose.

'Let me tell you one thing, my dear. If you want to break Pakistan into two clean pieces, this is the man for the job!'

'Sir, please,' Ishaan protests, embarrassed but also rather touched.

'What is this, sir – little bit of Pakistani dismemberment we are capable of doing also!' Raka laughs.

Carvalho's fiery gaze swivels to him.

'Maybe, Aggarwal Sweets, maybe,' he concedes. 'But I

don't need to flatter you in front of pretty girls any more!' He nods gallantly at Juhi. 'You're already married!'

Juhi blushes prettily, Raka kisses her hand and leads her away for a dance.

Carvalho turns back to Tinka.

'Baaz here' – he pats Shaanu on the back again – '*he's* the man.'

'Heartbreaker, Pak-breaker!' chimes in Deengu from beside him.

'I don't want to break Pakistan into two pieces, actually,' Tinka replies smilingly.

'His science is gol, ekdum gol, zero! But his instinct is sharp! Instinct, that's the ticket! Judgement! Audaci—what did you say?'

Tinka puts down her glass.

'I said I wouldn't want to break Pakistan – or any other country – into two clean pieces.'

'Yes yes, I heard.' Carvalho's face assumes a pained expression, one which any hostess who has ever placed a vegetarian dish in front of him would recognize.

'She's a pacifist, sir,' Shaanu informs him.

'Pah!' Carvalho rocks back on his heels. 'We're all peace-loving folk here! Arrey, even *I* don't want to break Pakistan into pieces! It is *they* who are intent on self-decapitation!'

'What's this?' enquires a soft voice from behind them, and Tinka turns to come face to face with Macho da, a lanky brown character with a sad monkey face, romantically long curly locks of hair and, incongruously, a pair of sunglasses on his nose. He is holding a very dark whiskey-paani in his hand. 'Is there a pacifist on the loose?'

Everybody in their little circle makes room to accommodate the Mukti.

'This young lady here shudders at the evils of war,' Carvalho says in a tone so patronizing that Tinka burns with indignation. She is about to make a cutting reply when she remembers that he's Ishaan's boss and Ishaan is her host.

'Surely you agree that war is horrible?' she asks instead, her eyes travelling from officer to officer.

There is an awkward silence. All the slickly Brylcreemed IAF Fighters look at one another shiftily. In the end Deengu bites the bullet.

'Yessssssnnno,' he says.

Tinka raises her eyebrows. 'Yes-no?'

He nods. 'We're fighting, which is terrible – to get the Bangladeshis their freedom, which is non-negotiable! No, boys?'

Everybody nods solemnly.

'O ya ya, absolutely!'

They're just boys with toys, Tinka thinks, disheartened. With nicknames like Baaz and Raka and what not. They're living inside a Commando comic, high-fiving and back-slapping and shouting *Gott im Himmel!* and *Schweinhund!* and *Die Nazi Dog!* It's no use talking to them.

'Sure.' She shrugs and turns away.

She's staring at the bottles placed on the bar counter, her eyes bleak, when she senses somebody coming up behind her. Thinking it must be Ishaan, or perhaps her aunt, she turns around.

'Joy Bangla,' Macho da says wryly.

Huh?

That's the war-cry of the Mukti Bahini, she knows, and also their way of greeting each other. Is he saying hello?

'I mean conjunctivitis,' Macho da says, tapping the frame of his sunglasses. 'That's why I'm wearing sunglasses at night. I could tell you were wondering. We call it Joy Bangla in the refugee camps. Kind of an affectionate nickname. It's rampant there, you know.'

'Oh,' Tinka says. Then she adds, conscious of sounding like a trite socialite, 'Is the situation in the camps very dreadful?'

He stares at her through the opaque glasses for a moment, then says abruptly, 'Are you really interested?'

'Of course she is!' Kung fui has spotted the romantic Mukti Bahini officer talking to her niece and materialized at her side. 'She's come from Bombay to help! We both have!'

Macho da absorbs this and then shrugs. 'Like you know, there are almost ten million people in the camps,' he says in his deep, soft voice. 'Joy Bangla isn't the worst disease we're facing, not by a long shot. That honour belongs to cholera. Which, if you aren't aware,' his gaze seems to flicker (disdainfully?) over their elegant attire, 'is high fever and painful, uncontrollable diarrhoea. It kills you through dehydration. Then there's malnutrition. The monsoon brought mosquitoes and malaria. Children and old people are dying every day. The corpses are piling up, the infections spreading. I would give anything for an electric crematorium.'

His voice throbs with an intensity that commands silence, and by the time he has finished speaking, a hush has fallen over the bar.

'That's horrible.' Kainaz Dadyseth's voice is stricken.

'Yes,' agrees Tinka softly.

'Christ, what a party-pooper,' the voice of Kuch Bhi Carvalho floats up from the back of the bar. He sounds like he has gone back to gnawing on his pork chops. 'Why would he bring up loose-motions on a party night? These Muktis grab any opportunity to hand-wring in public.'

'And that's why this war must happen,' Macho da continues, gesturing dramatically, his greasy curls flying this way and that. 'So that our suffering people can go back to our country after we have rid it of the tyrannical West Pakistanis – with the help of our friends in the Indian Army, of course! It is a just war, a necessary war, a good war...'

This is too much for Tinka.

'Oh *please*,' she says, louder than she intended. 'There is no such thing as a good war.'

The Mukti goes very still. Then he bows politely to her and goes back to talking to the senior officers.

Great, Tinka thinks resignedly. I've created a scene and probably got Ishaan into trouble too. It was a stupid, stupid idea to meet him today – this place is clearly a fauji watering hole.

She looks around impulsively for Carvalho and realizes with a start that he is at her elbow, wiping pork chop gravy off his chin.

'Please don't get mad at Ishaan because of anything I said,' she tells him.

He looks mildly surprised at this idea, then waves one hand tolerantly. 'You're entitled to your opinion.' Then his gaze grows keener. 'Dadyseth, eh? Not many of those around – are you Jehangir Dadyseth's sister, by any chance?'

Tinka nods.

Hosannah Carvalho's face grows sombre.

'Brave lad, brave lad. What a fight he fought! They teach it in the NDA, did you know?'

'Yes.'

'It's a masterclass in hand-to-hand combat. After his tank was destroyed by a direct hit, he crawled out and polished off six Pakistani soldiers with his bare hands.'

'I know.' Her voice is toneless.

'I'm sorry, babah,' Carvalho says heavily. 'It's always tough on the families.'

They sit side by side at the bar, not uncompanionably, and watch the room together. Dilsher Singh is chatting with the band members, who are on a break. Shaanu and Juhi are giving Kainaz Dadyseth pointers on the best shopping areas in the city. And Raka is holding forth to Deengu on precision bombing.

'Sir, it's so frustrating! Eight times out of ten, the damn S-5s drift. And of course, five times out of ten, they're duds. We can compensate for the duds, but how do we compensate for the drift? It's totally unpredictable.'

Deengu nods, his eyes getting a reminiscent gleam.

'Oh, things drift,' he says knowledgeably. 'You won't believe how much! Once at our base in Pathankot, back in the fifties, the ladies were having a mah-jong party. Alfresco, if you please, out in the spring garden of the AOC's house. Meanwhile, a bunch of us were taking on the Pakis way up north, near the Poonch Sector. To cut a long story short, there was a dogfight. They fired at me, I fired back, and got one bugger bang in the belly, and he blew up into smithereens, and one of his hands, severed at the wrist, spun and drifted all the way to Pathankot, where it landed right into Mrs AOC's punch bowl. Just as she had picked up the ladle, saying, Ladies, could one of you give me a *hand*?'

He bursts into gales of laughter at this punchline and everybody joins in. Even Carvalho gives a short laugh. Shaanu moves in next to Tinka, studies her sickened expression and slides her a fresh shandy.

'Are you okay?' he asks in a low voice. 'Don't mind Deengu. All his stories are made up.'

She rolls her eyes and takes a deep swig. Shaanu watches with some misgiving as the level of her drink drops rapidly.

'I haven't been around army guys for a while,' she says when she finally puts her glass down. 'I'd forgotten how they talk.'

'Hey, we're good folk,' he protests mildly. 'Gory but good.'

Tinka snorts.

'Your Deengu's a barbarian!'

'Nonsense!' Shaanu retorts. 'He's the best ballroom dancer at the base. His waistcoat's made of *velvet* and he smokes *cigars*. How can you call him a barbarian?'

She glares up at him only to discover the teasing light in his eyes.

'Ufff!' Tinka spins her barstool away from him.

Ishaan twirls it back gently.

'Also, we aren't Army guys, we're Air Force, the most elite wing of the Defence Forces.'

Tinka snorts.

'The most refined killers, you mean.'

The light goes out of Shaanu's eyes. He backs away, shrugging.

'For someone who talks so much about having an open mind, yours is pretty closed.'

She opens her mouth to argue this, then shuts it abruptly, shaking her head.

He continues, his tone friendlier, 'That haircut's a good decoy, by the way. Makes it hard for people to recognize you.'

She stiffens.

So he has seen the ad.

She wraps her arms across her chest, feeling oddly exposed.

'Is that why you invited me?' she says tightly. 'So you can show off the Freesia girl to your mates?'

Shaanu puts down his glass.

'Would that be so dreadful?' he asks, his eyes meeting hers with complete frankness. 'I mean, you're famous, you're gorgeous, I know you. Why wouldn't I want to flaunt that?'

This simple admission stumps Tinka. She stares at him, trying to pull her thoughts together, but it's tough because (and how galling is this for a feminist to confess!) all she can see are the frank grey eyes and all she can hear is that matter-of-factly uttered *You're gorgeous*.

'That is so shallow!' she finally manages to bluster.

'Oh, I'm not particularly deep,' he assures her, grinning. 'That's more Maddy's style – he reads poems and shit. But to answer your question, no, that's not why I invited you here as my guest, and anyway, nobody's spotted the likeness yet. You're still flying below the radar, so to speak.'

She scowls and dips her head. 'Thank God.'

Before he can respond, the musicians strike up a little intro and the singer speaks into the mic in her husky contralto:

'Time to play the last song of the evening, ladies and gentlemen! And as a delicate compliment to our lovely lady visitor from Bombay, we would like to serenade her with this year's most popular, supremely refreshing melody!'

She nods at the band and they grin and start to play.

'La...
la-la-la-la...
la-la-la-la-la...
la-la-la!'

People are confused but, as the singer points smilingly to Tinka, they start to nudge, point and, finally, applaud.

'Busted,' Shaanu says ruefully. 'Ah, well, Dilsher clearly recognized you. I believe he's been camping in the front stall of Tivoli cinema ever since your ad came out.'

'*Great,*' mutters Tinka.

She squares her shoulders, smiles and waves half-heartedly to the singer, who takes this as a cue to segue into '*Itsy-bitsy teeny-weeny yellow polka-dot bikini*'.

Across the room, Kainaz Dadyseth raises her brows and shrugs at her niece, her expression, even from this distance, clearly I-told-you-so.

'Dance?' Shaanu's gaze is quizzical. 'Or will I be accused of showing off again?'

'Hai, it was *you* na in the ad?' A random jolly lady rushes up out of nowhere, her voice squeaky with excitement. She is jumping up and down while, behind her, Macho da is staring at Tinka with a sardonic look upon his sunglassed face.

He definitely thinks she's a silly bimbo now.

Tinka, feeling cheapened and very flustered, with the eyes of the entire gathering upon her, snaps hurriedly, 'Uff, yes, yes! It was me! Please stop jumping!'

The woman freezes, her face clouding over. There is an awkward, uncertain pause.

'Look, let's just go to the floor and get it over with,' Ishaan whispers. 'I'll escort you out once we've danced for a minute or two.'

But Tinka shakes him off.

'Stop *telling* me what to do!' Shaanu goes very still.

'I owe you nothing, okay!' she says, suddenly feeling close to tears. 'I barely know you!'

His face closes down.

'You're right,' he says lightly.

He gives her a polite bow, turns on his heel and stalks away, his tarmac swagger very much in evidence as he strides across the dance floor and flat palms his way through the double doors.

Tinka sits down on a bar stool heavily.

Across the room, Kainaz disengages politely with the people she's talking to and starts to walk towards her niece.

'Pardon, but that wasn't very nice of you,' says a seething voice behind Tinka.

Tinks turns to confront Juhi.

'I don't know you,' says Juhi, the lights from the chandelier catching the flyaway curls around her face, making her appear almost angelic. 'Maybe you are having some problems or pressures, because everybody knows girls from decent houses don't do ads like *that*. Anyway, all that is your business. I only want to say one thing to you.'

'Say it, then.' Tinka is starting to feel pretty fed-up. God knows what this girl's problem is!

'You should be nicer to Baaz.'

Tinka stares at Juhi, her heart, for some reason, starting to sink.

'*What?*' she asks with an incredulous laugh.

'He lost the Sword of Honour because of you,' Juhi continues in her sweet, stinging voice. 'It was practically settled on him till he decided to help you out. The top brass got furious. They wouldn't even look at him after that. All his boxing medals and flying medals counted for nothing. He desperately wanted to fly MiGs but they didn't let him. He got assigned to the Gnats instead. They said it was because he was short, but that's silly, lots of tall men fly Gnats. He may never rise higher than a Wing Commander, thanks to the stuff your great Poncha uncle wrote in his permanent file. Kul mila ke, your influential family effectively crippled his career. And I'm not even getting into the taanas his stepfather threw at him. So when you say you owe him nothing, you're not being very correct.'

Tinka pushes back her short hair with a shaking hand.

'I didn't know,' she says stupidly.

Juhi shrugs, her eyes reflecting both sympathy and scorn. 'Well, now you do. What are you going to do about it?'

SIX

'Shaanu Bhaisaab?'

'Hmmm?'

It is early the next morning. Shaanu is lying prone on a folding cot, one arm flung up to cover his face, staring moodily at the ceiling fan.

'Who's your Mercury?'

He groans and turns his head. Sulo is sitting on the edge of his bed dressed in her best white dress and matching shiny sandals.

'Nice frock.' Shaanu dutifully joins index finger and thumb into an admiring circle.

'It's from Snow White,' she tells him, proudly smoothening the folds. 'My birthday frock. I've only worn it twice. So who's your Mercury?'

He pushes his hair off his forehead and smiles at her, his grey eyes warm with affection. 'You are.'

She gives a delighted little giggle.

'You're lying.'

'No.'

'But Sari said you told her that *she's* your Mercury.'

'The solar system,' Ishaan says, rolling onto his stomach and regarding her solemnly, 'is a very complicated thing. We learnt all about it at the Flying College. The planets keep changing their paths. Sometimes Mercury is closest to the sun, sometimes Venus is. Sometimes all of them even line up in one orbit, imagine! And sometimes a Halley's comet comes blazing in out of nowhere and throws the whole system for a six!'

Sulo gives up hope of extracting a clear answer from him and moves on to other subjects.

'Can we come watch you fly today?'

He sighs and sits up. He can hear Sneha in the next room, persuading Sari to surrender her beloved pants and change into a nice frock.

'But *why?*' Sari is wailing.

'Because otherwise everybody will think ki you don't have any good clothes,' Sneha explains patiently.

'How about I wear my pant-shirt only?' Sarita negotiates. 'But I carry my good frock along on a hanger? Then I can be comfortable, and people will still know I have good clothes.'

Shaanu chuckles, picks Sulo up from under her armpits, being careful not to crush the Snow White dress, and deposits her on top of his rolled-up fauji hold-all.

'The airfield is a dangerous place, gudiya,' he says. 'No little kids allowed. Suppose a big jumbo jet came down from the sky... and rolllled up to you ... annnnd ... *ate you up*, you baaawdi booch?'

He matches his actions to his words, and Sulo gives a delighted giggle and squirms away.

'*You* baaawdi booch! How can such a small girl fill its stomach?'

'That's also true,' Shaanu says, struck by this logic. 'So then we'll let it eat pitaji too.'

Sulo giggles, but Sneha calls out at once from the next room, her voice sharp.

'No making jokes about pitaji!'

'But we're serious!' Shaanu protests.

The Choudhary puts his head into the room at this very moment. Sulo's eyes grow round. She jumps up and runs out, circling around a harassed Sneha, who has entered behind her father, wringing her hands.

Shaanu gets to his feet.

'Namaste, pitaji,' he says formally.

The old man grunts and sits down at the little dining table. He is wearing a navy-blue bandgallah and looks curiously shrunken without his pagdi on his head. There is something oddly vulnerable about his exposed, bulbous forehead.

'Manne kuch baat karni hai taarse,' he grunts. 'I have to talk something serious to you.'

Shaanu's eyebrows rise. 'I would imagine so,' he says dryly. 'Since you decided to show up here with poor Sneha and four kids in tow when we're expecting war to be declared any moment.'

'What is war?' The Choudhary waves away war as a thing of no importance. 'The children wanted to meet you.'

'You've made them miss school,' Shaanu says.

'What is school?' The Choudhary waves away school as a thing of no importance. 'The thing is, Shaanu, ke I have found a bride for you. From a very good family in Jhajjar.'

He tries a fatherly smile as he says this, but it doesn't come out too well.

Shaanu just stares at him.

'Go on.' There is a dangerous edge to his voice.

The Choudhary's face starts to turn red and blotchy.

Slowly, he gets to his feet.

'Gori se, te kori se,' he says bluntly. 'She is fair and pure. Which is more than your mother was.'

Shaanu makes a hasty movement towards the old man, who steps nimbly behind the dining table.

'Shaanu, no,' Sneha says, distressed. 'Please! She really is a good girl. Sachhi. Her father is a very big jeweller in Jhajjar. See the photo.'

'The father's photo?' Shaanu demands. 'Or the jewellery shop's photo? I can't believe he's co-opted *you*, Sneha didi, I thought you were on my side!'

But Sneha looks offended. 'She *is* nice, Shaanu Bhaisaab!' she insists. 'She's a friend of mine. My prettiest, most popular friend! You'll like her! She reads books and newspapers and listens to English songs and all! And nothing is wrong with arranged marriage – I had one and look how happy I am with your jijaji!'

'*And* you'll bring in a decent dowry,' puts in the old man. 'More than that idiot Surinder brought in, at any rate! How much money I spent on the fellow's studies, thinking I'll get a doctor in the family! Colour pencils and geometry boxes and what not, and keeping the tubelight on all night to study – such big-big electricity bills I used to get! And after all that, he only became a wet! Spends all his time ramming the sperm of foreign buffaloes into desi bhains with an injection as big as a holi pichkari! Dhatt!'

'He's head of the animal husbandry team for all Haryana,' Sneha says hotly. 'It's a big post, pitaji!'

'Chuppp ke!' the Choudhary grunts. 'The girl's father is giving fifty thousand rupees and a brand new Fiat.'

'So what?' Ishaan says.

'So say yes.'

'I'd rather say yes to one of Surinder bau's desi bhains!'

'Shaanu Bhaisaab!' Sneha's eyes fill with tears. 'That's so *mean*! So my friend's a desi bhains? And *I'm* a desi bhains?'

Ishaan reels at this unexpected attack. Sneha and he never fight.

'No, no,' he starts to say weakly. 'That's not what I meant...'

The old man clears his throat authoritatively.

'I've already said yes.'

'What the fuck!' Shaanu whirls to face him. 'No! A thousand times, no!'

The old man points a shaky finger at him.

'If you say no to this girl also, I'll cut you off without a penny. No land, no money, nothing!'

Shaanu shrugs. 'Fine.'

The Choudhary's eyes almost start from their sockets. 'What do you mean, fine? *Chutiya* gain?'

Shaanu grins, his grey eyes glittering with anger. 'That was your trump card, wasn't it? Your father played it on you and it worked – you buckled. So you think it'll work on me. But it won't, pitaji, you're welcome to cut me off. I'll only marry a girl *I* like, *when* I like. Get this gori-kori-tijori married to Shelly instead.'

'Oh, I would have,' bursts out the old man, goaded into revelation. 'But they want an Armed Forces officer!'

Shaanu stares at him, incredulous. 'That was a *joke*! My God, what's wrong with you, Shelly's only fifteen!'

'What is age?' The Choudhary starts to wave away age as a thing of no importance, but Shaanu has had enough.

'Stupid bloody conversation.'

Saying which, he threads his belt through the loops of his overalls with unsteady fingers, yanks open the door and strides out of the room.

• • •

'Ishaan?'

He is running lightly down the wooden staircase, putting on his aviators, heading for the mess exit, when the hesitant voice halts him in his tracks.

Tinka Dadyseth, sitting at the edge of a rattan sofa, dressed in a black poloneck and a bright bandariya skirt, looking both pale and resolute.

Shaanu staggers slightly and has to prop a hand against the corridor wall.

Oh, great.

Like there aren't enough women in his life already!

Also, how come his name has never sounded so sexy before?

Also, why the hell is his heart thudding so fast?

He recovers and walks towards her, not bothering to modulate his voice or make it officer-like. 'Yeah? What can I do for you?'

She gets to her feet, slowly.

'I came to apologize,' she says.

He schools his face to register polite surprise. Inwardly, he is appalled by just how absurdly happy he is to see her again.

'Whatever for?' he asks incuriously.

'For...' She hesitates, then squares her shoulders. 'For saying I owe you nothing. It was ungrateful and uninformed. Because you let me run away that night, you didn't get the Sword of Honour.'

'Sword of Honour?' Ishaan is really confused now.

Is he being deliberately obtuse? Never mind, she can be clearer.

'The Sword of Honour. Back in Flying College. Juhi told me.'

'Juhi!'

She has been avoiding his gaze, but now she looks directly into his eyes.

'Yes.'

The cockiness, never absent for long, comes coursing back into Shaanu's veins. He folds his arms across his chest. As he's wearing his flying overalls and the sleeves are rolled up and his forearms are all sinewy, this is highly fortuitous.

'So you've come to thank the poor fool whose small dream of rising from bumpkin to gentleman you nipped in the bud? You're welcome.'

'Huh?' She looks confused and then annoyed. 'That's not what I meant!'

He puts on his aviators.

'Well, that's what I heard.'

'Okay, so maybe I said it wrong,' she capitulates immediately.

Sweet, strong exultation surges through him, seeing the general's daughter so eager to please. Facing down this girl is like facing that childhood train again. Somehow he contrives to hold his inscrutable expression.

'Maybe you did,' he drawls, his voice deliberately arrogant.

Tinka flushes but perseveres.

'And she said your dad got mad at you...'

Perfectly on cue, the Choudhary appears at the head of the staircase, leaning on his lathia, breathing fire.

'Shaanu!' he calls hoarsely. 'Ei, Shaanu!'

'And he's *still* mad at me,' Shaanu says, starting to grin a little. 'Look what you did, Dadyseth.'

She looks confused, then sketches a polite namaste at the old man and turns back to him.

'And she also said that Popo uncle wrote something nasty in your permanent file which will cripple your career—'

'Nothing can cripple my career,' he interrupts. 'Let alone your popat of an uncle.'

'Popo, not popa—' she starts to say, then frowns. 'You are really quite insufferably cocky!'

He rocks back on his heels. 'Careful,' he says, the grin getting wider. 'Remember you came here to apologize.'

But Tinka is not in the mood to apologize any more.

'You know what, maybe you didn't get that Sword of Honour because you just weren't good enough,' she flashes, irritated. 'And I'm the excuse you came up with.'

One dark eyebrow flies up. 'Really?'

'Really.' She nods firmly.

Shaanu takes off his aviators and leans in, his eyes sparkling intimately, openly letting her know how glad he is to see her.

'I'm the best there is,' he tells her.

She sniffs, looking away. 'The best don't fly Gnats, they fly Sukhois. Or BiGs.'

'You mean MiGs. Mikoyan Gurevich.'

'Speak in English, please, you sort-of know it.'

'It's not about the plane,' he says. 'It's about the pilot. Ask anyone—shit!'

Tinka frowns. 'Huh?'

He is no longer looking at her but behind her, where Jana-Gana-Mana and several other young Gnatties have just appeared. They're in jogging gear, laughing and talking, but stop abruptly at the sight of Shaanu in a tête-à-tête with the Freesia girl at this hour of the morning.

Meanwhile, on the staircase, the Faujdaar brood troops up, resplendently dressed, and takes position besides the Choudhary.

'Bloody hell,' mutters Shaanu, now caught between two sets of very interested spectators. Tinka gets the feeling he's holding himself back from using far more colourful language.

Ishaan glowers at his gawking squadron mates. They get the hint and slink away down the corridor. But the Faujdaars hold their ground.

'Look, seriously?' He turns back to Tinka, knocked off-balance by these intrusions, the tips of his ears a telltale red. 'Juhi is a sweet girl, but not very clever.'

'Can I tell her you said so?'

He ignores this. 'And Raka should stop obsessing about his bombarding technique and focus on his girl, so that she, in turn, stops focussing on my girl. Pay no attention to what either of them says.'

'You said my girl,' Tinka says.

Shaanu goes fiery red. 'What?'

'Just now, when you were talking about me, you said—'

'Yes yes, I know what I said,' he says hastily. 'My English isn't very good, like you just-now said. I make mistakes all the time.'

Tinka immediately wants to pull him in by the stripes of his navy-blue overalls and kiss him on his slightly open mouth, right where his lower lip dips in the middle, so firm and springy. Appalled by this highly improper desire, she steps back.

But Shaanu has something else on his mind.

'Look, do you need money?' he asks in a lowered voice. 'Is that why you did that ad? And you don't want to ask your family? I could organize some. We could ask Maddy or Raka – they're both rich, especially Maddy...'

'No!' Tinka says, startled. 'I didn't do the ad for money.'

'Okay okay. So then why did you do it? For a dare? I do shit like that all the time.'

Tinka groans inwardly, then decides he deserves an explanation.

'I did it because – well, yes, partly because I don't want to ask my aunt for money any more – but more importantly, I wanted to shut Ardisher up. He goes on and on about getting me married, and this seemed like a good way to get all the goody-goody Parsi boys off my back.'

Shaanu's lips twitch but he manages to keep a straight face.

'What's so funny?' she asks coldly.

His eyes are dancing as he asks, 'You thought bathing in a bikini under a waterfall on TV was a good way to get boys off your back?'

'Uff! You know what I mean.'

He nods, not unsympathetically.

'Just don't be embarrassed,' he tells her. 'Or regret doing it. It isn't immoral or illegal, and it's making a helluva lot of people, like your loyal fan Dilsher Singh, very happy. Why the hell should you be ashamed?'

How strange, thinks Tinka as a disproportionate wave of gratitude sweeps over her at these simple words, that it should be a Jat from rural Haryana who gives me this advice.

'Yeahhh,' she says feelingly, the childhood American twang suddenly prominent.

'Yeahhh.' He grins. 'It was fun, right?'

She grins back. 'Yes, it was, actually.'

They stare into each other's eyes for a long, rapt moment, before, somehow, Tinka manages to look away, pink-faced.

'I'll, uh, see you then.'

'Then,' Shaanu echoes her witlessly.

Tinka twinkles. 'When?'

He puts on his aviators again.

'Now,' he says bossily, striving for masterfulness and managing to achieve it. 'Why don't you come watch me fly today, and reassure yourself that in spite of your meddling my career is secure?'

'What?'

He gestures to the staircase.

'Join the gang. Watch the flight training today. I promise you a good show.'

'Hi, Tinka didi!' chorus Sari and Sulo from behind their grumpy father. Sneha smiles reluctantly. Jaideep Singh grins, blushing.

'*Hi*, kids!' Tinka waves back excitedly. Then she tosses her hair and walks snootily past Shaanu to join them, without saying goodbye.

Strangely unfazed by this cavalier treatment, he smiles and strides out into the balmy day to get his bike started.

'La…!' a Gnattie materializes at his elbow in the parking lot, crooning in a lilting falsetto.

'La-la-la!' joins in a second Gnattie, hoarsely happy.

'La-la-la-la-la-la-la!' chimes in what feels like the entire squadron. They inhale deeply and hit the crescendo, arms spread wide. 'La-la-laaaa!'

'Chupp chutiyon,' growls Shaanu, very red-faced, as he kickstarts the Bullet and rides away.

• • •

But when Shaanu and the rest of the Streaks report at the airbase, they are told that all training sorties have been suspended for the day. They are to spend another day all suited up, playing Scrabble, waiting for the order to scramble.

Shaanu shrugs philosophically, gets word out to his family that their visit to the ATC has been postponed, bolts down a huge plate of scrambled eggs, baked beans and bacon and sits back in a happy haze to savour the memory of his early morning encounter with Tinka.

She came to see *me*, he thinks exultantly. She must've had to set an alarm for five a.m., find out my schedule, organize a vehicle – shit, it was a huge step coming alone to the Officers' Mess. What a girl, what guts – she must really like me!

He springs to his feet and starts to pace up and down the room. Jana-Gana-Mana, who were squabbling over the Scrabble board, look at him and nudge each other slyly.

'Ants in Baaz's pants,' says Jana.

'Take a cold shower, hero,' Gana suggests slyly.

'Under a *waterfall*,' adds Mana and they start to guffaw.

Shaanu grins foolishly, flips them the middle finger and throws himself down on an empty settee near the huge glass windows. He stares up at the empty skies, dreamily hugging a conveniently placed packed parachute.

How pretty she is, he thinks with hesitant possessiveness. Not in that obvious, long wavy-haired, fair and lovely way, but somehow finer. Sleeker. More – he searches for the right word and finds one that satisfies him – *aerodynamic*. I bet, he thinks, his pulses leaping jaggedly at the thought, she has an incredible body…

Oh God, the moment he gets out of here, he's going to go buy tickets to whatever movie is running at Tivoli and see her ad again. But the damn thing is such a tease, the shots cut so fast, you can't see anything properly!

But then, he sits up, why should he see the ad? He can see her in person! Clothed of course, he clarifies to himself hastily. He is not some lecherous cheapie, the kind who're always ripping saris off Sharmila Tagore in the movies. He could swing by the club in the evening, *without* his friends this time, sweet-talk that dragon of an aunt and sneak her away for a ride on his bike. He's low on fuel though, but that's okay, Maddy will lend him the dough...

Kuch Bhi Carvalho comes barrelling out of the main ops room.

'Go go go!' he shouts. 'Now! Four of you, Cocktail formation. Baaz, you're leading. Over the Boyra salient. Get those Sabres today!'

• • •

'Don't tell me.' Mana's voice is hollow.

'I'm telling you,' Shaanu replies resignedly. 'Ghanta Pakis in sight. You lads see anything?'

'Nope.'

'Negative.'

'But we got here in six minutes!'

They are circling over the now familiar terrain of Garibpur again. The Forward Air Controller has greeted them as glumly as before, informing them that the strafing Sabres were right here, two minutes ago.

'But maybe I'm imagining them,' he says. 'Maybe living in this mud with these surds have turned my brain to curd.'

The Gnats circle over the salient cursing.

'This whole experience feels like when the missus went to the MH three times before the baby was born,' says Gana dispiritedly. 'Bloody false alarm.'

And then, just like that, Shaanu spots it.

A glint of gun-metal grey below him.

He sits up, electrified.

'Bogey!' he shouts over the R/T, his heart thudding like a drum. 'Below us – at three o'clock! Gana Gana Gana, d'you see him?'

'Negative!'

'He's right there, I tell you!' Shaanu swears, wishing he could bust through the glass, reach through the sky and point Gana's skinny neck in the right direction. 'Your three o'clock, low! Gana, you're right on top of him. *Take him out*, man!'

'Where's the fucker, *where*'s the fucker, where's the fucker?' Gana's adrenaline is up, but he hasn't made visual contact yet.

Shaanu swears colourfully.

Three seconds later Gana calls, suddenly steady and very cool, 'Okay, I see him. Mana, stay with me.'

The Sabre, which seems to be levelling off from a climb, is veering gently to the north. Gana, on the right side of Cocktail formation and best positioned to follow the Sabre, peels off behind him in pursuit, Mana on his wing and slightly behind.

'Baaz, bogey!' Jana's warning is sharp.

Shaanu's head jerks around. 'Where?'

'There's another bogey, *ahead* of the one we just spotted.'

'And one more, behind. Fuck! There's three of 'em!'

The Sabres, large, mean and steely grey, are in a circuit, the one in front flying in the same direction as Shaanu and Jana, the one in the middle now curving away, and the one behind, some way below the Gnats, pulling up, probably from a strafing run. The Gnatties of Cocktail formation are not yet close enough to see the nationality markings, but there is no mistaking the Sabre silhouettes. And they have to assume that the Sabres may be carrying missiles – Sidewinder heat-seeking missiles, the one weapon the Sabres have which outranges anything the Gnats can throw at them.

It's becoming clear that the Sabres are in a loose circuit pattern, taking turns to strafe the troops below. They are slipping in and out of sight, between small patches of cloud, even as the diminutive Gnats dart above, pursuing gun-firing positions in the rear quadrants of the Sabres.

Shaanu, staring at the Sabres, experiences the weirdest sensation of unreality. This is it, he thinks numbly, as tiny clouds go scudding past his Gnat. The real thing. When we press the gun button, real bullets will shoot out of our cannon muzzles. *Real* fire, *real* lead.

He grins.

Shit, how cool is this?

He hunkers down and focuses on locking in on the Sabre leader, who is fortuitously heading eastward, away from him. He is getting closer to firing range, sneaking up...

The Sabre slows down and Shaanu has to weave, using his rudder pedals, to stay behind it. Then he realizes the Sabre only *seems* to have slowed down; it is in fact climbing, he now realizes, as it pulls into a smooth curve and starts to gain altitude. Fuck, it's seen him!

Shaanu's fast-closing Gnat turns too, pulling higher and then into a wing-over, to stay behind the turning Sabre. He can feel the relentless weight of gravity tightening its grip on him and the reassuring pressure of the G-suit inflating against his abdomen and legs. And he knows Jana will be right with him, on his wing.

The tight-turning Gnat holds the turn and keeps Shaanu above and behind his quarry.

But then as the G-forces increase, Shaanu's vision blurs and the lead Sabre vanishes, melting into the clouds.

Huh? Shaanu blinks, his helmeted head swivelling as he searches for the enemy.

As he scans the skies, he spots Gana well and truly engaged with the Number Two Sabre which has peeled off towards the north, with Gana in hot pursuit, while Jana is now in a direct confrontation with the third, who is charging at them head-on. At the closing speeds of two jet fighters head-on to each other, the Sabre is on them in seconds, flashing past Jana at just a couple of hundred yards' range – close enough to see the green-and-white fin flash and the crescent moon and the star painted on his sides.

'Go, Jana!' Shaanu breathes.

Thanks to the Sabre's over-aggressive approach, Shaanu's wingman is the first man in Cocktail formation within firing range – and he seizes his opportunity. A sharp, bright line of tracer stabs from his ADEN cannons.

'*Dishoooom*,' Shaanu breathes, goosebumps pimpling his arms as his wingman's lethal burst of cannon-fire shoots across the blue. The armourers have loaded tracers at every fourth link in the ammunition belts, and their streak is visible even in the afternoon sun.

It is nothing, absolutely *nothing* like firing at the targets they've trained on at the ranges. Shaanu is conscious of wanting nothing more, at this moment, than to open fire himself.

Then Jana's voice, in a cry like ice-cold water.

'Guns jammed!' he is calling, his dismay audible even through the crackle. 'I had him in my sights, behenchod! My guns jammed after I fired!'

Ooooohhhhhhterrrri.

'Cycle gun dip switches, Jana,' Shaanu reminds his wingman through gritted teeth.

There is the kind of pause you only notice in slow motion, and the click of a mic in response. Then Jana's Sabre lurches, black-rimmed orange-hearted flames flaring out of its wing root.

It is a short burst, but it is enough.

'Woooohoooo!'

'*Got* the fucker!'

'Jai Mata di!'

Seconds later, the Sabre's canopy flies off, and Cocktail formation is rewarded by the sweet sight of a Pakistani pilot ejecting. The abandoned Sabre, well and truly on fire, is nosing over, almost directly underneath Shaanu.

That should make the 14th Punjab happy, Shaanu thinks with grim satisfaction. One down, two to go.

He is still scanning furiously for the lead Sabre when suddenly there's a sharp explosion below him. The abandoned Sabre has exploded. Jana's Gnat, behind the exploding Sabre, and Shaanu's above, are both peppered with debris, rattling against their fuselage sides and bellies. Rocking inside his tiny cockpit, Shaanu's eyes widen.

'Jana, you're streaming fuel! Drop tanks, drop tanks!'

Jana straightens for a moment and jettisons his holed auxiliary tanks, and is immediately and visibly flying lighter. Shaanu's head is still swivelling, looking for the lead Sabre, his neck and shoulder muscles beginning to ache.

And then Gana, from off to the north, crows blood-curdlingly over the R/T:

'Murder, murder, murder!'

It is the brevity code, signifying that he too has hit his target. In the distance, the Number Two Sabre, which Gana has been pursuing, is spewing thick black smoke and veering into a seemingly uncontrollable nosedive.

As Shaanu watches, whooping at this second kill, Gana fires again and his Sabre judders, turning helplessly over and over as it falls out of the sky.

In the midst of the smoke and debris and the belly of the dark grey cloud, Shaanu spots the lead Sabre again.

It has gained altitude and curved around, to lock-in behind Jana's Gnat. Jana has nosed down, to follow his own victim, and the lead Sabre is now well-positioned, behind and above him, ekdum Baaz-ke-maaphik.

The bastard waited for us to spend our ammo, Shaanu realizes with reluctant admiration, as he reefs around, grimacing at the rise in G-forces, pulling up into a wing-over to get behind the lead Sabre. But he doesn't know I'm locked and still loaded. Okay … here … I … come…

'Baaz, you're smoking!'

'Bail out, Baaz, bail out!'

Huh?

He looks around. The cockpit's hot, too hot, he realizes, it's coming from underneath; the metal of his ejection seat is actually scalding him, where the upholstery ends and his overalls are in contact with the metal edges.

He stares down in vague disbelief.

This is it.

You're gonna burn like a dry safeda leaf inside a red-hot chullah now.

If you're lucky, that is.

If you're unlucky, you'll end up legless, paralysed, good-for-nothing, a broken, pathetic vegetable.

For the first time in his short life, fear claws at his heart.

Should've prayed more, I guess. Too late now.

Shaking his head, he shifts in his seat and tucks himself on the cushion of his parachute pack, intent on getting the Sabre into his sight. His hands are slippery with sweat, the plane feels horribly imbalanced and hard to manoeuvre, but he has to get that lead Sabre before it gets his buddies.

'Bogey behind you, Jana, six o'clock high!' he shouts back into the R/T. '*Sabre*, Jana!'

Maddeningly, he doesn't respond.

The R/T, Shaanu thinks, his heart plummeting through his stomach like a stone. The bloody R/T's packed up.

He is in a classic tail-chase, tightening his turn for position behind the lead Sabre, who is in turn jockeying behind Jana. The Gnat can turn tighter, but the Sabre carries missiles and can fire from well over a mile away; Shaanu has to close to within a few hundred yards for his cannons to be effective. As Shaanu grits his teeth, pulling to shave off those last few degrees by which the Sabre is off-boresight, the Sabre itself is steadying behind Jana's Gnat, and Shaanu knows that the Sabre pilot is hearing the audio tone in his earphones, indicating missile lock.

'Mana, break!' Shaanu yells in frustration. 'Break, break, *BREAK*!'

Helplessly, in sickening slow-motion, he sees a flash, as one of the Sidewinder missiles carried by the Sabre ignites and arrows through the air, straight for Jana...

And misses.

'Yes!' Shaanu doesn't know why the missile failed to track and doesn't care.

The Sabre corrects, recalibrating, preparing to shoot again.

'Oh no you *don't*,' Shaanu breathes, ignoring the increasing heat as his Gnat closes in. The Sabre is expanding steadily and almost fills his gunsight.

And Shaanu fires.

'*Dishoooom.*'

His shells shoot out of their cannon muzzles with a short, thick growl that sounds like pure sex.

The Gnat judders with the recoil as a huge, red-hearted, black-rimmed fireball blooms in the sky. Throbbing, acrid and hot as hell.

Ishaan sags with a relief so exquisite he feels physically weak. Dimly, he hears the others' voices.

'Hain?'

'Where'd that come from?'

'Was he above us? Fuck!'

Shaanu grins.

'Three out of three, boys,' his voice crackles over the miraculously restored R/T, hoarse with triumph. 'We did it. Let's go home.'

• • •

News of their victory reaches Kalaiganga base before they do. The FAC from the 14th Punjab has radioed, jubilant. Two Pakistani pilots have been taken POW, and the Pakistani forces on the ground have been routed. Boyra salient has been wrested by the India-Mukti Bahini combine!

When the Gnats pull up over the airfield, Jana-Gana-Mana scooting ahead like over-excited escort vehicles, the lead Gnat lagging behind drunkenly, smoke still billowing from its belly, a cheering crowd is waiting for them.

Shaanu is given priority clearance and touches down first, while Jana and Mana get in line, and Gana cheekily zooms ahead to perform a series of victory rolls over the airfield, causing the ATC to austerely chastise him to 'please maintain circuit discipline, Mr Gonsalves'.

Shaanu pulls to a stop, flings back his canopy and

emerges, his sooty face exultant with triumph. He is immediately lifted out of his cockpit by a posse of cheering airmen and carried around the field on their shoulders.

In the verandah of the main building, pilots from the MiG squadron and the helicopter service come rushing in to congratulate the Streaks. Deengu talks incoherently about a similar air battle he had in the '65 war and Carvalho cackles, clapping Shaanu on the back so hard that he starts to cough. Even Pomfret cracks a sour smile.

And then the Faujdaar brood comes careening in, hysterical with excitement, and smacks into Shaanu, almost knocking him off his feet.

'What are *you* lot doing here?' Shaanu exclaims as they thud into him one after the other, like a cricket team that has just won a Test match.

They wriggle with delight. 'Oh, we were here anyway, so the ATC said might as well let them listen in! We heard all the R/T talk! We saw you land!' Sulo draws a deep ecstatic breath, her eyes glowing with hero worship. 'Shaanu Bhaisaab, you … are … *great!!!!*'

'Shaanu the *great*, born in a *plate*, in nineteen forty-*eight*!' Jaideep Singh capers around madly. 'Die paki paki, dhain dhain dhain!'

Shaanu scoops him up by the scruff of his collar and sits him on his shoulders. 'Whoa, hero, relax! Achcha,' he lowers his voice, his eyes searching the crowd hungrily, 'where's that train-wali didi?'

'She went to the bathroom,' Sneha says. 'She didn't look well.'

Jaideep Singh, clutching onto Shaanu's head for dear life, sucks in his breath excitedly. 'Oohh teeeeriiii! Raka bhaisaab and Maddy bhaisaab are here! *Daaru* gain?'

Because Raka and Maddy have rushed in, whooping excitedly, faces flushed with pride, bearing crates of beer. Everybody swoops down on it with delight.

'To the Streaks!' shouts Deengu, grabbing a beer and attempting to spray it about like champagne. 'To our heroes! To the Bottle of Bayra – I mean, the Battle of Boyra!'

'Yaayyyy!' shouts Jaideep Singh, and immediately has his bottle confiscated.

But before the four victorious pilots can get even a taste of the celebratory liquor, there sounds the throbbing of a motorcycle engine, and an official olive-green Enfield bike with a uniformed Dispatch Rider behind its handlebars, comes roaring with great pomp down the road. The DR parks the bike and strides down the verandah at a clip, bearing an olive-green satchel. He stops before Pomfret and salutes smartly.

'At ease,' Pomfret says warily.

The rowdy crowd quietens, lowering their bottles from their thirsty lips. DRs are sent out to deliver only very important, high-level messages. What could this mean?

The Rider, a tall, dark Rajasthani with a black pencil moustache and flashing eyes, inclines his head and holds out the satchel.

'GOC saab ne bhijvaya hai.'

Everybody looks at each other. The General Officer Commanding. From Calcutta. The biggest shot in this half of the country. What have they done to attract his attention?

Pomfret clears his throat, his Adam's apple bobbing uneasily.

'Whuh-what is it?'

The DR holds out the satchel again, his very white teeth flashing in a grin of benign bonhomie.

'To be cunjshoomed by the heroes of Boyra.'

And with a neat flourish, he rips open the satchel to reveal two glistening bottles of Johnnie Walker scotch whiskey.

. . .

Tinka waits only till the lead Gnat touches down and Shaanu is lifted out, safe for the moment. Then she walks out of the viewing room as unobtrusively as she can, runs full tilt down the four flights of stairs, makes straight for the foyer bathroom and is violently sick in the sink.

When she emerges, white-faced and clammy, the celebration has moved to the main dining hall. But Shaanu is waiting in the foyer, chugging water from a green jerry can. He lowers the can when he sees her, his face flushed, his Kota-grey eyes sparkling.

'Well?'

His voice is low and teasing and, like she had told him earlier, insufferably cocky. It's also incredibly hot.

'Congratulations,' she manages to say sincerely. 'You were fantastic.'

He takes a step closer. She takes a corresponding step back, bracing against the wall.

'So?' His tone is extremely meaningful.

'So?' she repeats.

'So I'm the best, right?'

The dimplets flash at this, but fleetingly.

'You're not ... too bad.'

Then her pointy chin wobbles and her eyes fill with tears.

'*Hey…*' Shaanu's voice is tender. He cups her chin gently and raises her face to make her look at him. 'What's wrong, Tell-me-na?'

Wordlessly, she lunges forward and grabs him in a fierce

hug. He laughs, surprised but also pleased, his arms closing around her slender body, hugging her back tentatively. And even though his smoking Gnat touched down a full twenty minutes ago, it is only at this moment, as he rests his chin on top of her head, that Ishaan feels he has truly come back home.

They stand like that for a long moment, her face mushed up against his chest, her heart thudding next to his.

When she pulls back, Shaanu's heart is in his eyes. He smiles down at her adoringly, like a man in a dream.

Tinka gives him a brief, tremulous smile and quickly looks away.

'Goodbye. And I'm sorry, but we can't meet ever again.'

'Wait...' Ishaan's smile falters. 'What?'

Tinka nods resolutely, wheels around and hurries away.

SEVEN

It doesn't take Kainaz Dadyseth long to notice that her niece is behaving in a rather odd fashion.

First, she has started avoiding the Anchor Bar. Whenever she has to cross it, she hurries past, head lowered, like a naughty child sneaking past the principal's office.

Second, whenever the club bearers climb up to their suite to inform her that there is a call for her from AFS Kalaiganga, she tells them to say she isn't in.

Third, she has started going to bed extremely early. She sets out for the refugee camp at six every morning, and when she comes back in the evening, she showers, gets into bed with a P.G. Wodehouse novel, polishes off a club sandwich from a plate placed atop her chest and goes to sleep.

Sick of the hollow giggling that accompanies the Wodehouse reading, the breadcrumbs on the bed and the general atmosphere of listlessness, Kainaz decides to tackle her niece.

'How are your Brylcreem boys?' she asks brightly one evening. 'Aren't you going to catch up with them? Shaanu has become quite a hero after Boyra!'

'No, yes,' says Tinka dully as she turns a page.

'Matlab?' Kainaz demands.

'No, I am not going to catch up with them. Yes, he has become quite a hero. Satisfied?'

'No!' Kainaz snaps. 'Why don't you just meet him if you miss him so much?'

Tinka turns another page. 'I don't miss him.'

'Balls!'

Tinka puts down her book.

'I cannot *believe* you've picked up that vulgar phrase.'

'Oh, don't be an old woman.' Kainaz moves closer. 'Why must you work so hard, darling? You rise at the crack of dawn...'

'Because the light is best then!'

'And spend the whole blessed day in those squalid camps! Surely you can let your hair down and indulge yourself in the evening?'

'I don't have any hair left to let down. And they aren't squalid!' Tinka's eyes blaze with indignation. 'They are *important*. They *matter*. Why don't you come with me tomorrow and see for yourself?'

'Fine!' Kainaz sits up. 'But only if you come down with me to the bar tonight and sip a beer and dance and chit-chat with young men like a normal person!'

'*No!*'

This is said so vehemently and in such a trembling voice that Kainaz's anger dissolves.

'Tinka,' she says, distressed. 'Bachche, what's up?'

'Nothing,' Tinka replies in a thread of a voice, whipping herself around to face the wall.

Kainaz looks at her small, stiff body and sighs.

'I'll come with you to the camp tomorrow,' she says. 'It's high time I see how you're spending your days...'

She is as good as her word. The next morning, when Tinka gets up, she finds the other side of the bed empty. When she walks down to the breakfast room a little later, Kainaz is already at one of the pretty antique tables, elbows on the red-checked tablecloth, ploughing martyredly through a platter of fresh fruit.

'You don't have to wear blue-and-white, Kung fui.' Tinka rolls her eyes. 'You're not a nun. It'll just be confusing.'

'I've worn what I've worn,' her aunt replies tartly. 'I've ordered you a cheese om— darling, why are you toting that big ugly bag?'

'It's my turntable,' Tinka replies. 'I don't want a cheese omelette. Let's go.'

The guard at the front gate greets Tinka like an old friend and helps them procure a cycle rickshaw to take them to the camp. The icy wind stings their cheeks as they coast downhill, bumping bone-rattlingly every now and then over potholes, clutching at each other for both balance and warmth. Impulsively, Kainaz kisses her niece's cheek.

'You're a good girl, Lily the tinka-tinka-tink!' she says. 'Lead me to these sad refugees!'

But she sobers up when they get to the camp.

Rows of thatched bamboo tents are lined up as far as the eye can see. Blank-eyed women, many of them pregnant, sit before woodfires, stirring pots of boiling rice. Half of them carry fitfully crying, painfully emaciated babies in their laps. Their bony, angry-eyed menfolk lounge sullenly on string beds under the trees. There is a pungent smell – a mixture of rancid rice, rotting sewage and burning plastic.

'Oh God,' says Kainaz in a subdued whisper as she walks through the scummy green, fly-infested puddles towards the tents, her patent leather pilgrim pumps already soiled.

'No wonder you're reading P.G. Wodehouse like a maniac. I would too, if I were you. Where do you practise?'

'Under those trees.' Tinka points to a scraggy row of kachnaar trees. 'C'mon.'

Hitching her bag higher on her shoulder, she hurries to the shade of the kachnaar. Once there, she puts down the bag, stands with her legs planted wide and claps her hands together authoritatively.

'Geetu Geetu Geetu!' she shouts.

There is a murmur within the silent tents, followed by an excited rustling, and then the flaps of almost half the tents part and children pour out in an animated flood.

'Geetu Geetu Geetu!' they chorus. '*Geetu Geetu Geetu!*'

'Oh. My. Goodness.' Kainaz fui has to sit down on a rickety bench.

Tinka laughs and claps again as the children rush up, pushing and tumbling, and stand before her in three bedraggled lines.

'Guh…' they burble. 'Gooh…'

A few stragglers rush in, throwing them off their rhythm, and they have to begin again.

'Gooh…' they chorus, more cohesively now.

'Goooo… d…' they gain confidence and volume, '*morning miss!*'

Most of them have faces only a mother could love, Kainaz Dadyseth thinks as she studies the line-up. They are thin, snot-nosed, chapped-cheeked, and all of them seem to have styes in their eyes. Their clothes are either far too big or way too small. Almost all of them are barefoot.

'Who is this?' they demand now that the formalities are over, swarming around the two women and looking the new visitor up and down with bright, curious eyes. 'Tomar ma? Didi?'

'Fui,' says Tinka. 'Uh, bua. Father's sister.'

'Pishi!' choruses the swarm. 'Good morning, pishi!'

And then they all demand individual handshakes from Kainaz. She has to shake about fifty-seven small grubby hands.

Meanwhile, Tinka squats on the ground to connect the turntable to a wooden plug point at the end of an open extension wire. After a couple of false starts, the *Aradhana* LP starts to revolve jerkily. Lightly, she drops the needle into the groove and the lively opening strains of '*Mere sapno ki rani*' fill the little shaded area under the kachnaar trees.

The children's faces grow solemn with concentration. They put stiffly straight hands to their lips and mime the blowing of a train engine.

'Whoooo hoooooo! Coooo hoooo! Twooooo hooooo!'

'But who's Geetu?' Kainaz whispers, mystified.

'Sharmila Tagore.' Tinka laughs. 'They think her name is Geetu. Because mere sapno ki rani kab aayee *Geetu*.'

Kishore Kumar's lusty singing kicks in and the dance starts with full gusto, if not full cohesion. Two small lads swagger forward, clearly playing the pilots in the Air Force Jeep, and proceed to do a credible job of lip-syncing to the lyrics.

Then, with a dramatic little swirl, the main girl makes her entry. Her face is tantalizingly obscured (exactly like in the film) with an Alistair MacLean novel. She moves the book away from her face, right on cue, and Kainaz tries to cover her gasp of distress.

'Oh God, what happened to that poor child's face?'

'Those are burns,' Tinka replies softly. 'Her family did that to her when they found out she'd been raped by the Razzakars. Who also made her pregnant. Her name's Mamuni.'

'She's *pregnant*? Oh God, of course she is, I can tell. How old is she?'

'Thirteen,' Tinka replies. 'There are thousands like her. Girls and women raped by the West Pakistanis. We've started calling them birangana, which means heroine, to signal that there's no shame in being one, but it's no good. They're already being shunned.'

'People are *evil*,' says Kainaz Dadyseth feelingly.

They watch the children swing and swirl with gusto, shouting 'Geetu' at periodic intervals. Presently the song ends and they freeze in a tableau, as poised and intense as professional dancers. They hold the pose for almost thirty seconds, then let go, laughing breathlessly and hitching up their loose pyjamas, all flushed with exertion and importance.

Kainaz applauds vigorously.

'Shabaash shabaash!' she shouts. 'Khoob bhalo!'

'They're bad, aren't they?' Tinka mutters.

'Dreadful,' Kainaz agrees, still clapping.

'Oh God,' Tinka sighs. 'What am I going to do with them?'

'Arrey, drill the little buggers hard,' Kainaz says, smiling and waving at the children. 'Tell them to do it again!'

'They'll never agree.' Tinka shakes her head.

The children come clamouring around her.

'Didi, didi, "*Haathi mere saathi*"!' they shout.

'Didi, "*Chin-chin-choo*"!'

'Didi, "*Dil deke dekho*"!'

'Hush!' Tinka says sternly. 'One song, toh, you can't do properly, want to learn ten more! We'll do *Geetu* again. Let's start.'

'No!'

'Didi, *once* only, "*Chin-chin-choo*"!'

'Didi, "*Haathi mere saathi*"!'

'Okay fine fine.' She produces another LP from her bag. '"*Chin-chin-choo*". But just once, then it's back to *Geetu*, okay?'

This time the dancing is a mad riot of improvised moves. The children gyrate and twist and shout and pout. Kainaz, watching Tinka match them step for step, sighs wistfully for her own giddy youth, now long past.

The song comes to its crazy climax and her niece collapses by her side, panting and laughing.

'You should buy more LPs,' says one saucy young fellow as he hitches up his pyjamas. 'Your collection's too small.'

'Ya,' chimes in another. 'We want new songs, *more* songs, *fast* songs.'

'In our house we had *five thousand* LPs. But we had to leave them behind when the Pakistanis came.'

'Abbey ja!'

'Liar.'

'It's *true!*'

'Enough,' roars Tinka. '*Geetu!*'

And *Geetu* it is.

'We're hoping to perform this live on Christmas day,' Tinka tells Kainaz as the kids start their train-like puffing again. 'There's going to be a show. Mother Teresa herself is coming. If they're good enough, that is.'

'They'll be good enough,' Kainaz replies. 'Your Mamuni is good as the coy Sharmila, and that little kid who's playing Rajesh Khanna, he's good too. The life of the show, actually!'

'Isn't he?' Tinka gurgles with laughter. 'You should have seen him at the audition, strutting about with a hanky knotted around his neck! He winked at me thrice! *So* saucily!'

'Quite the little stud-muffin.' Kainaz studies the skinny figure. 'He can't be more than eight or nine, no?'

'He's eight,' Tinka confirms. 'His name's Prasanto. His entire family was knifed to death, seventeen of them. His mother hid him underwater in a buffalo pond. He breathed with a length of pipe for three hours and survived.'

'Ugh.' Kainaz wrinkles up her nose. 'Spare me the gory details, darling. Do all of them have such dreadfully depressing back stories?'

'Pretty much.' Tinka's face grows thoughtful. 'Some of the other volunteers think Prasanto exaggerates, though. They've found inconsistencies in his story. They say it's entirely possible that *nobody* in his family died and he's making up these lurid details out of sheer competitiveness.'

'I can't decide which is worse,' Kainaz says darkly. 'A genuine tragedy, or a kid so screwed up that he makes up tragedies! So, what else do you do around here besides being the dance teacher?'

Tinka sits down beside her.

'Well, I shoot photographs mostly. And when the good light fades, I help with vaccinations and pest control. But dance is the main job the nuns have given me to do. They say the kids need cheering up. Anyway, there are tons of volunteers around. Some Indians, some foreigners.'

'Any cute ones?'

'Kung fui!'

Her aunt raises her beautifully plucked brows.

'What? One can't romance in a refugee camp?'

'One can, I suppose,' Tinka says doubtfully, looking about the dusty, depressing world spread out around them. 'If the suffering of other people is what turns you on.'

'Oh, don't turn into such a self-righteous little prig!'

Kainaz says robustly. 'In the midst of death, we are in life! See, over there, that woman in the patched sari with the three skinny kiddies in her lap is exchanging amorous glances with that one-legged man. And if you don't think romance has no place in a refugee camp, why'd you pick the *Geetu* song for the show?'

'The kids picked it,' Tinka says.

'But it features an IAF Fighter! Like your Ehsaan.'

Tinka's face shutters over immediately. 'I don't want to talk about Ishaan.'

• • •

'Raks...'

'Hmmm?'

'What's wrong with Baaz?'

The Aggarwals are snuggled up under the velvet honeymoon razai in their little bedroom. It's late in the night. Through the fly-mesh screen windows comes the sound of crickets chirping. A cool breeze stirs the olive-green mosquito netting overhead. Juhi is stroking Raka's hair and sneaking looks at the new silver anklet around her shapely ankle. She's quite pleased with it.

Raka groans. 'Baaz? There's nothing wrong with him. He's strutting around pleased as punch and is probably in line to win a Vir Chakra.'

Juhi pulls his hair.

'Ouch!'

'Stupid,' she says severely. 'I didn't ask you about his Vir Chakra. I asked why he's looking like his mummy just died.'

'His mummy died fifteen years ago, as far as I know,' her aggravating husband replies.

This is rewarded with a harder yank on his hair. Raka rears up on his elbows indignantly.

'What, wifey! D'you want me to go bald before my time?'

She leans in to kiss his forehead, then raises her shapely leg and points to her toes. 'Isn't my anklet pretty?'

'Very pretty,' he agrees with immediate appreciativeness, his calloused hands sliding down her smooth calf. 'Lemme take a closer look...'

Juhi arches her dainty foot and pushes him away. 'Something's *wrong* with Baaz,' she repeats, wrinkling her smooth forehead. 'He's wandering about smiling automatically, talking mechanically. He's worn the same shoes to the club three days in a row, there are shadows under his eyes and he never wants to dance.'

Raka finally sits up, sighs and strokes his moustache. 'You mean he's suffering from some kind of delayed reaction from the dogfight? His Gnat exploded, you know, three minutes after they lifted him out of it. That could have shaken him.'

'Uff!' Juhi sits up and stares at him in acute exasperation, her unbound hair cascading about her naked shoulders. 'It's not the dogfight, Raks, it's that girl.'

Raka continues to look blank.

'*Tinka!*'

'Oh, her...' he responds unenthusiastically. 'She left, no? Or she got busy somewhere, shooting something.'

'He likes her,' Juhi says positively. 'And she likes him.'

Raka looks doubtful.

'I didn't notice him paying her any special attention.'

Juhi stares at her husband in disbelief. 'What is *wrong* with you?'

'Nothing,' he retorts. 'Anyway, Baaz couldn't possibly like her seriously. I mean, everybody's seen her in a bikini. She's not a decent girl.'

'Stop talking like a halwai and talk like an Air Force officer,' says his wife brutally.

Raka grows belligerent. 'So I should've married a bikini model too? Instead of a girl from a good middle-class family?'

Juhi throws up her hands, her pretty bosom swelling with indignation.

'Tinka's family is very good!' she says. 'They're wealthy and high-class and respected.'

Raka sighs. 'That's what I'm worried about,' he says, glumly. 'Did you see her snooty aunt that evening? She only talked to Maddy. Because he's rich and English-medium. She had no time for the rest of us, including Baaz.' He sits up straighter, tugging at the razai, tucking it around his shoulders and under his butt. 'And anyway, *you* didn't like her, Juhi! You sunaoed her so much that night and were pleased with yourself for doing it! You said she had it coming.'

Juhi's eyes grow troubled. She is silent for a while, playing with his hair.

'Yes, but then she came and asked me for Baaz's address, and she seemed nice. She was so sorry for all the trouble she got you boys into. And she didn't seem at all stuck-up even though her ad is such a big hit. Besides, Mrs Carvalho said her brother died and that messed her up.'

'So now she wants to mess *my* brother up,' Raka says resentfully. 'I don't like it, Juhi.'

'Arrey, but even our families didn't get along at first,' his wife reminds him. 'We had to elope – and Shaanu helped! You have to help him too.'

'That was a totally different thing,' he replies. 'We were same caste, same community, same social standing! This girl's some rich Parsi Bombay bitch—'

'Raks!'

'And you've toh seen Shaanu's pitaji. Now try and imagine him and that snooty flower-waali auntie together! What will they *talk* about? What do they have in *common*?'

'She smokes and so does he,' Juhi suggests after a moment.

He gives an incredulous laugh.

'Virginia Slims and Haryana ka hookah? C'mon, yaar.'

'I don't know all that,' she says crossly. 'And stop hogging the razai ... gimme some! Point is, he *likes* her. And she likes *him*.'

Raks maintains his hold on the razai and starts to hum '*Pyar kiya toh darna kya*'.

She hits him with her pillow.

'Raks!'

'What?'

'Help Baaz! Talk to him about Tinka!'

He throws up his hands.

'Why *me*?'

'Because Maddy's gone off to do that helicopter flying course. Or I would've asked him. He's *much* more sensitive than you.' She pauses, then adds pensively, 'Better-looking too.'

'Achcha!' He rears up, outraged.

Giggling, she hits him again.

Laughingly, Raka wrests the pillow away and grabs her by the wrists. 'And if I don't talk to him, then *what*, madame wife?'

Juhi's pretty face grows stern. 'Then no sex for you.'

'Whaaat?' Raka's jaw drops. 'No!'

'Yes,' she says ruthlessly, lying back on the bed, her expression resolute. 'Till you talk to him.'

Raka rolls on top of her, pinioning her to the mattress. 'Pukka?'

It's his sexy bedroom voice, the one that always makes her toes curl up in helpless longing, but now she resists it.

'Pukka.'

He buries his head into her bosom and groans.

'Oh Baaz ... you baaaztard! Mera KLPD kar diya!'

Juhi giggles and tugs at his hair to make him look up at her.

'Just *talk* to him, Raka. Please.'

He sighs.

'Okay.'

He kisses her neck persuasively, but she pushes him off and scrambles away to sit against the headrest, arms and legs crossed primly over her luscious body.

'But talk *sensitively*. Feel your way into it. Okay?'

Bitterly informing her that he'd much rather feel his way into something else, Raka rolls over and goes to sleep.

But the next evening, he seeks Shaanu out at the Officers' Mess.

He finds him hanging out with the Gnatties, all of whom have grown irritatingly cocky since Boyra. They don't snigger openly when they see the MiG pilots, but only just.

Which is probably why I've missed the fact that Baaz is low, Raka thinks defensively. Besides, it's not like I don't have issues of my own.

He says as much to Shaanu, as a prelude to poking about in his personal life.

'Those damn K-13s are refusing to behave,' he says, sliding into the bar counter next to his friend. 'The Tactical Aviation Centre guys are stumped. The whole precision bombing programme is turning into a guessing game.'

'That's because they're fitted with parachutes,' Shaanu responds listlessly. 'They make 'em drift. You need a shell that falls like a stone. And you need to set the fuse detonator correctly.'

'Yeah yeah,' Raka responds impatiently. 'We have nothing like that in the ordnance factories. So why are you looking so fucked ya, Baaz?'

Because this is his best attempt at 'feeling his way into it'.

A haughty expression slides across Shaanu's haggard (how could he have not noticed it all this time?) face.

'I'm not fucked.'

Raka responds to this by glowering at the other Gnatties until they sidle away. Then he lowers his voice and says, 'Juhi tells me you're in love with this Tinka from Bombay. Are you?'

Shaanu stares at him for a moment, his jaw taut, his grey eyes glittering strangely, then gives an unamused laugh. 'You *do* know how to drop a bomb, brother,' he says. 'Just like that ... *thapaaak!*'

He suits the action to the word, raising one arm and dropping an imaginary bomb dramatically to the floor.

'*That's* how your S-5s should fall.'

Raka holds his gaze. 'Are you?'

Shaanu flings back his head, looks Raka in the eye and shrugs. 'Yeah.'

'Hain?' Raka almost drops his drink. His jaw sags, making him look, even with his gallant hussar moustache, a little ridiculous. 'Arrey, aise kaise? How can you be? You've met her what, twice?'

'Five times, actually.' Shaanu's gaze doesn't falter, the grey eyes sparkle with conviction. 'I just ... know.'

'Does *she* know?'

Shaanu shakes his head. 'No.'

Then he adds, 'But she loves me too.'

'Arrey wah!' A harassed Raka mops his forehead. 'Phir toh kuch problem hi nahi hai! Let's call a pandit and start handing out laddoos! Everything's hunky-dory!'

'No.' Shaanu shakes his head again. 'Nothing's hunky-dory. In fact, she told me she never wants to see me again.'

Inwardly rather relieved, Raks manages to put on a troubled face.

'Oho ... is she engaged to somebody else? Family pressure?'

Shaanu shakes his head.

'It's something else.'

He knocks back his drink and Raka studies him, concerned.

'So where is she now?' he asks finally.

'At Sarhind Club only, but she's refusing to take my calls.'

This doesn't sound like the behaviour of a girl who loves you, Raka feels.

'Did you guys fight?' he asks.

'I don't ... *think* so,' Shaanu replies slowly.

In the background they can hear Deengu's hearty voice booming over the general hubbub of conversation.

'So the CO said, have some shame! The Israeli Army is an Orange Juice Army! Powered on the goodness of pure OJ and nothing but pure OJ, they mow down the Palestinians like wild grass! So then I told him, sir, we are also an Orange Juice Army! But we are an Orange Juice and *Rum* Army! Jaiii shri rummm!'

A burst of laughter greets this sally.

'Have you tried showing up in person?' Raka asks.

'Yes,' Shaanu says gloomily. 'But I can't get into the

resident guests-only areas, and she never seems to come out to the restaurants or the Anchor Bar.'

'Try harder, man!'

Shaanu glares.

'Arrey, it's a long ride to the city, and I'm flying CAPs all the time! *And* my family is visiting. Whenever I have free time I have to do bachha-party duty. Not that I mind,' he is quick to clarify. 'Besides, they're leaving tomorrow. *And* of course,' he shoots a dirty look at Raka, 'my best friends are too busy being happily married to help me.'

Poor Raka thinks back to the sleepless night he has just endured, but nobly says nothing.

'Sorry, yaar,' he says instead. 'We'll figure something out! What about this refugee camp she's volunteering at? Isn't that closer?'

'That's closer.' Shaanu's hand grips Raka's shoulder painfully. 'We could go there! Why didn't I think of that? What a good idea! Tomorrow?'

'Sure!' Raks assures him heartily, then sobers. 'Aur sun, Baaz, there are Sabres sniffing around our skies. Your photo's come in the *India Post*, grinning from ear to ear, all four of you! The Pakis must've seen it. They'll make it personal. You need to stay focussed.'

'Yeah yeah.' Shaanu nods in an offhanded fashion that Raka finds far from reassuring. 'So in the morning then?'

'In the morning.'

They clasp hands and Raka gets to his feet.

'Stay for a drink, yaar,' Shaanu says.

'Not tonight,' Raka replies firmly. 'Now that I've spoken to you about this, I need to go home and, er, catch up with Juhi.'

He hurries away, and immediately the Gnatties come

surging back, brimming with beer and good cheer, and bear
Shaanu away to play billiards.

'Make way for the Sabre slayers!' they shout good-
naturedly. 'Make way for the innnnn-vinnnnn-cible heroes
of Boyra!'

• • •

The train carrying the Faujdaars back to Chakkahera is
scheduled to depart at ten in the morning. Eight a.m. finds
the family cranky, constipated and clingy, and in no mood
to say goodbye to their beloved Shaanu Bhaisaab.

The Choudhary is holed up in one suite, enjoying the
hot running water while all the children have been bundled
into Ishaan's quarters, a messy, noisy space strewn with
hold-alls, suitcases, cloth bags filled with Kalkatta shopping
and everybody's washed-but-still-wet chaddis. At regular
intervals, children emerge from Ishaan's bathroom with
chattering teeth, wet hair and scrubbed skin and present
themselves to Sneha to be cold-creamed, combed and
clothed. Sneha herself is ready, having bathed and dressed
at the unearthly hour of four a.m.

Ishaan straddles a chair and watches his sister keep her
cool perfectly in the eye of the storm.

'*You* should've been in the Army,' he tells her. 'You're
drill captain, quarter-master and commanding officer all
rolled into one!'

'Don't you be condescending,' she replies tersely as she
holds Sulo's chin firm and bisects her hair into a perfect
middle parting. 'I may not wear a uniform, but if a man
had to do as much work as I do in a day, na, his *manhood*
only would fall off!'

His eyebrows rise. 'Ouch.'

She smiles grimly. 'I mean it.'

'You're right,' he agrees peaceably. 'Anyway, I believe women are superior to men.'

Sneha sniffs. 'No, you don't,' she says darkly. 'You believe *some* women are superior to men. Just the rich educated ones.'

Ishaan sits up interestedly. This seems to be going somewhere.

'From *big* families…'

'Matlab?' He wrinkles his forehead.

'Who pretend to be *Muslims* and talk like *Amaaricans* and dance around in wet *bikinis* and give my brother sleepless nights.'

'Sneha behenji!' Ishaan is surprised. 'I thought you liked Tinka!'

'*I* like Tinka!' Sulo, who they've both forgotten about, pipes up. She turns to her eldest sister. 'You're just jealous because she's his Mercury.'

Both Ishaan and Sneha gasp in indignation.

'I am *not*!' Sneha blazes.

'She is *not*!' Ishaan protests.

Sneha whacks Sulo smartly on her rounded bottom, propelling her towards the door.

'Go eat your breakfast!'

The little girl rolls her eyes, but rushes away without a fuss. After all, there's shahi tukda for breakfast today.

Brother and sister look at each other in the momentarily empty room.

'What's all this?' he asks lightly.

Sneha puts down the comb and ribbons.

'Shaanu Bhaisaab, I know she is nice – she was so nice on the train! But she's complicated, and she's not like us. She talks too easily to men, roams around alone. She's bold and she's trouble, and she's wrong for you.'

'You mean she's too hep for me.'

'I knew you'd say that.' Sneha reaches for him, distressed. 'That's not what I mean at *all*.'

He shakes his head. 'You've got it all wrong. First, she's *not* my Mercury! And second, it's silly for you to worry because she's not trouble, and she's not complicated or any of those things, and she's definitely not wrong for me.'

She stares at him in disbelief.

'You're contradicting yourself,' she says bluntly. 'You're saying you don't like her, and then you're saying she's right for you.'

But this is too much for her older brother.

'Don't speak to me like that, Sneha behenji!'

'Why not?' Sneha snorts. 'Tinka does! You're trying to patao her by acting very modern, but actually, Shaanu Bhaisaab, you're *not*. You have one set of rules for girlfriends and another set for sisters.'

'That's not fair,' Ishaan says, stung.

'Achcha?' She's really upset now. 'I've been here so many days now – when did you ever take me dancing to the Club?'

He stares at her in total non-comprehension.

'You said you didn't want to go!'

'But you could have insisted! *Made* me go!'

'But then you'd say I was bossing you around and not letting you decide for yourself! And you'd call me a chauvinist!'

She shakes her head, staring at the floor.

'I said no because I felt little under-confident, but if you'd asked me a few more times, I would have gone. I even brought my good saris to wear to the Club. But you didn't, because you're...' her voice drops to a despairing whisper, *'ashamed of me.'*

He rises from his chair so fast it falls backwards and drops to his knees before her.

'That not *true*,' he says urgently, the grey eyes agonized. 'You're amazing, you're beautiful, everybody envies me my sisters!' He grabs her hands. 'Let's go dancing tonight!'

She shakes her head. 'I'm leaving in ten minutes.'

'We'll change the tickets.'

'No!' She pushes past him and starts to comb her hair with trembling hands.

'I *insist*!' Shaanu says determinedly, thinking that maybe this is what she wants him to do.

But she just ignores him and starts checking the locks on her attaché case.

Ishaan's troubled eyes follow her around the room.

'Sneha behenji, you're ... you're happy in your marriage, na?' he asks finally.

She gives a little laugh, but says nothing.

'You don't ... regret it?'

'No no.' She shakes her head. 'I just wish ... I had something *more*.' She looks up at him, her eyes bright. 'I'm a good teacher, no, Shaanu Bhaisaab? I taught all the little ones so well?'

'You did.'

'I could be a teacher!'

'Yes, yes of course you could...' Ishaan's eyes rake her face. 'Doesn't jijaji take you out to parties and all?'

'We live in *Jhajjar*, Shaanu Bhaisaab. Where will we go?'

'I'm sorry,' he says wretchedly.

She turns to face him. 'It's just...' She pauses, then continues in a softer voice. 'It's just that you've never fallen in love before, and you'll do it like you do everything else – with *all* your heart and soul. I'm worried you'll get hurt.' Her voice drops even lower as she confesses, all in a rush, 'And I'm worried you'll forget all about us.'

'I'm *not* in love with her.' Thus, Shaanu, fervent and frazzled, completely contradicts what he told his friend last night.

'Yet,' Sneha replies sadly.

'Okay, yet,' he admits. 'But she's nice. She's so different. I'm the envy of the entire Air Base. All the guys are crazy about her, heck, the country's crazy about her!'

'Just because the country jumps into a well, you don't have to jump into the well.' Sneha rolls her eyes as she murmurs the old aphorism.

'And I don't want her to be my girlfriend just so I can show off,' he continues doggedly, ignoring this interruption. 'I liked her before she did that ad, you know, ne, I *told* you the story. When I was in Jodhpu—'

'Why can't you just marry my nice friend from Jhajjar and be *happy*?' The words are wrung out of her.

Shaanu stares at her hopelessly, not sure what to say, when they are interrupted.

'Beta Shaanu?'

The Choudhary's voice is so cooingly sweet that both Shaanu's eyebrows and his antenna rise immediately. He looks at Sneha, his eyes comically conspiratorial, but she just tosses her head and looks away.

'So we are leaving!' Chimman Singh states the obvious as he enters the room at the head of a wave of children, wiping shahi tukda syrup from his chin.

'Yes,' Ishaan says formally. 'Thanks for visiting, pitaji.'

The older man sits down on the edge of the bed with a grunt.

'Maybe I am too strict,' he says.

Ishaan's jaw drops. 'Hain?'

'Too strict with you!' the Choudhary repeats after letting out a small burp. 'After all, you are an afsar, a Flying Officar ne, I can tell, after living here, seeing your life and all, that a girl from our village just won't fit in.'

'That's not the point.' Ishaan addresses his stepfather, but his eyes are on his sister. 'It's not about a girl from a village or a girl from a town. I just want to pick my girl myself.'

The younger girls giggle. Jaideep Singh nods stoutly.

'Shaanu Bhaisaab wants to do *love marriage*,' he explains to his grandfather. 'Because when you do love marriage, your wife loves you. When you do arrange marriage, she *arranges* you.'

'Yes yes,' the old man says tolerantly. 'Shaanu Bhaisaab feels like that because his mother loved his father.'

'And you?' Jaideep Singh demands.

The Choudhary shrugs. 'Our marriage was arranged.'

'Oh.' There is a world of pity in the toddler's voice.

Shaanu stares at his stepfather.

'So I won't force you to marry anybody,' Chimman Singh declares. 'You find your own girl, chhore, and you marry her and bring her to the haveli for my blessing, bas!'

Ishaan goggles, rendered absolutely speechless. Has somebody body-snatched Chimman and replaced him with this paragon? He stares at the old man in disbelief, then at Sneha, standing by the window.

Her lips twist into a bitter smile.

The old man leans in. 'Theek se, ne?'

Ishaan blinks. 'Thee-theek se, pitaji.'

'Aur haan.' The Choudhary looks meaningfully at Sneha, who nods, walks to her attaché case, extracts a red velvet box and hands it to her father. He opens it, revealing a chunky gold chain. 'This is for you. I bought it yesterday from Senco jewellers, Kalkatta, because I'm so proud of you. Here, wear it!'

'For … me?' Shaanu asks in wonder.

The old man cracks a rusty smile.

'For you. I'm proud of you, chhore. Pakistaniyon ke plane gira ke, you have made my chest double in size with pride.'

Ishaan's grey eyes grow painfully intense. Starting to his feet, he lets the old man drop the chain around his neck.

'And *your* chest?' To cover the awkwardness of the moment, Ishaan grins at his sister. 'Did it double with pride too? Looks the same to me!'

'Chupp.' Sneha goes pink with embarrassment.

'There's a flying eagle ka pendant on it,' the old man says from behind them gruffly. 'Because Baaz…'

'… means eagle. I know.' Shaanu turns back towards his stepfather, his voice equally choked.

Chimman Singh looks him full in the face and smiles. Shaanu smiles back, his heart in his eyes.

The old man clears his throat self-consciously and shouts, 'Eiiii bachhaa party, camera lao! Let's have a family photu!'

EIGHT

When Tinka reaches the refugee camp on Saturday morning, she finds the children in an unusually cranky mood. They are usually cheerful after breakfast, their stomachs filled with rice, the winter sun warm on their backs, but today is a cold, wet day and everybody is sluggish and surly and out of sorts.

When she drops the needle into the groove and claps her hands, they all sort of dwaddle forward, picking their noses and scratching at their mosquito bites, and start to sway half-heartedly to the beat.

Tinka raises the needle of the LP.

'You can do better than that! Didn't you eat breakfast?'

'I'm sick of rice,' somebody grumbles.

'It's always burnt and smelly.'

'I want to sleep. This is stupid.'

Not in a particularly sunny mood herself, Tinka is tempted to add several of her own woes to this list. But she's the grown-up here.

Shaking off her lethargy, she laughs, restarts the music and roars, '*C'mon*, kids! With *feeeeling*!'

This time, things go a bit better. The upbeat music energizes the maidan, and the long line of smaller 'uns playing the 'train' finally get the hang of huffing and puffing and *cooo ... chookk-chookk-chookking* in unison. Strung between them like a pendant on a pearl chain, Mamuni performs her coy act perfectly, flipping the pages of her book while casting flirtatious glances at the two 'IAF Fighters' chasing the train in their 'Jeep'.

Mere sapno ki rani kab aaye gee tu?
Aayee rutt mastani kab aaye gee tu?

'Good, very good!' Tinka shouts as the 'train' runs merrily around the maidan. 'Stop now, everybody, let Mamuni do her thing. Mamuni, smile at Prasanto! Prasanto, stop drooling on the mouth organ, it belongs to your friend. You just have to flirt with Mamuni. Smile at her ... *smile!* Arrey, why aren't you smiling?'

'Because she's pregnant,' announces Prasanto, who has been hanging out with older boys, smoking beedis and downing hooch, and is privy to information he didn't have at a more innocent time when he'd assumed Mamuni was just fat. 'She's dirty! *And* ugly! I won't flirt with her! Change her!'

There is a shocked silence. Some of the kids giggle nervously. Prasanto, perhaps horrified at his own temerity, puts his fingers into his mouth and starts to suck on them.

Tinka strides forward, her mouth set in a grim line.

'She's pregnant, yes, but she's *not* dirty,' she says sternly.

'Pregnant without marriage means dirty!' yells back the boy, puffing out the frail cage of his ribs.

'*No!*' Tinka, thoroughly rattled, reaches for the explanation the Missionaries of Charity always give in this situation. 'All babies come from God!'

'Oho, so God is a West Pakistani rapist?'

Shocked gasps greet this blasphemous statement.

Tinka, appalled at the crudity more than the blasphemy, slaps Prasanto across his sneering face.

'Chupp!' she thunders, aghast at the ugliness of the scene but also aware that she has to make an example of this child or risk losing her authority for good. 'Say sorry to her.'

The little boy shakes his head, holding his stinging cheek. 'I won't!'

Tinka's face darkens.

'Say sorry *now*,' she growls, 'and I'll let you be in the show. Or *don't* say sorry and I'll throw you out.'

'You can't throw me out!' he exclaims, startled. 'I'm the main!'

'Yes, and you're a good main, *very* handsome and an excellent actor,' Tinka says in a kinder voice, sensing that behind his bluster, he is actually quite close to tears. 'But if you're ugly inside, I can't use you. Your choice, kiddo.'

They stare at each other, locked in an impasse – the scrawny orphan in loose pyjamas and the privileged young woman in a bright orange kurta – and then Prasanto's eyes drop.

'Sorry,' he mutters sullenly to Mamuni.

'Fuck off,' is her cordial response.

'Mamuni!' Tinka swivels to glare at her. 'That was rude! Say sorry.'

Mamuni stares at Prasanto out of her good eye for a few seconds and then blinks.

'Sorry.'

'Good children!' Tinka says, relieved. 'Now let's start from where we left off, shall we? Music!'

Tinka restarts the music and they're off again, like nothing untoward has happened at all. Things go much better this time, everybody remembers their cues and performs with full energy. In fact, things go so well that they start to attract a crowd of spectators who clap their hands to the beat and cheer lustily. Tinka's heart almost bursts with pride.

But halfway through the third verse, just as they're approaching what the entire troupe agrees is the best bit of choreography, the LP jerks convulsively, Kishore Kumar's voice starts to drag ominously.

'*Kyaaa hai bharrrrr-o-saaa...*'

And the little green light in the gramophone blips off.

Prasanto and Mamuni stand frozen in the sudden silence, hands stretched towards each other to start the sizzling salsa Kainaz has taught them.

Damn, Tinka thinks, disproportionately disappointed. They were in such a flow! Everything was going so well! God alone knows when the electricity would come back now.

She gets to her feet and starts to call the children off the 'stage', when a pleasant baritone sounds from the gathered crowd.

'*Kya hai bharosa,*
Aashiq dil ka,
Aur kisi pe, yeh aa jaye...'

The singer has picked up the verse exactly where Kishore Kumar left off. His voice is tuneful, vibrant and very cheerful. Everybody starts to clap.

Mamuni grins at Prasanto, who swings her into the salsa, careful of her bulging belly.

The singer's pleasant voice rises to hit the high notes of the last line:

'*Aa gaya toh, bahut pachhtaye...*'

And the crowd joins in with gusto to sing the only word of the song they know, which of course is

'Geetu!'

As the troupe swings into the final chorus, the lyrics of which all the children know, Tinka turns around and scans the crowd for the man who'd started the singing.

And spots him.

Standing in the back, leaning against a broken-down water pump, wearing a rather dashing black leather jacket over a tight blue T-shirt and jeans faded in just the right places.

It is Fabulous Shaanu Bhaisaab. Clearly, he can hit the high notes as easily as he can hit a guava from forty feet. He is looking right at her, his Kota-grey eyes steady and questioning and curiously alight.

As Tinka waves to him, tentatively, apologetically, he smiles at her briefly, and then very deliberately turns around and walks away.

• • •

'You should have struck when the iron was hot, yaar!' Raka is really upset. 'Spoken to her then and there!'

They're gathered around the dining table of his tiny quarters. Maddy, back from his helicopter flying course, has just been given a full report of Shaanu's inexplicable behaviour at the refugee camp by the disgusted Juhi. She has now gone off to cook dinner, her attitude that of one who no longer wishes to place good money on a lame horse.

'It's his old we're-the-coolest-cats-in-the-place logic,' Maddy drawls as he sips his drink. 'Why should *he* go chasing the girl? She should come chasing *him*.'

'Oye hoy!' exclaims Raka. 'Is that it, Chakkahera? You're too hep to chase the general's daughter, now?'

'No ya, buggers,' Shaanu says good-naturedly. 'Nothing like that! I just thought...' His voice trails away as his expression softens. '... that she looked like she needed space.'

'Space? The final frontier?'

'To think,' Shaanu explains. 'To be alone, and spread out a little, do her charity shows and all. So I let her be.'

'Balls.' Raka snorts rudely. 'Teri phat gayee. You chickened out basically! Made so much fun of me for not telling Juhi I liked her, and now you're doing the same thing yourself!'

Shaanu, reddening slightly, retorts with spirit. 'At least I'm not a rakhi brother!'

Maddy snickers. Raka glowers.

Shaanu grins. 'Also, I let her have a good look at me, in case she'd forgotten how hot I am. *Then* I left.'

'Hey Bhagwan, he thinks he's Miss India!' Juhi marvels from the kitchen. 'So cunseeted ki I can't imagine! Uff!'

'Did you give her the full 360-degree view?' Maddy wants to know. 'You know, the slow twirl?'

'Of course.' Shaanu grins. 'I'm a professional.'

'Chutiya strategy.' Raka looks glum. 'All this dur-dur-se space-giving. It'll never work.'

Chutiya strategy or otherwise, it's the one Shaanu has decided upon. And he sticks to it consistently over the next two weeks.

'Have you noticed,' Kainaz says to her niece over tea at the Sarhind Club lawn one evening, 'that your young Jat seems to have huge sympathy for the refugees? He's there practically every day, God bless the boy.'

She then spoils the effect of this entirely straight-faced speech by giggling so hard that she snorts tea through her nose.

Tinka puts down her cup in disgust.

'You are *so* juvenile,' she tells her aunt.

'Why shouldn't I be?' Kainaz retorts. 'You're grown-up enough for the two of us.'

Tinka glares at her, very red-cheeked, and picks up her tea again.

'He was playing cricket with the kiddies yesterday,' Kainaz continues. 'The ball ended up on the dispensary roof so he hoisted up one of the boys to get it down. The child scrambled wildly and your Jat's T-shirt rode up, and I got a teensy-weensy peek at his yummy chest and tummy. He's *delish*, darling.'

And Tinka, who had seen Shaanu hit the six that sent the ball flying to the dispensary roof, has to admit, even as she sinks her teeth into a wonderfully moist shammi kebab, that he *is* delicious.

And that she is constantly hyper-aware of his presence in the camp. Playing a merry game of teen-patti with the biranganas here, sharing an argumentative cup of tea with the Muktis there, whistling as he goes about digging and lifting and cleaning everywhere.

And often she senses his watchful grey gaze upon her, quietly confident, biding its time, saying nothing but drawing her to him as surely as he has hooked her with high-strength, tensile, steel wire.

And still Tinka resists.

December comes to Calcutta. The mornings grow colder and mistier, the hot boiled eggs sold at street corners topped with salt, chopped onion, green chillies and lashings of raw mustard oil grow more irresistible, and the Sabre-rattling from across the border grows louder and nastier. Pakistan, red-faced over the ignominious downing of their Sabres over Boyra and the coverage this downing received in the

Indian press, is intent on revenge. At the United Nations General Assembly, West Pakistani politicians indignantly point out that India is the real aggressor, interfering in their internal matters and providing succour to separatists while it piously pretends to have nothing but sympathy for the East Pakistani refugees at heart. World opinion is divided on the matter. While the Soviet Union backs India, the US and China, worried about the increasing influence of the Soviet bloc, insist that the reports of loot, rape and genocide in East Pakistan have been wildly exaggerated, and continue to stand staunchly behind Pakistan.

On the morning of Friday, the third of December, Shaanu flies his usual CAP over Dum Dum, comes back to eat a mammoth breakfast at the Officers' Mess, opens the *India Post* randomly to page 5 and finds that all talk of war has been pushed off the page by a quarter-page photograph of Tinka in her emerald-green bikini.

'People are just people,' says bathing beauty.
'I will never shout Pakistan Murdabad!'

Were you charmed by the innocent beauty and energy of the girl in the Freesia ad? Did you, like millions of Indians, wonder who this child-woman is and what she does when she isn't frolicking winsomely beneath a waterfall, revelling in the tingling freshness of Freesia?

Well, we did. We were so captivated by the bathing beauty that we sent out our reporters to bring her story to you. The story they have come back with, however, is a saddening and shocking one!

First, our desi bathing beauty is not a desi at all, but an American born, American citizen.

Second, in these highly sensitive times, when India is on the brink of war with Pakistan, Tehmina Dadyseth has declared: 'People are just people. Before they are Indian or Pakistani or Hindu or Muslim. Any religion, any nation or any person who tries to make itself or himself bigger by putting down another nation, religion or person is to be condemned. I will say Hindustan Zindabad a million times and with full feeling, but even if you put a gun to my head, I will never say Islam Murdabad or Pakistan Murdabad.'

These statements were made during a debate at her alma mater Miranda House, three years ago. A senior student, pursuing an M.Phil from Delhi University said, 'I am not at all surprised that she ended up half-naked under a waterfall, titillating men to buy an American soap. She's an America-crazy Pakistani sympathizer, like so many of the stuck-up Miranda House girls, who are all crazy for good looks. They swoon over American rockstars and Muslim film heroes and turn up their noses at patriotic Hindu boys.'

Perhaps it is no coincidence that the titsy-bitsy bikini Tehmina is wearing in the Freesia ad is a traitorous Pakistani green?

• • •

'They've painted a Pakistani flag on your titsy bikini,' Kainaz Dadyseth says in a dazed voice, pointing to the large Freesia ad photograph that accompanies the article. 'Look.'

'Oh God.' Tinka throws down the paper in disgust. 'What rubbish! I'm going to write a letter to the editor!'

'Excellent idea!' her aunt agrees. 'Camp cancelled for the day! Here, sit down and compose your thoughts. I'll get you pen and paper and a nice cup of tea.'

Tinka looks at her suspiciously. 'Why don't you want me to go to the camp?'

Kainaz sits down heavily.

'Oh bachche,' she says. 'Some crazy may throw acid on you.'

Tinka stares at her in astonishment. 'Don't be silly, Kung fui! It's just a stupid article, that too on an inside page. Nobody'll read it.'

But when they get to the camp, it seems like everybody has. The sentries glower at Tinka as she walks in, the women who are queuing up for medicine and their daily cupful of raw rice hiss at her as she passes, and when they get to the maidan, they find that none of the children has showed up for rehearsal.

'Stupid, ungrateful *brats*.' Kainaz sits down on a fallen lamp post with a thump. 'How much you've done for all of them...'

'It's Friday,' Tinka says. 'Maybe they're all at the mosque or something.'

'They're mostly Hindus,' Kainaz retorts. 'Still, let's wait.'

And so they wait. Alone in the muddy maidan with the cold creeping in through their sneakers and Kainaz fui complaining that her backside is in danger of freezing to solid ice.

But not a soul shows up. Well, until eleven o'clock anyway, when a deep voice drawls out from behind them lazily.

'So Pakistan Murdabad will never be your slogan, eh?'

They turn around to see a lanky, wild-haired figure studying them sardonically.

It's whatsizname, Tinka thinks dully. Macho da, the Mukti Bahini major. He is still wearing his dark glasses, even though his conjunctivitis must've cleared up days ago. I bet he wears them just for style.

'Yes,' she says calmly. 'Do you have a problem with that?'

He grins, showing a large amount of teeth. 'It seems a lot of people do.'

'C'm'ere,' Kainaz snaps. 'Help me up. I'm all stiff. Can't you round up the children for Tinka?'

He comes forward gallantly, his black curls bouncing, a faint whiff of whiskey fumes on his breath.

'I wish I could,' he says, as he draws Kainaz to her feet. 'But this theatre class is voluntary, I can't force them to come.'

'So they hate me now,' Tinka says.

'They hate West Pakistanis,' Macho da tells her. 'And you don't.' After a moment he says, 'Tell me, couldn't you stretch your principles a *little*, to at least say Nikka Murdabad?'

General Nikka Khan, also known as the Butcher of Bengal, is the commander of the Pakistani Armed Forces in Bangladesh and is bitterly hated by every fleeing refugee. Though nominally subordinate to the Governor of East Pakistan, he virtually rules the area. Every kind of atrocity has been committed under his regime.

'I don't think so,' Tinka says slowly, really considering the question. 'Violence breeds violence. I don't believe in *anybody* murdabad.' Her chin comes up. 'Nor does Mother Teresa, for that matter, and I don't see any of you boycotting *her*.'

'Ah, but she isn't young and beautiful and dancing under waterfalls.'

Tinka's eyebrows rise at the randomness of this statement.

'What does that have to do with anything?' she asks.

Macho da looks irritatingly enigmatic.

'Nothing and everything,' he says. He turns to Kainaz, his tone meaningful. 'It would be advisable to take your niece away from here now, ma'am.'

And much to Tinka's disgust, this is exactly what Kainaz Dadyseth does. Moving swiftly for a middle-aged lady with an allegedly frost-bitten backside, she has them out of the camp and on a cycle rickshaw in the next fifteen minutes.

'Hurry hurry hurry,' she harangues the rickshaw-wallah, poking him in the ribs with her bony fingers as he starts to toil up the hill to the city. 'Uff, we should have got a more muscular fellow! Dum lagao, bhaiyya!'

'Kung fui, you're being rude.'

'You're being a *fool*. Can't you see those people behind us?'

Turning around, Tinka sees that there is indeed a scrum of people following them. They're about fifty feet away. They look shabby and crabby, and they're muttering loudly. Unease grips her heart.

'It's just the Friday sabzi mandi,' she says unconvincingly. 'They gather here to sell fruits and vegetables every week. Can't you hear? They're chanting *mandi mandi mandi*.'

'God, give this girl some sense,' mutters her beleaguered aunt. 'It's a mob, idiot child. They're chanting *randi randi randi*.'

And indeed they are. The word spews out of them, chanted repeatedly to a staccato beat, full of hate.

Tinka gives a shaky laugh.

'Wow. Why do they dislike me so much?'

'They're just lecherous beasts, darling.' Kainaz rootles around in her handbag for anything that could be used as a weapon, produces a dainty mother-of-pearl nailcutter and chucks it back into the bag in disgust. 'Your being *unpatriotic* has just given them an excuse to act upon their lecherousness. Oho, why are you stopping? Haw, coward, blackguard, *dog!*'

Because the rickshaw-wallah, who has just figured out that the mob is after the women in his rickshaw, has pulled to a stop, grabbed the small tiffin carrier hanging from the handlebar of his rickshaw and taken to his heels.

'Shit.' Kainaz looks sick with fear. 'Tinka, darling … *run.*'

'You too,' Tinka says fiercely as she scrambles down from the cycle rickshaw. Holding her aunt's hand firmly, she looks up and down the deserted road. The darkness is coming down fast and the crowd, looking larger than it was before, is less than forty feet behind them. There's a line of upended thelas up ahead and, behind it, a small clump of trees.

'Quick, behind those trees.'

They race down the lonely road to a scanty thicket and duck behind the foliage.

The mob, about thirty people strong, is moving closer. The two women can now make out individual figures in the gloom. One of them, unmistakably, is eight-year-old Prasanto.

Kainaz sucks in an outraged breath.

'That little snake!' she rages. 'Must have been nursing a grievance for *days.*' She clutches at the grass in impotent anger, makes a dreadful discovery and wails aloud, 'Oh no, this is a shit spot! Tinka, people do chuchchu-potty here!'

'Shush, fui,' Tinka whispers fiercely. 'They'll hear you.'

She wraps her hand around a large, empty ketchup bottle she's found in the thicket.

Kainaz eyes her uneasily. 'I thought you were a pacifist? If they spot us, just run, okay? Promise me.'

Tinka's eyes are intent on the approaching crowd, but she grips her aunt's hand hard. 'Promise. I'm not an idiot. I'll run – as fast as the rickshaw-wallah did. Faster.'

'What a pig, that bloody rickshaw-wallah…' Kainaz says feelingly.

'Yeah, well, at least we didn't have to pay him.'

Kainaz laughs shakily, her face white to the lips.

'They're here,' she says grimly. 'They'll come straight here, of course, there's no other logical place we could be.'

Sure enough, the mob comes panting up, looks about wildly, then thunders up towards their thicket.

'Traitor!' the mob bawls. 'Paki-lover! Prostitute!'

'Run!' gasps Kainaz, stumbling to her feet. 'Run *towards* them, Tinka! But from behind the thelas so they can't see us! They'll be expecting us to run away from them – stay *behind the thelas*, Tinka!'

The mob spots them and sets up a howl of ecstasy. The two women whirl around and start to pelt down the road as fast they can.

'Split up!' pants Kainaz. 'We must split up…'

'I won't leave you!' Tinka pants. 'Fui … *wait*!'

The mob is practically at her heels now. She gives a little sob, willing her muscles to move faster, cursing the fact that she's not as fit as she should be. Spotting a sidelane, she veers into it, hoping the mob will keep going straight, and realizes abruptly that she's reached a dead end.

In front of her there is a rubbish dump against a bare brick wall, an unhitched tonga, a looming neem tree and nothing beyond. Cold to the bone, she internalizes that this dark lane is the perfect venue for what the inflamed mob has in mind for her.

The mob reaches the head of the lane. She can hear

hoarse shouts as they argue about whether to go ahead or turn into the lane.

I've got to lure them away from Kung fui.

She straightens her shoulders, her young face set in grim, timeless lines, and smashes her ketchup bottle hard against the wall.

The shattering of the glass galvanizes the mob. It turns away from her aunt, who has continued down the straight road, and stampedes towards her, reaching her in a hot fetid rush.

The figure at the lead of the herd grabs her by the throat and slams her against the wall. Her head hits the unplastered brick so hard she sees stars. The violence is sudden and absolute.

'Say Pakistan Murdabad!' growls a man she has seen peacefully selling vegetables at the camp gates every day.

'Balls, I will,' Tinka gasps out. She is flat on her back on the ground now. Her mouth feels bloody.

And then a child's tight, breathless voice comes to her ears.

'No, you can't! Don't, don't hit her!'

'Prasanto!'

Tinka's eyes fly open only to see the little figure being flung roughly into the crowd.

She rears up.

'You sick *bastar*—'

'*Say* it!'

She grits her teeth and glares at him, eyes blazing with helpless anger, and shakes her head.

'No.'

Curses. Snarling. And then more pain as something that feels like a chowkidaar's iron-tipped lathi is slammed hard against her side.

'*Will you say it or not?*' The man's voice is a scream of thin, violent ecstasy.

And in that moment of pain and fear, Tinka suddenly comes to the clear, calm realization that it is she who holds the power in this situation, the power to say yes, or to say no.

'Not!' she snarls out, smiling savagely, eyes closed, muscles clenched, ready for the worst, hoping it won't hurt too horribly.

She senses him drawing his arm back and braces for a fist to slam into her face.

Nothing happens for a moment.

Then another.

And then a weird gurgling sound comes to her ears, the sort of sound a sink makes when it's clogged with gunk.

Warily, Tinka opens her eyes...

And discovers that her assailant is now bent backwards like a bow. His eyes are huge and bulging, and his free hand is clawing the air, trying desperately to break free of the chokehold on his throat.

As she watches, his grip on her weakens, his eyes roll back and he crumples to the ground. Tinka pushes his limp arm off her, grabs the strong hand stretched down to her and scrambles to her feet.

'Can you walk?'

The voice is urgent and vibrant and very familiar.

A wild gladness sweeps over Tinka. She almost stumbles, then laughs and slides down to sit on the muddy ground in a relieved heap.

'It's you.'

'You said you could walk.' Concerned grey eyes scan her face. 'Can you?'

'My aunt?' Tinka looks up, her face fearful.

'She's with Maddy,' he replies gently. 'Look, up there – are you all right?'

Dimly, she becomes aware of the thrumming of motorcycle engines and realizes that shrouded headlights are glowing dimly in a semicircle all around her. Robust north Indian cuss words float into her ears, and she laughs again, her breath catching painfully in her throat. A chorus of deep, gleeful male voice rings out joyously in the darkness, making nonsense of the baying of the mob.

'*Doggggfighttt!*'

Unsteadily, she gets to her feet, surrounded by the sweet sound of thuds, crashes and whimpers for mercy as the contingent of young officers work through the mob, reducing it to chastened, cringing single figures that scurry away into the gloom.

And then a sinewy arm hooks around her waist, plucks her off her feet and swings her onto the front of a running Enfield motorcycle.

'I can walk,' she protests breathlessly.

'To the MH?' His voice is wonderfully growly in her ear, his stubbled cheek rough against her skin, his breath warm in the December cold. 'We're going there now, to the Emergency.'

'But I'm fine,' she insists. 'Well, except that everything hurts, and I think I bit my tongu—'

'It's not your physical condition I'm worried about,' he replies tersely, his voice reverting to its native cadence in his anger. 'It's your *mental*. I saw what happened back there. You baaawdi booch, Tell-me-na, why couldn't you just say what the madman asked you to!'

But Tinka is beyond answering. Shaking with shock, she slides her arms into the warmth of his open leather jacket, buries her face against his wonderfully taut chest and bursts into tears.

• • •

'That board says no visitors after eight p.m.'

She is sitting cross-legged in a large hospital bed, dressed in the blue-and-white striped pyjamas that are standard Military Hospital issue. There's a rough, checked blanket swathed about her, making her look rather Jat-ish, he thinks, suppressing a grin.

'I pulled some strings,' he replies.

Tinka sniffs. Her face is very pale, a big purplish-blue bruise stands starkly on one side of her forehead, which her shaken aunt has informed her makes her look like a devout but demented mullah, with his prayer bump a little askew.

'Flirted with the nurses, you mean,' she says faintly.

'That's sexist,' he retorts with a grin.

'You're right,' she says, conscience-stricken.

'I can leave if you like,' he offers, stretching out lazily in the uncomfortable metal chair. 'And you could take a sleeping pill, like the kind they gave your fui. It'll put you out for the night.'

Tinka pulls a face and looks out of the window.

'Hmmm.'

Shaanu draws up his chair closer.

'What's a hmmm?'

'It's a non-committal sound meaning no comments.'

'I know that much English.' He tweaks the tip of her nose gently. 'And if you'd hmmed more and ranted less during college debates, you wouldn't have got into this mess today.'

'I didn't *rant*!' Tinka rears upright indignantly. 'That was a piece of yellow journalism! You can't possibly blame me for it!'

In reply, he stands up, tucks her blanket more securely under her chin and looks deep into her eyes.

Tinka swallows nervously. 'Wha-what're you doing?'

'Relax,' he says. 'You're safe.'

She wriggles awkwardly below the rough blanket.

'Oh, I know *that*.'

'Good. Now tell me about this wild, wild life you lived in Dilli University.'

She rolls her eyes and hunkers lower.

'Please, DU is full of idiots. The guy they quoted in that article is the president of the students' union. He hates me because I hit him on the head with a temple bell.'

'A what?' Shaanu repeats, confused.

'A temple bell from Muradabad. Cast iron, with copper plating.'

'Well then, you can't really blame him for hating you.'

As he says this, he sits down on the bed beside her. This is done so casually that Tinka feels it would be absurdly prim to object. Besides, he is radiating warmth, and it is a cold night.

She continues talking, as naturally as possible.

'I had provocation. Besides, it's wrong for the paper to make it sound like I said those things *now*, when we're in war mode, when I actually said them three whole years ago.'

'Ah, but you weren't famous three years ago.'

'True.' She sighs. Then her head comes up.

'Was there anything wrong with what I said?'

He is silent for a long time. So long that she turns towards him to read his expression.

'No,' he says slowly. 'But then, you're a civilian, you can afford to take that point of view.'

'People are just people!'

'No. For us in the fauj, things are more black and white.

Abusing the dushman is a cherished ritual for us. It creates a bond and a common enemy and gets the men all fired up.'

Tinka frowns.

'Shouldn't love for one's nation suffice?'

Shaanu shakes his head, very sure of himself.

'It can't. See, we've studied this and heard countless stories from the trenches, of how when the chips are down and your comrades lie dead around you, only the thought of avenging them helps you find an extra reservoir of strength, a sort of sixth gear – and that's essential in giving you the winning edge.'

'You become an animal, you mean.' Her voice is tight.

He looks at her, his eyes amused.

'And you didn't become an animal when you hit this guy on the head with a temple bell?'

'That isn't the same thing at all!'

'Hypocrite.'

But he says it very lovingly.

So lovingly that she flushes and looks away.

'You're too smooth,' she mutters darkly.

'Matlab?' One dark eyebrow flies up.

'Chatting me up. Getting into my bed.'

'Saving your life. Helping you run away.' He grins. 'Your debts are piling up, Dadyseth. How d'you plan to repay me?'

She frowns, then smiles.

'You can have some of my blanket.'

She lifts a corner of it and holds it out to him.

But he doesn't take it, just stares down into her face, his expression oddly moved.

Tinak looks up at him, confused.

'You want or you don't want?'

But Ishaan can't reply. The simple gesture, so redolent of

trust, has silenced him utterly. He stares down at her, feels the sweet heat rising from the slender body in the striped, too-big pyjamas beneath the blanket and swallows.

'Yeah sure, I want,' he says casually.

He pulls the blanket over his chest and tucks it firmly over both of them.

Tinka sighs contentedly.

'So you *have* to hate the enemy to get the job done?'

He shrugs.

'Look, when you're going down in flames, the only thing that gives you satisfaction is the knowledge that you're taking the dushman down with you.'

'And who decides who the dushman is?'

He throws up his hands. 'Air Headquarters. The government. The President of India.'

Tinka's lips curl scornfully.

'At least I picked out my enemy myself! When *you* joined the Air Force, you basically surrendered your brain in exchange for the thrill of flying and a cute uniform.'

He turns to face her too, his white teeth flashing.

'I'm glad you think I look cute in my uniform.'

Tinka chokes.

'Why do you refuse to take anything seriously?' she demands.

'Because I like to be *happy*, yaar,' Ishaan replies rousingly, clapping her on the back in a buddy-buddy manner she can't possibly object to. 'Don't you?'

This very simple question, for some reason, silences her utterly.

She stares at him with mute, hurting eyes, before tears start coursing down her cheeks.

Shaanu's been expecting this, somehow. He pulls her

onto his lap and hugs her close, her back against his chest, rocking her and stroking her goosebumpy arms with the flats of his palms, like he does for his little sisters when they have nightmares.

'Shhhh,' he whispers into her ear. 'Snooty Miranda House girls who dig American singers and Muslim movie stars and have no place in their heart for patriotic Hindu boys don't break down like this.'

Which makes her laugh.

It is a ragged pathetic excuse for a laugh, but a laugh nonetheless. Presently, her tears subside, and she blows her nose vigorously on the blanket.

'I'm not howling like a madwoman just because of the mob, you know,' she mutters. 'I have a pretty solid reason for crying.'

'I'm sure you do,' he replies. 'You don't have to tell what it is if you don't want to.'

'I don't want to.'

'Okay.'

She sniffs and pulls her knees up to her chest and rests her chin on them. The loose pyjamas slide, revealing an angry bruise on her thigh.

Shaanu's face darkens.

'Bastard,' he mutters, running his hand over it gently.

'What about him?' She looks at him worriedly. 'How badly did you guys beat him up? Did you bring him to the hospital?'

He stares at her in disbelief.

'Are you really that nice?' he demands. 'Or do you just *pretend* to be?'

Tinka blinks, confused. 'He was maddened by mob mentality, Ishaan. He's just a vegetable seller.'

Ishaan.

That sexy thing that happens whenever she says his name happens again.

Ishaan.

Ishaan.

He is smiling at her foolishly when she adds, with a slight hint of apology, 'Achcha, how come you've been volunteering so much at the refugee camps? You're there almost every day.'

Shaanu stares at her for a second, then says, 'Because my heart bleeds for the poor refugees. Their situation is tragic, and I feel it's every human being's moral duty to help them.'

'Oh!'

It is a small, disappointed sound that makes his heart quicken with triumph.

'Why oh?' he asks.

She twists around to look at him.

'I thought that maybe...'

'Maybe?' Shaanu parries, trying not to be distracted by the fact that her full, soft mouth is right within kissing reach now. Old Kuch Bhi Carvalho rises up inside his head, all skinny and manic-eyed, urging him to swoop down on it, ekdum Baaz-ke-maaphik.

Tinka colours, bites her lip and makes to move away.

'Nothing!'

He laughs and pulls her back against his chest, hugging her, his hands warm and snug over her belly.

'I come there to look at you, Dadyseth,' he whispers into her ear. 'Every free moment I can get. My friends think I'm nuts. So does my family. I come even though you told me you didn't want to meet me any more. Why did you say such a stupid thing?'

For the life of her, Tinka can't think of a logical answer to this question. Wordlessly, she snuggles into him, sliding her hands down to cover his and tilting back her head to inhale the clean soapy smell emanating from the warm place where his neck joins his ear.

'I forgot why.'

'Good.'

They sit like this for a while, her head on his chest, his arms holding her close.

Then, very slowly, he bends his dark head and drops a kiss on her shoulder.

It is a soft, gentle question mark of a kiss. It is clearly going someplace, though, because when she turns to look at him, he is looking at her already, and the light in his eyes is like a slow burning fuse leading inexorably to a powder keg.

She smiles, an implet with dimplets, closes her eyes and tilts up her face obediently.

Shaanu, staring down at her upturned face, feels the exultation he'd felt the very first time he executed a full vertical flip in a cloudless blue sky.

Tinka opens one eye. 'You want or you don't want?'

He laughs, his arms tighten about her, and his lips land on hers.

Neither of them is prepared for the kiss that follows. They'd been bracing for an explosion, but what follows is annihilation by tenderness – a laying down of arms, a totally unexpected, unconditional and mutual surrender.

Stunned by the miracle of it, Tinka falls back against the hard hospital pillow, taking Shaanu down with her.

He continues to kiss her, his hands cupping her face – his arms are shaking slightly, her hands are in his hair, her lips are welded to his, there is that scent of wildflowers again, there is all the time in world, and, underlying that, there is a throbbing urgency setting the pace.

And then a weird, ominous thrumming fills the air.

Tinka's eyes fly open.

'What's that? Can you hear it?'

'Huh?' Ishaan blinks, his gaze unfocussed, adorably confused. 'What?'

'*That*. That sound.'

He sits up straighter, then clambers off the bed and strides to the window to look up at the sky.

'It sounds like…' He frowns. '*Shit!*' His voice grows savage. 'Not *now*, damnit, when we're sitting ducks!'

The throbbing grows louder. Through the window, they can see the shadows in the valley grow sharper and start to move towards them with shocking speed. Tinka puts a hand to her head, feeling disoriented, as though the earth is running beneath her feet.

'Take cover!' Shaanu's voice is like a whipcrack. He grabs her by the arm and pulls her down with him below the windowsill.

'It's an air strike, isn't it,' she says hopelessly. 'It's the Pakistanis.'

'Yeah,' he replies without looking at her, his eyes scanning the skies. 'They picked a Friday knowing we'd be off-guard, thinking they'll never strike on their holy day. And this is the hour at which the shift changes at our signals unit.' His voice is reluctantly admiring. 'Smart bastards.'

She glares at him, suddenly angry.

'You sound so happy,' she says accusingly.

'Huh?' Shaanu denies this, his eyes still on the starry sky. 'No no, not *happy*.'

'Excited, then,' she says hotly. 'You want to go up there in your stupid little plane and *kill* people.'

He is about to answer when there is a sickening scream of jet engines, and several dark glowing shapes whizz by above them, flying low and fast.

Shaanu pulls Tinka closer.

'Sabres,' he breathes. 'Six of them. They're doing us proud.'

'Stop talking like that!'

'What?' He is genuinely bewildered. 'This is what I've been training for, for five whole years! Would you prefer if I pulled a long face or shook with fear?'

'That would at least prove you're not an unfeeling robot!'

The grey eyes gleam in the dark.

'Oh, I have feelings,' he says meaningfully.

Tinka hastily looks up at the sky again.

'Where are they heading to?'

Shaanu looks up too. 'The airfield. The ordnance stockpiles. Our planes. *Damnit!*'

Because the shells have started to explode, bright and hot and loud even at this distance. The ground shudders beneath their feet with each impact. Orange flames, lined with thick black acrid smoke, lick the sky.

'Well, we're officially at war now.' Shaanu pulls Tinka to her feet, his young face grim. 'Jumma Mubarak.'

NINE

There can be no doubt, Prime Minister Indira Gandhi declares in her midnight address to a groggy, reeling nation, that by carrying out air strikes against India's Forward Air Stations on the night of Friday, the third of December, 1971, Pakistan has declared war on India.

'Lekin, mere pyaare bhaiyon aur behno,' her nasal, imperious voice rings with conviction, 'our brave Armed Forces are more than equal to the task! These people think that by attacking us in the west, they can weaken our resistance to the atrocities they are committing in the east. But that will not happen. In both theatres of the war, the western and the eastern, we will teach them a lesson they will never forget! Jai Hind!'

As dawn breaks over Kalaiganga Air Force Base, airmen and the Garrison Engineers repair the damaged runway as fast as possible. Debris is cleared, concrete slabs moved into place, road rollers deployed. The smell of hot tar fills the air. Inside the briefing room, all the fighters have reported for duty. The room is packed with young men – taut, alert, clear-eyed, as straight and sharp as bayonets. The sense of excitement is palpable.

'Gentlemen, the enemy launched strikes against *eleven* air force bases last night.' There is nothing dreamy or comical about Wing Commander Dheengra this morning. 'Except Kalaiganga, all the other bases they picked are stationed in the west – Pathankot, Amritsar, Ambala and Agra are the ones worst affected.'

A hubbub of conversation breaks out at this information. None of the pilots had anticipated that the strikes would be so widespread.

'We've learnt that the strike was code-named Operation Chengez Khan and that its purpose was to paralyse the IAF ahead of land strikes by the Pakistani Army on Indian territory, thus leaving the Indian Army unprotected from the sky.' His voice rises. 'Will they succeed?'

'No, sir!' the fighters roar back.

'They're also hoping that, by striking in the west, they will be able to dilute the headway we've been making here in the east.' His voice rises even louder. 'Will that happen?'

'*No, sir!*'

He pauses, scanning their young faces. They look calm and focussed, he notes. No fear, no panic, no stupid animal excitement. He nods in approval.

'It is imperative that we retaliate swiftly, strongly and sharply. Our engineers have been working all night, the runway will be usable in an hour from now, when four MiGs will take off to bomb Dacca's primary air base, Tezgaon, with our S-5 missiles.'

A ripple runs through the room. The Gnatties seem to slump a little, while the MiG squad sits up even straighter, their chests swelling perceptibly as they sneak snide looks at the 'heroes of Boyra'. A smile of distinct smugness spreads across Dilsher Singh's pimply face.

How young they are, Pomfret thinks. Well, they'll be years older before this day is done.

'Your Operations Officer, Wing Commander Carvalho will brief you on your targets,' he says and steps back.

Sitting in the front row, his heart bursting with pride that it is to be the MiGs that strike the first blow for AFS Kalaiganga, Raka nevertheless feels a twinge of misgiving. Bomb Tezgaon airfield with the undependable S-5s? Those things float like seed puffs in the springtime.

Old Kuch Bhi bounds forward to take over, his eyes glittering hungrily.

'Gentlemen, you've been practising the steep-dive glide for weeks. You know what to do. Crater the hell out of the airfield and put those goddamn Sabres out of the bloody equation. Clear?'

'Yes, sir!'

He starts to pace the room, wheeling about as he reaches the wall.

'You'll have to watch out for two things – Sabres from above and ack-ack guns from below. Tezgaon will be expecting us, and they'll have both ready. The ack-ack you'll have to take on the chin, but we'll give you some Gnats to provide you top cover.'

'Wooo-hoooo,' the Gnatties whoop as one.

Carvalho's keen gaze assesses them one by one. Then he gives a curt nod in Gana's direction.

'Gonsalves,' he says.

Shaanu's face falls.

Dilsher Singh can't resist a tiny snicker.

'And...' the Wing Commander continues.

The tension builds.

Carvalho allows himself a small tight grin.

'Chakkahera.'

Shaanu's fist shoots up into the air triumphantly.

'Yes, sir!'

'Calm down, Fighter,' Carvalho growls. 'Your role will be just to stay, scan and report.'

Balls, thinks Shaanu privately.

'Yes, sir!'

'The rest of you will stay here on standby, fully fuelled and armed, to be deployed for further strikes, or to provide Close Air Support to the troops as and when the Army asks for it. All clear so far?'

'Yes, sir!'

'Like I said, gentlemen, expect a warm welcome. They know Tezgaon is our number one target and they'll be waiting. Dive in steeply, ekdum...'

'Baaz-ke-maaphik,' Raka says with him, sotto voce.

'Drop your bombs and don't hang about. Go over it once, if you can't hit it, the next bunch of pilots will. Clear?'

'Sir!'

'In case you're shot down, head for the closest red-light area, nobody asks any questions there – just keep your pants on and, if you're a Hindu, your foreskin hidden!'

Muted, nervous laughter greets this injunction. Even Pomfret, standing at the back of the room, allows himself a nostalgic smile.

'Mix with the low-life there, and find a way to contact our embassy. Understood?'

'Yes, sir!' everybody shouts back.

Carvalho wheels around, his manic, glittering eyes jabbing into each one of them, and continues, 'Do the *maximum* damage you can to their 'craft, their armoured vehicles, their radar and their runways. Civilian targets are of course totally out of bounds. Is that clear?'

'Yes, sir!'

Carvalho's hungry gaze probes the posse of fighters.

'Any other questions?'

There are many what-ifs on their mind – mortality, injury, malfunctioning parachutes. Nobody asks them.

'As the Sabres came calling at dinner time last night, I doubt any of you got fed,' Pomfret puts in mildly. 'So eat a decent breakfast before you leave, please.'

'Sir!'

'The call sign for the MiG formation is Black,' Old Kuch Bhi decrees. 'Javed, you're Black one. Raka's your wingman, Chatrath is Black three and Dilsher is Black four. Baaz, your formation's call-sign is Thunder. You're Thunder one and Gonsalves is Thunder two. Jai Hind!'

• • •

'Black one to ATC. Requesting permission for formation Black to take off, please.'

'Permission granted, Black one,' says the ATC.

'Thunder one requesting permission for formation Thunder.'

'Permission granted, Thunder one. Happy hunting, lads. Jai Hind!'

And with a roar of jet engines, the formation is up in the sky, a spray of stubby silver bullets against the blush-pink dawn.

'Not a bad way to spend a Saturday morning, eh guys?' J-man's chirpy voice sounds on the R/T. 'Feast your eyes on that sunrise and think beautiful thoughts!'

Which, of course, makes Raks think of Juhi. She had been very calm when he left, tucking Pakistani currency into his wallet, tying a black thread tightly around his wrist and lining his eyes with kajal to make him look like a pukka pathan.

'You're tall enough to be one,' she'd said, her voice trembling just a little, her eyes suspiciously bright. '*Such a good-looking man!* Here, eat this prasad. It's from the Kali-bari, it'll keep you safe. And this gond-ka-laddoo from mummyji's Satyanarayan ki pooja. And drink this Gangajal. Okay, bye now. What do you want for lunch?'

'Egg curry,' he'd replied huskily, hugging her tight. And before she could scold him for these less-than-vegetarian cravings, he had strode out of the little quarters, got onto his bike and left.

'Speak for yourself,' he says wistfully to his squadron. 'I had plans for my Saturday. And none of them involved hanging out with you hairy buggers.'

'I had plans too,' chirrups Dilsher.

'You had booked a facial, hadn't you, Black four?' Chatty snickers. 'To cure the acne?'

'I was going to see *Goldfinger* again,' Dil says indignantly. 'I had balcony seats.'

'Aren't you tired of it yet?' Raka asks.

'No,' retorts Dilsher, and adds slyly, 'I'm not tired of the Freesia ad, either.'

Then he starts to hum.

'*You ... are ... my ... theme, for a wet dream, a very lovely wet dream...*'

Nobody says anything, so after a while, he remarks with deliberate outrageousness, 'What hot tits she has.'

Raka sits up, a furious response ready on his lips, but he needn't have bothered. Pat comes Shaanu's cool response.

'Talking filth to cover up for the fact that you're shitting yellow on your first real-life mission, Black four? You ain't fooling anybody.'

'I'm not scared!' Dilsher retorts a little too quickly.

'No?' Shaanu says interestedly. 'Then you should be. 'Coz if the Pakis don't break your balls, *I* will.'

'And I,' Gana growls ungrammatically.

'And I,' adds Raka.

'Maintain R/T silence please.' Chatty's voice is sharp. 'Approaching Tezgaon.'

They cross the twisting silver ribbons that are the Meghna and Padma rivers, expertly led by J-man, who has flown in this area before. Soon, Dacca is sprawled out below them, bathed in morning sunshine like a lush-green buffet spread.

'Let's keep it short and sweet, guys,' J-man says breezily as he starts the descent.

'Just like the action on Black two's wedding night,' Dilsher snickers again. Everybody ignores him.

The MiGs sink, a posse of squat steel birds, claws outthrust, eyes searching keenly for their prey. The two Gnats continue to circle above.

'There it is!' says Chatty. 'No wait, that's a road. What a wide road – double lanes and no traffic. So much better than ours!'

'Don't miss the imported cars. Daimler! And also Subaru, I think. Is that a *Benz*?'

'*There's* the airfield. They tried to hide it, but we see it.'

'We *see* it!' everybody choruses musically. 'We see it *good*!'

'Good morrrrning Pakistaaaaan!'

While the others circle at a height, J-man swoops lower, approaching the airfield as if to land on it. This is what makes steep-dive gliding so hazardous. Unlike the usual technique, in which jets fly criss-cross over the targeted highway, dropping their bombs only when they are directly above it, steep-dive gliding involves flying over the entire length of the runway. The chances of your bombs hitting the target are thus maximized, as it is always below you, but so are also the chances of being hit. There's only one path you can take, and that makes it easy for the guns on the ground to predict your position and pick you out. Now J-man, his belly completely exposed to the anti-aircraft guns on the ground, gauges how the wind is moving, mutters a silent prayer and drops the S-5s.

Suddenly, puffs of black-and-white smoke bloom all around him. The anti-aircraft gunners have kicked in!

Grimly, he hunkers down and continues to barrel down the length of the runway. He still has the element of surprise, they haven't quite got him in their sights yet. Things will be tougher for Raka and the others, so he must make the most of this vital first chance.

The S-5s drop, J-man can't really see where, and then he rises, made buoyant by the loss of weight.

Raka swoops down into the sea of swirling ack-ack fire to take his place...

Circling at a higher altitude, Gana and Shaanu are clueless of what is taking place below. Things are eerily quiet up here, and they're idling in a clear sky the colour of milk when Shaanu feels the hair at the back of his head prickle and, slewing sideways, spots a Sabre lurking at eight o'clock.

The pilot seems intent on the MiGs below. He hasn't spotted him or Gana. Shaanu can't even tell if Gana's spotted him. And he can't warn Gana on the R/T because the Sabre may very well be on the same frequency.

Silently, Ishaan rises higher, scanning the skies for more Sabres. They usually tend to hunt in pairs.

Nothing.

Below, the anti-aircraft fire has turned brutal. It is

thudding into wings and fuselage, making the MiGs judder and mush madly as they dive. Not a single S-5 seems to have done any damage to the gleaming runway below.

'I'm clean out!' Chatty yells. 'Nothing more to hit them with!'

'Let's go!'

'Is anybody hit?' J-man shouts.

Miraculously, nobody is.

'I've got a load to drop still.' Dil's voice crackles. 'Hang on, guys.'

He dives audaciously low, flying right over the field into the punishing ack-ack fire, and releases the S-5s about halfway down the length of the runway. The MiG squad watch, hearts in their mouths, as an improbable magic unfolds before their eyes. The erratic S-5s fall sweetly, as straight and predictably as they would have in a perfect vacuum, smack smartly into the runway and explode on impact.

A black-lipped crater blooms right in the middle of the runway.

Dil lets out a triumphant yell.

'Yesssss!'

'Fuckin' beginner's luck!'

'Strike *One* for the MiGGies!'

'I *love* you, you pimply bastard!'

'Let's go, let's go, let's go!'

Triumphantly, the MiGs rise up and away, breaking through the clouds to level around the circling Gnats.

'Did you see that, Thunder one?' Dilsher demands excitedly. 'We *punctured* the thing, we *destroyed* it, we—'

'*Watch out, Dil!*'

Shaanu's voice is like a whipcrack on the R/T. Even as

he speaks, he fires a one-second burst at the Sabre locked onto Dil.

Bracing for the now familiar recoil, he watches the tracers hiss through the sky…

It nails the Sabre unerringly, but not before the Sabre releases its air-to-air Sidewinder straight at Dil's cockpit.

The sky curdles into a smoking ball of bucketing red heat.

Debris flies everywhere.

The battle moves forward, the planes zooming ahead, buffeted madly by the explosion, stone-blind in the black smoke, orange flames and swiftly hurtling clouds.

As the smoke clears, the IAF Fighters swivel around in their harnesses to see the Sabre falling out of the sky, sunlight bouncing off its crescent moon fin flash. The struck MiG is still flying, streaming fuel, emitting thick black smoke, and from inside it, on the somehow still perfectly functioning R/T, they hear the hair-raising sound of Dil screaming in agony.

• • •

There are front-page pictures of the downed MiG in all the Pakistan dailies the next morning, in sweet revenge of the jubilant coverage given by the Indian media to the Battle of Boyra. The headlines, big and bold, scream all about how Pakistan will never succumb to the vile aggressors from across the border.

Indian newspapers carry a black-edged photograph of Pilot Officer Dilsher Singh in his passing-out-parade finery, grinning the bashfully lustful grin all the ladies at Kalaiganga know so well.

At a memorial service conducted on a misty Sunday morning at Air Force Station Kalaiganga, a grim-faced knot of airmen and officers swear they will return the favour to Pakistan, and soon.

Most galling of all, when the engineers examine the photographs taken by the MiG cameras, they decree that Tezgaon is still operational. The crater punched by Dilsher Singh in his first

and last flight has still left 5000 metres of runway clean – sufficient
enough for its Sabres to continue flying out in a steady stream to
dominate the eastern theatre of what is now a very official war.

• • •

'Oder modhye keu ki tomar boyfriend chhilo?'

Not understanding any word in this sentence except
one, Tinka nevertheless gets the gist of Mamuni's shyly
asked question. Even if she hadn't understood one word,
the glow in the girl's good eye, the coy manner in which
she is hiding behind the bouquet of multicoloured roses and
mor-pankhi she's brought for Tinka and the giggles of her
little delegation would have been enough.

Is one of the officers who scattered the mob the other
day her boyfriend?

Is *Ishaan Faujdaar* her boyfriend?

Tinka ponders the question. She hasn't heard from Ishaan
since late Friday night, when he left her at the hospital after
the air strike. He had got her back into bed, reassured the
shaken nursing staff that all would be well, then turned to
scan her face with grave eyes.

'Sleep well.'

'Where are you going now?' Anxiety had made her voice
abrupt.

He'd shrugged, smiling, backing out of the door.

'Back to base. An enemy strike is a de facto order to
report for duty.'

'Will … will you come see me tomorrow?' Her voice had
been a whisper, but inside her head it felt like a scream.

'Tinka.' He had stopped, his face growing serious. 'Leave
for Bombay as soon as you can. Tomorrow morning, if
possible. Promise me.'

'I don't make promises to people I've just met!'

His handsome jaw had set.

'You owe me.'

She'd thrown up her hands.

'I'm not going *anywhere*,' she'd blazed. 'Besides, Bombay would be just as unsafe.'

And then she'd pulled the white hospital sheet taut over her head, for all the world like a corpse at a funeral pyre, and spent the entire night wide awake.

Now, three days later, she has no news of him, and Dilsher Singh is dead.

Tinka still can't process this information. Dil is dead, she repeats numbly to herself even as she urges piping-hot potato wedges and bottles of Coca-Cola on the visiting children. Like Jimmy. No more hungry lunging backward and forward on the dance floor for him, no more furtive glances at the bosom of his dance partner, no more matinee shows of James Bond movies. Packed into a wooden box, draped with a flag ... and maybe, at the Republic Day parade next month, his weeping father or stoic mother to be handed India's second- or third-highest medal for bravery.

Just thinking about it sucks the strength from her muscles.

And yet ... that tiny, guilty, sustaining relief that Ishaan has been spared.

How did he even blindside her so fast? Why does she care?

He stands for everything she most despises, she tells herself resolutely: swaggering, cocky machismo, a crude way of looking at the world as either friend or foe, an obsession with adrenalin.

But then her mind goes back to the way he'd stroked her arms with the palms of his hands, so gently, and made her laugh and hushed her tears away.

And then kissed her with such thoroughness that her toes haven't quite uncurled yet.

Stop it.

'So, will you continue with your dance practice in Meerut?' she asks the children brightly.

Everybody ignores this pathetic counter-question. Though they had been very subdued when they arrived at the Sarhind Club, huddled together in a worried, hesitant little knot, they have all recovered their spirits after meeting her and guzzling large amounts of fizzy Coca-Cola.

'Tell na, didi!' they demand impatiently. 'Tomar boyfriend!'

Tinka crosses her hands across her chest. 'There's nothing to tell!' she says sternly. 'Now, listen, just because you're all being shifted to a new camp far away from the air strikes doesn't mean you should stop singing and dancing and being happy, okay?'

'Okay,' they chorus.

'Good.'

An odd pause follows. Clearly, something remains unsaid. Finally Mamuni edges even closer, pins Tinka with her beady eye and says earnestly, 'You're not angry with Prasanto?'

Tinka has been aware of Prasanto all along, sullen-faced, hanging back from the rest of the group, holding a hand drawn *Get Well Soon* card so tight it is all crumpled and dented. Now she sinks to her knees and addresses him directly.

'No,' she says softly, 'I know it wasn't your fault – you didn't know how badly it would go, and you tried to stop it later.'

The other kids turn to look at Prasanto. There are dark

circles under his troubled eyes, Tinka has already noticed, and bruises on his arm, just below the edge of the half-sleeved sweater.

'So, basically, thanks,' she says. 'Thanks, yaar, Prasanto.'

The children murmur to each other, surprised and happy. But Tinka's eyes are on the boy. His face works, he gives a massive gulp and a sort of convulsive shudder. For a moment, it seems that he may break down. Then, with valiant effort, he manages to school his face back into its usual smug grin, shaking his head, scratching his nose and saying nothing.

'Well?' Mamuni demands of him belligerently. 'Say something!'

Prasanto grins, his impudent eyes rising to meet Tinka's.

'Kawta chokh,' he blurts out.

Which immediately sends the little contingent into gales of laughter.

Grey eyes.

Laughing, threatening, shaking her head, Tinka hushes them and ushers them out of the lawn. They troop down to the Club's main gate in a boisterous band, growing sober as the time comes to say farewell. Tinka feels a pang as she shakes each little brown hand and kisses every grubby face goodbye. Then she heads for the reception to ask for a vase for the roses and mor-pankhi, damp-eyed and sniffy, and feeling decidedly deflated.

Because with the refugee kids gone and Ishaan on full-time war duty, what is there for her to do in Calcutta, really?

This is silly, she tells herself sternly as she climbs the wide marble steps that lead to the reception, you didn't come here to befriend children or get embroiled in romantic relationships. You came here to *work*, to make the world aware of what's going on here, to get some pictures and pieces printed. Luckily, WWS finally seems to be interested in your pictures, though, let's face it, this is basically because (1) their regular war photographer has been shot dead at the border, (2) they've just discovered that you're a famous pin-up girl in India.

'Only thing is, we don't want any more sweet artsy pictures of refugee children and Mother Teresa, Tinka,' they'd told her over the phone last night. 'We need *action* pictures. You know, of bombs exploding, planes burning, people dying, guerrillas chucking grenades. Can you manage that?'

When she'd told them that that wasn't really her sort of thing, they'd tried to wheedle her into it by offering her all sorts of seductive perks.

'The press corps are all holed up at the Intercontinental Hotel in Dacca – it's very close to AFS Tezgaon, and it's a five-star with fantastic room service and a fab pool. We'll pay for your suite and organize all your permissions. You have an American passport, so that'll be easy. And don't worry, it's been designated a neutral zone by the International Red Cross, so it's perfectly safe…'

'Hah, if it's so very *safe* and so very *neutral*, why aren't *they* rushing there to feast on the five-star food?' Kainaz fui had sniffed when informed of this offer. 'Because they are scared the bombs meant for Tezgaon will land on their heads, that's why! You saw how bad that Maddy's aim was! He kept trying to put a bread roll into his mouth and kept missing. Don't fall for it, Tinka!'

Tinka had asked for a little time to think the offer over.

Not, as she'd let her aunt think, because she was apprehensive of the security situation in Dacca, but because (humiliating though it is to admit this!) her thinking processes have been suspended till she meets Ishaan again. Once she sees him and is reassured that he is safe, her life, which seems to have been thrown into a sort of clenched, agonized limbo, will start moving forward again.

But how much longer to wait? Should she just drive down to the base and demand to see him? She's done it before, she can do it again. Maidenly reticence has never really been her style, anyway.

I'll check once again if he's called for me, she decides, and if he hasn't, I'll just go down there and find out.

At the reception she asks for a vase and, when they're handing it to her, enquires casually (though her cheeks are flaming) if there have been any phone calls for her.

'No, but a gentleman has called to see you ma'am.' The receptionist beams at her. 'Your aunt asked him to go up to the suite. He's with her now.'

'Oh!' Tinka's hands fly to her hair, fluffing it up, while her heart starts to thud hard against her ribs. 'Did he give a name?'

The receptionist shakes his head. 'No, but he looked like a military gentleman. I think he came from the base.'

Tinka flashes a smile of such wattage that the young receptionist staggers back, instantly infatuated, then hurries up the staircase taking the wooden steps three at a time. *Thank God he's safe ... How do I look? Should I nip into the ladies' ... no, that's silly ... Okay, here goes.*

She stumbles over the last step, smoothens out her clothes, takes a deep breath and pushes open the door to the suite.

To come face to face, not with Fabulous Shaanu Bhaisaab, but a much older man. Square-shouldered, thick-waisted, dressed in a striped T-shirt and khakhi pants, his bushy white moustache bristling under a big hawk nose and quarrelsome, rheumy eyes.

A man whom she'd naively imagined to be pottering about in his large white kothi in Defence Colony, 'knee-deep in Punjabis' as his sister disdainfully puts it.

Major General Ardisher Dadyseth (retd) to be exact.

Tinka sags against the doorjamb, the joyous lurching of her heart transforming neatly into a dismal lurching of the stomach.

'Hello, Dad.'

• • •

'What nice flowers,' Kainaz Dadyseth says in a tinkling, fake-cheerful voice. 'Where did you get them, darling?'

Tinka shoots her a burningly reproachful look, and Kainaz, who is wearing a tie-and-dye dressing gown, a tilted eye mask and a guilty expression, hurriedly looks away.

Tinka enters the room, shuts the door and faces her father.

He looks older. And distinctly grumpier. His white handlebar moustache, that symbol of pride and pompousness, seems to have taken over his entire face. He seems to be lurking behind it, like a soldier behind a shield, eyeing his daughter resentfully.

'Put down that foliage,' he tells her without preamble. His voice is as rusty as it used to be, and his habit of clearing his throat every now and then as he speaks has got more accentuated. 'And, *arrrrhum!* get your bags. You're coming back to Delhi with me. I'm going to *arrrrhum!* get you married.'

'No,' Tinka says, softly and steadily, then she strides across the living room and slams the bedroom door shut with a shaking hand.

Damnit!

Ardisher bloody Dadyseth.

With his usual dampening aura of 'duty' and 'patriotism' and 'no-backtalk, if you please' and general party-pooperness.

Just when things were going so well. (Of course, there is a war on and everything, and people are dying on both sides of the border, but still!) She is taking pictures and helping people deal with the horrors, and she might even have met someone special.

Tinka rakes her hands through her short hair and slides down against the wall to sit on the bedroom floor.

Even through the heavy teak door, she can hear her father grousing and blustering. Stray phrases reach her ears – 'totally irresponsible of you' and 'shameless' and 'running wild' and 'that bloody draft-dodger Muhammad Ali' and 'those ridiculous John Lemon songs'.

They are followed by 'everybody is laughing at us' and 'childless women like you don't know how to handle children'.

Tinka rolls her eyes and throws open the door, making the general's eyes start from their sockets.

'First, she's not childless, she has *me*,' she snaps. 'And second, she does a much better job of parenting than *you*.'

His lips curl, but he doesn't react. Instead, he asks irritably, 'Are you packed?'

Tinka stares at him in disbelief. 'I'm not coming.'

Ardisher Dadyseth glares at his sister. 'Why isn't she packed?'

Kainaz, who has recovered her composure, raises a haughty eyebrow and shrugs. 'Don't ask *me*. I'm just a childless woman who doesn't know how to handle children.'

He glowers across the room at both of them, his moustache bristling with frustration.

'I've spoilt you,' he says finally. 'All this American living and Miranda House and *arrrhmm!* riding lessons and *"You've come a long way baby"*. I should have put you in a putri pathshala and married you off when you turned eighteen, that's what they do to girls in the families your *arhhhm!* new friend comes from.'

'What?' Tinka blinks, then turns to look at her aunt with huge betrayed eyes. 'You told him about Ishaan?'

Kainaz fui spreads out her hands helplessly. 'Bachche, he is your *father*. He has a right to know. And after what happened that day, with all those men chasing us, screaming *randi randi randi…*'

'*What?*' the general roars, looking from daughter to sister, his face reddening alarmingly.

'Oh, don't be such a pompous ass, Ardisher,' Kainaz says. 'I called you here because I thought you could help with the situation. But if you're going to jump like a stuck pig every time we tell you something, you might as well not have bothered.'

The general's face grows even more livid (red as a chukandar, thinks his unloving sister uncharitably. And with his flashy white moustache festooned across it, he looks a lot like a tastefully wrapped Christmas present).

'From what I can tell, you have been encouraging her to behave disgracefully, Kainaz,' he thunders. 'This assault in the mandi—'

'She's exaggerating,' Tinka interrupts impatiently. 'And anyway, Ishaan saved us.'

'So what?' The general pulls at his massive moustache. 'If you hadn't done that *arrrhmm!* stupid, shameless ad, nobody would have been chasing you in the first place.'

'Well, if you hadn't put so much pressure on me to get *married married married*, maybe I wouldn't have done it!' she flashes. 'I can't *believe* you got him to come here, fui!'

Kainaz looks desperately ashamed of herself.

'I'm sorry, darling, I panicked…'

'It was the only intelligent thing you've done in years!' roars the general.

'But maybe it's all for the best?' continues Kainaz like there's been no interruption. 'I mean, now that there is a war on, maybe you should go home with him.'

Up shoots Tinka's chin.

'I'm going to Dacca.'

'Oh no, you're not.' Brother and sister spring to their feet, looking remarkably alike.

They *are* alike, Tinka thinks, feeling betrayed and furious as she looks from her father's beetroot-red face to Kainaz's distressed one. I thought Kainaz fui was different – broad-minded, liberal – but I should have known that anybody who says Betty Freedom instead of Betty Friedan could only be a farzi feminist.

'You can't stop me,' she says quietly.

'I don't think young Ehsaan will let you go to Dacca either, darling,' Kainaz says in a gentler voice. 'It isn't safe.'

'I don't need young Ehsaan's *permission*,' Tinka snaps. 'And it's *Ishaan*!'

'Yes yes, Ishaan the kisaan,' grunts Ardisher Dadyseth, thoroughly disgusted. 'From Haryana, I believe. Typical bloody bumpkin.'

This makes Tinka so angry that for a moment all she can do is gape. Then she pulls in a quantity of air and says, her tone blistering, 'You are *such* a hypocrite! You go on and on about patriotism, but you think some Indians are better than others. You think Shaanu's good enough to die for India, but not good enough to enter your social circle!'

'I'm not a hypocrite!' General Ardisher throws out his chest. 'My son died for India, too!'

All the fight goes out of Tinka.

'Oh no, he didn't,' she says in a tired voice. 'You bullied your son into joining the Army even though he didn't want to, and he went to Chhamb to defend a stupid little border—'

'Borders are *not* stupid!' the general roars, starting to his feet, veins sticking out of his forehead. 'Soldiers live and die to protect every inch of border!'

'… and he killed six Pakistanis with his bare hands and was so shattered that he came home and shot himself.'

General Dadyseth's eyes bulge out frighteningly. 'He was cleaning his gun,' he thunders. 'It was *arrrhm!* an accident.'

'Yeah yeah,' says Tinka wearily and stalks out of the room.

• • •

Shaanu is attacking his boxing bag with savage energy when there is a knock on the door of his quarters. He ignores it and continues to punish the bag, his hair slick with sweat, his eyes glazed with concentration. But the knocking continues.

'Damnit!'

He throws one last punch, leaving the bag swinging, then strides to the door and throws it open.

Tinka Dadyseth is standing in the corridor.

He barely has time to shut the door before she hugs him. 'Thank God you're safe.'

Shaanu finds he can't speak. Filled with a profound gladness, he clasps her in his arms, rests his cheek on the top of her head and gives into the pleasure of just holding her.

She frowns.

'You've cut your back.'

'Minor flak,' he says into her hair. 'You should see the other guy.'

She pulls back, upset.

'Is he dead?'

'Would you rather I was?'

It is flippantly said, but there is an edge to his voice.

'No.' Tinka shakes her head fervently and hugs him again, shutting her eyes tight. Oh God, it feels so good to hold him! She wants to cry, but she ... will ... *not*. She's cried all the way to Kalaiganga and that is really enough crying for the day.

As she leans into his warm, rock-steady body and inhales him gratefully, she makes a discovery.

'You're shirtless.'

'Uh, yeah. I'm also sweaty, sorry, I was working out – I'm a bit offended it took you so long to notice, actually.'

She smiles against his chest. She could get used to this chest. It is smooth and firm and sculpted and highly touchable. It also features a gold chain with a small eagle pendant, which she isn't too mad about.

'I've noticed now.'

'Can I put a shirt on?' he asks formally. 'It's ... a little cold.'

Reluctantly, she lets him go. He walks down the corridor to the bedroom and shuts the door behind him – with unnecessary emphasis, Tinka thinks, piqued.

Alone for the time being, she looks slowly around the room. It is painted the pale MES yellow of her early childhood homes – Wellingdon, Dinjaan, Babina. There is a round dining table with four chairs, a well-worn sofa before a fireplace stacked with dry firewood and a makeshift divan created out of two battered black trunks, with letters stenciled out in white paint.

I. FAUJDAAR

There is a mantelpiece with passing-out-parade pictures, the entire Faujdaar brood posing in a blooming mustard field, several trophies and ribboned medals, and through an iron jaali-ka-darwaza, a balcony overlooking the parade ground, with a battered red boxing bag suspended from the fan-hook.

'It's not Ultimate Road, but it's home,' Shaanu remarks as he emerges from the bedroom, freshly showered and very properly covered in grey track pants and a cream cable-knit cricket jersey. 'Should I light a fire? I have to fly a sortie in two hours, though, so it'll have to be a small one.'

Two hours. Is he trying to tell her something? And why hasn't he phoned her all these days? Surely he could've taken out time to tell her he was safe?

'Yes, please.'

Five minutes later, a crackling blaze is throwing up jumping shadows all over the room. Tinka settles down on the couch, kicking off her shoes, staring at the flames and sucking her thumb pensively.

'How did you get it going so fast? It always takes me ages.'

'Arrey, I'm a gaon-ka-gora.' He flashes her a quick grin and hands her a small glass filled with hot brandy. 'Besides, commando training. Cheers.'

She doesn't sip the drink. Putting it down beside her, she asks, her voice ragged with emotion, 'Can you please tell me what is so goddamn holy about a wretched border?'

He looks at her in surprise.

'Arrey, surely you know! Borders keep order. All

countries have borders. If we don't protect our borders, the Pakistanis and the Chinese would soon be sitting in Delhi. And if they don't protect theirs, we'd swarm up sooner or later and gaardo a tiranga at Lahore Fort.'

'So what?' she demands passionately. 'It's all one planet!'

He sighs, looking like he would like to roll his eyes, but instead he picks up her glass and hands it to her.

'Just have your drink, hmmm?'

She stares at him mutinously for a moment, then snatches the glass from his hand and takes a gulp.

'Good girl.'

He doesn't sit beside her, though she's left space for him. Instead, he drops down on the floor, resting his back against the couch.

Then he adds, 'To friendship.'

Tinka splutters and lowers her glass.

'*Friendship?*'

He nods guardedly, stirring the flames with his foot. 'Yeah.'

Tinka starts to get a very bad feeling in the pit of her stomach. She sits up. 'Why friendship now, suddenly?'

He looks at her, the Kota-grey eyes troubled, and quickly looks away. 'Well, I've been thinking this over, and I feel that, given that the war is now officially on, it would be better if you and I were just friends.'

Tinka's eyes kindle dangerously.

'D'you usually go around kissing your *friends*?' she enquires. 'Is that a Chakkahera thing, an IAF Fighter thing, or just a Baaz Faujdaar thing?'

He stares into the fire and says in a quiet voice, 'That kiss happened by mistake.'

'*Oh!*' It is a hot, angry exclamation. She puts her hand on his shoulder and twists him around to face her. 'By *mistake*. So you were, what, aiming for my cheek?'

His jaw tautens.

'Yes.'

'You know, I find that really hard to believe.' Her voice is scathing. 'You can hit a guava at forty feet, and you downed a moving Sabre through the clouds while your own plane was bouncing up and down like a ping-pong ball, and yet, you missed a *cheek* at close proximity, even though it's at least four times as large as a mouth?'

He doesn't say anything.

'Ishaan?'

Why, each time she says his name, does his heart turn over inside his chest? He has tried to hold out, not phoning her, keeping busy, busting the shit out of his punching bag. But now that she's here, he knows that he's been only half alive since the last time he'd held her in his arms.

He turns towards her, grasping her hands, his grey eyes agonized.

'Please don't make this harder than it already is!'

'Please be talking about your erection!'

Shaanu's jaw drops. Practically incandescent with embarrassment, he manages to utter one scandalized word.

'Tinka!'

'What?' she demands, fighting back tears.

'You can't just *say* things like that!'

'Why?' She is half-crying, half-laughing, as she falls into his lap. '*What* are you telling me, Ishaan?'

He pushes her away gently to the other side of the couch, places a cushion firmly between them and begins stroking the hair off her forehead with unsteady hands.

'Dilsher's dead. He died even before his zits cleared up, the poor bastard.'

'Which is horrible and tragic,' she replies swiftly, 'but that's got nothing to do with—'

'I got hit by flak again this morning,' he interrupts her. 'Raka's engine flamed out when he landed. And we fly again tonight – anything can happen.'

She hugs a cushion fiercely and stares ahead of her with blind eyes.

Shaanu continues to speak, his voice toneless.

'Poor Raka's all messed up with worry about Juhi. He told me on the ride back home that I should thank my lucky stars I'm an unattached bachelor.'

She snorts rudely.

'What? I *am* unattached.'

'Really?' she says witheringly. 'Then why did you say on the dance floor that evening that we have a connection?'

Shaanu, valiantly trying to stick to his resolution to have nothing more to do with her, replies unwisely, 'Because your ad is so hot. Hell, I bet the country's full of men who feel they have a connection with you.'

'Fuck you.' She scrambles to her feet, furious.

'I didn't mean that!' The words are torn out of him. 'Okay, look, listen, it would never work out between us, Tell-me-na,' he says pleadingly. 'You hate what I do. Don't you?'

'Where are my shoes – where are my shoes?' She is weeping, wiping her nose on her sleeve. 'I want … to … *leave.*'

'You despise the fauj.'

'Yes.' She stops scrabbling around the floor and looks up. 'D'you want to know why?'

He sits forward, the grey eyes sympathetic. 'I've got a theory,' he says gently. 'But tell me, anyway.'

So she tells him. It is a jerkily told story, with many pauses.

About how, after the '65 conflict, Jimmy, the golden war-hero son General Ardisher was so proud of, hadn't been able to cope with the enormity of what he'd done. How he'd been wracked with guilt, tracking down the families of six Pakistani soldiers he'd killed, staring at the pictures of their widows and orphans, aching to make amends. And how, in spite of psychological counselling and everything, he'd finally shot himself in an attempt to find the peace that eluded him.

By the time the story has been told, they're lying on their sides, facing each other, all thoughts of leaving forgotten.

'Wow.' Shaanu kisses the palm of her hand. 'That explains a lot.'

'Yeah.'

'So now you don't talk to Ardisher at all, huh.'

'Ardisher's just a *moustache*,' she says hopelessly. 'I can't explain it – he's getting more and more shrunken, and it's getting bigger and bigger – it's *growing* on him like a parasite, eating him alive! A big luxuriant moustache, flourishing on a diet of pride and pompousness and warped patriotism! I hate it – and him.'

She goes silent now, all talked out. Silence reigns in the room for a while.

Shaanu drinks in the sight of her, revelling in the pleasure of looking at her so openly. The neckline of her navy blue dress has dipped, the hem ridden up above her knees, her short tumbled hair seems to have golden highlights. He strokes the length of her body, committing to memory the smooth calves, the narrow knees, the generous swell of thigh and hip. He can tell, from the way she moves below his touch, that they could be making love right now, here, beside the fire.

Finally he says, his voice tender.

'So much love for Pakistanis and so much hate for your father?'

Her head comes up with a jerk, her eyes kindling.

'Meaning?'

He shrugs. 'If you're *such* a pacifist, show some understanding for him too, ne?'

'But you hate Chimman!'

'I'm not so sure of that any more.' He says slowly. 'Besides, okay, you lost a brother, but your father lost a *son*, he must be grieving also! He has no other children – he *needs* you.'

She's sitting bolt upright now.

'He wouldn't have lost a son if he'd been a better father!'

Shaanu sits up too.

'That *very* thought must be driving him crazy!'

Silence.

Ishaan leans in, closer to her.

'Tinka, it seems to me that your brother was a sensitive type. Like you. Poetic and all. Mein maanta hoon, your father shouldn't have forced him to join the forces, but—'

'My brother wasn't weak!'

'Arrey, did I say he was? He's a hero. They teach about him at the IMA.'

'They teach all the *wrong* stuff,' she says fiercely. 'All that crap you were telling me that day about hatred for the enemy, channelling your bloodlust, Pakistan murdabad. That's animal behaviour!'

But this is too much for Ishaan.

'Look,' he says frankly. 'Say what you want, but I *won't* hesitate if I have to kill some Paki soldiers – and I won't be racked by guilt afterwards either! They're enemies of India, and it's my job to kill them, to protect our civilians and keep the country safe. It's that simple. Trust me.'

She sits up, her eyes swimming.

'Can't you just quit?' she says desperately. 'Leave the IAF and get a job in, oh, I don't know, Air India?'

His jaw tautens stubbornly.

'I love my job. This war will probably be the most important thing to happen to my batch from the College. The timing's perfect – people go for years waiting to see action, and we've been handed a full-scale war on a platter! Why should I miss out on any of the fun?'

She pulls away, her expression sickened. 'You said *fun*.'

'It was just a figure of speech,' Shaanu says, not very convincingly.

Tinka backs away.

He looks at her, worried.

'I didn't mean it that way, I meant action, fighting, striking a blow for my country … Damnit, don't go … don't *misunderstand* ya!'

But she has risen to her feet and made it to the door, and this time she finds her shoes.

'You're just like my father.'

He knows this is the worst thing she can say – and it hurts like hell that she's saying it. But he doesn't argue, although his Kota-grey eyes flood with regret.

'Tinka, go back to Delhi, or Bombay – and take your aunt with you. This area isn't safe for civilians any—'

'I'm going to Dacca,' she cuts him off in a tight little voice, 'to report on the atrocities. To get the world's eyeballs to swivel to this part of the world. To somehow get the insanity to end.'

'You're doing nothing of the sort!' He gets to his feet in a flash. 'You can't—'

'Oh yes, I can. And *you*,' her voice grows bitter, biting, 'can *enjoy* the war.'

TEN

Pomfret's wife, a stringy, battered battle-horse of a lady who spent her peacetime days pottering dreamily about her garden and pretty much letting the younger women run things, has now shaken off her inertia and resumed charge of the Air Force Wives Welfare Association.

'To prepare you for war,' she explains with grim earnestness, clad in a smart navy-blue cardigan and a chic grey silk sari that reeks fearsomely of mothballs. 'Because you're fighting this war as much as your husbands are, my dears.'

Everybody nods, including Juhi, who is seated bang in the middle of the circle.

'No weeping!' says Mrs Pomfret sternly, inhaling through flared, battle-ready nostrils. 'No whining! Remember, this is real life, not *Sangam* or *Aradhana* in which IAF officers die ekdum phataak se, after getting the heroine pregnant. Statistics show that eight out of ten IAF Fighters survive war. So please don't panic!'

Hai hai, shubh shubh bol, chudail, Juhi thinks resentfully.

Eight out of ten, indeed. *Your* husband survived three whole wars, why won't mine? Do you think I won't fast and pray to Laxmi-Ganesh as hard as *you* did? Cow.

'Cry as much as you like in your bathroom,' Mrs Pomfret continues, 'on the phone to your mother, or here in this strong supportive circle of women – but never let your husband see your tears. Nor your children! Continue with the homework and make sure they brush their teeth twice daily! If you break down, they will too. In the three wars I have lived through with my husband, I have never *ever* let him see me cry!'

Chalo, main toh already fail ho gayi, Juhi plunges into despair. Raka sees me cry every time he leaves! But it's not easy for me – if I were married to a miserable, dried-up old stick like Pomfret and there was a chance that he might die during a sortie, I would wander around the house with a stupid grin plastered to my face too. But I'm not married to an old stick, I'm married to *Raka*, who is handsome and loving and funny and has the most darling gappuchee cheeks and the bravest moustache in the world...

'Unlike our sisters in the Army, whose husbands fight at the borders, far away from home, we Air Force wives are in a privileged position,' Mrs Pomfret says. 'We stay right here at the Air Force Station, and our menfolk fly back home to us every night. Therefore it is not just our duty but also our *privilege* as Indian Air Force wives,' Mrs Pomfret waxes eloquent, 'to be a calm harbour away from the stormy seas of war, which is a navy metaphor, of course, but will serve for us as well. If your man comes back confused and guilty, reassure him that he is only doing the morally correct thing, the patriotic thing, that his nation is counting on him. If he comes back shaken or aching or mentally broken, resurrect him as only a woman can, so that he rises again...'

Juhi's eyes widen. Around her some of the teary-eyed young wives smother giggles. A vision has risen before their eyes, unbidden, of Mrs Pomfret resurrecting Pomfret and making him *rise* again...

'Umm, Mrs Pandey, are we talking about, er, the *bedroom*?' asks one of the young wives.

Mrs Pomfret smiles, showing ancient, wizened dimples.

'Yes, my dear. We're talking about the bedroom – and about romance and marvellous highs and lows and all that fluff.' She gives a long, dreamy sigh. 'It's one of the few – in fact the *only* perk – of wartime.'

That's true enough, Juhi thinks, doleful again, her mood mushing up and down as badly as Raka's MiG on a steep-glide dive. Her nights under the olive-green mosquito netting have been reaching ecstatic heights. There is a new edge to their love-making now, and all the stress Raka is under has melted the slight pudginess that had started to creep around his tummy, thanks to her ghee-laden cooking. Hey Bhagwan, what kind of evil wife is she, rejoicing in her husband's newly taut tummy when he could be shot out of the sky any time?

All in all, she thinks as she surreptitiously wipes tears from her downcast eyes, she prefers the ho-hum, slightly pudgy, peacetime sex.

'And please use contraception, ladies, unless you're planning to have a baby without the government-advised three-year gap. We aren't a bunch of village women here!'

With a few last words on keeping an eye on the poor bachelor officers who have no womenfolk at home to look after them, Mrs Pomfret winds up her act. The ladies sip tea, nibble on little snacks and then trickle out.

Raka is out on sortie, so Baaz is waiting to drive Juhi home. His Gnat needs some solid repair work, he brought it back so leaky and battered and riddled with shrapnel that he's on the ground for the next two days.

With Mrs P's winding up remarks very much on her mind, Juhi makes Baaz come into her quarters, brews him a hot mug of adrak ki chai and places a stack of homemade matthri at his elbow. He demolishes them with mechanical gusto.

'How are you, Baaz?' she asks, watching him eat. 'Sleeping well?'

'Oh, yes,' he assures her, chewing busily.

He looks so drawn, Juhi thinks with a guilty pang. But then, they all are. And there are shadows under his eyes.

'Are you drinking enough water?'

He glances up with the ghost of a grin.

'Yes, doc.'

She ignores this crack.

'And showing off on sorties. Raka said you took too many risks yesterday.'

He shrugs. 'Somebody told me to enjoy the war.' He looks up with a savage little smile. 'So I'm doing just that.'

'Thhhutt!' she says, distressed. 'Wing Commander Carvalho also na! What a stupid thing to say.'

Silence. Shaanu chews. Juhi watches him with some unease.

'Any news from your family?'

The grey eyes light up a little.

'All fine,' he says. 'The girls have started at Sophia Convent now. Sulo was offered a double promotion, but she decided not to take it. Pitaji got angry, because it would've saved him one whole year of fees, but she said no. She's smart, that girl.'

'That's great,' Juhi says brightly. 'And how's your pitaji?'

'As kameena as always!' Shaanu rolls his eyes with a flash of his old affectionate energy. 'And how are *you*? You look thin. Your cheeks aren't as pink as they used to be!'

'Yours aren't too pink either, okay!' she retorts, her vanity piqued. 'It's because I worry about all of you. Raka, of course, but also Maddy and you – because you're my bachelors and I'm supposed to watch over you. How's Tinka?'

She slips the name in as quickly and as naturally as she can, but it is no use – it emerges from her mouth clumsily, clunkily, calling attention to itself, the elephant in the room suddenly acknowledged, demanding discussion and closure.

Shaanu, who has been layering his matthri with achaar, puts it down and glances at her, the grey eyes so vulnerable Juhi has to look away.

'I don't know.'

Hai hai, Juhi thinks, her heart sinking at the dispirited tone of this confession. He is in love with that complicated female. Hamara Baaz! How horrible.

She reaches for his hand.

'She's … in Dacca, right?'

He nods. 'That's all I know.'

'Are you okay?'

'Yes,' he says shortly.

'Baaz…'

'Do you know' – he looks up at her restlessly, his gaze painfully intense – 'what Napalm can do to human skin?'

'What? No.' She looks confused.

'Yeah, well, it's petroleum jelly mixed with gasoline, so once it's ignited, it sticks to your skin and burns there at temperatures as high as 1,200 degrees centigrade. Water boils at—'

'100 degrees, I know.'

'So it's a terrible, unnecessarily cruel way to kill. Our Hunters have been dropping Napalm on the Pakistanis. If they ask me to drop it, I'll quit.'

If Kuch Bhi Carvalho had been present, he would have told Shaanu to shut the fuck up. Nobody stresses out the ladies with this kind of information, and besides, Shaanu's puny Gnat is too small to carry the massive Napalm bombs anyway. But Old KBC isn't here. And nothing Mrs Pomfret has told Juhi has prepared her for this.

'Baaz,' says Juhi, deeply distressed. 'Baba, don't think about things like this. You can't just quit, abandon your duty! You're being silly, and anyway, what you're saying doesn't even sound possible. Are you an ordnance expert now? How do you even know what different bombs do?'

He looks evasive.

'I read it somewhere.'

Quickly, he downs the rest of his tea.

'Stay for dinner,' Juhi says inadequately, because she doesn't know what else to say.

'I'm going down to the boxing ring.' He gets to his feet and gives her a reassuring grin. 'Don't look so worried, Juhi. Everything's fine. I'm way too good for anybody to down me, and the maintenance crew is superb, so the machines will never let us down! And you're praying for us, aren't you?'

She nods fervently. 'Every day.'

He hugs her.

'Thanks for the matthri.'

'Anytime.'

• • •

Hosannah Carvalho has inherited a stash of pornographic magazines from Pilot Officer Dilsher Singh. There had been a stack of them under the mattress of his bed in the Officers' Mess, and his room bearer had dutifully cleaned them out before Dilsher's mother arrived, teary-eyed and heartbroken, to pack up his room. The shattered room bearer, who had been very close to his Officer, had handed the sordid little bundle to Wing Commander Carvalho wordlessly at the funeral ceremony. It is sitting at his desk in the office.

Idly, during his lunch hour, Carvalho leafs through them.

It's the usual collection. One glossy imported *Playboy*, its pages well-thumbed and stiff with dried fluids, a couple of *Debonair*s and some assorted pin-up posters, all creased and folded up. From the dog-ears on the magazines, it is easy to see that Dilsher had a type – leggy, big-bosomed, blonde.

Carvalho is about to consign the whole lot to the dustbin when, slipped into the pages of a *Debonair*, he discovers something that looks like a leaflet from an ordnance manual.

Frowning, he scans the sheet.

It is literature for a missile of some sort, he realizes after studying the sheet for a while. FAB500 M-62. That's a Russian coding number, Carvalho knows, but he doesn't remember the missile off-hand. Why would Dilsher have kept its literature under his mattress?

He reads through the leaflet again, more closely this time.

The bomb weighs 1000lbs, he learns, is elongated and streamlined, hence is wind-resistant, which, the leaflet claims, will ensure high speed of delivery and minimum drift.

Very interested now, Carvalho flips the leaflet over and finds one word written in ball-point pen ink, in Dilsher's unformed scrawl.

Tezgaon?

An hour later, Carvalho is scouting feverishly through

the ordnance depot with the supplies team and Rakesh Aggarwal.

'Er, what exactly is this missile, sir?' Raka asks.

'It's the only free-fall weapon in the IAF's Russian Fighter's inventory,' Old Kuch Bhi tells Raka, manic eyes glittering. 'I can't believe we overlooked it all this time!'

Neither can Raka. But now is not the time to gripe.

'Is it accurate?' he asks, tugging on his moustache.

'Totally, Aggarwal Sweets! And we'll get the armourers to reset the fuse setting. They'll be set to explode *after* impact, once they've ploughed through the earth – they're strong enough to cause damage even to a hardened runway. Just dive down, ekdum Baaz-ke-maaphik, drop 'em on the sweet spot, and we'll be home!'

But dropping 'em on the sweet spot is easier said than done, Raka points out. These are bigger, heavier bombs – they will make the MiGs sluggish, and worse, when the pilots go into a dive, could cause the aircraft to mush dangerously.

'They're better than the S-5s, that's all I know,' Carvalho snaps crankily. 'I think Dilsher was onto something. Let's try them out on your sortie today.'

Raka agrees – but not without reservations, which he confides to Shaanu outside the briefing room a little later.

'Basically, your nose is pointing somewhere, and these heavy bombs are pointing somewhere else, so the aircraft flight path becomes a total hotchpotch. Accuracy suffers. Carvalho insists we can achieve accuracy if we can manage to start off very very straight, and *then* as we dive downwards, approaching release range, we'll gain speed naturally and mush less, so we can drop the things off easily, rise up and zoom away.'

The flaw in this plan, Shaanu knows, is that when you come steep-glide diving straight down the length of the runway, you are effectively a sitting duck. The gunners know you're committed to coming in from a certain direction, so they point their guns in that direction and then just sit pretty, singing '*She'll be coming round the mountain, when she comes*'. When you show up, they can spot you, take aim and pick you out of the sky at leisure.

He tells Raka this, and Raka nods grimly. The MiG fighters have already experienced this twice before, getting hit smack in the belly with ground fire as they dropped the largely ineffective S-5 missiles.

'Matlab ki, it's total madness, Baaz,' he tells his friend. 'Every moment you're thinking *laga!*, you've been hit, and every *other* moment you're thinking *phew, nahi laga*. It's a constant chant in your head, and bloody unnerving, but you get used to it – so much so ki when somebody *actually* gets hit, it comes as a sort of surprise.'

They both go quiet, thinking about Dilsher.

'I just hope Dillu's wet dream doesn't end up killing us all,' Raka says gloomily. 'What was the fucker doing, jerking off to missile manuals, anyway?'

'I've got an idea,' Shaanu says abruptly.

'What?' Raka demands suspiciously. 'Your puny plane is too small to carry these missiles, so please don't offer Carvalho your services!'

'Maybe, maybe not.' There is an edge to Shaanu's voice. The smallness of the Gnats is a sore point. 'But I've got an idea on how to distract the Tezgaon gunners…'

He explains his plan to Raka, who listens, then shakes his head vigorously and entreats his buddy to get admitted to the pagal khana in Agra.

But Shaanu keeps talking, grabbing Raka's arm and gesturing animatedly as they walk down the tarmac together.

'Okay, if all else fails, we'll try it,' Raka reluctantly tells Shaanu as they reach their jets and clamber up their respective ladders. 'Jai Mata di!'

The formation sets off – four MiGs strapped with the massive FAB500s and two diminutive Gnats flying top cover to ward off any marauding Sabres – and descends at four in the afternoon over Tezgaon.

• • •

The Intercontinental Hotel squats self-importantly like a fat slice of birthday cake in the dusty plate that is Dacca, the other structures of the city heaped deferentially around it like lesser snacks that know their place. A wraparound colonnade, a glittering swimming pool and several elegant lawns seek to soften its uncompromisingly rectangular structure, with uneven results.

WWS has done Tinka proud, procuring for her a room on the highest floor, with a view of the city. When she pushes back the curtains as far as they can go and stands at a certain angle, she can just about make out the occasionally shimmering sky above AFS Tezgaon, home of the PAF's F-86 Sabrejets.

The official conflict, which began on Friday, the third of December, is ten days old now and on the brink of being won by either India or Pakistan, depending on which version of the news you choose to believe. The pro-Pakistan brigade, mostly the mainstream American press, insists that China is set to intervene *now*, at this *very* moment, even as we *speak*, and will teach the cheeky interfering Indians a lesson as sharp as the one they taught them in '62. Meanwhile, the

Bangladesh sympathizers (which include the International Red Cross and the United Nations teams, even though they are ostensibly neutral) insist that the India-Mukti Bahini alliance is set to win and end the genocide, oppression and misrule of West Pakistan once and for all. The career journalists, a wise, weathered non-partisan crew, shake their heads and talk of how Dacca is starting to resemble Berlin at the end of the Second World War – a city to which the battlefront has arrived. It'll end badly for Dacca, they predict, and bloodily too, unless somebody has the sense to rise above the hubris and cry *Enough!*

India, slugging it out on both fronts, is showing no sign of climbing down. Neither is Pakistan. Seemingly unaffected by the mounting casualties, General Nikka Khan and the figurehead Governor he supposedly reports to continue to talk tough, insisting that Pakistan is in the right and will prevail.

Tinka, who's been here for a week now, is not finding things easy. First, the entire hotel staff insists on watching over her with a sort of avuncular lust. Apparently, the head bellboy (a seventy-five-year-old grandfather who should be thinking more about jannat and less about hoors) travelled to Calcutta last month and chanced upon a Freesia poster in a grocery store. He ripped the thing off the wall, carried it home and hung it up with great ceremony in the hotel pantry. And now, every time the azaan sounds, she can't shake the feeling that the hotel staff (ninety-five per cent male) are on their knees praying for a particularly hot day, so that she will don her emerald-green bikini and frolic in the hotel pool while they hum laaa la-la-la, la-la-la-la...

Then there's the fact that her editor won't stop griping over the fact that her stories aren't 'balanced' enough.

'What the hell d'you mean not balanced?' Tinka demands for the nth time. 'I'm telling it like it is!'

'Tinka, you've filed *one* story about the horrific effects of Napalm bombing – which is something both sides are using – and *three* stories about Pakistani violence against the Bengalis. We need something from the other side as well. Aren't the Bengalis butchering the Biharis? Why can't you get us some dope on that?'

'I can't create an artificial balance when none exists,' Tinka snaps. 'Yes, the Biharis have suffered at the hands of the Awami League supporters and the Muktis, but the sheer magnitude of the violence inflicted upon the Bengalis is far far greate—'

'Yeah, so let's have a story on these poor oppressed Bihari sods,' her editor cuts her off briskly. 'And we want pictures of bombs falling and dogfights and all that. Those always sell well.'

And then he cut the line, leaving her to stare down at the phone in disbelief. Does he even realize how difficult it is to get through to him on the phone? There's always a gaggle of journos waiting to use the erratically functioning line – her turn came after four solid hours of waiting – how can he just brush her off? What the hell is wrong with the world? Why doesn't anybody give a damn about anything that's really important any more?

And finally, of course, there's Ishaan, or rather, the absence of Ishaan, which she's carrying around with her everywhere she goes – a horrid, hollow uneasiness bobbing about in the middle of her stomach, making her feel constantly clenched and yet gapingly open at the same time and curiously removed from everything that happens around her.

'Editor's being a pain in the arse?'

The crusty, quavering voice belongs to Julian Arnott, an ancient freelance correspondent from the UK. He is bright-eyed and bird-like and incredibly wrinkled, with a fondness for loud batik shirts and silk scarves. He has been ensconced in the telecommunications room's only armchair, legs crossed dapperly at the knee, waiting for her to finish, but now he seems to be in no hurry to place his call.

Tinka nods gloomily. 'He wants me to write a story on oppressed Biharis. You know what, I think you were right, they hired me because they saw that idiotic I-will-never-say-Pakistan-Murdabad article in the *India Post* and thought I'd toe the official American line.'

'And you turned out to be a Ted Kennedy supporter!' Julian tsk-tsks. 'Aah, women are so fickle! Just because the fellow's better-looking than Nixon.'

'D'you know any oppressed Biharis?' Tinka asks, ignoring this jibe.

'Hundreds,' the old journo replies promptly. 'But surely writing about the Indian de Havilland Caribou, a transport aircraft pressed into military action, that dropped a bomb on an orphanage in Tangala yesterday would be a better idea?'

Tinka sits up. This is brand new information.

'Are you serious?'

'Oh, yes,' Julian says calmly.

'But India wouldn't do something so foul!'

He raises his eyebrows. 'It was an accident, I think,' he says mildly. 'Also, my dear, you're supposed to be neutral.'

She flushes. 'Well, yes of course, except that ... no, actually you're right. I'll chase the story. But *can* you really drop bombs in a Caribou? Isn't it some sort of flying bus?'

'You'd have to ask an expert,' he replies. 'D'you know any fighter pilots?'

Her expression grows oddly wooden at this. Julian Arnott's old eyes don't miss this, but then, they don't miss much.

'No.'

Before he can quiz her further, the door of the lounge bursts open and Leo Stepanov, a chubby young Russian cameraman who works for the Russian daily news station Solntse, peers into the room.

'Our Nikita's at the military club next door, addressing a big crowd,' he announces with relish. 'Everybody's listening to him with bated breath.'

'Nikka Khan?' Tinka grabs her bag and jumps to her feet. 'Oh my God, is it an important announcement? Maybe he's asking for a ceasefire!'

Julian looks unconvinced. 'Are you sure?' he asks Leo.

'I'm sure, grandfather.' The Russian grins. 'But if you're too decrepit to totter out to see for yourself, I'll give you one of my pictures for free.'

'Pictures!' the old man snorts. 'Any monkey can press a camera button! But to *describe* a scene, to bring alive the *mood*, to *paint with words*, as it were...'

'Are you coming or not?' Tinka asks.

'I'm coming,' is Julian's crusty response. 'You, Ivan the fool, gimme a hand!'

'My name's Leo.'

'Don't babble,' Julian snaps thanklessly even as Leo pulls him up from the squishy embrace of the armchair. 'Whuff! Yes, yes, you can let go now, I'm not a bloody invalid. Come now, let's go.'

They make their way down the pillared colonnade to the club, flashing their press badges at the security staff at the gate, and emerge onto a beautiful green lawn, abloom with late chrysanthemum and winter roses. A beautifully turned-out crowd is sitting on white cane chairs, listening riveted to a man speaking from a podium.

A very suave, elegant man this, sporting a nattily tied cravat, a navy-blue beret and a sharp blazer that does a decent job of skimming over his small paunch. His features are very fine, they would be womanish if not for the harsh lines that link the corners of his thin mouth with his chiselled nose. He's talking into the mic in the most insufferable pommy accent Tinka has ever had the misfortune to hear.

'A naice cup of tea,' says Nikka Khan sonorously. 'Fort-teh-three.'

Tinka blinks.

'Ultah pultah,' continues Nikka, in the same ghastly British accent. 'Ultah pultah, sixty-nine!'

'Is he announcing *Tumbola numbers*?' Tinka asks in disbelief. '*Now*? Why?'

Leo's chubby face splits in a grin of pure glee. 'I *told* you he's making important announcements, and everybody is listening!'

'Never trust a Russian,' Julian says resignedly. 'Making me walk all this way for nothing.'

'The sun's good for your old hide, grandfather,' Leo grins. 'You're getting as pale as a snake's belly in that hotel.'

'Shush!' An elderly lady with a hennaed bouffant bun frowns at them fearsomely. 'We can't hear the number calls.'

They subside, cowed, in the second-last row of seats.

Tinka glares at Leo.

'*Why* did you drag us here?' she whispers.

'Shammi kebabs,' he replies reverentially. He is looking beyond her, his gleaming eyes seeking a bearer. 'The goats in Dacca were made to be minced. You have to try them.'

'Aaah.' Julian's old eyes gleam. 'Our Ivan's not such a fool, after all.'

Tinka, uninterested in the kebabs, is watching Nikka do his thing.

'Unbelievable.' She shakes her head. 'General-saab has a fondness for Tumbola!'

'General-saab has a fondness for the sound of his own voice,' says Julian, his quavery voice not as low as it should be. 'He reads out the numbers every Sunday at the Defence Club. Nobody else is allowed to do it, even though he's now in charge of the defence of all East Pakistan and most definitely has more important things to do.'

'Some upstart tried to take over the number-calling once,' Leo chimes in. 'Conducted an entire Sunday Tumbola and was very funny and charming. Came up with some very original rhymes. Everybody loved him. He was found dead on the banks of the Buriganga the next morning dressed only in little shorts. His testicles had been cut off and stuffed into his mouth.'

Tinka chokes.

'Nuts on a plate,' Nikka announces from the podium serenely. 'Num-bah eight.'

Tinka stares at him in horrid fascination. She has the creepiest feeling that he is staring right back at her.

'Double D,' says the general next with a knowing smirk. 'For-ty!'

Somebody calls out that they have a jaldi five, and the number-calling halts for a little while. Shammi kebabs and Coca-Colas find their way to the little press gang's table.

Tinka, staring at the Butcher of Balochistan, now crowned the Butcher of Bengal, can't help feeling a bit underwhelmed. She has read up on the general – a childhood spent in grinding poverty in a small village in undivided Punjab, seventh of eleven children, missionary school education, recruitment into the British Army, campaigns abroad, the rape of his mother and sisters during Partition and the subsequent reign of terror in the two provinces. None of that seems to tally with the cummerbanded, cravatted caricature before her.

'I can't help feeling there's some deep psychological explanation for his behaviour,' she says.

'Never romanticize a bastard,' Julian Arnott snorts through a mouthful of shammi. 'The man's a despot, pure and simple. A cold-blooded killer. So, naturally, also a narcissist. His office is always calling us asking for cuttings of his pictures and interviews for his several voluminous scrapbooks. The *moment* he sights camera crews, especially international camera crews, he turns his best angle towards them, smoothens down his dyed black hair and starts flashing his sinister, thin-lipped smile. Hold up your camera, Tinka.'

She does.

Nikka preens immediately. Squaring his shoulders just a wee bit more and batting his eyelashes like a female pop singer competing on Eurovision.

'You're right,' Tinka says, fascinated. 'What a diva!'

She presses her 'shoot' button several times and is rewarded by several poses. The general moves just a little every time she clicks, now stroking his eyebrow meditatively, now leaning forward thoughtfully, now shaking the numbers drum in a pensive fashion.

'Maybe he finds you attractive, wench,' Julian tell her. 'Maybe looking at you has made him come alive with the freshness of Freesia.'

'Shush!' Tinka whispers back. 'You'll get us thrown out of here.'

'Son-of-a-gun,' says Nikka. 'Twen-teh-one!'

They giggle and the people seated in the next row glower at them. Quickly, they compose their faces.

The game gets over a little later, a large lady with maroon hair cleaning up the bumper prize, and then Nikka is free to circulate.

'Don't go to him.' Leo puts a restraining hand on Tinka's arm. 'He'll come to us, never fear – he can't resist the international press. He's like a moth to our flame.'

'Wonder what pearls of wisdom he'll let fall today,' Julian murmurs. 'My favourite so far has been "East Pakistan gets flooded in the monsoon because it's a low-lying land full of low, lying people". Haha.'

Meanwhile, the general has scooped up a glass of whiskey-paani and is conversing with the crowd around him. Somebody cracks a joke and he throws back his head and laughs, a semi-neigh semi-bray of a laugh. Everybody chimes in dutifully.

'Sycophancy at its peak,' Julian sighs, suddenly looking every one of his rumoured eighty-three years. 'How many many times I've seen scenes like this! They always end badly.'

And Tinka, looking at him, is suddenly rocked by a very bad feeling, a premonition of horrors to come. She isn't at all surprised when the air raid siren kicks in.

WooooOOOooooOOOoooo!

It is a keening, see-sawing wail, rising and falling in pitch like an animal in pain, and it never fails to fill her with dread.

'Clear the lawns please!' Nikka's security detail barks out. 'Take cover! Everybody, take cover!'

The posh, perfumed people scurry to the nearby clubhouse, two of the bearers carefully carrying the Tumbola numbers and drum. The three journalists move in the opposite direction, making for the hotel.

'Hurry hurry hurry!' Tinka urges the doddering Julian in an agony of impatience. 'Faster!'

'Run ahead then, girl,' he replies crankily. 'No need for you to dawdle with me!'

Leo and Tinka exchange frustrated glances, then the Russian mutters under his breath, slings the old man under one arm and runs with him all the way to the hotel lobby.

Tinka laughs and runs too, her shoes in her hands.

The regal, moustachioed doorman doesn't bat an eyelid when he sees them, merely opening the massive bevelled glass doors without comment.

In the lobby, Leo sets Julian down and eyes him apprehensively.

'Sorry for, um, mishandling you,' he says.

'Get the lift door!' grunts the old man ungratefully, adjusting his rumpled clothes. 'The best view is from the terrace.'

Leo grins and rushes to press the elevator button. A minute later, the three of them are shooting up to the top floor.

'A live show.' Julian practically licks his chops as the doors slide open smoothly. 'Have you two got reel in your cameras?'

'Yup.' Leo nods, his mouth full of shammi kebab. He has stuffed them into his pockets without even wrapping them in paper napkins. He proffers them to the others. 'Tinka?'

'No, thanks.' She shakes her head, getting her camera ready. 'Did you even *pay* for those, Leo?'

'How could I?' He grins. 'The waiter ran away.'

'Disgusting.'

The other journos are already clustered around the terrace wall when the three of them arrive at the rooftop, all of them oohing and aahing like they're at a fireworks display.

Tinka immediately wants to slap them.

Leo clambers onto the water tank with practised ease and quickly adjusts his camera to zoom in on the action.

'MiGs!' he shouts. 'Indian.'

Tinka's heart slams into her ribs in relief.

Thank God.

It can't be Ishaan.

'See how proud our Ivan sounds.' Julian nudges Tinka. 'Just because they're made in Russia.'

'Well, the Gnat's almost a British plane,' she tells him, her fingers trembling a little as she tracks the jets through her viewfinder. 'And it has the best record against the Pakistanis, better than anything Mikoyan Gurevich's come up with. Tell him that.'

'Hmmm, how come you're so jet-savvy?' Julian raises one desiccated old eyebrow.

'I'm generally savvy,' she shoots back and lowers her camera with a sigh. 'Damn, they're too far away. I'll get nothing with my crappy zoom feature.'

'They're aiming for the airfield!' shouts a German cameraman, who is positioned on top of the air-conditioning shafts. 'They're trying to crater it again! Whoa, hark the ack-ack guns!'

• • •

The moment the gunners hear the unmistakable roar of the Tumansky engines, the ack-acks start to fire, causing the

MiGs to bounce and check. The puffs of smoke exploding around them are bigger than last time, clearly the Pakistanis have brought bigger guns into the game. The MiGs rise to higher altitudes, cursing colourfully, until they are level with the circling Gnats.

'Too hot for you down there, brother?'

Yeah,' comes the terse reply.

'Can we try my idea now?'

'No. We're gonna try out Dillu's missiles first. We're going in again. You stay, scan and report, okay?'

'But Raka, yaar...'

The MiGs drop height, vanishing below the thin cloud cover. Shaanu curses but stays put.

Hearing the roar of the MiGs returning, the Pakistani gunners up their attack. The MiGs barrel through grimly, taking the only route they can – right down the length of the runway, wide open to gunfire.

At Shaanu's altitude, all that can be heard is an eerie silence.

The Gnats circle...

The silence stretches out...

The sky stays empty....

'Fuck this.' Shaanu's voice is brisk. 'C'mon, Gana.'

• • •

Peering through his zoom lens from his vantage point atop the water tank of the Intercontinental, Leo Stepanov gives a sudden exclamation.

'Gnats!'

His cry is followed by a chorus of others.

'Shit, yes, Gnats! They're Indian.'

'Where? Where?'

'Look! Those little flashing ones swooping around close to the ground! *Hooly-doolies*, that was close!'

With a sinking heart, Tinka watches the three diminutive jets dive in perfect synchrony towards the airfield. Though there is no logical way she can tell from this distance, she is sure one of them – probably the cocky one that's flying the lowest – is being piloted by Ishaan. Shakily, she turns her back to the scene, leans against the parapet wall and swallows hard.

Julian chuckles. Resting one hip comfortably against a water tank, he is watching the action with one wrinkly hand shading his eyes.

'Cheeky bugger! Fancy some gum, Tinka?'

He proffers a pack of Wrigley's Spearmint. Tinka pulls out a stick with unsteady hands.

'Aren't you watching?' he asks her.

'The sun hurts my eyes,' she replies, popping the gum into her mouth.

Julian glances at her.

'Man up, young woman!' he says rallyingly. 'Hey, maybe a small bet would spice things up for you. How about you wager a small sum on either the PAF or the IAF coming up tops today?'

'I'm not going to pick sides,' she replies tightly. 'War is stupid.'

'Agreed,' he replies. 'But vastly entertaining and good for selling newspapers.' He draws in a sharp breath. 'Phew, that was close, too close for comfort!'

• • •

At this lower altitude, the air is thick with puffs of gunfire. Shaanu can see the MiGs – two smoking, one limping and one flying higher than the others, divested of its missiles. Down below, the airfield looks intact, except for the massive crater created by Dilsher Singh on his first and last sortie.

'Missed!' Shaanu says savagely. *'Damnit!'*

'Here we come, boyssss,' Gana shouts over the R/T as he dives even lower, right above the area where the ack-ack fire is the thickest, to a height where they can practically see the whites of the gunners' eyes. Thach-weaving now, they criss-cross each other, confusing and distracting the gunners, strafing them mercilessly. The air around them explodes with AA fire, but not a single ack-ack touches the tiny, weaving Gnats.

'Coast clear, Raka, go!' Shaanu yells over the R/T, but he needn't have bothered, the MiGs are already swooping in, engines screaming, dropping their deadly cargo.

'Dishoom,' mutters Raka, his MiG mushing madly as he drops the first FAB500 slap-bang in the middle of the airfield. 'Annnnddd ... *dishooom* again!'

As he watches, pulse throbbing, muscles clenched, the missiles plummet straight down towards the tarmac, straight as stones.

'No drift!' Raka mutters triumphantly. 'Oh, well done, Dillu, no drift at all!'

And land smack in the middle of the runway.

There is an odd little pause.

Raka scans the ground in his buffeting MiG, his heart as heavy as his 'craft is light...

It's a dud, he thinks, devastated, his mouth as dry as cotton wool. Shit, so much risk and effort, and the damn thing went phuss ... God alone knows how long it had been rotting in the depot...

• • •

'It's a different sort of missile,' Julian reports, shading his eyes with his hand. 'No parachute attached.'

Tinka isn't interested in the missiles. She's on her feet too, all pretence of disinterest gone, trying to spot what the Gnats are up to. They're flying at a lower height, below the MiGs, zig-zagging merrily. The cocky one makes a particularly audacious dive, and, as the terrace full of spectators gasp in awe, she gives a choked laugh.

Mad, she thinks to herself, torn between pride and despair. Quite, quite mad.

'That's a remarkably well-thought-out strategy,' Julian wheezes from beside her. 'See, the Gnats are doing that sexy little shimmy to keep the AA gunners distracted while the MiGs drop their bombs.'

'What bombs?' somebody asks. 'Nothing's exploded yet.'

They stare at the airfield, eyes straining against the sun. As they watch, it seems to glow a dim but unmistakable orange and, a moment later, a dull booming sound reaches their ears.

Julian gives a dry chuckle.

'There she blows.'

• • •

The force of the explosion rocks Shaanu's Gnat. He goes higher, wincing at the deafening noise. Thick smoke has risen in a mushroom cloud from the tarmac, rendering him momentarily invisible to the gunners.

Above him the MiGGies are cheering on the R/T.

'It wasn't a dud!'

'Yayyyyyyy!'

'Rakaaaaa! Patakaaaa!'

Suspended in an envelope of heat and smoke, Shaanu shoots forward to clearer skies, then peels around and peers down gleefully to see what's happening below.

The airfield is still obscured, but it seems to be aflame. There is no sign of Gana. Has he been hit?

Shaanu noses in, looking anxiously for his wingman.

'Baaz, you idiot, get the fuck out of the area!' Raka yells from above him. 'They'll kill you or we will, you crazy basta—'

His voice is abruptly drowned out by a new blast of AA fire. The gunners who, confused by the Gnats, had started to fire unevenly, have regained their savage rat-tat-tat precision.

• • •

'One of the Gnats is hit,' Julian murmurs. 'See, he's limping away from the fight, I hope he makes it home.'

Tinka finds that she suddenly cannot breathe.

'The other one's wreaking havoc though.' Leo chuckles. 'Clearly enjoying himself, the cocky little bastard.'

She draws a ragged breath and gets to her feet.

'You're right,' she manages to say quite calmly even as she grips the parapet wall hard, so hard her knuckles turn white. 'He's definitely enjoying himself.'

• • •

'All four sets of twins delivered, ladies?' Shaanu enquires over the R/T, his voice steady but bubbling with adrenalin. 'Or are any of you still waiting to drop your load?'

Two of the MiGs still are, and they now dive and drop their bombs with pinpoint accuracy. The impact of the missiles shakes the earth and sends up a new mushroom-shaped cloud of smoke and debris.

'All done now,' Raka says. 'We *could've* managed without your little chin-chin-choo cabaret dance, but I admit it did help. Thanks, buddy.'

'Save the ass-kissing for when we get home,' replies Shaanu lazily. 'Drinks are on the MiGGies tonight.'

Smoothly, the formation rises up, up and away. There is

a hoarse cheer over the R/T when Gana limps in from the left, one wing hanging wonkily. As they begin their flight back to base, a pall of dust and smoke lifts from Tezgaon, and an incredible sight greets their eyes.

The FAB500s have lived up to their name. Circular craters, easily fifty feet in diameter, have opened up all along the tarmac – great gaping mouths with up-thrust, concrete lips. Deep, black cracks radiate out from the epicentre of each crater, like lightning bolts spread in a monstrous spider's web.

The Sabres of Tezgaon are well and truly grounded.

ELEVEN

With the PAF rendered more or less toothless in the eastern theatre of the war, the IAF's role changes somewhat. It now settles down to providing Close Air Support to the Army as it makes its way slowly through the countryside, avoiding the bigger towns, towards Dacca. Fighters from the MiG, Hunter, Sukhoi and Gnat squadrons circle over the fighting below, strafing with impunity, their Forward Air Controllers guiding them from the ground. Transport aircrafts paradrop soldiers and supplies. Sukhois carry out sorties by moonlight, and even the lumbering Caribou are enlisted to drop bombs in the pitch dark of night.

The strategy of the Indian generals is to harass and demoralize the Pakistani Army, keeping them jittery and off balance, constantly watching the skies, wondering where the IAF will hit them next.

The Caribou squadron is mighty chuffed at this new development – it's an exciting change from dropping food and ammunition. Only the best pilots are picked to drop the bombs – and Maddy is one of them! He tells Juhi this very proudly when he drops in to see her, in-between mouthfuls of the French toast and cold coffee she has prepared for him.

Her pretty face falls.

'Oh, now I have to worry about you too. Here I was thinking that what *you* do is safe at least!'

Maddy checks, fork halfway to his face, then continues to eat. He is certainly grateful for the piping-hot French toast, but what she's just said is mildly offensive. Flying the de Havilland Caribou is no easy task. It entails low-level flying through valleys and mountain passes in calamitous weather. Night flying in formation, the lights on each aircraft your only marker to prevent you from banging into each other! Inching through treacherous passes and ravines in the northeast, with the rain pelting down and cloud cover so thick it might as well be a brick wall.

'Well, it's less dangerous than the sort of stunts Raka and Shaanu are required to pull,' he says lightly.

'Raka told me you guys have a STOOL,' Juhi says, producing the newly learnt technical term with evident pride. 'It helps you get up and down easily, na?'

'STOL,' he corrects her gently. 'Short take-off and landing. Basically, we don't need runways. And we have a really tight turning radius too. So yeah, that does make life a bit easier for us.'

'I'm *so* glad.' She says it earnestly, and she really means it – but Maddy's ego takes a denting nevertheless, because clearly she thinks the job he does is less glamorous than the stuff the other two pilots in her life do.

'But *I* also want be a hero, Juhi,' he says in an uncharacteristic burst of self-pity. 'Save the day, win a medal. Gain the respect of all those crazy Kodavas back in Madikeri!'

The usually sympathetic Juhi snorts at this ambition.

'Just stay *alive*,' she says tartly as she picks up his empty glass. 'We don't need any more heroes – we need you to play the piano.'

Which, of course, makes Maddy feel even more deflated.

To make things worse, when he gets to the base the next morning, he finds his fellow pilots in the doldrums. News has come from across the border that one of the bombs the newly co-opted Caribou pilots dropped a couple of days ago landed in the civilian quarter and hit an orphanage. Children were hurt, some died. And model-turned-journalist Tehmina Dadyseth has just written a brilliant, damaging piece about it for WWS.

Damn, Maddy thinks disheartened, as he enters the briefing room. I should've stuck to growing coffee. Embraced the civilian life, never tried to pull this macho shit. Because, let's face it, I'm just not cut out for heroics.

He gets even gloomier when he discovers the mission for the day – dropping a small band of para-commandos close to Dacca. If anybody could be cooler than IAF Fighters like Raka and Shaanu, it is these guys with their dashing red berets and devil-may-care attitude. Hanging out with them will make him feel even more of a loser.

He is striding down the tarmac with his navigator when a hand lands heavily on his shoulder.

'My man, Subbiah!' a deep voice drawls into his ear. 'Thanks for the lift. Appreciate it.'

'Macho da!' Maddy's eyes widen as he turns around. He reddens at once. 'Shoot, uh, sorry, I mean Major Maqhtoom, *sir*!'

The lean, dark face, sunglassed as always, cracks into a dazzling white smile. 'I prefer Macho da,' says Macho da heartily.

Maddy is confused. The Mukti's all suited up and packing a parachute. His romantic curls have been pulled back into a no-nonsense ponytail.

'You're with the para-commandos?' he asks.

'Surrrre!' nods the Mukti, rolling his r's flamboyantly. 'They're landing in unfamiliar territory, so I'm going along to guide them. We'll have a blast, won't we, guys?'

The paras react to this question with expressionless faces. They're a crack team, the most elite force in the Army, and notoriously clannish.

Maddy puts on his aviators.

'Right, let's do this, Macho ... er, da. Load up, gentlemen!'

The paras board swiftly and noiselessly, like a well-oiled machine, and less than three minutes later the Caribou's Pratt and Whitney Twin Wasp engines kick in, it lifts off and rumbles towards Dacca.

The paras get busy in the rear, their leader barking out instructions, while Macho da sits up front with Maddy and his navigator, a forty-three-year-old Tamilian who doesn't talk much.

'So what do you make of the young lady's article on your 'craft?' the Mukti asks, his sunglasses glinting in the slanting morning sunshine.

Maddy shrugs. 'Fair, I suppose. She seems to have done her homework. She mentions that, overall, India has a pretty decent record as far as steering clear of civilian areas is concerned.'

'She's sweet on your friend, isn't she?' Macho da asks. 'That short guy – whatsizname, Gurbaaz? Shahbaaz?'

'Just Baaz.' Maddy grins. 'Maybe she is, I wouldn't know. Should we really be gossiping about who's crushing on who right now? I mean, there's a war on, and you're about to be flung out into the wild wild east.'

'Nah, I know this area like the back of my hand.' Macho da is all macho nonchalance.

'Then you probably recognize this terrain,' Maddy says, leaning forward and pointing. 'There's the fork of the Meghna and Padma rivers, and between them...'

'... is my sweet city,' the Mukti says softly. 'Oh, I've been away from home too long.'

As they begin to descend, he bounds away to the back of the Caribou, where the para-commandos are readying for their drop, doing last-minute checks on their rig and equipment, fussing over the massive crate of rum their quartermaster has packed. Maddy lowers the ungainly 'craft over the green jungle cover below, holding it as steady as he can.

He pulls the lever to activate the rear doors, but as they start to slide open, a furious hail of anti-aircraft fire rocks the Caribou.

It lurches and tilts forward dangerously. The para-commandoes are thrown forward, colliding right into Maddy and his navigator.

'Fuck!'

'Where'd that come from?'

'Take her up, sir, take her up!'

'Get out of my goddamn way!' Maddy shouts. 'I can't work the levers. Okay, here we go...'

Slowly, the Caribou starts to rise, and again it is rocked by an angry volley of ack-ack fire. Maddy's good-natured, grey-haired navigator slumps over on his controls, suddenly, decisively dead.

The mighty 'craft judders and drops sickeningly. Maddy can feel his ears pop.

'Sir, she's going down.'

'We have to jump!'

'*Now*, or we'll never land clear of her!'

The leader's voice sounds like a whipcrack.

'*Jump*, men!'

The damaged Caribou lurches again.

'You guys get out!' Maddy shouts. 'I'll hold her as long as I can!'

The paras start to drop off the plane, their commander bellowing instructions until he jumps off too, leaving Maddy and Macho da alone in the plane.

'Go!' Maddy tells Macho da.

'Not without you. Put the damn thing on auto.'

Maddy feels rough stubble against his cheek and smells warm whiskey-laced breath as he is dragged up the ramp and to the open rear doors beyond. Freezing cold air sweeps into the 'craft, reeking of the fuel that is leaking out of the fuselage. He can see the fluttering bodies of the para-commandoes falling into the flat dark-green earth below, their parachutes blooming *phut phut phut* like exotic mushrooms over the jungle.

'Not ... good,' Maddy chokes in a small dry voice. 'I don't ... like ... heights.'

A mighty gust of red-hot flame and oily black smoke shoots out of the doomed Caribou.

Macho da grips Maddy harder and takes a flying leap, right out of the flaming plane.

'Joyyyy Baaaaangla...!'

• • •

Patriotic jeweller casts solid gold medal for war hero son-in-law

In a touching move, Mr Om Pal Gehlot, a jeweller from Jhajjar, has cast a medal out of solid gold for his soon-to-be son-in-law, a fair, handsome IAF Fighter who is far away from home and loved ones, fighting Pakistanis at India's border with Bangladesh.

'My daughter's fiancé, Flying Officer Ishaan "Baaz" Faujdaar, led India to a mighty victory during the air battle over Boyra,' Mr Om Pal told this reporter. 'His picture came out in the papers, standing in front of his plane, wearing the gold chain and medal which we presented to his family as rokka. The medal was created by myself for him, out of solid gold. It has an etching of a soaring eagle on one side and the Ashoka lions on the other, along with the legend "Baaz pe Naaz hai". Even the Param Vir Chakra – India's highest military medal – is not made out of solid gold – but this is.'

Replicas of the medal, engraved with the message 'Har Baaz pe Naaz hai' are available for sale at Gehlot and Sons, Jhajjar Main Market Sarai, Haryana.

'I would request all families with serving sons to buy these for them,' Mr Gehlot said.

In these dangerous days, some fathers would cavil at giving their girls to our air warriors, but not Mr Gehlot. When quizzed on this, he replied, 'I am a deeply patriotic man. I dreamt of joining our Armed Forces but couldn't because I have flat feet. Even if my daughter is widowed, she will be the widow of a patriot.'

He also mentioned that he will cast another Baaz-pe-Naaz-hai medal in a teardrop shape if Flying Officer Faujdaar perishes in the conflict.

'I hope families buy it for the widows/children of their fallen sons,' Mr Gehlot said.

'What the fuck is this?' Ishaan is white-faced with anger. 'What is this crap, Sneha behenji? Who is this vulture Gehlot, and what is he *talking* about?'

'Oh, that.' Sneha's voice sounds faraway. 'Yes, what about it?'

Shaanu strides about the sentry box, walking as far as the short phone cord will allow him. 'What *about* it? He tricked me, and you *knew* – don't deny it – and you let me think the chain was a gift—'

'It wasn't a gift,' she interrupts him, her voice still listless. 'The family came home and did a rokka. They gave us fifty thousand rupees and a brand new Bullet. Shelly has been driving it around for a month now. I told you about the girl, she's my friend. She's kind and pretty, and she knows English.'

'Sneha behenji!' Shaanu's voice is raw with betrayal. 'How could you?'

'How could I *what*, Shaanu Bhaisaab?' Her voice grows teary. 'Arranged marriage is good enough for me but not good enough for you? Where was all your modern thinking when *I* was being married off?'

'*What?*' He rakes the hair back from his forehead, then takes a deep breath. 'Sneha, are you unhappy?'

'*No,*' she replies wretchedly. 'But I want to do my B.Ed., and they say I cah … cah … *can't!*'

'Shit.' Shaanu slumps to sit on the pavement.

'My mother-in-law says she won't have a masterni in the house.'

And so? Shaanu thinks to himself. You're miserable, so you decided that I should be miserable too?

Aloud he says. 'I'm sorry, behenji, I let you down.'

'It's fine,' she says. But her voice is flat.

'What do you want me to do?' he demands. 'Do you want to *leave* him? I'll support you, if that's the case! You can do a B.Ed., get a job—'

'I'm perfectly happy, thank you very much.' Her voice grows hostile. 'And as far as your rishtaa is concerned, it's just a rokka. Nobody has married you off yet, have they? Say no to pitaji and call it off, if you want.' Her voice grows bitter. 'You're a man, you have that choice.'

And she cuts the line.

Ishaan stares at the phone, racked with disbelief and frustration, then slams it down with a bang.

Damnit!

He sits down heavily on the barrier, indifferent to the gaze of the sentries.

She's right, he thinks, through a haze of disappointment and pain. I *can* call it off. It's a childish trick and I won't be trapped into it.

What hurts, though, is the deceit. He'd actually thought that bloody Chimman Singh and he were finally in a good place. That maybe the old man, the only parent he's had since he was eight, finally had a little respect and even love for him.

But he'd been fooling himself, clearly. The so-called gift – he'd torn it off his neck as soon as he saw the article – had actually been a noose round his neck.

And Sneha had known! Had the little ones known too? Sari and Sulo and Shelly? Do any of them love him at all?

He rakes his hands through his hair and stares down at the road with furious, unseeing eyes.

'Baaz?'

'What?' Ishaan snaps, too angry to look up or modulate his voice. '*What* is it?'

Raka shambles up, his gait very unlike his usual crisp stride. 'Nothing.'

Ishaan looks up and frowns.

'What are you doing here? Don't you have a sortie in half-an-hour?'

'I do,' Raka says, his voice subdued. Slowly, Ishaan takes in the fact that his chubby cheeks are sagging, his eyes look bewildered. 'Baaz, buddy, we just got some bad news. Maddy's plane went down. Nobody knows what happened to him.'

• • •

Gawky, sixteen-year-old Maddy, clasping hands for the very first time with Raka in the NDA dining hall. Bewildered when the servers asked if he was a 'Meater or a Non-Meater'. Persuading Raka to say he was a Meater too, so he could scarf down Raka's quota of meat as well as his own. Guffawing shirtless in his bed as Raka scrapes away at his plentiful stubble in their cracked mirror, thanking his south Indian gods that he isn't as hairy as his friend. Getting teary-eyed when he hears the national anthem play, then swearing at his mates for laughing at him. Banging on the piano keys, looking incredibly handsome, an unlit cigarette dangling from the corner of his mouth, singing 'Why why why Delilah?'

'Gentlemen, we have received information that the PAF Sabres are back in the skies. The Hunters from Hashimara encountered three of them early this morning. As Tezgaon has been totalled and there is no way the PAF can fly here from West Pakistan without stopping to refuel, we can only surmise that they have carted their Sabres by road from Tezgaon to the small, disused runway of Kurmitola close by. The Mukti Bahini reports movement along the road linking Tezgaon to Kurmitola and feverish activity in Kurmitola itself. Your task today is to crater this airstrip and nip the nascent revival in the bud.'

'Yes, sir!'

Aerial shots of the runway at Kurmitola appear behind Carvalho on a slide projector screen.

'Raka is leader. Chatty, you're wingman. You will replicate the steep-glide dive pattern and bombing procedure we employed at Tezgaon. Of course, you'll have to watch out for Sabres. A piece of good news, though – the PAF's anti-aircraft guns are running low on ammunition so they can no longer do the sort of damage they did in the first few days of this conflict. So you're flying safer now than you were before, lads!'

The MiGGies nod.

On the football field, shirts versus skins. Raka in possession, racing towards the goal, Maddy coming in out of nowhere, knocking down a defender Raka hasn't seen. A goal, a triumphant roar, and a bloody-nosed Maddy being carried away on a stretcher, their sweaty hands clasping as he grins. 'Nobody fucks with you except me.'

Ten minutes later, they strap on their parachute packs and stride out to the waiting jets.

'Not bad for the Pakis, eh?' Chatty tells Raka. 'They're putting up a fight! I'm glad this happened – things had gotten a bit flat, na Raks?'

But Raka is staring ahead of him blankly.

Chatrath leans in. 'Raks?'

Raka looks around.

'I heard about Subbiah.' Chatrath's voice is sympathetic. 'Hard luck. I know you guys were course mates.'

'Yeah.' Raka voice is hollow. 'Course mates and roommates.'

Chatty claps him on the back. 'They'll find him, yaar,' he says bracingly. 'Before New Year's Eve, for sure. I can't imagine a New Year's party without Maddy on the piano, making the rest of us look like a bunch of charmless yokels!'

This makes Raka smile. Then he says, his voice slow

and deliberate, like he's making a solemn vow, 'Chatty, I'm not coming back down till I've pulverized the last of those bastards to talcum powder.'

Chatrath looks a little taken aback at this vehemence, then nods determinedly. 'Me neither, brother. Let's *go*.'

They slap palms, mount their ladders and drop lightly into their leather seats. As he pulls on his fighter gloves, Raka's notices that his palms are damp.

'Happy hunting, sir!' his airmen shout out as they stand away from the MiG.

'Jai Hind,' is his terse reply.

Twenty minutes later, they are flying over the location where Carvalho and the other strategists in the briefing room suspected Kurmitola to be. But there is nothing below, just the usual tangle of silent greenery. The MiGs descend lower, keeping a watchful eye out for the large circular water tanki that had figured prominently in the photographs from the briefing. It is nowhere to be seen.

Maybe they've camouflaged it somehow, Raka thinks as he scans the landscape below. If we could camouflage the entire Taj Mahal, what's one measly tanki?

He drops even lower and fires an exploratory round of fire into the wilderness below. Chatty follows suit.

Immediately, AA fire bursts up around them in angry white puffs. It's like they've stirred a hornet's nest.

Idiots, thinks Raka scornfully as he accelerates, zooming up and away, gaining G, burning fuel, so he can come back in his steep-glide dive. I know where the tanki is now, it's that extra-smooth bit of roundness just *there* beside the gunners, covered in green-and-brown gunny bags. I can't possibly miss it, it's so *obvious*, how dumb do they think we are – shit, where is it?

He blinks, rubbing his eyes. The 'tanki' has merged back with the rest of the foliage. Whoever has done the camouflaging has done a good job.

Lemme just go by the coordinates provided, he decides. Forget about identifying the thing.

He does as much, dropping his bombs on what he hopes is the right spot. So does Chatty. The AA guns don't let out so much as a splutter. Maybe they've run out of ammo, or maybe they've realized they're giving their location away.

'Do you think we got it?' Chatty asks Raka, breaking radio silence as they start to approach Kalaiganga.

Inside his cockpit, Raka shrugs, too cheated to reply. He'd really wanted to notch up a scalp or two today, but it seems their luck is out. On top of that, the weather has just gotten weirder. Dark clouds are floating around them, and the MiG is bouncing like a madman, the springs inside Raka's leather-upholstered seat squeaking madly with every bumpity bump.

'I hope so…' he starts to say, when some kind of sixth sense makes the hair at the back of his neck prickle.

And then a Sabre rises out of the mass of cumulonimbus swirling around them, engines screaming, claws out, glinting a gun-metal grey that's almost the same colour as the clouds.

'Holy shit!' Raka veers madly.

The thing is filling his gunsight – he can take a shot, but if he hits it, the debris will explode right in his face, taking him down with it.

Cursing dementedly, Raka starts to barrel upwards. The Sabre keeps pace with him, its heat-seeking Sidewinders trying to get a lock onto the moving MiG. Raka rolls and roils, moving constantly, trying to increase the distance between them. Chatty's plane is nowhere to be seen.

Utterly disoriented, with no bearings of what is horizon, earth or sky, Raka continues to climb, bouncing against the rolling clouds. Then he levels off and, manoeuvring hard, manages to position himself behind and above the Sabre, though it costs him so much fuel he's worried his Bingo lights will come on any moment now. Miraculously, they don't. The Sabre fills his gunsight again, and he presses the release button.

The MiG recoils as the missile shoots out, and, in delighted disbelief, Raka watches the Sabre judder as it takes a direct hit.

He whoops as gleefully as a chubby little boy whose Holi balloon has found a hapless target.

'Take that, you bastard! That's for Maddy – and that's for Dil and—'

And then the MiG lurches sickeningly and falls out of the sky...

• • •

'Apparently he was very brave.' Juhi's voice is high and tight.

'He downed a Sabre. Chatty told us.'

'That's...' Ishaan voice is a savage whisper, 'great.'

Juhi sniffs. Her pretty face is very pale, the flyaway hair that always manages to come free of her plait fluffing up like a halo around her face.

'He'll get a medal for sure,' she continues in the same thin, tight voice. 'An MVC, maybe even a PVC – won't he?'

'Yeah,' Ishaan agrees.

She smiles brightly.

'That would be so cool!'

They are standing in the corridor of Ward No. 4 at the Military Hospital. Raka's MiG went down very close to Kalaiganga, and he was rushed to the MH by the villagers.

He has second-degree burns, two fractured ribs and severe oxygen deprivation. He also told the hospital staff, just before passing out, that there was no sensation in his arms and legs. The doctors don't expect him to make it.

'Juhi.' Mrs Pomfret and Mrs Carvalho come hurrying down the corridor, out of breath. 'Juhi dear, we're so sorry.'

'Don't be,' Juhi says with frightening poise. 'I'm a Fighter's wife. I know what I signed up for.'

Bade risk waala job hai, beta! They fly such small, undependable planes, not even pressurized properly. His ears will burst, his lungs will rot, he'll be dead before he's thirty.

The two older women exchange distressed looks.

'Yes. Uh, beta, we've sent for your mother. She'll be here by tomorrow.'

'My mother!' Juhi says blankly, like she's forgotten she has a mother at all. Then she frowns. 'Baaz, Raka has to shave. He says you can't appear before your father-in-law-mother-in-law with stubble on your cheeks, it's not respectful.' She whirls around. 'I have to go home and get his shaving kit.'

'I'll get it, Juhi.' Ishaan's voice is steady. 'Just tell me where it is. I'll get you everything you need.'

'No!' Juhi grabs Ishaan's arm, her soft brown eyes blazing with sudden fire. 'This is not the time for you to be running stupid little errands!'

'Okay,' he replies in the same steady voice. 'If you don't want me to, I won't.'

She shakes him hard.

'*You* report back to duty and go up in the air and kill as many Pakistanis as you can! You hear me?'

Mrs Pomfret makes troubled tut-tutting sounds at this bloodthirsty speech and tries to hug the girl, but Juhi shakes her off and moves away, wrapping her arms around her body, shaking with fury.

'Just *get them*, Baaz.' Her voice is shrill. '*Promise* me!'

As the older women watch, distressed, Ishaan nods at Juhi, his young face growing resolute, his grey eyes hardening.

'Mujhe Jezu, kaale sangta yeh chedu?' Mrs Carvalho looks suddenly haggard behind her jauntily applied make-up. 'Is this some melodrama going on over here? You're both talking like foo—'

'I promise.' For once Ishaan Faujdaar forgets his impeccable officer-and-a-gentleman manners and rudely cuts off a senior officer's wife mid-speech. Then he places a hand over Juhi's trembling one and adds, his voice unusually grim, 'I'll get them, Juhi. I really will.'

• • •

Squadron Leader Bilawal Hussain's father, a retired lieutenant colonel from the British Indian Army, often told his son that there are only two types of officers in any army: Come-ons and Go-ons. Come-ons are the officers who stride ahead of their troop towards the enemy lines, every now and then turning around to exhort their men to 'come on, come on!' while Go-ons are like the officers who lag behind their men, prodding them forward from the rear, urging them to 'go on, go on'.

Bilawal has been raised by the old soldier to be a Come-on, and that is why he now finds himself, yet again, in a situation where he has to persuade a bunch of doubting, pessimistic people to follow his lead.

He is a tall, dark and brown-bearded man, an ace pilot who cut his eye-teeth during the 1965 war against India. He is a proud recipient of the Sitara-e-Jurat, Pakistan's third-highest gallantry award. He has no religious beliefs as such, believing more in basic human goodness than in anything he's ever read in the Quran. He is twenty-eight years old, a fan of West Indian all-rounder Gary Sobers and famed Indian tragedy queen Meena Kumari. He is also the second-in-command of the Sabrejet Squadron at Tezgaon and a very frustrated man.

'Sir, our runway is beyond repair, to be sure, but the good news is that our jets are unharmed. We have here seven Sabres, fully fuelled and equipped, with skilled pilots on standby, itching to fly them up and strike a blow for Pak sarzameen! All I ask for is a chance to use them.'

His boss looks at him irritably. He has no great affection for Bilawal. It's a pain in the arse having a junior officer who has won so many medals for valour.

'Bilawal, don't rabbit on like a goddamn Byronic hero,' his boss snaps. 'Those Sabres are grounded. They might as well not exist.'

Bilawal sticks out his jaw mutinously.

'We could get them airborne.'

'How?' demands his commanding officer. 'The runway's as pitted as a golf ball with smallpox.'

Bilawal Hussain hesitates, his lean cheeks flushing. 'Sir … with your permission, I have a little idea.'

The CO throws up his hands. 'We've already tried your little idea! We carted the wretched Sabres to this dump just like you wanted us to! But the Muktis figured out our location and gave it away to the Indians, and they bombed our ass off yesterday! We're running low on AA ammo! I don't think anybody will point fingers at us if we throw in the towel now.'

But to Bilawal, this is unthinkable. He has lost two of his

closest friends in dogfights with the Gnats. Several of his course mates have been injured. He *has* to get back into the sky and even the score.

'We got them good day-before-yesterday,' he says doggedly. 'Three kills in all. Two Hunters, and I'm pretty sure that MiG didn't make it back in one piece! It put the josh back into our lads.' He leans in, his gaze intense. 'We can still destroy them, sir!' Then he hesitates – the time has come to mention a particularly wild scheme that has been cooking in his head for a while now. 'Sir, there's a pretty good four-lane road right behind the airfield, the one that links us to the national highway. We could take off on that...'

'The highway!' The CO looks appalled. 'Some rubbish East Pakistani highway? That is the stupidest idea I've ever heard! That road wasn't built to withstand so much pressure. It'll crack on the first take-off!'

Bilawal's long dark face grows even darker.

'But sir, I've already stationed three Sabres there—'

'Enough!' roars the CO. 'I've had enough of this stupid, glory-hunting crap! We're closing this place down! Are *you* my 2-I-C or am *I* your 2-I-C?' He glares at his second-in-command, veins bulging terribly inside his temples.

Bilawal doesn't reply, choosing to avert his gaze and glare furiously at a spot above his CO's head.

They stand there, clearly at an impasse.

And then, through the carbon-papered window, drifts in the distinct sound of a Bristol Orpheus engine...

• • •

It doesn't take Ishaan long to locate Kurmitola. The sun is out, visibility is good and the water tanki shows up cleanly as he makes a low pass in his Gnat over the coordinates given at briefing.

The airstrip, painted a dull camouflage green, is easily identifiable from the air. It is thoroughly cratered, a sight so sweet that Ishaan's heart tightens exultantly in his chest.

'Oh well done, Raka, mere tiger,' he mutters. 'Good for you.'

A repair crew is hard at work over the tarmac, jointing slabs and pouring cement, but even from here, Ishaan can tell that the airstrip will not be repaired before the Indian Army appears on the scene. Further, the AA guns are silent, one more thing for Ishaan to be happy about.

The mission he's been given this morning is to assess the damage done by Raka and Chatty yesterday, and this has already been accomplished. Kurmitola is clearly ruined. Ishaan can go back home and make his report. But he is loathe to leave the site of what could be Raka's last fight so soon.

'Yoo-hoo!' he crows as he pulls up from his pass over the silent, defeated airfield. 'Sucks to you, bastards! Take *that*, Pakis!'

Somehow, this doesn't feel as good as it should. There is a savage satisfaction tightening his chest, to be sure, but also a distinctly sour, hollow feeling in the pit of his stomach.

Determined to make the moment count, Ishaan turns to do a second pass and executes a series of victory rolls directly over the ruined runway. Light and nippy, the Gnat can famously roll faster than any other comparable aircraft, and Ishaan's manoeuvre is an unmistakable gauntlet thrown down at any other pilot watching.

'Fuck you,' he yells inside the dizzyingly rolling aircraft. 'Fuck *you*, and *you*, and *you*!'

• • •

Bilawal Hussain rushes to the window and eyes the gleeful Gnat with a mixture of anger and disbelief.

The cheek of the Indian bastard! Performing victory rolls over our ruined airfield!

As he watches, AA fire kicks in from down below, but the Gnat seems to be impervious to it. It comes back for a *third* pass, audaciously, and fires a short burst at the AA gunners.

Bilawal wheels around and snaps to attention. 'Permission to take down that johnny, sir!'

The CO sighs and waves a hand in dismissal. 'Permission granted.'

• • •

The Sabres come out of nowhere. Three of them, gleaming like airborne sharks, sunshine bouncing off their gun-metal grey flanks. A weird adrenalin-fuelled gladness surges through Ishaan at the sight of them.

'Perfect,' he whispers to himself, stepping on his rudder pedals and starting to weave this way and that. 'Here we go.'

The Sabres are still a mile or so away, within missile range but all in his front hemisphere, so not in position to lock missiles on him yet. He heads challengingly towards the lead Sabre, the one in the middle of the formation, weaving just enough to keep the angles between them changing, frustrating any chance of missile lock.

But the Sabre refuses to peel away, as it would if it were trying to find a safe position from which to launch missiles. Instead, it bores equally determinedly in towards Shaanu, making him blink and purse his lips in reluctant admiration.

'Ready for a knife-fight, eh?' he mutters. 'But I'm here to kill, not get killed, you bastard.'

He will have to play it smart. He is low on juice already, having done all those passes over the airfield, while these blokes are fully fuelled and daisy fresh.

As the four fast-moving Fighters flash together into a

head-on merge, all four break. Ishaan and Bilawal pull into tight, twisting turns, each trying to get behind the other. The other two Sabres go wider – an obviously calculated tactical move.

Ishaan is pulling hard, five Gs … now six Gs, perilously close to the Gnat's rated maximum; and as his vision blurs, he indistinctly registers a smoke trail as a Sidewinder shoots out at him. The missile doesn't track; he is probably too close, and the angles are changing too fast as he pulls Gs. But it feels good. Since Tinka left, since Maddy vanished, since Chimman revealed himself to be a total asshole, since Raka got injured, this is the best Ishaan has ever felt.

Inside the lead Sabre, Squadron Leader Bilawal Hussain is pulling equally hard, intent on getting behind the upstart Gnat. He recognizes the pilot's aggressive style, and is as sure as can be that it is the same cheeky upstart who distracted the AA gunners on the day Tezgaon was cratered. The Indians got lucky that day, but Bilawal is determined to squash this bastard today. The stretch of highway he and the other two Sabres lifted off from has shattered from the impact of their take-off. Bilawal is not even sure he'll be able to land back on it safely. He pops his manoeuvring slats open, sets his sights on the diminutive Gnat and grimly waits for his gunsight predictor to light up.

Bilawal's wingmen have pulled wider, not attempting to close to guns range, their missile seeker heads still looking for the heat sources that are enemy exhausts. 'I have tone,' Bilawal's wingman calls shortly over the R/T, using the American codes the Pakistan Air Force has adopted. 'Fox Two!'

Sidewinders hurtle at Ishaan from two different directions. Reflexes on hyper-alert, he breaks to the east, straight at the morning sun.

'Goodness gracious, great balls of fire!' he chortles as he hurls his aircraft literally straight at the sun. This is a much-discussed Indian tactic, which sometimes works to confuse the heat-seeking sensors of early-model Sidewinders. The missiles lock mindlessly onto the intense hotspot of the sun, in preference to the tiny exhaust of the little Gnat, and go ballistic, speeding past Ishaan's Gnat, hissing angrily like the snakes for which they are named.

Bilawal's Sabre, powerful as it is, cannot quite match the Gnat's whiplash break, and he has to watch the Gnat dwindle and vanish into the dazzling brightness of the sun. He closes his manoeuvring slats, to maintain speed. Has the Indian gone home?

For a few moments, all is quiet above Kurmitola. The Sabres circle, scanning the skies like gliding eagles. Bilawal's Number 2 and 3 formate back on him. Time seems to stand still. The sky glimmers golden, shot through with streaks of pigeon-blood red.

And then Ishaan Faujdaar comes screaming out of the sun, releasing one short 30mm cannon burst and then another into Sabres 2 and 3. Both are mortal hits, sending them spinning and plummeting out of the sky.

Bilawal is dumbfounded. Blinking rapidly, loathe to believe what he is seeing, he struggles to get behind this devilishly accurate Indian. The good part, he tells himself, is that the bugger's almost certainly run out of ammo – the Gnats carry only about three seconds' worth of shells. This is the perfect time to get him.

Ishaan's slashing attack has carried him well below Bilawal's Sabre. Bilawal plunges after him, satisfyingly on the Gnat's tail for the first time in this combat. He frames the Gnat in his sights, hears the missile tone change and then lets the Sidewinder go.

It shoots out in a blaze of heat and slams, sweet and straight, into the tail of Ishaan's Gnat.

'Gotcha!' Bilawal's voice is hoarse with triumph. 'Take *that*, you bastard!'

The Gnat starts to plummet, looping crazily as it tries to recover. Inside the bucking plane, Ishaan curses, wrestling with the controls, hanging practically upside down as he tries to turn his nose back onto the Sabre.

But it's no use. He's all out of ammo now, dangerously low on fuel – his Bingo lights have been on for several moments – and the aircraft is only just responding to the controls. The Plexiglas of his cockpit is starred and cracked in a dozen places, and he can barely see out of it. The Gnat is lurching in a sick, random, non-rhythmic fashion, and he will probably lose control completely before long.

The Doors start to play inside Ishaan's head.

'Unborn living, living dead,
Bullet strikes the helmet's head.
And it's all over for the unknown soldier.
Aanhaaa!'

'Chutiya bloody song,' he mutters, shaking his head like a puppy that's got water into its ears.

There is only one last thing he can do.

For Maddy. For Raka. For Juhi.

He pulls back on the stick, the gain in G almost making him black out. The lead Sabre is behind him, pulling up to follow, but cannot match the Gnat's pull-up.

With a blood-curdling yell that would've frozen Bilawal's blood solid if he could've heard it, Ishaan drags one last wing-over out of his doomed Gnat.

Bilawal feels the heat before he sees it. Imperfectly controlled but still lethally, the belly of the Gnat crashes against the canopy of his Sabre, shattering it into a hailstorm of fragments and leaving him exposed to the blast of the bitterly cold air.

'Taraan!' gasps Bilawal. He has heard of aerial ramming, a technique employed by Soviet pilots during the Second World War, but he's always thought of it as a demented, vodka-fuelled fantasy. It is a last-ditch manoeuvre, frankly suicidal, using your whole plane as a weapon against another in the sky. He has never seen anybody do it before, and here is this cocky Indian, half his size, taraaning the shit out of him!

Bilawal cannot breathe, the blast of air at hundreds of knots pinning him back in his seat, but in the few seconds of consciousness left to him is ready to return the compliment. Two can play at this game. If the Indian wants to end it like a pair of drunk drivers banging their trucks together on the Lahore–Rawalpindi highway, Bilawal is more than willing to give him a run for his money. He's done for anyway, at least he'll take the bastard down with him.

An image of his two beautiful young daughters, dressed as Little Bo Peep and Little Miss Muffet for a fancy dress competition, rises before his eyes. He closes his eyes – he can barely keep them open against the roaring slipstream, but he savours the memory for a moment – and when he opens them again, just a crack, they are pitiless. With hands and arms already stiff from the icy air blasting through his broken cockpit, he points the Sabre higher. Then he slams his throttle forward and smashes his nose straight into the belly of that goddamned bhinbhinaoing Gnat.

TWELVE

The hospital ward is quiet, the only audible sound in the still of the night the chirruping of crickets outside and the beeping of monitors within. It is a cold, sterile, tubelight-lit space, the faces of the occupants seeming to reflect the green of the curtains and linen.

Here, on bed number four, flanked by a JCO with a badly shattered femur and a young major half eaten away by frostbite, lies Flying Officer Rakesh Aggarwal, stretched out almost at attention, dressed in the Military Hospital's regulation-issue striped pyjamas, his brave moustache meticulously trimmed and curled, his chubby, cheerful face curiously still and defenceless.

Slumped on a metal armchair beside him is Juhi, pale and exhausted, too emotionally wrung out to do more than hold her husband's hand and listen without really listening to the conversation in the corridor outside, where the relatives of various patients are huddled together on a row of wooden benches.

'Bauji, the leg will have to be cut off for sure.' The voice belongs to the JCO's elder brother. 'Bata rahe hain ki the whole femur is khokla, khattam, finished! I've seen the X-ray, some pieces of the bone are so small you could use them as toothpicks.'

'But Munna won't let them cut it off,' replies a thin, anguished voice. It is the JCO's father. 'Keeps asking for his gun and saying ki if those AMC butchers come near him, he'll blow their heads off.'

'They'll sniff him some chloroform and pass him out,' says the first voice calmingly. 'Otherwise the poison will spread, you understand. The wound's got infected – if they don't cut it off, he'll die.'

'He's dead already!' the father cries out with violent grief. 'Such a fit, handsome lad, newly married, so good at volleyball. His mother shouldn't have let him play langdi taang – it was a *bad bad* omen!'

'At least he's already married,' his elder son points out practically. 'You have a tidy dowry all safe and invested, and a good daughter-in-law. And now he will get a gas agency also – the gourmint will give. He won't have to work again his whole life.'

'Finished,' says the father bitterly. 'It's all finished! Mera Munna, my boy, my pride and joy, can a bunch of gas cylinders compensate for several strong grandsons? Who will take forward the family's name now?'

The brisk, rallying voice of the matron-on-duty floats into the ward.

'Arrey, he's only lost one leg. Middle wicket intact hai uska! Don't lose hope! Take him home, his wife will manage it all very nicely, I promise you.'

'I'm your son too, you know,' the elder son says quietly.

'Chup kar!' replies his father aggrievedly. 'Pretending

to be so sad, but inside your heart, big big laddoos of joy are bursting! You were always jealous of Munna – brave, intelligent, handso—'

'Is this any way to talk?' the matron interrupts in disgust. 'Shame on you, uncle! This fellow is your son too, and your other son's elder brother!'

'Oh I'm used to it, sister,' the son replies easily. 'Bauji despises me because I've only produced three daughters, but they're my pride and joy!'

'Daughters!' The old man gnashes his teeth. 'Bah!'

After a moment the son says, 'Bauji, Munna's afsar told me that he's recommended him for a medal, a Vir Chakra. If he gets that he will be awarded five acres of fertile agricultural land by his home state, isn't that good news?'

There is a long pause.

'Really?' There is strength in the old man's thin voice for the first time.

'I wouldn't get my hopes up on that, you know,' remarks a fourth voice, a deep, clipped rumble that belongs to a colonel from the infantry. 'They'll find some excuse not to give you the agricultural land – or they'll say there isn't any land available right now, so please take money instead. And the rate they will offer you will be rubbish – only about thirty paisa per acre or something equally dismal. *I* know, it happened to a course-mate's son during the '65 war. He got *both* his legs shot off and was awarded a Mahavir Chakra. I'm not trying to be competitive, you understand, just giving you the exact facts so you're clear – and he's *still* chasing the IAS babus for his ten acres in Punjab.'

This long speech is met with much tsk-tsking (by the matron) and several aggrieved mutters.

'At the end of the day,' the colonel sighs gustily, 'a medal is just a metal disk, while a leg … well, a leg's a leg.'

Silence. The colonel has comprehensively ended all conversation for the night.

Inside the ward, Juhi's attention wanders. She stares at Raka and remembers a picnic Raka, Maddy, Baaz and she had gone on at the beginning of the year.

They'd zoomed out of the base at five in the morning on three motorcycles, zipped up in leather jackets and swathed in mufflers.

She'd packed boiled egg sandwiches with lots of coleslaw, their favourite, and a big pineapple upside-down cake. On the back of Baaz's bike was an icebox stacked with chilled beer and Fanta.

They'd played Frisbee and cards, and (on Juhi's special request) a rather raucous game of Stappoo. Once they'd polished off the food and drink and were sitting tired and happy by their warm campfire, Maddy had produced a mouth organ and played it as the sun went down. She'd looked at the three of them, laughing, joking, sharing the chores with such easy camaraderie, and felt … full. With these three men in my life, she'd thought, I am complete. Please God, let Baaz and Maddy marry nice women – not prettier than me but not *too* plain either, or they'll resent me – women I can get along with, basically, and then we'll all have lots of children, and when the boys retire we'll get houses close to each other in some nice, green and leafy Jal Vahu Vihar-type Armed Forces scheme and be happy forever.

And now, this.

A cold, white hospital ward, the smell of disinfectant, the reek of blood…

Baaz lost, Maddy lost, and Raka…

Here with her, but not here with her at all.

She grips his unresponsive hand tighter, her eyes dry, beyond tears.

I'm responsible for Baaz crashing. I am, I really am. I said some very stupid things to him – I realize they're stupid now. Are you listening?

Her eyes scan his face. Raka lies there, his chest rising and falling gently.

'Come back to me,' she is whispering out loud now, her voice fervent. 'The doctors say that's almost impossible, but doctors don't know anything, do they – all that studying makes them stupid. You'll get up, Raks, and you'll be fine, and even if you're not initially, you'll *become* fine! And look at the bright side,' she gives a wild little laugh, 'at least your middle wicket's intact! I'm praying and fasting for you. Ma says that's silly because I need my strength, so I sent her away, I sent away Mrs Carvalho and Mrs Pomfret too. I'm praying for Baaz and Maddy and all the others. My prayers have great power, Ma always said so, and it's true – I used to pray for easy questions in the board exams and they always came, and I used to pray that you would fall in love with me and you did, and whenever we played teen patti, I prayed for good cards and I always got a trail! Remember?'

'Didi?'

She looks up.

It is the JCO's elder brother.

'I'm going to the canteen to get chai. Would you like a cup?'

Juhi nods.

'Yes, please.'

He gives her an awkward sympathetic smile and walks away, the sound of his chappals echoing down the corridor, and Juhi goes back to her vigil, the little burst of earnest bargaining with God over, the sick, cold numbness descending again, more desperately unhappy than she's ever been in her young life.

• • •

There is mud in his mouth. Gritty, squelchy mud. When he tries to spit it out, the back of his throat hurts agonizingly. Ignoring the pain, which feels like somebody has taken his tonsils out, grated them raw with a kaddoo kas and shoved them down his throat again, he manages to spit, cough and rise to his hands and knees.

It is dark.

How can it be dark? It was morning just fifteen minutes ago.

One of his shoulders is hurt, he can't tell which one. It is throbbing with a pulse that is beating through his whole body as loudly as a parade ground drum.

He stays on his hands and knees for a while, like he is about to take young Jaideep Singh horsy-back riding, and scans the little bit of Bangladesh he's fallen into.

It smells green and clean and wet.

And doable.

Pushing down on the moist ground with his palms, he tries to get on his feet and ends up flopping back weakly on his face into the mud.

When he awakens again, the sun is out and a trio of very Indian-looking crows are studying him with their heads cocked to one side, swaying on the ends of a long grassy plant.

Putting out a hand, Ishaan tries to greet the crows, and immediately wishes he hadn't.

His throat is on fire.

The crows fly away and study him from a distance, their eyes brightly enquiring.

Clutching at his throat to make it hurt less, he manages to roll over onto his stomach and stare up at the sky.

It is a clear day, perfect visibility. But nary a plane in sight.

He props himself on his elbows and surveys his surroundings.

There's the tangle of parachute ropes and material in a little puddle around him, and beyond that, fields of paddy as far as his eyes can see.

It's almost ready to be harvested, Ishaan can tell. The ears are heavy with grain. He breaks one off and chews on it; it is like chewing particularly crunchy grass. Rice *is* a sort of grass, he remembers. Nanaji had told him that years ago.

Damn, his throat hurts.

Wiping the sweat off his face with his sleeve (why is he sweating, it's really cold!) he unbuckles his parachute and sits up shakily.

His mind starts to issue nagging little instructions.

Drink some water.

Piss.

Ditch your IAF overalls.

After doling out these orders, it also feels the need to update him on other stuff.

Tinka hates you, you poor bastard.

Raka's probably dead.

So is Maddy.

You knocked down three Sabres.

This last makes him pause and grin.

Three fucking Sabres!

Yes!

He scans the field of ripening rice. It is alive with humming insects but not much else. Even the crows seem to have flapped off somewhere. Surely the Pakistani pilot he'd taraaned should've fallen around here too? Where is the bugger? Lurking in the long grass clutching some lethal weapon?

'You'll never know if you don't get to your feet, Shaanu,' he says out loud, his voice sounding raw and croaky even to his own ears. Also, he has reverted to Haryanvi, which is weird because he hasn't spoken it in years. He repeats the sentence in Hindi and in English, feels a little more in control of the situation and manages to haul himself to his feet.

Panting lightly from the effort of standing up, he studies the area. The paddy looks flattened in several places. It is high enough to hide a human being, but certainly not high enough to hide a downed plane.

'East is thataway,' he mutters to himself, squinting at the sun. He has some dim recollection of the fork between the Meghna and Padma rivers – surely it lies in the east? 'So then … I should go … *this* way.'

As he stares blankly at *this* way, he spots, through the gently swaying ears of paddy, the unmistakable glitter of sunshine on water.

Water!

Electrified, he stumbles towards the water through the squelchy paddy and drops down at the edge of what turns out to be a gushing tubewell. Plunging his hands into the stream of bubbling water, he takes several long reviving gulps and then slumps down in relief onto the wet earth, leaning back against the tubewell's cemented wall.

There is a body in the tree.

Ishaan's ragged breathing catches, for almost an entire minute.

The body is hanging head down, the legs tangled among

the lower branches. Its parachute is draped limply on the top branches, filled with puddles of water. Its hands dangle, almost touching the earth, its fingers look cold and white and clearly dead.

It is dressed in PAF overalls. There is a name stitched into the slightly singed lapel on its chest.

Bilawal Hussain.

An hour later, Shaanu in leaning nonchalantly against a milestone on a winding country road lined by fields of verdant paddy. He is dressed in the uniform of an officer from the Pakistani Air Force, with the insignia and pips of a Squadron Leader. Under his overalls is a white Bangladeshi kurta-pyjama and around his throat is a silver tabeez on a black thread.

A black three-wheeler tempo, tricked out as gaily as a bridegroom on his big day, comes phatpatting merrily down the broken road.

Wincing a little at the throbbing in his left shoulder, Ishaan puts out his arm and raises his thumb stylishly.

• • •

The Tempo Traveller driver is singing a song about lovers rendered asunder. It features a beautiful village belle, a dashing potter and a lustful older woman who is obsessed with the dashing potter. When our hero spurns the older woman's advances (because she's married to his elder brother), she chham-chhams sneakily into his kiln and poisons the clay he has been working with. The poison leaks into his blood through his fingers and kills him. The village belle, seeking to feel closer to him, drinks from the last pot he had been shaping and dies too.

The chorus, a maudlin, lustful piece about how we all come from clay and return to clay is sung by all the passengers in the tempo in mournful gusto. They close their eyes, shake their heads and thump their hand against their chest to the beat. They all sit up, rather put out, when the tempo slows down.

'Ki holo?' one of the passengers, an old gentleman, hunkers lower and peers through the windscreen.

'Soldier,' the driver grunts. 'West Pakistani.'

The ancient gent, travelling with a bevy of veiled womenfolk, leans forward, breathing heavily. In a tone far removed from the mood of the song he has been singing, he growls, 'There's no space for him here.'

Having said this, he closes his eyes again and goes back to giving the chorus all he's got.

On the road, the soldier now holds out a crisp ten-rupee note.

The driver slows to a wistful crawl. Customers are customers. He's pretty sure he can squeeze in the soldier if everybody would just adjust a little.

He says as much.

The passengers start to argue loudly. Some men are in favour of stopping for the soldier, some are against. Then the burly burqa-clad lady sitting next to the ancient gent points with a shaking finger, and exclaims, in blood-curdling accents, with an exquisite flair for the dramatic:

'Rokto!'

'There's blood on his shirt. Look!'

Everybody peers at the soldier. Some offer the opinion that the 'blood' is just a design on his overalls, others think it might be mud.

Meanwhile, the soldier twiddles his fingers a little, and the one ten-rupee note reveals itself to be *two* ten-rupee notes. The thin, angular face of the Great Leader, very distinguished in his karakul hat, twinkles benignly at the driver in the sunshine.

The driver halts.

'I cannot insult Quaid-e-azam like this!' he declares decisively, beckoning to the soldier. 'You! Soldier! Come!'

The elderly gent grunts disapprovingly.

'Anything for money,' he shakes his head. 'Pull your veils down properly, all of you! Too much wind is blowing today!'

The Pakistani soldier runs lightly up to the tempo and clambers in beside the driver, squeezing onto half his seat and putting his unhurt arm around the driver's neck chummily.

'Shukriya,' he says. 'I need to get to Dacca.'

The driver takes the tenners that have been dangled so negligently and slips them into the breast pocket of his Pathan suit.

'Work the gears,' he tells the soldier laconically.

'With pleasure,' the new arrival responds.

'What happened to your shoulder?' one of the slimmer veiled ladies ask.

The soldier smiles, a brave, dashing smile.

'Just a small wound that I was proud to get for my country,' he says whimsically.

'*Which* country, that's the question,' grumbles the ancient gent.

The soldier turns to face him.

'I'm a loyal son of Pakistan, janab.'

'*Which* Pakistan, that's the…' the old man starts to mutter, but he is drowned out by a loud whisper from the burly lady beside him.

'Oho, can't you see he's wounded? He can't do us any harm. Let him be!'

The old man subsides.

The soldier smiles gratefully at the lady and then reaches forward and squeezes the bhompu of the tempo. It responds with a musical wail.

The soldier turns and grins at the driver. It is possible that his grin is met with an answering gleam, somewhere behind the beard and the kohl and the inscrutable stare, but one cannot say for sure.

The driver proffers a small tin of jet-black kohl. The soldier, without missing a beat, dips his little finger into the goo and lines the rims of his lower eyelids with it.

'Bah! Ki bhalo kawta chokh,' murmurs the burly lady, who clearly seems to think the Pakistani soldier is cute.

And truth be told, he is. Very cute.

The tempo restarts.

The driver resumes his plaintive love song. The passengers join in with gusto on the chorus, swaying as one to the beat.

• • •

'Two an' two – twenteh-two.'

'Four an' five   forteh-five.'

'Seven an' three – seventeh-three.'

'Nikka's heart isn't in it today,' Julian whispers wheezily. 'What is this bland, monotonous calling out? Whatever happened to two little ducks, twenty-two, and goodness me, forty-three and all that?'

'I'm surprised he's even here, grandfather,' Leo drawls in reply. 'Everybody knows he's up shit creek without a scrap of toilet paper.'

'The crowd's looking thinner too,' Tinka whispers, looking around the Defence Club lawns. 'Hardly any people today – wow, things are moving fast.'

Things are indeed moving fast. In the eastern theatre of the war, the PAF has been brought to its knees. The Indian Army is surging forward, knocking on the gates of Dacca. The Pakistani generals' gamble – that attacking India in the west would result in weakening her focus in the east – has failed dramatically. Rumour has it that President Yahya Khan and Foreign Affairs Minister Zulfikar Ali Bhutto, the man who was so comprehensively defeated by Mujib ur Rahman in last year's election, have stopped taking Nikka Khan's calls. Nikka and his boss, the Governor of East Pakistan, are increasingly being isolated. There is no sign of Chinese intervention either, and the Americans seem to have restricted their support to mere sword rattling.

'He keeps licking his lips today,' Julian whispers. 'Look – like a snake, there he goes again, *sshviccck!*'

'All men are snakes,' Tinka says suddenly in a hollow voice.

Her two colleagues exchange glances.

Tinka has been acting very strange recently. Ever since she received a phone call from her aunt two days ago, to be exact. Julian and Leo don't know what she said to her, but whatever it was, it has turned her all dark and care-a-damn-ish. Yesterday she had rushed out to click pictures of a flare-up between the Pakistani Army and the Muktis in the street behind the hotel without even bothering to put on a bulletproof vest, and almost got herself killed. And tomorrow, she's planning to visit a very unsafe part of old Dacca, where none of the other journos have yet dared to go.

'Surely not?' Julian says gently. 'I grant that some men are like this seedy, ancient lecher here, but some are sporty and healthy and clean – like me. Just keep the faith, eh, Tinka?'

'Shushhh,' she replies, her eyes still on the general. 'Ugh, he does flick his tongue over his lips rather snakishly.'

Nikka shakes the numbers drum and produces another number.

'Six an' nine – six-teh-nine.'

'No risqué sixty-nine jokes?' Leo rues. 'Aah, poor Nikita Khan, my heart goes out to him! But why are the shammi kebabs taking so long to come?'

'Maybe because your credit here isn't good,' Tinka says tartly.

'There he goes again!' Julian nudges Tinka. '*Sshviccck!*'

Now that Julian has pointed it out to her, Tinka finds Nikka's lip-licking quite hypnotic.

'Five an' three *sshviccck!* Fif-teh-three.'

'Seven an' eight *sshviccck!* Seven-teh-eight.'

'Two an' nought *sshviccck!* Twen-teh.'

'That has got to be the quickest Tumbola ever,' Leo remarks as he studies the little group of players, all struggling to keep up with the speed of the call-outs. 'These poor ladies are moving their heads so fast from line to line, I'm worried they're going to give themselves whiplash.'

'They should just discontinue it,' Tinka says crossly. 'It's so silly, all this false bravado when basically everybody is shivering in their shoes, waiting for bombs to drop on their heads.'

Presently the game gets over and the crowd rises to its feet to line up for the buffet lunch that has been laid out. On the stage, Nikka puts away the numbers drum and downs a glass of water.

'Do you think he'll talk to us?' Leo's chubby face looks doubtful. 'He's not mingling with the guests, and he has all those gun-toting guards. Not to mention that massive-impassive ADC – the fellow looks seven feet tall.'

'We'll talk to *him*,' Tinka says firmly. 'C'mon!'

The others look at her uncertainly.

'What?' she demands.

'Are you counting on flooring him with your charm?' Julian asks diffidently. 'Because, unchivalrous as it is to point this out, you're not exactly looking your best.'

This is putting it politely. Tinka, since the afore-mentioned phone call from her aunt, has turned into a bit of a slob. She has been wearing the same baggy food-stained shirt for the last three days, her hair looks greasy, her eyes wild and bloodshot. They are pretty sure she hasn't bathed in a while.

Tinka snorts.

'I can handle generals. My dad's a general. C'mon.'

She strides up to Nikka as he descends the podium and calls out in a cheery, impossible-to-ignore voice from behind her camera, 'General, surely not a good time to be playing Tumbola?'

Nikka stops, looking cornered, but the presence of the two white men behind her has its usual edifying effect. He smoothens down his hair and smiles for the cameras.

Sshviccck!

'I don't see why I should disrupt my regular schedule because of a few fractious Indians,' he says smoothly, even as he checks out Tinka from chest to toe, then looks away dismissively.

'You were sort of rushing through the number-calling today,' Julian remarks in the plummy, uber-brit voice he adopts during interviews. 'Any particular reason?'

'I never rush,' Nikka replies superbly.

Leo tries a different tack.

'Looking a bit black for Pakistan, though, isn't it, sir?' he says sympathetically.

Nikka draws himself up.

'Not at all.'

This is met with a stumped, incredulous silence. The general licks his lips again and continues smoothly, 'It's pretty much even-stevens at the moment, I would say.'

Tinka almost snorts aloud but manages to control herself.

'Could you please elaborate?' Julian asks politely.

'Kindly do me the courtesy of not interrupting,' says the general, rather unfairly, because Julian has not been interrupting. 'Fatalities on both sides are equal. You must be aware that our ally America is pushing for ceasefire resolutions in the UN Security Council. When that happens, India will have to immediately stop its forces from advancing and capturing Dacca. International pressure will force them to sit at a negotiating table, vacate all captured territories *and*,' he licks his lips again, 'pay us millions of dollars in war damages.'

'The Soviets will never let that go through,' Leo says immediately. 'They'll veto it for sure.'

'But *why*?' Nikka's eyes bulge. 'India poked its nose into our private business, *they* attacked our country without any provocation whatsoever!'

'General, refugees have been streaming into India right through the years—' Julian starts to say when Tinka interrupts him.

'But won't there be less loss of life if you just surrender now?'

He has more or less ignored her so far, talking only to the blond and blue-eyed 'foreigners', but now he deigns to make eye contact with her.

'We will never surrender, madam,' he says disdainfully. 'Pathans do not know the meaning of surrender.'

She shakes her head impatiently, dismissing this for the hyperbole it clearly is.

'But sir,' she leans in, her voice soft, her bloodshot eyes sympathetic. 'Your mother and sisters suffered so much during the Partition. Surely they wouldn't wish that sort of horror on other women and children?'

Nikka's jaw drops.

His face goes white, then very red.

Behind him his guards tighten their holds on their guns.

'Bluddy hell,' Julian mutters, putting up his hands and pulling Tinka back. 'You have no concept of personal space, wench.'

'We were just leaving,' Leo chimes in cheerily. 'Nice meeting you – goodbye.'

The two of them turn around, tugging at Tinka to come too.

But she stands her ground, refusing to look away from the general.

'Break that woman's camera,' Nikka says in a strangled voice.

It is done in a moment. Nikka's ADC, a seven-foot-tall, wooden-faced man-mountain, steps forward, plucks the Lecia out of Tinka's hand and breaks it in one economical move.

It makes a noise like a bone being crunched.

'If you are *so* troubled by violence against women and children, madam,' the general's voice is all silky malevolence, 'may I suggest you leave this country during the four-hour Red Cross-mandated ceasefire tomorrow night? Because after that, things will get, how should I put it, *messier*.'

• • •

Shaanu's tempo rolls into the city of Dacca late in the evening. The other passengers have disembarked along the way, and he is now sprawled right across the back seat. As the tempo travels down the largely deserted streets, the driver turns around and addresses him, his voice faintly ironic, 'Where now? Hospital?'

'You could call it that,' Ishaan says. He is tired, his body feels clammy, his shoulder is throbbing. The bumpy ride has confirmed what he already suspected – something jagged and sharp is lodged inside his wound. He sits up and rubs his knuckles into his grimy eyes. 'You know, the kind of hospital where I can get girls, booze and a good time.' He winks.

'A red-light area?' the driver says, puzzled. He jerks his head towards the bloody shoulder. 'Shouldn't you get that attended to first?'

Shaanu shakes his head. 'Too ... many ... questions ... will be ... asked.'

There is a short silence. Then the driver gives a nod.

'Okay. I'll take you someplace.'

They drive on in silence and turn into a crowded, noisy street some ten minutes later. Chaat and boiled-egg thelas jam the pavements, doing brisk business. Groups of men mill about in the small booze and beedi shops beyond, their eyes glued to the ladies lounging in the wooden balconies upstairs. Naked bulbs twinkle overhead gaily, adding a festive touch. Skinny yellow street dogs nose about busily in rubbish heaps. Music plays loudly. A decrepit yellow board declares the place to be English Road.

'Is there a party?' Ishaan asks, peering out of the tempo.

'There's a party every night.' The driver chuckles. 'You should be safe enough here, they don't mind Indians.'

Shaanu's eyes widen

'I'm not Indian.'

'And I'm not a fool.' The driver's voice is dry. 'Only an Indian infiltrator would stand at the road waving brand-new ten-rupee notes. Who carries so much money around in these hard times?'

Shaanu chuckles and pushes his hair off his forehead. He is starting to feel rather feverish.

'Th-thank you.'

'Mention not,' the driver replies. 'I used to have a wife and sisters. Now, I don't. I hate these bloody West Pakistanis.'

Ishaan clasps his hand, his eyes glowing with gratitude.

'Please … you've being so helpful … tell me where to go!'

The driver pulls his hand away. 'Go to the Dawakhana,' he says hurriedly.

'Dawakhana?' Ishaan repeats. 'For treatment, you mean? I don't believe in all that quakery.'

But the driver's eyes have started skittering around nervously. He gives Ishaan a little push. 'I've said enough. Now, go. Go!'

'Shukriya.' Shaanu gets out of the tempo.

It feels both strange and commonplace to be walking along a crowded street in the enemy's city. Everybody looks so … *Indian.* The street dogs. Even the food. Shaanu still has some Pakistani currency left, so he heads for a food stall and places an order. Sitting on a low parapet around a peepal tree a little later, he chews on a bread pakoda, watches everybody have a good time around him and wonders what to do next.

Should he try and get to the Indian High Commission? Or make for the border? Or stay put? Dacca is clearly tottering. If he can get the treatment he needs and lie low for even a week, the Indians will get here and take the city. Yeah, lying low and staying put is the best plan.

Except that he is not very good at lying low. Should he look for this mysterious Dawakhana?

What would be *really* good, he thinks restlessly as he strokes the edge of his wound gingerly through his overalls (it feels hot and wet and sore), is if he could *help* in some way, be a part of the final assault, strike a blow against the guys who got Maddy and Raka! Yes, that's what he will do!

But after he has sat here for a while and rested himself.

It's nice here under the peepal tree. His belly is pleasantly full with bread pakora as good as any he's had at home, and his body seems to have untensed itself. If only the pain in his shoulder wasn't so intense. It's started to throb like a bastard. He can feel a pulse beating between his ears, a pulse so loud that it has drowned out all other sound.

Sweat trickles down Shaanu's brow.

His eyes droop, he slumps against the peepal tree.

Around him, English Road continues to party.

• • •

The three girls have the evening off. They are to entertain nobody but themselves tonight, their madam has decreed in a fit of uncharacteristic generosity, and that is exactly what they intend to do. Like a trio of buzzing hummingbirds, they descend upon English Road, in their net chunnis and bright nylon ribbons, and get down to milking its many pleasures with gusto. Nine plates of sweet-sour puchkas have been consumed, some pretty wool purchased to knit sweaters for their children, and now they're sitting under the big peepal tree, leaning against its wide trunk, sucking on bright orange ice lollies and arguing about whether they should see a picture or take a walk down the sari-sellers' street, which is looking so pretty tonight, all festooned with glowing gas hurricane lamps.

'I want to buy a yellow silk sari, the colour of marigolds,' declares one of the girls.

'To get married in?' asks another.

This is met with gales of laughter. Marriage is an institution none of them believes in any more.

'I want to see *Shakuntala*,' says the third decisively. 'It's mythological, not like other pickchures. Watching it is like praying or going to the temple.'

'You've never been to a temple in your whole life!'

More laughter.

'Cholo cholo, what should we do?'

'Open the rum!'

'Oh! And dip our orange bars in it!'

'Good idea, here, take the bottle ... arrey, where did it—*ore baba re*!'

A shocked hush follows as they take in the young man lying unconscious against the other side of the peepal trunk, a big patch of blood staining the front of his shirt.

'Is he dead?'

'No, he's breathing, look.'

'But barely. He's hot.'

The other two giggle.

'Horny girl! I mean he has *fever*.' Her voice goes from concerned to doubtful. 'Do you think he could be from ... *across the border*?'

The other two giggle again, unfazed by the suggestion.

'Let's pull down his pants and check.'

But before they can act on this tempting suggestion, a rough voice calls out from behind them.

'What's all this? What's going on here? Who's that fellow? What are you girls up to?'

Girl number one quickly throws her chunni over the bloodied chest of the unconscious man.

'He's had too much to drink,' she calls out to the policeman saucily. 'No capacity, you know. Don't worry, officer!'

The portly cop frowns at them for a moment, then nods and passes along. The girls breathe a sigh of relief.

One of them sprinkles a few icy-cold drops of the melting orange bar on the unconscious man's face.

He winces. His lashes flutter open. They all suck in their breath admiringly.

'Ki shundor chokh!'

Ishaan coughs weakly. His gaze flits from one hard, bright face to the other, then he decides to take a calculated risk.

'Joy ... Bangla,' he says hoarsely.

The girls look at each other and nod.

'Let's take him to the Dawakhana.'

• • •

The decrepit two-floored old house stands in the middle of a small scraggy garden full of thorny grey rose bushes set around a broken birdbath. It is small and surly looking, with the flat roof typically found in north Indian kothis. There are ornate cement jaalis and exposed plumbing pipes with pigeons roosting in them. Yellow pigeon droppings streak the walls.

The hand-painted sign at the gate reads HARRY ROSE KHANDAANI DAWAKHANA but somebody has scratched out the original writing to read HAVASKHANA instead. Indeed, there are signs of lust everywhere, or rather posters proclaiming the efficacy of Harry Rose's remedies for:

- small pennis
- dry vageena

- nightfall
- penile limp
- premature ejection

The three good Samaritans hustle Shaanu into the house through a rickety door and sit him down on a bench in what seems to be a reception area. They give the metal bell placed there a vigorous shake, then turn around and hurry out as fast as they can.

'If we rush we can still catch *Shakuntala*.'

'But I want to buy a bright yellow silk sari…'

'To get *married* in?'

As their giggles fade away, Ishaan opens his eyes and looks around the waiting room dazedly. It is lit with a harsh tubelight that casts an uncompromising light on its occupants – a thin, miserable-looking, gulping youth, a middle-aged merchant in a too-tight coat and a wiry old man sitting hand in hand with a burqa-clad girl. On the wall is a black-and-white portrait of a moustachioed gentleman who, Shaanu assumes, must be Harry Rose himself, standing next to Jawaharlal Nehru in front of Lahore Fort.

A blue bulb lights up above the iron door at the end of the reception and, immediately, both the merchant and the old man spring to their feet.

'We're next. Come, begum!' The old man pulls his young wife to her feet.

'Rubbish! *I'm* next!' huffs the portly merchant.

The miserable boy sits there listlessly, clearly resigned to going last.

The old man turns on the merchant.

'Ei lala! I came earlier than you!'

'Dadu, get some treatment, or you'll be coming early your whole life,' the lala says rudely.

Shaanu, weaving in and out of consciousness, nevertheless manages to chuckle at this sally. This enrages the old man even more.

He waggles his cane combatively.

'Better early than never, fatso!'

This causes a giggle to emerge from within the young begum's burqa. Mortified, the lala throws out his chest, ready to explode when the door below the flashing blue bulb flies open. Framed inside it is the most beautiful woman Ishaan has ever had the good fortune of beholding.

She has huge, doe-like eyes, full lips, a heaving bosom and a figure that swells and dips in alarmingly voluptuous curves under a jewel-toned silk kaftan. A lock of grey runs through her mane of glowing dark hair. She could be any age between thirty-five and fifty.

'Quiet please, dearies.' Her voice has the soft, husky-musky melody of small-town Bihar. 'Let the compounder decide who the next patient is, hmmm?'

She turns towards the front door and bellows in a voice as imperious as it is unexpected, 'Abbe, compounderrrrr!'

And vanishes back into her room.

A moment later, the front door opens with a slow, complaining wail and a sleepy-looking man in a monkey cap puts his head into the room.

'Tea break,' he explains apologetically to the room at large. He sounds like he has a cold. He also sounds very familiar. Shaanu whirls to look at him, forgetting his shoulder for a moment and regretting the sudden movement instantly.

'Let's do this one by one, in an orderly first-come-first-served basis, please!' the compounder continues with the air of somebody who does this every day. 'The doctor will see everybody, beginning with…'

He pauses. He has just noticed the newest patient.

Ishaan stumbles to his feet, a hesitant, painful question in his fevered eyes.

The compounder stares at him for a moment, then slowly removes his monkey cap to reveal a dark, handsome face. A face that bears a remarkable resemblance to Pat Boone.

Ishaan's face lights up.

Flying Officer Madan Subbiah sags against the wall, swallows hard and says simply, 'Beginning with *this* very sick man here.'

• • •

'How bad are his injuries?'

Ishaan sighs. 'Bad, brother. Second-degree burns, two fractured ribs and severe oxygen deprivation. Also…'

He pauses, shaking his head.

Maddy leans forward.

'What? Tell me, Baaz!'

Shaanu looks up, his eyes tortured.

'Also he told the hospital staff, just before passing out, that there is no sensation in his arms and legs.'

'*Jeezus.*'

Thoroughly depressed, Maddy slumps against the edge of Shaanu's stretcher.

They are in the makeshift operating room inside the inner office. Behind them, the beautiful lady doctor is busy preparing all the equipment she requires to dress Shaanu's wound.

'How's Juhi taking it?' Maddy asks. 'Is she okay?'

'Stop badgering him.' The doctor's voice is severe (but

still sexy). She pushes him aside and moves closer to Shaanu, unbuttoning his overalls and easing them off his upper body. 'Can't you see he's in pain? Just hold the tray and stop worrying – worrying is an absolute waste of time. As for *you* – oh my, you're a handsome one.'

This, on sighting Ishaan's exposed torso.

He grins up at her lopsidedly.

'Yuh ... are ... Bihar or east UP, no?' he asks as her tantalizing perfume assails his nostrils. 'You don't talk ... you sing.'

Her winged eyebrows fly up.

'Quite the flirt aren't you, dearie?'

Ishaan's grin widens. 'You started it. Are you ... a *proper* doctor?'

She throws back her head and laughs. A rich, strong laugh. The silver streak in her hair tumbles forward, and she has to tuck it behind her ear.

'No!'

'I like your hair,' he says next. The shot of rum she'd given him to dull the pain has taken full effect by now. He feels like he's floating on a cloud of candyfloss.

'Thank you.' But her voice is distracted. She feels around his wound with quick, cool fingers, her touch oddly soothing.

'It isn't infected, is it?' Maddy asks worriedly from behind her.

'No no.' She raises her large doe eyes to meet Shaanu's. 'You washed it?'

He nods. 'In cold water, several times, just like they taught us in the commando course.'

'*Good* boy!'

'I want to see,' Maddy demands.

She sighs. 'Have a peek then.'

Maddy pushes his way in and peers down at the exposed wound.

'Ugh.' His face goes an unhealthy white. 'Baaz, brother, I...'

He backs away quickly, his expression queasy.

'Wimp,' she scoffs. 'Run away if you can't handle it.'

'I'll stay.' Maddy sets his jaw.

'It doesn't hurt that badly.' Shaanu struggles to sit up and stares down at his wound critically. 'It looks like the cakes my sisters turned out when they just started baking – kind of cracked and uncooked and oozing in the middle.'

'Well, that's put me off cake for life.' Maddy looks green now.

'Hold the tray steady.' Her rich voice is calm but commanding. 'Can you feel something in there, dearie?'

Shaanu nods.

'Shrapnel. A chunk of Sabre fuselage, I think. I couldn't get it out.'

'But I can.' She feels around the wound, palpating it, and snaps her fingers together. 'Tongs.'

Maddy stares down at her 'instruments' tray and doubtfully holds up something that looks suspiciously like a chapati turner.

'This?'

She nods and reaches for it.

'Yes.'

Maddy wards her off.

'Promise me you're not living out your doctor-doctor fantasies by using my friend as a guinea pig.'

Her dark eyes snap.

'Give that to *me*!'

But he holds it away, out of her reach.

'You heard what he said! My one best friend's already badly injured. Baaz is the only other best friend I've got left.'

She leans in, all earnest sympathy. 'I'll *fix* him. And your other friend will recover too, inshallah. We're wasting time. Give me the cheemta.'

'I *knew* it was just a bloody cheemta,' Maddy says, handing it over. 'Tongs, indeed!'

'*Thank* you.'

She takes it, bends down and looks into Shaanu's pain-glazed grey eyes, her own liquid and luminous. Her husky voice, which was surely made for saying far sexier things, whispers, 'Dearie, your tissues have already started growing around this thing, so this will hurt. Be brave now…'

• • •

Shaanu wakes up with a start to the sound of a loud crackling, followed by an equally loud clearing of the throat, and then the sonorous call of the muezzin rings out with full vim and vigour in his ears. Clearly there is a mosque right next door.

He groans, raises himself up on one elbow and looks around the tiny room drowsily.

It is a spartan little space. Early morning sunshine slants in through the latticed window high up in the wall, highlighting the grey Young India underwear drying on a washing line running diagonally across the room. There is a stove on the floor, in the corner. Next to it lies a cloth bag, lumpy with onion and potatoes. A tin, dusted with flour around the rim. And at the foot of Shaanu's bed, a prone figure, sprawled out face down on a cotton gadda.

Maddy.

Thank God the bugger's alive and okay.

Even as Shaanu gazes down at his friend with a full heart sending up this heartfelt prayer of thanks to the Almighty, Maddy stirs, farts and covers his head with his ratty, grime-stained pillow.

'Man, how deaf are the faithful?' he grumbles. 'This guy's gonna burst my eardrums one of these days.'

The muezzin probably hears this complaint through the paper-thin walls, because the azaan cranks up a notch, now becoming so loud and high-pitched that Ishaan can feel his back teeth rattle.

'What the hell.' He sits up. 'How long will this go on?'

'Oh, he stops and starts and stops and starts the whole blessed day,' Maddy says. 'Just get used to it. How're you feeling, buddy?'

Shaanu thinks about his injury for the first time since he woke up.

'Good,' he reports in surprise. 'The pain's kind of dull now. Not stabbing through me, like before.'

'Excellent!' Maddy's brown face lights up with relief. 'Now sit up and have some tea.'

Ishaan looks at his friend questioningly, there's no tea in sight – but then footsteps sound on the stairs and a large, fat man in a white kurta and no pyjamas appears in the doorway. He is carrying a tray on which are three chipped enamel mugs, brimming with tea. Smiling gently, ruddy cheeks glowing, he holds it out to Shaanu.

'Shukriya.' Ishaan takes the tea, privately thinking that the man looks exactly like Santa Claus. Or Guru Nanak, for that matter.

'Who's he?' he asks Maddy, as they both sip their tea a little later, sitting in a patch of sunshine. The pyjama-less man has wandered away to wring out wet clothes from a bucket and hang them on a wire stretched across the terrace.

Maddy scratches his head. 'I think he's a bit retarded,' he says finally. 'Everybody calls him Front Room – because he lives in the front room downstairs, opposite the dispensary. Sometimes he comes out in the evening to light crackers with the street kids.'

'He looks Afghani,' Shaanu says. 'A full kabuliwallah. Or Russian or something – what *is* this place anyway? A dawakhana or a safe house for Muktis?'

Maddy sips his tea.

'Both, I think.'

There's a pause.

'Maybe Raks is getting better?' Maddy's voice is determinedly cheerful as he returns to the topic that has been troubling him all night. 'I mean, you thought I was dead, and here I am, safe and sound! Maybe the AMC guys are taking too grim a view of his condition?'

His soft dark eyes probe Shaanu's painfully.

Shaanu looks away.

He thinks of Raka, still and waxen. And Juhi, her eyes glazed and fevered, sitting by his bed. A shiver runs through him, despite the warm winter sunshine beating down on his back.

'Maybe.'

'When I get back, we'll get him the best treatment,' Maddy declares in the same doggedly cheerful voice. 'I'll make my dad cough up the dough! Forget the Base Hospital, we'll fly him to the best centre, in Bombay, abroad, in London, even!' A thought strikes him. 'Arrey, what am I saying? When he sees I'm alive and well, he'll be so happy he'll recover at once! Like *you* did, right, Baaz?'

'Uh, right.' Ishaan shifts restlessly. He doesn't want to talk about Raka. 'Listen, tell me what happened with you, yaar. All we heard was that your Caribou got hit while it was dropping off a team of paras.'

Maddy puts down his mug, immediately distracted.

'Yes, that's what happened,' he says. 'And I had a scenic little ride down – except that I had to inhale the aroma of Macho da's armpits all the way, which sort of marred the beauty of the experience a bit. But whatever! We landed, unhurt. And *then* things started to get strange.'

Shaanu's eyes narrow. 'Matlab?'

'Matlab Macho da guided the paras to where 14 Punjab was holed up, all right and tight. Then he told me he had a secret mission in Dacca and that I should accompany him to help fulfil it. He says he's my commanding officer now.'

Shaanu's jaw drops.

'What the hell! You could've seen such great action with the paras! Those guys are the best!'

'No, Baaz.' Maddy shakes his head. 'Macho da's right, he *is* the senior officer, and he says that his business in Dacca is extremely vital to the cause and that I should help him achieve it.'

Ishaan looks dubious. 'What cause?'

'*The* cause!'

'Didn't he tell you what it is?'

'He will, eventually. But not now because he says we might get captured and reveal it to the enemy, under torture.'

Shaanu throws back his head. 'What a load of war movie crap!' he says in disbelief.

'War movies aren't crap.' The deep drawl makes them both turn around. Macho da is standing in the stairwell, dressed for prayer, in an exquisite chikankari kurta pyjama, a white namazi cap perched on the back of his head. 'Most of them are based on real events. And reality is mostly stranger than fiction. Coming to this particular situation, I saved your friend's life. I saved *your* life too – that isn't an exaggeration. My doctor tells me your wound would've turned gangrenous if it hadn't been attended to. Why not trust me a little?'

His eyes, revealed to be bulgy, thin-lashed and honey-brown now that he's no longer wearing dark glasses, bore into Ishaan's.

'I'm not ungrateful, sir,' Ishaan says steadily. 'But our loyalty is to the Indian Armed Forces. The Mukti Bahini is a separate, independent outfit...'

'Working in tandem with the Indian Army,' Macho da reminds him. 'We've joined forces. Together, we're now called the Mitro Bahini, remember.'

Shaanu continues to look doubtful. 'Yeah, but—'

'Can you repair wireless radios?' Macho da changes the subject abruptly.

Ishaan shakes his head, surprised. 'No, sir, I can't. Is yours giving trouble?'

The Mukti's expression stays unchanged, but Shaanu gets the sense that he's disappointed.

'Never mind. Hopefully I'll get hold of a new mechanic today. I have to go say my namaaz now. We'll talk later.'

He jerks his head at the pyjama-less Front Room, then turns around and goes down the steps. Front Room smiles his saintly smile at Maddy and Shaanu, scoops up the enamel mugs and exits too, his empty bucket slapping against his bare legs. Ishaan stares after them.

'When did Macho da get so namaazi?'

Maddy shrugs. 'I think he always was.'

Shaanu continues to look sceptical.

'And what happened to the old radio op?'

'They had to shoot him. He was a traitor.'

Shaanu's jaw drops.

'What the fuck!'

Maddy grins. 'Just kidding. The guy went AWOL.'

'What does he need a wireless radio for, anyway? Is he spying on the Paki radio chatter?'

'I guess,' Maddy replies. 'Maybe that's part of the mission.'

When Shaanu says nothing, he adds, his voice slightly pleading, '*She's* nice though. I like her, she has a certain…'

'… *je ne sais quoi*,' Shaanu completes the sentence automatically, his accent honed by years of practice. He looks at his friend, and his frustrated expression changes to a fond one. 'You'll never change, will you, bastard? But yes, for once, I agree, she's lovely. But is she a proper doctor?'

'What's proper?' Maddy's expression grows dreamy. 'My thoughts about her are highly improper!'

'A quack, then?'

Maddy frowns at his friend. 'She's a BAMS,' he says with great dignity.

Ishaan throws up his hands.

'Matlab? Whamz Bamz, thank you maamz?'

'A Bachelor of Ayurvedic Medicinal Science,' Maddy rattles off glibly. 'A five-year degree, including a one-year internship.'

'Tujhe bada pata hai,' Shaanu smirks.

Maddy flushes.

'Nothing like that, yaar. She's with Macho da, anyway. I *think*.'

He shoots Shaanu a speculative sideways glance.

'How about you?'

Ishaan looks away.

'What about me?' he repeats truculently.

Maddy glares.

'*Tinka* about you!'

'I don't fancy the lady doctor, if that's what you're worried about!' Shaanu sweeps on, ignoring this interjection. 'She's all yours, and she likes you, I can tell!'

But Maddy refuses to be distracted, even by this delicious bait. 'What about Tinka, Baaz? She's in Dacca – you know that, right?'

'Is she?' Shaanu says indifferently.

Maddy sneaks him another sideways look and says, with careful casualness, 'In the designated neutral Red Cross zone. She wrote a piece on our Caribou bombing an orphanage. Did you see it?'

Shaanu's lean cheeks flush. 'No. And anyway, that doesn't sound like she's sympathetic towards India.'

'Tinka is the most sympathetic person I know,' Maddy replies, a little surprised.

The blood starts to throb inside Shaanu's ears.

'Yeah, you two got along so well,' he hears himself say. 'Both so *rich* and so *educated* and such great readers and writers and *cultureds*.'

Maddy looks at him uncomprehendingly.

'Baaz,' he says finally. 'Whatchu *saying*, brother? There's nothing like tha—'

'Let's drop it!' Shaanu interrupts him, suddenly very fed-up. 'I'm not interested in girls. There's a bloody war going on, and a mysterious mission, and a muezzin going ballistic behind us. Let's just focus on that, shall we?'

• • •

'*Balls* I'll leave the country,' Tinka says the next morning. 'Why should *I* leave the country? Who does that pig Nikka think he is?'

'Call me old-fashioned, but I find the sound of a woman swearing deeply unattractive,' Julian says, clinging onto the brace handle at the back of the bumpy taxi with all his might. 'Do desist, my dear. *Please.*'

'You *are* old-fashioned,' she returns darkly from the front seat. 'Sexism! Chauvinism! Pathanism! All men are snakes.'

'What's with this constantly recurring all-men-are-snakes motif, huh?' Leo speaks up from the back. 'What is bothering you so much, Tinka?'

But she just wraps her arms tighter over her chest and doesn't reply.

The taxi hurtles on for another twenty minutes or so, then comes to an abrupt stop at a seedy street in Dacca's old town.

'Oh Lordy.' Julian peers out of the grimy window. 'English Road. Indeed! There doesn't seem to be anything very English about it – remind me again why we're here, Ivan?'

Leo rolls his eyes and fiddles with his camera.

'Ask *her.*'

But Tinka has already wrapped a shawl over her head and shoulders, leapt out of the cab and headed down the street like a woman with a purpose.

'Harry Rose?' She grabs a lounging rickshaw-puller by the arm. 'Harry Rose Dawakhana? Kothai?'

He points wordlessly. Tinka thanks him and moves on. Julian and Leo attempt to follow in her wake but are swamped by a crowd of half-cajoling half-threatening pimps, each one insisting the goras visit their house for a heavenly ride at the princely rate of ten rupees each. They call out to Tinka, but she continues to pick her way through the thickening press of pigs, people, policemen and garbage.

'Damn the wench!' Julian says when they finally break

loose, dishevelled and rattled, from the clutches of the pimp army. 'I've no idea which way she went. Do you?'

'No.' Leo shakes his head, letting his camera arm sag. 'All these lanes look alike – wait, there she is!'

They scramble down the lane to catch up with her. Together, all three of them turn into a narrow sidelane and stop in front of a dilapidated two-storeyed house with a broken iron gate.

'Cures for sterility, impotence and premature ejaculation.' Leo scans the various posters as they enter the shabby premises of the Dawakhana. 'You've come to the right place, grandfather!'

But Julian is too out of breath to come up with a response.

Leo purses his lips tactfully, places a hand under the older man's elbow and propels him into the reception area.

'So how did you track down the legendary Harry Rose?' Julian demands of Tinka once they're all seated. 'I'd begun to think he didn't exist.'

Tinka shrugs. 'I chatted up the waiters, who knew somebody who knew somebody who knew Harry. I sent across a cutting of my last three articles and I was granted an audience. That's it, really.'

They sit bolt-upright the bench, staring at the metal door opposite. Tinka gets the feeling they're being watched.

'I was told to meet the compounder,' she says after a while. 'But there's nobody here…'

'Sambadik?'

Tinka springs to her feet. 'Yes!'

It's a small, dishevelled boy, not more than twelve years old. He nods, opens the iron door in the wall opposite and announces in a high-pitched voice, 'Sambadik.'

'Oh and by the way,' Tinka tells the other two as they enter the office. 'Harry's a she.'

'Hullo, dearie.'

The voice is rich and earthy. Tinka blinks, eyes adjusting to the gloom, and beholds the wonder that is Harry Rose.

Her first thought is one of intense regret – if only Nikka Khan's minions hadn't broken her camera!

Harry Rose had floored Shaanu by night and she is no less fabulous by day. Dressed all in red and black, her gorgeous hair cascading all about her, she is busily decapitating a huge mound of bright orange flowers, tossing the heads into a bowl on her lap and discarding the leaves and stems on the floor. The acrid, slightly astringent scent of flowers fills the room and makes everybody's heads swim a little.

'Woof,' moans Leo from behind Tinka longingly. 'Woof woof.'

'Shut up,' Tinka whispers. 'Hullo, I'm Tehmina.'

'I'm Harry.' She smiles, showing slightly chipped teeth. 'Who are these two, Tehmina?'

'My friends,' Tinka replies. 'They can be trusted – and please, everybody calls me Tinka.'

'Tinker Tailor Soldier Spy,' says Harry Rose unexpectedly. 'It's the name of a book one of my, uh, *friends* is writing,' she explains.

'I want to know about your friends,' Tinka replies at once. 'Not that I'm writing a book or anything – just a piece on what the women of East Pakistan have endured during this conflict.'

'Same old idea,' Harry Rose sighs as she continues to de-head the flowers in her lap efficiently. 'Really, if I had a kaala tika for every writer, screenwriter, journalist, poet and director who wanted me to tell the story of the men in my life I would be as black as a negro by now.'

Tinka apologizes humbly for being so unoriginal. Harry

Rose waves her sorrys aside and accepts a hundred-rupee note, tucking it securely inside the neckline of her red-and-turq kaftan.

'Where do you want me to begin?'

'At the beginning,' Tinka replies. 'I want to hear everything.'

'Me too,' Julian choruses.

It's the first thing he's said, Tinka realizes, amused. Harry Rose's beauty has clearly got him gobsmacked.

'And me,' Leo adds. 'Err, what are you doing with those flowers, by the way?'

'They're calendulas,' Harry replies, gently fingering the petals of one bright flower. 'I'm making a poultice. To disinfect and heal flesh wounds.'

'Flesh,' Julian repeats idiotically.

Harry Rose's luscious lips part in an enchanting little-girl grin. Then she stretches luxuriantly. Marvellous undulations occur beneath the silk kaftan. In the manner of a Great Teacher stating an undisputable, eternal truth, she declares, 'All men are dogs.'

'Hear hear!' Tinka bursts into spontaneous applause.

'But Tinka says all men are snakes,' Leo objects.

'Snakes, dogs, same thing.' Harry Rose waves one manicured hand dismissively at this petty quibbling.

'Yeah, don't be so literal.' Tinka twinkles at him. 'Would you care to expand on that statement, Harry?'

Harry Rose puts aside her bowl of decapitated calendulas, leans in and rests her chin on her hands. The change in position causes her bosom to squish between her elbows, increasing her generous cleavage to Grand Canyon-like proportions. A waft of perfume drifts towards them, mingling with the scent of calendulas.

'My father married me off to a thirty-year-old man when I was twelve, and my husband sold me into prostitution two weeks later. Don't look so shocked.' This is addressed to Leo. 'It's a very ordinary story, happens to many many little girls in rural Bihar.'

'You're Bihari?' Tinka looks up from her scribbling.

She nods, a faraway look in her doe-like eyes. 'Bi-*harry* Rose,' she explains. 'And my name is Gulab Kali. Which means—'

'Rosebud.' Tinka nods, writing again. 'I get it.'

'No, you don't.' Harry Rose chuckles and raps Tinka's scribbling hand, stilling it. 'I was the sauciest, sassiest thing in those days – not the withered-up crone I am now.'

She pauses graciously so they can table fervent protests against this modest statement, then continues:

'There was this one feeble, consumptive fellow, just come out of England and *so* homesick! None of the girls could get his worm to stir, no matter *how* hard they played the pungi, so finally, his pals brought him to me, and I fixed him. His name was Harry and that's why I'm called Harry Rose – because Harry finally *rose* to the occasion.'

Tinka's dimplets flash. 'This time I *really* get it.'

Harry laughs again and continues to talk. Her life has been a rich, eventful one. She tells the story of her lows and highs, her brush with drug addiction and how, finally, she decided to learn some other profession besides the one she was engaged in and settled on Ayurvedic medicine – 'Because dearie, half the fellows who came to me had some sexy problem or the other, and I had to help them deal with it!'

Then she expands her theme to larger topics.

'What is liberation?' she demands as the small boy

re-enters with cups of sweet strong coffee. 'All *these*,' she indicates the men in the room, keep saying we are suffering under the zulm of dictators like Yahya Khan and bloody naak-mein-dum Nikka Khan, and we should fight for our freedom and be liberated, but what I want to know is, how can a nation be free if fifty per cent of it are kept subjugated and battered?'

'Fifty per cent?' Julian asks, puzzled.

She rolls her magnificent eyes.

'I mean all of us women, of course! There's a petty Yahya Khan or Nikka Khan in every Bengali home – *they're* the ones who have to defeated! That's the war of liberation I'm interested in, not this my-penis-is-bigger-than-your-penis rubbish!'

'*Yeaaah!*' Tinka's American accent, that relic of her childhood which resurfaces whenever she is particularly moved, kicks in with a vengeance. 'Rrright *on*, Miss Harry!'

'Hey, hang on…' Leo tries to protest. 'All men are not the same…'

Harry Rose turns to face him.

'Dearie, I've seen plenty, and believe me, they're *all* the same! Except for race and colour, of course, but those differences are superficial. I mean, if you had to buy a banana and a couple of plums, would you care if the thaila they came in was black or white or brown?'

'Not at all!' Tinka assures her as the men splutter into their coffee. 'You're right again!'

'Surely, there are *some* points of difference…' Julian tries to protest.

'Maybe.' Harry has lit a cigarette. She inhales deeply. 'Like the West Pakistani soldiers are the vainest, the Bihari Razzakars the cruellest, the Indians the horniest, and the

Muktis are the cheapest, always asking the girls for free fucks because they're "liberating the homeland". She leans in, the doe eyes sparkling playfully. 'I tell them, "Dearie, I don't give a *fuck* – especially a free one!"'

She laughs uproariously, and everybody joins in.

'Anyway, I'm like the Red Cross – I'm neutral and helpful and on nobody's side!'

'Except your own?' Tinka suggests with a ghost of a twinkle.

Harry Rose twinkles back. 'Except my own!'

Tinka smiles, then asks in a slightly altered tone, 'Harry, there are whispers that this place is a safe hous—'

'Your bra's all wrong,' Harry Rose interrupts her, smoke streaming from both nostrils. 'It's too tight. Let everything *breathe* a little, and don't worry that your boobs will get saggy if you do. They won't.'

'Sure.' Tinka takes this without a blink. 'Uh, why do people say your place is a safe house—'

'At least, they won't if every time you take a bath, you sprinkle them first with very hot water and then immediately with very cold water. Then they'll stay as tight as young buds in the springtime. Like mine.'

'...that your place is a safe house for Indians and Muktis?'

The older woman stubs out her cigarette, her expression pained.

'I don't want to answer that question,' she says. 'Don't you get it?'

Tinka looks her right in the eye.

'I don't want to talk about boobs,' she replies. 'Don't *you* get it?'

Harry Rose folds her arms over her chest.

'You're looking for somebody, aren't you?' she says

bluntly. 'That look in your eye – hopeful, desperate – I saw it as soon as you came in. Do you even want my interview or was all that just a cover?'

'I *do* want your interview,' Tinka replies steadily. 'All that stuff you said, it's great. But—'

'Brother or boyfriend?'

Tinka bows her head, her eyes shuttering.

'I don't have either.'

'She's lying,' Julian says chattily. 'She's a real liar, our Tinka – she has a laddie somewhere, I know. This has to be about him. He broke her heart, so she's given up eating and bathing.'

Harry abandons her aggressive stance and bends over Tinka.

'Really?' she asks gently.

Tinka's head comes up.

'I'm *done* with men,' she says fiercely. 'They're liars and they're fools and all they want to do is kill each other. I'm going to adopt a few children from the refugee camps and raise them alone, without fathers or foolishness.'

'Now *you're* being foolish,' Harry Rose points out practically. 'As if *any* orphanage – even your great Mother Teresa's – will let you adopt children after you came on screen with no clothes on, full guddi-fuddi showing!'

Tinka looks totally deflated.

'Shit, you're right. Now what should I do?'

'Make some babies the old-fashioned way,' the older woman advises. 'It's the *best* way to do it!'

'Maybe you'll find a suitable procreating partner at tonight's Twelve-days-to-Christmas Ball,' Julian suggests rallyingly. 'All business, no pleasure, eh?'

'Yeah,' Leo chimes in. 'The UN-mandated ceasefire kicks in at midnight. Make the most of the lull before the storm!'

'The *lul* before the storm!' Harry Rose chuckles. 'Haha!'

'Haha,' Tinka responds politely. 'Desi joke,' she adds for the bemused men. 'You won't get it.'

There is a little pause. Then Harry Rose bends over Tinka again.

'So who *is* he?'

Leo and Julian, hoping somebody else will have better luck getting this question answered, go very quiet.

'Just ... somebody,' Tinka mutters finally.

'Why did he break up with you?' Harry demands, eyes flashing. 'Because of your ad? Men are so narrow-minded!'

'He was ... cool with the ad,' Tinka says slowly. 'We stopped talking because, well, he gave me some noble, bullshit reason, but now I realize that, really, it was because he was engaged to somebody else all along. Which is information he neglected to give me.'

'Khankir pola.' The curse words come out sounding tremendously sympathetic. 'And how did you know this?'

'My aunt phoned and told me,' Tinka says hopelessly. 'It was in the *India Post* apparently. And now...' Her voice trembles, she swallows, hiccups, then continues, 'He's missing. Maybe even dead. His plane went down close to Dacca four days ago.'

Julian and Leo stare at each other over her head, finally enlightened. Then Leo puts his arm about her shoulders.

'So why do you care, eh? He cheated on you – he's past history!

Harry Rose stares at him like he's a moron.

'Of *course* she cares!'

'I *don't*,' Tinka insists unconvincingly.

Harry Rose squeezes Tinka's hand.

'Of course you don't. Was he very good-looking, dearie?'

Tinka sighs gustily. 'He was ... all right.'

'Find an ugly fellow next time,' Harry Rose advises. 'They're more faithful. More grateful. Besides, other women leave them alone.'

She gets to her feet as she says this. The audience is clearly over. As they walk to the door, Leo asks curiously, 'So *is* this a safe house for sympathizers of an independent Bangladesh?'

Harry Rose stares at him in genuine surprise. 'You'll never get answers if you frame your questions like that, dearie! What kind of journalist *are* you?'

'He's just a photographer,' Julian explains. 'A blunt instrument. A witless fool.'

'Thank you for your time.' Tinka gives her a smile. 'Let's go, guys.'

At the door of the little office, Tinka turns to look at the older woman, her heart in her eyes. 'If you hear anything...'

Harry nods. 'If I do – which is highly improbable because this isn't a safe house, you know, just an Ayurvedic clinic – I'll let you know.'

THIRTEEN

'Ramblin' rose,
Ramblin' rose,
why you ramble, no one knows,
wild and wind-blown, that's how you've grown,
who can cling to, a ramblin' rose?'

Maddy is lying on the parapet wall, singing, his eyes closed, arms thrown out dramatically, a singularly lovesick expression on his face.

Three floors below him, English Road is getting ready to party.

The impending ceasefire has added urgency to the evening's revelries – the shop signs seem to glow brighter, the women's laughter sounds sexier, richer, full of promise. Even the reclusive Front Room has emerged from the front room and, kurta flapping around his bare legs, is sending rockets shooting up into the air out of an old beer bottle. One of them misses Maddy narrowly and lands hissing on the terrace. He ignores it and continues to sing, swelling his lungs, shutting his eyes, giving the second verse all he has got.

'*Ramble ON,*
Ramble onnnn…
When your ramblin' days are go—'

Shaanu bounces out onto the terrace.

'Oye, Maddy!'

The warbler starts, almost falls off the parapet, recovers himself and sits up, cursing.

'What?' he asks with as much dignity as he can muster and reaches for the mug of tea Shaanu has offered him. Looking at Shaanu, he narrows his eyes. 'Why're you wearing those overalls, bastard?'

Shaanu tells him.

Maddy slams his mug down with a loud clatter.

'Behenchod, be reasonable!' he says agitatedly. 'You can't just gatecrash some Paki party at the Intercon! You'll get yourself caught and killed!'

But Shaanu just shakes his head and starts to comb his hair before the cracked, soap-caked mirror hammered lopsidedly into the terrace wall.

'She thinks I was just fooling around with her, Maddy. She thinks I'm engaged to somebody else – I have to find her and clear up that misunderstanding.'

'She thinks you're *dead*,' Maddy says bluntly. 'Which is okay. Wait for the war to finish and then clear up the misunde…' He pauses, frowning. 'Wait a second, you're engaged? To whom? When did *that* happen?'

'It didn't,' Shaanu says. 'I'll explain later.'

Maddy looks at him like he's a moron. 'So explain to *her* also later! Why risk your life now?'

Shaanu's face grows stubborn. 'I don't want her going

around thinking I'm a narrow-minded asshole. Suppose she falls for somebody else?'

'Saale.' Maddy can scarcely credit his ears. 'If you wanted to talk to her so badly why didn't you do so while she was *here* and you were doing compounder duty? Why did you hide?'

'I couldn't have talked to her *here*.' Ishaan shakes his head impatiently. 'First, there were these two goras with her – I didn't know who the hell they were! Supposing they hauled me away and it blew Harry Rose's cover? Besides,' he looks a little sheepish, 'I wasn't exactly looking my best, brother. I was unshaved and dirty, I hadn't even brushed my teeth.'

He dips his comb in a jar of Brylcreem and goes back to combing his hair in the cracked mirror, leaving Maddy to splutter into the tea he's finally started sipping.

'Bastard, are you man or peacock?' he demands when he can speak.

Shaanu grins, throws out his arms and lets out a piercing squawk, an eerily exact replication of a peacock's mating call.

'She still loves me.' He grins. 'I could tell.'

Maddy can't help grinning back.

'Why not?' he says. 'You're the coolest cat in the place.'

Shaanu laughs, jumps up on the parapet and hugs him hard.

'Tu bhi chal,' he urges, his grey eyes alight with that daredevil gleam that always makes Maddy uneasy. 'Come on, it'll be fun! We'll eat Pakistani food and encroach on Pakistani hospitality and dance with pretty Pakistani girls. Hey, maybe they'll have a piano so you can wow the dames!'

Maddy shakes his head.

'The only dame I want to wow is right here.'

This gives Ishaan pause. He loosens his manic grip on his friend's shoulders.

'Maddy, she's too old for you. Besides, I'm pretty sure Macho da and she have some chakkar.'

'No,' says Maddy with conviction. 'It's a work-only relationship. Don't be so goddamn narrow-minded, Baaz!'

'What *is* this work anyway?' Shaanu demands. 'What are they up to? What's this great mission they're on?'

Maddy looks away sullenly. 'I don't know,' he admits.

'I say we try and get in touch with the Indian forces,' Ishaan says. 'That's another good reason to go to the Intercon tonight! *Hundred* per cent there will be people there who'll get word across and connect us to the Indian side—'

'You're talking like a madman!' Maddy interrupts angrily. 'And you're wounded – that cut on your shoulder hasn't healed yet.'

'Harry's given me a really phaardu painkiller,' Shaanu tells him. 'I don't feel a thing!'

Maddy throws up his head.

'Fine gratitude you're showing her then, sneaking off once she's helped you!'

Ishaan sighs, pushes his hair off his forehead, ruining all his hard work with the comb and the Brylcreem.

'Maddy, I'm grateful, I really am! I'd fix their radio if I could – but I *can't*. And I really, really want to meet Tinka. Come with me!'

Maddy stares at Ishaan for a long time, then takes the comb from him, dips it in the Brylcreem and starts to comb his own hair before the mirror.

'What will we call ourselves?'

'I'll be Bilawal Hussain.' Ishaan taps the name stitched in white stencilled thread on his PAF overalls.

'Mad,' says Maddy resignedly. 'Ripe for the pagal khana.'

'Come with me, brother,' Shaanu urges. 'C'mon! I'll pass you off as my civilian friend.'

'Arrey yaar, why do I have to be a bloody civilian?' Maddy demands irritably. 'Civilians suck. When I was a child our batman never let our spaniel Benji mate with the civilian dogs, even though all the civilian bitches thought Benji was so hot!'

'Behenji was a lesbian?' Shaanu is momentarily distracted. 'Wow, that stuff happens in dogs?'

Maddy turns around and stares at him blankly for a moment.

'*Benji*, you farmer,' he explodes. 'Not Behenji.'

'Whatever…' Shaanu waves this explanation away. 'Chal na, yaar, I *have* to meet Tinka…'

'And I'll take you there,' Maddy capitulates suddenly and totally, much to Shaanu's delight. 'I'll take you there in *style*, so nobody will suspect you're a ratty Indian, and I'll wait for you outside. And in case you get into a mess, I'll whisk you away in my getaway car.'

Shaanu's face brightens.

'Getaway car?'

Maddy turns around, leans on the parapet wall and directs Shaanu's gaze to a snazzy silver Ford Mustang convertible parked in the driveway below.

'*That* baby.'

'Wow! Whose is it?'

Maddy winks. 'Just a lady who happens to be a Pat Boone fan. She thinks I do a mean imitation.'

Ishaan's jaw drops.

'Bastard, what have you been *doing* here on English Road?'

'You want the car or not?' Maddy demands. 'I'll pretend to be your driver and drive you to the Intercon. They're sure to let you in when they see those wheels.'

'Okay, okay.' Shaanu nods, bouncing on the balls of his feet. 'Thanks, man.'

Maddy snaps his fingers together.

'And let's take a couple of those Sten guns stashed downstairs!'

Ishaan's eyes glow with gratitude.

'Thanks, man. You're a real hero.'

'No, I'm not,' Maddy says gruffly. 'You and Raka are the heroes. Not me.'

'You're Harry Rose's hero,' Shaanu insists, grinning.

Maddy's face grows wistful immediately. 'Harry rhymes with marry,' he sighs.

'And rose rhymes with woes.' Ishaan finishes lacing his shoes and straightens up with the air of one expecting flashbulbs and applause. 'How do I look?'

Maddy takes in the cocky stance, the lean, sinewy arms emerging from the rolled-up overall sleeves, the dark hair slicked back to carefully careless perfection and the laughing grey eyes.

'Not bad.'

Shaanu's eyes narrow. 'What d'you mean *not bad*, fucker?'

Maddy grins.

'I mean a tiger had sex with Zeenat Aman, and the baby that popped out was *you*.'

• • •

The Crystal Ballroom at the Intercontinental Hotel is living up to its name. Crystal glitters in its ornate chandeliers, twinkles in the champagne flutes borne on silver trays by uniformed bearers, flashes tantalizingly from perfumed bosoms and delicate earlobes. The very laughter of the ladies tinkles like crystal, as distinguished-looking gentlemen bend over their hands and lead them to the dance floor, while the five-piece orchestra plays '*On the first day of Christmas my true love sent to me, a partridge in a pear tree...*'

Descending the red-carpeted double staircase, Tinka is conscious of a feeling of complete surreality. Not far away from here, Indian soldiers are crawling on their bellies through mud and slush. In the lanes of Old Dacca, West Pakistani soldiers and Bihari Razzakars are engaged in bloody clashes with student leaders and Muktis. Aircraft carrier *USS Enterprise* has led a section of America's Seventh Fleet into the Bay of Bengal, and Soviet warships have been sent from Vladivostok in retaliation. The Soviets have vetoed America's resolution to have a ceasefire declared in the region by the United Nations Security Council – a ceasefire upon which all of Yahya Khan's hopes were pinned. The only ceasefire happening at the moment is the four-hour mini-break decreed by the Red Cross to allow stranded civilian expatriates to flee the city. In spite of all this teeming activity, here is the Intercontinental Hotel, brimming with Christmas spirit.

'Aren't you leaving?' one of the scruffy journos, almost unrecognizable in his spruced-up, 'party' avatar, asks her as he plucks two champagne flutes from a passing waiter and hands her one. 'I thought all the Americans were on the flight to Islamabad.'

Tinka feels a jolt on hearing herself being described as an American. But that *is* what your passport says, she reminds herself. And your employer is American too.

'I'm staying till the bitter end,' she replies gaily.

She is, however, sending out some of her precious negatives and voice recordings on the Islamabad flight. Everybody is. It's their last chance to send out material. After tonight, it's going to be a fight to the finish.

Now she clinks flutes with the man beside her, takes a big swig and looks about for Leo and Julian.

'Well well, that's quite a transformation!' exclaims a slightly inebriated voice behind her. 'The grubby prawn has become a swan! There must be a *very* grotty rim of grime around your bathtub, wench! I hope you rinsed it clean!'

It is Julian Arnott, looking dapper in a tweed jacket with leather elbow patches, nursing a balloon-sized glass more than half full of sherry. He is holding out both arms in an extravagant gesture and gazing at Tinka in unconcealed, donnish delight.

It must be admitted that she *has* sort of pulled out all the stops tonight. Dressed in a long, clingy, ridiculously Hollywoody sleeveless dress, she is easily the most dazzling thing in the room. Her arms are smooth and glowing, her lips Christmassy red.

'Clearly the ravishing Harry Rose has got Tinka's competitive juices flowing,' Leo smirks from besides Julian. 'Eh, Tinka?'

'You're both looking very smart yourselves.' Tinka smiles. Then she adds, 'I shopped at the boutique downstairs. I've decided to stop moping and move on.'

Julian beams. 'Excellent decision! You look lovely.'

She winks at him. 'I know.'

She smiles brilliantly around the room and quite a few men go red, clear their throats, throw back their shoulders and stand up straighter.

It does feel lovely to look good again, Tinka admits to herself, basking in the glow of a hundred sucked-in paunches. Really, I've been behaving ridiculously! I do *not* get all dressed up to attract the male gaze or retain it – I get all dressed up for *myself*!

'So, how deep does this transformation actually go?' Julian asks presently.

'I'm wearing sexy lingerie,' she replies. 'And I've slathered myself liberally with Afghan Snow. Does that answer your question?'

'No. But I'll retract it and ask you another.' He cocks his head to one side like a bird and twinkles at her. 'Do you think I'm too much of a spring chicken for you?'

Tinka throws back her head and laughs. 'Yes!'

'Tinka!' Leo's cheery voice comes floating out to them. 'Abandon that shrivelled-up bag of bones and come meet some delicious young West Pakistani officers! Why do you insist on giving them bad press all the time, huh?'

Tinka looks at Julian.

He puts a thin, wrinkled hand into the small of her back and propels her forward.

'Go, go!'

With a laughing rebuttal on her lips, Tinka walks over to the group Leo is standing with, very conscious that she is sashaying seductively. What is *wrong* with me, she wonders, even as she offers her hand to the handsome officers, recalling Harry Rose's assessment of the men in this war.

West Pakistanis are the vainest.

And at first glance, it does indeed seem this little contingent from Lahore has a lot to be vain about.

'The lovely lady journalist from WWS,' Leo announces. 'Tehmina Dadyseth. Say hello, boys.'

'Hello, ma'am,' the officers chorus, gazing at her with open admiration.

Tinka smiles back at them, feeling decidedly big sister-ish. Except for the fact that they're undeniably cuter, they are practically indistinguishable from the Indian officers she's met in Kalaiganga.

'How are you all?' Tinka asks. 'Looking forward to the little break from the fighting tonight?'

'Yes, ma'am!' they chorus.

Tinka sips her champagne, not knowing what else to say. A bearer stops at their group with a plate of hors d'oeuvres and everyone focuses on picking kebabs with toothpicks.

'So, have you seen *Play Misty for Me*?' one of the officers gulps out finally. He's very young and Tinka is vividly reminded of Dilsher Singh. 'What a scary movie it was, to be sure! Scarier than even *Psycho*!'

He ends his question with a nervous laugh.

'No, I'm afraid I haven't,' Tinka replies politely.

'Oh really?' They are all surprised. 'We've seen it! And *Fiddler on the Roof* too. Don't you see cinema in Amaarica?'

Tinka explains that she's basically from Bombay.

They receive this news with sympathy.

'Oh, then, of course, you wouldn't get to see the latest Amaarican movies,' one of them says somewhat condescendingly. 'You must be watching only Russian Circus and all over there.'

Which is actually true, Tinka has to admit to herself. How mortifying!

Aloud she says, 'Don't you think life is scary enough at the moment without watching scary films?'

The posse of officers registers surprise.

'Scary?' scoffs the youngest one, the nervous gulper.

'Oh no no no,' says the tallest.

'What's there to be scared of?' demands the fairest (who is a bit too fair to be lovely, to be honest).

'Not *Indians*, surely?' says the largest. 'Indians aren't scary in the least! Not to full-blooded Pathans like us, anyway!'

Tinka smiles politely at this cocky sally, though she has started to feel oddly deflated inside. In fact, she realizes as she sips her champagne again, she is fighting a feeling of utter desolation.

What did you think, you little idiot? That if you dressed up and looked your best, you'd summon him out of nothingness with the magnetic force of your beauty alone?

She feels like slipping off her high heels right there on the edge of the wooden dance floor, throwing them across the room and running back to her room to cry her heart out.

And then a relaxed, curiously vibrant voice speaks up behind her.

'*I* think Indians are bloody scary, personally.'

The hair at the back of Tinka's neck prickle. Goosebumps form on her smooth bare arms. She turns and sees a slight, straight figure dressed all in PAF green standing behind her. His dark hair is swept back from his handsome forehead, his lean body somehow radiates both complete casualness and tightly suppressed energy, and his eyes are agleam with pure, cocky enjoyment.

'Squadron Leader Bilawal Hussain.' He clicks his heels gracefully and holds out his hand. 'We have common friends, I believe, Miss Tehmina. Such a pleasure to meet you.'

Tinka takes the proffered hand like a girl in a dream. It grips hers firmly, his grasp cool but somehow intimate. Her head is whirling. She has to put up a hand in a vain attempt to steady it.

'How … how…'

Ishaan's eyes widen warningly. The pressure on her hand increases.

Tinka pulls herself together, wishing she hadn't downed two glasses of champagne.

'How nice to meet you, Squadron Leader!' she manages to say, with perfect aplomb.

She is rewarded with an appreciative gleam from the laughing Kota-grey eyes.

'Please call me Bilawal,' he beseeches. He drops her hand and looks at the little knot of officers hovering protectively around Tinka. 'So you don't find Indians scary? Weren't you taught, in your very first term at Kakul, that underestimating the enemy is the gravest blunder in armed combat?'

'No, sir,' says the nervous gulper. 'I mean, yes, sir.'

'You look too young to be a squadron leader, sir,' says another, immediately infatuated.

But the tallest of the officers, a major, isn't impressed.

'Respect is one thing, fear another,' he sneers. 'Are you from Tezgaon? You lot didn't exactly cover yourself in glory before the enemy.'

'Yeaaah,' chimes in Tinka, who has just remembered that she hates Ishaan Faujdaar. She plucks another glass of champagne from a passing bearer, knocks it down in one smooth gulp and squints down at him, her cheeks flushed. 'You got *wiped* out by the IAF! I marvel you can show your face at parties!'

The army men snicker.

'We do all the heavy lifting around here,' the major says martyredly. 'PAF is just faff.'

Ishaan ignores this crack, spears a shammi kebab from a plate at the bar and raises his eyes to look directly into Tinka's. 'I've showed my face at this party,' he says deliberately, 'because there's someone here I absolutely *had* to speak to. And there was no other way to get to them.'

Tinka's heart gives the oddest thump. She stares at him, her eyes reflecting anger – and fear for him – and helpless longing. 'Then I won't detain you any longer,' she says jerkily. 'Please go and find this person you're looking for.'

She waves her hand in a you-are-dismissed gesture, leaving the snubbed Shaanu with no option but to bow politely and walk away. Her eyes follow him, angrily, hungrily. Then one of the Pakistani officers addresses her, and she turns to him, her manner arch, her smile glittering.

Julian Arnott, who has been watching this exchange with interest from the sidelines, now makes a beeline for Shaanu.

'Hello there, friend of Tinka.'

Shaanu wheels around.

'I wish,' he says with a rueful smile. 'Actually, we just have common friends.'

'I have common friends too,' Julian admits. 'Everyone does, you know, it can't be avoided nowadays, but it's terribly common to call them common. What you *meant* to say, I think, is that you have *friends* in *common*, which is a different thing entirely.'

'If you say so.' Ishaan's eyes have skittered back to Tinka. 'My English is pretty basic.'

You're pretty basic, Julian thinks but doesn't say. He likes this young fellow. Could he be the mystery man who has got Tinka all wound up? But this fellow claims to be a PAF Fighter. His dungarees look loose though. Borrowed?

He decides to probe a little.

'What plane do you fly?'

'F-86 Sabre,' is Shaanu's glib response. 'They're the backbone of our air defence here in Pakistan. We rig 'em out with Sidewinder missiles or Browning machine guns or Napalm bombs – well, at least we used to, till the bloody Indians cratered the crap out of our airfield. Now we are grounded and outnumbered, and the fate of our fair nation is in the hands of those ... those *army men* there.' He glowers at the officers still talking to Tinka.

'Your fate is actually in the hands of that army man *there*.' Julian directs his attention to the doors of the banquet hall, through which Nikka Khan has just made his entry, followed by his gun-toting guards and the massive-impassive wooden-faced ADC. 'Nikita Khan, as the Russians like to say. What do you make of *him*?'

For a moment, Shaanu doesn't recognize the Butcher of Bengal. The man looks so shrunken compared to his newspaper photographs, almost a non-entity. Then,

'He's my biggest hero!' declares Shaanu, deciding that if a thing is worth doing, it's worth doing well. 'What a man!'

Julian looks at him quizzically.

'*Really*?' he drawls. 'So tell me, what do you admire the most about him? His fake British accent or his hideous human-rights record?'

'Well, a leader needs to be a leader,' Shaanu says easily. 'With no self-doubt or namby-pamby squeamishness.'

He produces the last word rather proudly – he has picked it up from Maddy, who once used it to describe the ruthless manner with which Dilsher Singh used to press out his pimples in the bathroom mirror of the Sarhind Club.

Julian's gaze grows even more quizzical.

'No wonder Tinka didn't like you.'

Shaanu's eyes grow stormy. He starts to deny this charge, then changes his mind and settles for a flat, resigned, 'Yes.'

'Would you like to meet him?'

The question comes from Leo, who has just joined their group, arm in arm with the major who has been fawning over Tinka.

'Oh, I hardly think—' Julian starts to say hurriedly, but Ishaan interrupts him.

'General Khan? Sure.'

The major raises an eyebrow. '*Absolutely* sure?'

Shaanu's grin grows challenging.

'Why? Don't you know him well enough to perform an introduction?'

Leo bursts out laughing.

'PAF man is cocky, huh?' he says appreciatively. 'So *do* you know the general well enough to introduce people to him, Major?'

The Pakistani major has stiffened in outrage, but now he chuckles and drops his arms about Ishaan's and Leo's shoulders. 'Come along.'

'No-no,' Julian says agitatedly.

'*Relax*, grandfather.' Leo grins good-naturedly. 'I'm with the Army now – the general won't eat me!'

The old man watches them go, consternation writ large on his lined face. Then he curses colourfully under his breath and follows them.

The two officers stride over to where Nikka Khan is conversing with a knot of balding white dignitaries.

'General!' says the West Pakistani major easily. 'Here's one of your dashing air warriors from Tezgaon. Squadron leader Bilawal Hussain.'

Ishaan clicks his heels together smartly. 'Sir!'

'At ease, soldier, at ease.' Nikka waves a gracious hand, his Tumbola accent very much in evidence. 'Squadron Leader, eh? You must be the 2-I-C … I've heard of you, your boss says you're a real fire-eater.'

Shaanu ducks his head gracefully. 'Thank you, sir!'

Nikka looks him up and down and slowly licks his lips. *Sshviccck!*

'He also called you a bloody giraffe.'

Julian, hovering at the back of the group, groans inwardly. From the soles of his polished shoes to the top of his Brylcreemed head, this so-called PAF Fighter can't be more than five-feet-six inches tall.

Shaanu throws back his head and laughs.

'Sarcasm! Our CO's a real joker, sir!'

'He also reported,' Nikka's voice grows softer, more speculative, 'that your plane went down a couple of days ago...'

'And so it did!' Shaanu agrees. 'Crashed into a paddy field, taking a pesky Gnat down with it. I hitched a ride into the city with a party of farmers.'

'Hmmm.' Nikka's face twitches like he's smelt something fishy. In a distinctly silky voice he murmurs, 'You know what, Hussain, it's the most vexing thing, I seem to have forgotten your CO's name...'

'I won't tell him you forgot, sir,' Shaanu reassures him. 'It would be too much of a blow to his vanity.'

But Nikka isn't to be deflected so easily. From under his peak of over-dyed black hair, his small pouchy eyes bore into Ishaan's frank ones.

'What was his name again?'

There is a horrible, almost one-second-long pause.

'It's...' Shaanu begins, then stops.

Nikka's too-black eyebrows snap together.

'It's...?'

Ishaan's grey eyes have started to sparkle, a strange, cool, fuck-you sparkle. He locks gazes with the Butcher of Bengal, clearly enjoying himself.

'It's...?' Ishaan Faujdaar says outrageously.

'Wing Commander Iqbal Farooqi,' a dulcet voice speaks up from behind them. 'Such a charming man. Pity his airfield got bombed out from under him.'

It is Tinka, of course. Ignoring Ishaan, she extends a hand towards Nikka, smiling brilliantly, her tousled cap of hair shining like a knob of silk skeins beneath the chandeliers, her eyes limpid pools of hero worship as she gazes up breathlessly at the older man.

Well, well, who's *this* tall drink of water, thinks the general as he licks his lips. And why does she look vaguely familiar?

'Have we met before, ma'am?' He bows gallantly.

For a moment Tinka is tempted to say no. Then her eyes flicker to the ADC standing behind Nikka. He has clearly recognized her, she can tell. Besides, she has to do her best to deflect attention from the clearly suicidal Ishaan Faujdaar.

She gives a tinkling little laugh.

'We met just yesterday, gennerrul,' she says, her American twang suddenly prominent. 'One of these muscular gentlemen standing behind you broke my camera into itsy-bitsy bits.'

Nikka Khan looks confused, then amazed. But not at all suspicious.

Tinka continues smoothly, 'I'm a special correspondent with WWS. I'm sorrry I was so insensitive yesturrday. Do grrant my publication an exclusive, one-on-one innerrview?'

With great alacrity, Nikka reaches for this bathed-and-beautiful Tinka with both hands.

'On the contrary, I am sorry I was so boorish yesterday,' he says smoothly. 'It's not often that I meet a journalist who goes to the core of the issue, to the source of the suffering so unerringly. You saw, with your searing woman's gaze, the pain that lies at the centre of my soul, and I, poor brute, lashed out like the animal I am. But today, granted a second chance, I will do better!'

Bollocks, you horny old goat, thinks Julian Arnott, from the sidelines. You've realized the girl is beautiful today, so you've changed your tune! The pain at the centre of your soul is just your throbbing hard-on. Suddenly, Julian wishes he were fifty years younger and could put the oily bastard out of commission by punching him in the nose.

And while he was at it, he would punch that fool Leo Stepanov till he was out of commission too! What was the moron thinking, dangling Tinka's laddie under Nikka Khan's suspicious nose?

'Wonderful!' Tinka breathes, holding onto the Butcher's hands determinedly and staring deep into his eyes. Which is pointless, really, thinks the harassed Julian, because *his* focus is on her breasts beneath the silver stuff of her high-necked, sleeveless gown.

'So, can we set up a tête-à-tête?'

'Certaihn-ly, certaihn-ly, my dear!' Nikka is all suave graciousness. 'Let's have some fun, one on one!' He seems ready to say more, but Julian Arnott breaks into the conversation, his quavering old voice determinedly commanding attention.

'General Khan, the BBC would like you to appear in our radio series *Great Generals through History*. We've done Julius Caesar and Napoleon, and now we want to do you.'

Nikka's gaze flickers away from Tinka for a moment. 'Great generals, eh? Why not?'

'Step this way, please, and we can discuss it,' chimes in Leo who has finally got with the plot.

Nikka lets go of Tinka's hands with obvious regret. 'Why wait till tomorrow? We can talk tonight itself – say, in half-an-hour, when the party wraps?'

Tinka gives a purr that makes the hair at the back of

Julian's neck stand on end. What the hell is she playing at?

'You don't beat about the bush, generrul!' she says.

'No, I don't.' Nikka grins with grotesque playfulness. 'Ask the East Bengalis.'

'General Khan?' Leo's voice is firm.

'Yes yes…' And Nikka allows himself to be led away.

Shaanu and Tinka, left alone, eye each other warily.

'Thank you,' he says finally.

'*Fuck* you.' Her voice is shaking.

For the very first time ever, she sees his usually smiling grey eyes smoulder with anger.

'What d'you think you're doing?' he says grimly. 'Get out of here before that old dog comes back for you!'

She snorts.

'*You* get out of here before they recognize you for the fraud you are!'

'Tinka…' He moves in closer, his voice urgent. 'I'm *not* a fraud.'

'Spare me. I owed you, so I saved you there. Now we're even.'

He ignores this and says, his tone insistent, 'Please, you have to believe me! I didn't even know about that engagement – it was all Chimman's doing!'

She tosses her head. 'I have absolutely no idea what you're talking about.'

Shaanu steps back, confused. 'I thought you were angry with me because you found out I was engaged. Aren't you?'

His eyes scan her face anxiously.

She stares at him in disbelief.

'Is that why you've come here?' she asks finally. 'Into this … this *den* of Pakistanis? Just to tell me you're not engaged? What if they catch you?'

He grins. 'They won't. And den is a bit harsh, don't you think? Matlab, this place is classy. The snacks are *good*.'

He spears another kebab from a passing bearer and pops it into his mouth.

Tinka watches him chew, trying to deny the queer, wild gladness in her heart. But she can't.

He's *alive*, she thinks. He's engaged, he's cocky, he's crazy – but he's alive, and so, I'm alive too.

He catches her staring and smiles. She flushes and looks away.

'Well, technically I am engaged,' he clarifies. 'But it happened behind my back and I don't plan to go through with it.'

'Please, spare me the update on every event of your little life,' she says haughtily. 'And it comes as no surprise to me that your family fixed your engagement. I know that's how marriages are arranged in the,' her voice grow deliberately withering, '*dusty backward village* you come from.'

'Chakkahera is *not* a village,' he says, hurt.

She sniffs.

'If you say so. The jeweller's unlettered daughter and you will suit each other very well, I'm sure.'

'Really?' he drawls. 'And how do *you* know her father's a jeweller?'

Tinka flushes. Shaanu grins.

'Oh, *fine* then,' she says in a furious little rush. 'I admit it, I read the piece. And I thought, aaaah, so *that's* where he got that vulgar gold chain!'

His wound has started to throb again, the pain an unrelenting pulse beating through his entire body, but Shaanu ignores it.

'Look, you're jealous and hurt,' he says. 'It's justified, I suppose. But there's a very simple explanation. And it is *not* that all men are dogs.'

Tinka, who is starting to feel a little ashamed of herself, starts to give a half-hearted retort, dismissing the accusation of jealousy as both baseless and laughable, then stops abruptly.

'Dogs?' she frowns. 'Were you listening to me at Harry Rose's door?'

He reddens self-consciously. 'Something like that. Well, actually, I was…'

But Tinka is no longer listening. Instead, she is sniffing the air. Cautiously, then openly, inching closer to him, her eyes widening.

'Calendula!'

'What?' He looks at her blankly.

'Oh my God, she was preparing the poultice for *you*.' She draws in her breath sharply and clutches his arm. 'Ishaan,' she says in an entirely altered voice. 'Are you *hurt*?'

'Ma'am.' He draws away, his eyes reproachful. 'The name's Hussain. Bilawal Hussain.'

She pushes her hair off her face with a trembling hand, looking about the room with anxious eyes and a brilliant smile.

'*Tell* me!'

'Whenever you say my name, I get this peculiar swooping sensation inside my stomach,' he responds, his voice wavering unsteadily. 'Like I'm long-jumping across an open well.'

'Only a complete moron would jump across an open well,' she says, her voice even more unsteady than his. Tears have sprung to her eyes. 'Why are you swaying like that? Are you wounded?'

'No biggie.' His voice is a little faint. Running a hand over his shoulder, he grins at her crookedly. 'I'm gonna have a very sexy scar. Would you like to see it?'

He pitches forward as he says this and she has to put a hand to his chest to steady him.

'Whooophf.' Shaanu's eyes close. 'The painkiller must be wearing off.' He opens them and looks interestedly around the banquet hall. 'Wow, this is a revolving ballroom. I didn't know they had those in Dacca.'

'They don't.' Her voice is teary. 'Could you please stand up straight? Nikka's looking right at you.'

'He's looking right at *you*, the horny old toad!' Shaanu struggles upright, wincing.

'Shushhh!' Tinka hisses, moving forward hastily to cover him from Nikka Khan's suspicious gaze. 'Take this.'

She slides something into his hand.

Ishaan looks down at the embossed brass key and his eyebrows fly up. 'Miss Tell-me-na Dadyseth!' he drawls. 'How very forward of you. Slipping your key into the hands of a stranger you've just met!'

'Run along, Bilawal,' she tells him, her eyes scanning the ballroom like it's a battlefield. 'Just *go*. I'll come up as soon as I can.'

• • •

Tinka spends twenty minutes more at the party, mingling, sparkling, talking feverishly to as many people as she can. Then she hurries out, kicking off her shoes so she can run faster up the stairs, stumbling as she rushes down the corridor, flat-palming her way into her room, flipping on the lights and coming to a dead halt at the sickening sight of Ishaan Faujdaar passed out cold across the bed.

She drops to her knees, her heart in her mouth.

'Ishaan!' Her voice is a sob. '*Ishaan.*'

Wanting to shake him but not very sure where his injury is, she looks wildly about his body and settles for slapping him briskly on both cheeks.

Shaanu winces and opens his eyes.

'Painkillers ... in my right ... pocket,' he replies through clenched teeth, before his eyes shutter over again.

'Good boy.' Almost weeping with relief, she reaches for his pocket.

'Your room's so fancy,' he sighs, stretching out more comfortably on the crisp white sheets. 'So rich! Like Freedom.' Bringing up his hands and waving them from side to side, he hums, '*Freedom is a rich girl, daddy's pretty sweet girl, Freedom is a sunny day...*'

'It's a hotel room,' she replies. 'Not mine. My room in Bombay is very basic, believe me. Pull yourself up a bit, or you'll fall off the bed.'

His hand closes over hers on his chest. She can feel his heart thudding through his overalls. His eyes open suddenly, curiously alight, glazed over with pain.

'*Freedom what would you do, if I said I loved you, Freedom would you run away?*'

Tinka has to fight back tears as she pries her hand out of his to retrieve the tablets.

'Swallow this,' she says firmly, once she's got hold of them. 'Here's the water, quickly now.'

He swallows the tablet obediently, chases it down with the water and lies back again, his eyes fluttering shut.

Outside, the wail of the siren signals the start of the four-hour ceasefire.

'You should never have come here,' she says wretchedly. 'It was a stupid *stupid* thing to do!'

There is no response from the figure on the bed.

'How bad is this wound?' she asks. 'Where is it?'

But Ishaan seems to be asleep, his chest rising and falling evenly.

Cursing the complicated PAF overalls, she undoes as many buttons as she can and slips her hands inside to feel for his injury. Harry Rose had mentioned a flesh wound, and from the way Shaanu had lurched forward downstairs, she suspects it is somewhere on his chest or shoulder.

Shaanu stirs under the pressure of her searching fingers.

'Are you outraging the modesty of a serving officer?' His voice is faint.

'I need to find this wound. No arguments, okay?'

He chuckles. It is a ghost of a chuckle.

'Be ... my ... guest.'

Her head comes up, her eyes blazing with frustration.

'You could tell me where it is!'

'But this is much ... more ... fun.'

She gives a despairing little laugh, and then, finally, her fingers find the rough texture of the crepe bandage. It feels dry and firmly tied.

'I'm okay, Dadyseth,' Ishaan murmurs. 'Harry Rose fixed me up good.'

'Thank God,' she sighs with relief. Then she wriggles out of her clinging dress, snuggles in next to him, rests her head on his good shoulder and, for the first time in a fortnight, falls into a deep, dreamless, healing sleep.

FOURTEEN

Downstairs in the Crystal Ballroom, General Nikka Khan is smouldering like a lecherous bomb whose fuse has been lit. He props himself against the bar, smoothens back his hair and covertly rakes the gathering for the namkeen journalist who had solicited an interview with him earlier in the evening. His gun-toting guards lurk behind him, trying (but failing) to look inconspicuous. The air around them buzzes with talk of war, peace and intrigue.

'He's increasingly being isolated,' a Red Cross official whispers to a colleague as they both eye the restless general. 'Yahya Khan and Zulfikar Bhutto have virtually washed their hands off him! They've left him – and East Pakistan – to sink or swim alone. The poor bastard's slow-roasting on a spit, only he doesn't know it yet.'

Blissfully oblivious to this talk, Nikka sips his scotch and pursues his own chain of thought.

How unerringly she put her finger on the root cause of his pain, he marvels. She knew that behind his tough exterior he was but a puddle of mush!

He would order his soldiers to light a fire in his chambers, sweep her back there in his motorcade like a silvery trophy and spend the ceasefire telling her of his sufferings during the Partition – the death of his mother and the rape of his sisters. Ah, how many women he has seduced with those stories! He would describe the carnage he had unleashed in retaliation in a bid to quench his pain – that always got women horny. While he spoke of all this, and so eloquently, in a combination of fine English and mellifluous Urdu, her eyes would soften with sympathy and adulation, her silver gown would ride up her thighs and, seduced by his machismo, his suffering and his power, she would surrender herself to him – like Balochistan, like Bangladesh, he would have mastery over her!

Definitely one of those eager young sluts who can't resist a man in uniform, thinks Nikka, giving the medals on his chest a self-satisfied pat and smiling blandly at the clutch of VIPs around him. I'll put her out of her misery, give her what she's clearly asking for with that tight dress and those moist lips, and those frantic, restless hands that had clung to mine so tight!

Sshviccck!

She had talked to the Sabre pilot for a while – he'd clearly been trying to snow her, but she hadn't been impressed, snubbing him so hard that he'd actually left the party. Then she had joined those two foreign journalists – that old British fool and the rude Russian – and after that she had gone … *where?*

Behind him, a bespectacled lady in a violently pink burqa castigates her husband in a hoarse voice.

'Seven pieces of reshmi kebab! Fried in pure ghee! You might as well eat poison and die!'

The harassed husband, a very senior bureaucrat, replies softly but stoutly, 'But the waiter keeps coming around. I can't resist.'

His wife crumples up a paper napkin violently.

'Cultivate some self-restraint! And don't blame the waiter! He's just doing his duty!'

The senior bureaucrat sticks to his guns. He has a toothpick in his hand and is clearly looking for something to spear it into.

'It's too tempting. So plump and juicy. My hand reaches out automatically. I can't control.'

The pink lady's eyes well up with angry tears.

'*This* is the reason we women are in purdah!' she declares bitterly. 'Because men can't control! I suppose reshmi kebabs should also simper sweatily behind burqas at parties? So that hungry animals like you don't leap up and rape them? Hullo, General Saab, I believe Squadron Leader Bilawal Hussain has been found?'

Startled at being included so abruptly in the conversation, Nikka nods stiffly.

'Yes yes, it appears that Hussain has indeed survived his crash. He's claiming a kill too – a Gnat, or a Hawker Hunter, I forget which.'

The pink lady's tears, already in position, now start to fall fast.

'He's my nephew,' she sniffles proudly. 'My brother's wife's sister's son! A darling boy! With a heart of a lion and,' she looks pointedly at her husband, '*so much* discipline and self-control! Somebody told me he is here tonight?'

Nikka meets her eager gaze with a sour smile.

'He is. But I entreat you to curb your excitement, madam, we haven't verified his report yet. This downed Gnat may very well turn out to be a figment of his imagination. Besides, one downed Gnat does not a summer make! These PAF jokers have been absolutely decimated here in the East.'

The pink lady is too busy looking around the room for Bilawal to reply, but her husband, irritated at having his kebabs rationed, sucks unhappily on his toothpick and says fretfully, 'Be fair, General! PAF was allocated just one Sabre squadron in East Pakistan. *One* lone squadron against the might of the IAF's Eastern Command! Not your fault, of course – all this is decided at a level much above yours – it's a fall-out of Yahya Khan's idiotic the-defence-of-the-East-lies-in-the-West theory! If East Pakistan had been better equipped to defend itself from the air, it would have done so easily.'

Nikka, red-faced at the insinuation that there are levels above his, says with icy dignity, 'Quait so. Luckily, the army has things well in hand, and when the Chinese join the fighting...'

The bureaucrat removes his toothpick from his mouth. 'The Chinese will never become directly involved in this conflict, because they know that if they do, the Soviet Union will crack down on them in the Sinkiang region.'

'No Chinese for you!' the lady in the pink burqa rejoins the conversation. 'All Chinese food is deep-fried in cornflour, you might as well—'

'Eat poison and die,' her husband concludes resignedly. 'Maybe I will.'

'Nonsense,' she says absently, and then clutches his elbow hard. 'Look, there's Bilawal! Haiii ... Allah ka shukar hai! It's soo good to see him! Hain?' She leans forward, adjusting her spectacles. Her face falls. 'Oh! It's someone else.'

As she lets go of her husband's arm, disappointed, Nikka frowns.

'You thought that tall dark chap was Hussain?'

She nods, too disappointed to speak.

'But he's a short, fair fellow with light eyes.'

'*Light* eyes?' she repeats. 'No no. Bilawal's eyes are black. And he's tall – the tallest boy in our family.'

Nikka licks his lips.

Sshviccck!

'You're *sure*, madam?'

She nods, her face has clouded over.

'I told you, he's my brother's wife's sister's son.'

'I see.' The general's eyes narrow. He says softly, almost to himself, '*And* he didn't know the name of his CO! If the girl hadn't come up and saved his baco—' He stops abruptly. 'Excuse me.'

Saying which, he wheels about and walks away.

'Haw!' gasps the lady in the pink burqa, very put out. 'That was rude of him! And what about Bilawal?'

Her husband, hot on the trail of a waiter serving bhuna ghosht, his toothpick in his hand, doesn't bother to reply.

Nikka stands alone in the middle of the ballroom, the party milling around him, smoothing back his hair and thinking furiously. What does all this mean? Where has the impostor vanished to? Is there a larger conspiracy? All his paranoias – and he has many, being a man who has risen to his current post by surviving purges, succession battles, back-stabbings and intrigues – stir to life.

'Sir,' a rumbling voice sounds from behind him. It is his massive-impassive ADC, sprung miraculously to life.

'What?' Nikka says irritably over his shoulder.

The ADC comes around to the front and plunges into ponderous speech.

'Sir, the journalist lady with the dimpals, whom we met yesterday...'

'She doesn't have dimples,' Nikka snaps.

The ADC stands his ground. 'She does, sir. Two small-small dimpals. Maybe you were looking at, er, something else of hers and didn't notice. *I* noticed particularly, because I too ... ahem!' he clears his throat and continues coyly, 'have the same kind of small-small dimpals. My missus always tells me.' He bares his teeth in a wide smile. 'See!'

Staring dementedly at his massive ADC's impressive rictus, General Nikka Khan, the Butcher of Bengal, has to shake off the feeling that the world is going insane around him.

'Stop babbling about dimples, man! You don't know what you're talking about!'

But the massive, no-longer impassive ADC shakes his head.

'She went off with the impostor,' he says. 'I was observing them all evening. They met and argued, he left and then she followed him out. They're in her room now. I'm *sure* of it.'

• • •

Ishaan awakens peacefully an hour later to find moonlight slanting over the crisp white sheets of a tumbled bed. It is an incredibly soft bed, nothing like the metal fauji bunks he is used to – soft yet firm, huge and fluffy. And in the middle of said bed, her head resting on the pillow of his unhurt shoulder, one slender brown arm thrown possessively across his chest, sending up waves of sweet, drowsy heat like the kind that rises from a just-baked cherry bun, lies India's sweetheart, Freesia girl Tinka Dadyseth, her sumptuous bits gift-wrapped just for him in skimpy grey lace as delicate as a spider's web.

Staring down at her sleeping face, he is rocked by waves of gladness and gratitude so intense they are physically painful.

He turns and pulls her to him almost roughly, pinning her under him. She acquiesces sweetly, her body accommodating his, her limbs limp and willing.

Ishaan bites her ear gently.

'You realize you're not leaving this bed till I've had my evil way with you?'

She smiles, arching against his body, her eyes closed, her cheeks flushed.

'Yes.'

Heart constricting with exultation, he speaks against her softly parted lips.

'And you're okay with that?'

Her body strains towards him, her arms cling tighter.

'Yes, please.'

He gives her a little shake.

'I'm engaged to somebody else, Dadyseth.'

Her lips curve upwards. She smiles – an implet with dimplets. Then, pushing out her lips, she whispers one word.

'Balls.'

Ishaan laughs.

'Really? But you were so angry about it downstairs.'

Her eyes fly open. They're alight with a glow so wanton and tender that he catches his breath.

'There's a ceasefire on,' she whispers. 'All warring parties have to lay down their arms by decree of the United Nations.'

Staring down into those openly vulnerable eyes, Ishaan feels his heart flip over inside his chest. Wordlessly, he buries his face in her shoulder, hugging her, too moved to speak. Tinka feels a telltale wetness against her collarbone.

She raises a hand to his hair, tousling it with fingertips that feel hyper-sensitized.

'Isn't this your maiden flight, Flying Officer? D'you even know what to do?'

Shaanu raises his head and smiles, the sparkle in the damp Kota-grey eyes bashful and eager and confident.

'I'll figure it out,' he tells her. 'But you'll have to be a good navigator.'

• • •

Dressed in a brown Pathan suit and grey monkey cap, Maddy has been hanging about the parking lot of the Intercontinental all evening, befriending the drivers and bellboys and chatting up the tall, snooty doorman with the handlebar moustache. This maharaja-like personage is a hard-core snob who remembers the good old days when this entire hotel was a white-people-only property and darkies like Maddy (who is particularly brown, being the colour of the Kodava hills from whence he springs) were allowed in only from the service entrance.

But Maddy's soft southern charm slowly has its usual effect. By the time the Twelve-days-to-Christmas ball is in full swing, his story of being the new driver of one of Dacca's major personages has been bought, and he is warming his hands over the glowing orange ring of an electric heater owned by Nikka Khan's driver himself, engaged in a heated discussion on the Indian cricket team's tour of England.

'Bhagwat Chandrasekhar's performance was just a ruddy lappa,' says one of the drivers. 'Sheer, stupid luck.'

'And he ran out of luck with Luckhurst!' chimes in another one. 'The thing is, you see, that Indians lack the killer instinct. *Pakistan* now…'

'Is there going to be a Bangladesh cricket team?' Maddy asks. 'Who'll captain it?'

There is a nonplussed silence. Everybody looks at everybody else.

'Hassan?' someone hazards doubtfully. 'He played for the Quaid-e-Azam trophy. But only as twelfth man...'

'We'll have a *football* team!' another driver says vigorously, to much applause. 'Football, now that's a game to warm the blood of every Bengali! Why, I rem—'

But nobody gets to hear what he remembers, because at that moment, the sound of a heated altercation comes to their ears. It seems to be coming, not from the street, where the plebeians dwell, but unbelievably, from inside the glass-fronted lobby of the posh hotel.

'The soldiers are roughing up the lobby manager,' one of the ancient bellboys comes panting up to report. 'Not that I'm fond of him or anything – but what is this hotel coming to?'

Unease stirs in Maddy's heart. Making some casual excuse, he walks away from the group of drivers, picking up speed as he nears the lobby. Peering through the glass-fronted windows, he sees a posse of West Pakistani soldiers manhandling the front office manager, a portly young Bengali in a dark suit and black-rimmed spectacles. He is standing behind the marble-countered lobby desk, flanked by two smiling thermocol Santa Clauses, shaking like a leaf, but looking resolute.

'What's happening, janab?' Maddy asks the snooty doorman. 'What do they want?'

That worthy shakes his head.

'These West Pakistani scum are such uncultureds. No manners, no ettikate.'

'But issue kya hai?'

The snooty doorman shrugs grimly.

'Issue is ki their general wants to know the room number of a lady journalist who is living here and the lobby manager is refusing to give it.'

Maddy's heart sinks. *Tinka.*

'Why won't he give it?' he asks as incuriously as possible.

The snooty doorman strokes his moustaches, his dark eyes glinting militantly.

'Because that is the *rule.* This a proper hotel. A British-era hotel where we respect the privacy of our guests. And their general is a horny goat. Everybody knows. And also, this is a neutral zone. These lechers have no standing here! Besides,' he adds after a pause, 'we are broad-minded people, not like these narrow Punjabis, and we think-so she is entertaining her boyfriend in the room and will not appreciate being disturbed.'

Baaz, thinks Maddy. Fuck, I have to get in there before they do.

A scream of agony reaches his ears. The lobby manager has been bent backwards like a bow and is sobbing aloud. The leader of the soldiers is bellowing at him.

'Tell us the room number, or we'll go from room to room shooting your guests!'

The lobby manager raises his head, his chubby face as white as thermocol.

'It's 1152!' he gasps. 'Her number's 1152. I swear it is. Let me go!'

The soldiers drop him and he crumples on the marble-topped desk, his glasses broken, his hands trembling.

The watching bellboys suck in their breath in sympathy.

As the soldiers make for the stairs and the elevator, the doorman rushes to the lobby manager, urgently asking if he is all right. He is rewarded with an irately hissed, 'Yes, I'm fine. Please do not make a scene and kindly return to your post! This is a five-star hotel, the *only* five-star hotel in Dacca!'

Rather shamefacedly, the doorman returns to his position by the door. The portly young manager finger-combs his hair back into its sleek side-parting, straightens his tie and sits down at his desk, avoiding eye contact with anybody.

Meanwhile, Maddy gets to his feet and walks away slowly, picking up speed as he rounds out of the vision of the other drivers.

1152 means the eleventh floor. The soldiers would be working fast to cordon it off from within. But there is a *without*. All the rooms at the Intercon have a huge glass-fronted picture window facing the Race Course, easily accessible by air. And Maddy has seen a Medicines Without Borders helicopter parked at the corner.

He stops at his car in the darkness, feels around for the Sten gun Macho da has provided and starts to run full pelt.

He has to get there before they do...

• • •

'Who's your Mercury?'

They are lying in the big fluffy bed, staring up at the panelled ceiling, their clothes strewn on the floor. His arm is around her and he is running the backs of his fingers lightly against her bare shoulder, but at this question he groans, throws his head against the pillows and slaps his forehead. 'Not you too! Who taught *you* that stupid game?'

She props herself up on her elbow and twinkles down at him.

'Sulo did. On the train to Kalaiganga. So, who is it?'

Ishaan pulls her atop him.

'Who's *your* Mercury?'

'Careful!' she cries. 'You don't want to hurt your shoulder!'

He ignores this protest.

'Tell me.'

Tinka gives a defensive shrug, and gently lays her head down on his chest. Fingers caressing the bandage on his shoulder, she says, 'Well, my solar system's pretty small. My mother's dead, my brother's dead, my dad...' Her voice falters to a stop.

'How's that going?' He asks with careful casualness. 'Are you not talking to him at all? Still?'

He feels her shrug against his chest. 'Oh I *talked* to him.' She says crossly. 'Because of what *you* put in my head! Maybe I'll even go live with him when all this is over. In Defence Colony, buried knee-deep in Punjabis. So okay fine, Ardisher is my Earth.'

Shaanu catches her hand and kisses it.

'Fine.'

'Kainaz fui gets to be my Venus because she's so beautiful.' She lifts her head to look at him. 'That's only logical, right?'

'Right.'

She lays her head back on his chest. 'And so, in the position of the planet that's closest to the sun, which is *me*...' Her fingers twitch within his grasp, she takes a breath so deep that he feels the pressure of it depress his chest and says lightly, 'There's you.'

There is silence for a long moment and then Shaanu hugs her so tightly that she has to protest in a muffled voice.

'What the hell, lemme go, I can't breathe!'

'Then *don't* breathe,' he growls laughingly even as he loosens his grip enough for her head to come up and her eyes to glare down at him reproachfully.

'Who's *your* Mercury?'

The grey eyes start to sparkle.

'Mine?'

'Uh-huh.'

She stacks both palms upon his chest, rests her chin atop them and regards him expectantly.

He makes a loose fist and cuffs her gently against her nose.

'Well, you know, I studied in this very bakwaas school in my *dusty backward village*,' he emphasizes.

'I'm a cow.' She kisses his chest contritely.

'And the teacher wasn't really qualified so I'm not at all sure about the order of the planets...'

'My Very Educated Mother Just Showed Us Nine Planets.'

'What?' He has been sliding his hands down her back, but at this he stops and looks up at her blankly.

'It's to help you memorize the order,' she explains. 'My-Mercury, Very-Venus, Educated...'

'Ooooh teeeriii!' He throws up his hands. 'Why didn't anybody ever tell me that before?'

'You don't know it?' She is surprised. 'I learnt it in grade two.'

'In America.' Shaanu looks wistful. 'Wow, you're so rich, Tell-me-na.'

'Shut up.' She frowns, embarrassed. 'I'm not.'

He smiles, pulling her down to him, his hands sliding down smoothly to grip her bottom.

'My very educated *mistress* just showed us nine planets,' he whispers, pushing her up against him, his eyes darkening to smoke.

She shakes him. 'Tell me!'

Ishaan groans and shifts her weight slightly.

'Okay, let's see. Pluto would be ... my Flight Commander, Hosannah Carvalho. At Neptune, my brother Shelly, who's a bit of a donkey. Uranus would be Surinder bau, my brother who's training to be a vet. At Saturn ... Juhi, she's practically like a sister, Jupiter would be Jana-Gana-Mana, my fellow Gnatties – what's next?'

'Mars.'

'Mars is Maddy and Raka, Earth my little sisters, Venus is...' He checks abruptly, then goes quiet.

'Sneha!' Tinka predicts confidently.

Ishaan stays silent for a long moment, then draws a long, shuddering breath.

'Yes.' he says simply. 'That's only logical because she's so beautiful, right?'

Tinka smiles. 'Right.'

He lies back.

'And so we come to the top position. There *are* other contenders for it, but in this new spirit of love and forgiveness-for-fathers, I'll grant the top spot to my mother's husband, Choudhary Chimman Singh.'

Tinka gives a gasp of outrage and rears up, her hair whirling around her face.

'Chimman!'

'He's my stepfather, after all,' Ishaan says piously. 'I have to give respect—'

'Fuck you!'

'Hey, don't get so upset...'

But Tinka has already scrambled to her knees, a pillow in her hands, whacking him across the face with it as hard as she can.

'Jat! Dog! Jog!'

'Stop!' Shaanu protests, trying to sit up. 'Hey, my shoulder, Tinka! Stop, be careful! You'll bust open my wound!'

But she continues to hit him steadily.

Laughing, ducking, protesting, Shaanu finally manages to wrestle the pillow from her and throw it across the room. Foiled, she whirls away from him and flops down on the bed on her stomach, her chin on her knuckles, staring at the moonlit wall.

'Why so much physical violence, yaar?' Shaanu demands as he drops down beside her, slightly out of breath. 'You hit the DUSU president with a copper bell, then the first time we met you camel-kicked me right me in the crotch…'

Tinka rolls her eyes.

'Uff, how much you whine about that one kick in the crotch! What d'you want, a written apology?'

'You could kiss it better,' he suggests.

She considers this, tucking her hair behind her ear, her expression serious. Then she smiles.

'Later. First tell me, if you didn't know about the engagement, how come you were wearing the chain with the eagle locket that day?'

He interlaces his fingers with hers and stares down at them sombrely.

'He said it was a present from him to me,' he says lightly, trying, but unable to keep the hurt out of his voice. 'Because he was so proud of me. Because I'm his oldest son.'

Tinka looks first appalled, then furious. 'What a *pig!*'

What a *girl*, Shaanu thinks, staring at her besotted. What a *woman*. What a way she has with words!

'Yeah,' he says feelingly.

'To tell you the truth, I didn't really like that locket,' she continues. 'It was too loud.'

Ishaan's tender feelings vanish instantly.

'Arrey, what's wrong with loud, now?' he demands.

'Why would anybody wear a *soft* locket? It was heavy, solid gold!'

She kisses him.

'Jat.'

As he stares at her, wondering whether this a compliment or an insult, she stretches languorously in the slanting moon shadows, her body tan gloriously smooth, and slides a hand to his belly.

'*Ishaaan...*' she coos.

He groans. 'Don't Ishaan me! I don't like what it does to my stomach.'

'Ishaan...' Tinka murmurs in tones even more dulcet. 'Who's your Mercury?'

He grins.

'Maddy would say you're the Venus my penis has been waiting for.'

'Never mind Maddy,' she whispers fiercely.

He cups her face in his hands and looks down at her, the grey eyes grave and steady.

'You are.'

• • •

'Fuck fuck fuck,' Maddy mutters to himself as he approaches the Medicines Without Borders helicopter standing in a darkened parking lot behind the hotel. 'Don't screw this up, Subbiah!'

He saw the chopper's American crew leave a while ago, yawning and slapping mosquitoes off their arms. Now he approaches it stealthily, just in case there are Pakistani soldiers stationed around it, heart slamming hard against his ribs, his Sten gun in his hands.

What if I've got this all wrong, he wonders as he edges closer to the makeshift cordon around the chopper. Suppose

Tinka isn't the lady journalist they meant? Or what if she's got a new boyfriend? What if I'm putting two and two together and making two thousand? Fuck, I should've stuck to flying my Caribou. Even better, I should've stayed in Coorg, growing poinsettias and brewing coffee. Except I know nothing about coffee.

'*Halt-hu-khamba-phrend-uffo?*'

'Excuse me?' says Maddy, one eyebrow raised comically, even as he grips his gun harder.

The hoarse, definitely nervous voice repeats its musical litany, its accent clearly rustic Punjabi.

'*Halt-hu-khamba-phrend-uffo?*'

The bugger sounds even more petrified than me, Maddy thinks wryly.

'Halt, who comes by...' he mutters aloud, and his brow clears. 'Ah, now I get it – halt, who comes by, friend or foe? Well, the answer to that would have to be foe, I'm afraid.'

And he fires the Sten right where the voice has been coming from. The gun rattles, splutters, then shudders into silence.

Maddy stares down at it in disgust.

'Shit!'

But the noise it has made is enough to alert the nervous guard up ahead. Seconds later something whizzes past Maddy's head, missing him narrowly. He drops to his knees, cursing. Up in the hotel, a series of lights come on all along what looks like the eleventh floor.

Maddy rises to his feet. Staying low, he rushes forward and tackles the dark shape, throwing it to the ground. There's a grunt, some robust swearing in Punjabi, and then comes a blow to the side of his head. Maddy sees stars but manages to raise his useless Sten and slam the soldier across the temple with its butt. He gives a gurgle and goes limp.

'Stun gun!' Maddy pants, half-surprised, half-satisfied, and staggers to his feet. The chopper is just metres away, and thanks to the helicopter flying course he's done recently, he's pretty sure he can get the thing started and up in the air. But what if the tank is empty?

Abandoning all attempts at stealth now, he flat out runs towards the chopper and reaches it without incident. Placing his palms against its cold, bulbous flank, he draws several steadying breaths, then starts to move around it, feeling for the door.

As he rounds the tail and emerges onto the lee side, away from the chilling wind, he is faced with a circle of at least twenty chowkidaars, cosily frying kebabs in a saucepan suspended over a little campfire.

'Fuck!'

They stare at him for a moment, as taken aback as he is, their kebabs sizzling on their forks, and then, spotting the gun in his hand, they get to their feet with a collective roar.

Maddy takes to his heels. Racing around the chopper, with the chowkidaars hard on his heels, he comes around at the back, yanks at the pilot's door and is flooded with sweet relief as it yields to the pressure of his hand.

Diving into the cockpit, he slams the door shut behind him and feels around for the ignition wires, even as the chowkidaars start to whack the perspex of the chopper with their iron-tipped lathis. He connects the wires, the engine fires, and the rotors whir to life. Maddy stares down at the instrument panel, blinded momentarily by the sudden light in the cabin, then jabs tentatively at various buttons. The chopper lurches, pitches randomly towards the right and remains stubbornly grounded.

Maddy stares down at the controls dementedly. What is he doing wrong?

Outside, the chowkidaars, pushed backwards by the whirring rotors, have managed to get their hands on some kind of weaponry. Shots slam into the chopper's perspex, starring it in seven places. Illuminated by the light in the cabin, Maddy is as exposed as the ladies on the first-floor balconies on English Road.

And still the chopper refuses to lift off the ground.

• • •

Upstairs, the West Pakistani commandoes, lean mean killing machines in their OG camouflage uniforms make their way through the corridor of the eleventh floor, towards room 1152. There are ten of them, an unnecessarily large number to take down just one IAF man and a woman journalist, but General Khan's instructions had been very specific. As they file down the corridor, their boots thudding hard against the soft pile carpet, an elderly Swiss gentleman in a white towel bathrobe, who happens to be putting out his room service tray at that very moment, hails them in an outraged voice.

'Hey hey, this is a neutral zone, if you please! By whose authority are you here?'

The officer at the lead of the line of soldiers turns away his crew-cut head and keeps walking.

But the old man sticks out one frail arm and grabs him by the shoulder.

'*Excuse* me? I asked you a question!'

'Sir, please let us do our work!' the officer replies curtly.

'You have no work here, sir!' bellows the old man, now very red-faced. He sucks in a big breath, then, chest fully inflated with air and authority, he says, 'I work for the International Red Cross, and I tell you now that you need to turn around and leave this building *immediately*.'

There is a moment's pause. The soldiers look at their

leader. The officer, his face impassive, looks at a point behind the old man's perspiring head.

'Immediately!' the old man repeats.

The officer raises the butt of his Lee-Enfield rifle and knocks the Swiss out with it. He collapses, right next to the shells of the boiled egg he has just eaten, an expression of intense surprise on his face.

• • •

'Tinka?'

There is no answer. Shaanu sits up drowsily, feeling around the bed for her.

'Where d'you go?'

It is the darkest hour, the one before dawn, and she is sitting cross-legged on the floor next to the bed, wrapped in a bedsheet, her tousled hair glowing in the pool of golden light thrown by the bedside lamp. In her hands she clutches the overalls Ishaan had been wearing.

'Look.' There is a strange edge to her voice. 'This must be his family. They look so happy.'

Shaanu rolls over the cool white sheets to look at the little photograph she's holding.

'Where did you find that?' he blinks in surprise.

'Half falling out of the inner breast pocket. Didn't you see it?'

He shakes his head and leans over to kiss her shoulder. Then he leans even further and studies the picture.

A smiling woman in a floral hijab, a tall, dark bearded man and, sitting on his shoulders, two solemn-faced little girls in party frocks.

Ishaan chuckles. 'No wonder Nikka Khan looked so confused last night! I look nothing like this guy.'

Tinka doesn't smile. Her fingers are stroking the little girls' faces. 'They're so young,' she says softly.

Shaanu's grey eyes register pain, then harden.

Wordlessly, he reaches for the overalls in her hands and puts them on. Then he strides to the window. The now-familiar wail of the air-raid siren rises to their ears.

'The ceasefire's over,' he says roughly. 'I should go.'

Tinka looks up from the photograph, her eyes still far away. 'Hmmm?'

'Yes.' He bends down to put on his shoes.

'What happened?' she asks, confused.

'Nothing,' he says evenly. 'You're clearly all set to mourn the tragic demise of Squadron Leader Bilawal Hussain. And I'd rather not. Honestly, I don't feel he would even want your sympathy. I fought him in the skies, and I *know* the bugger was having fun when he died. It was a *good* death. We should all be so lucky.'

Tinka, sitting in the pool of light, shakes her head, bewildered. 'Why are you so *angry?*'

Is he angry? He stares down at her helplessly, clenching and unclenching his fists, and realizes he is.

'Tinka – I shot him down, I cut down his body and yanked the clothes off his charred corpse. I do *not* want to look at pictures of his little daughters!'

'Shaanu...' She rises to her feet in one swift move, clutching the bedsheet around her. 'Listen...'

If Ishaan sounded good on her lips, Shaanu sounds knee-bucklingly devastating, but he manages to ignore it. Raising a hand to ward her off, he says, 'Why the hell should I feel guilty, anyway? Sure, I chewed up Bilawal Hussain – the others ejected, I saw their chutes, so I know it was just the one guy. But what about Raka? They shot him up so badly, he'd be better off dead, the poor chap.'

She raises her chin, her face mutinous.

'Raka will get better,' she says firmly. 'Also, that's bullshit logic and you know it.'

They stare at each other for a while, then he turns away to look out of the big glass windows where the Dacca landscape is slowly glimmering into sight. 'Before I met you and you put all these ideas into my head, I *loved* my career. It was my childhood dream, all I ever wanted to do or be. My father was a freedom fighter. He hid from the British in my mother's village because he was wounded, and she nursed him – but he died before they could get married. Chimman says that story isn't true. But Chimman ka kya bharosa?'

Wordlessly, Tinka hugs him from the back, resting her chin against his shoulder.

Staring out of the window, Shaanu continues, 'But then you started talking about Jimmy and writing about Napalm, and about the kids in the orphanage ... and I got more and more confused ... and now you're nosing about in my overalls while I'm asleep, and you've dug out this bloody photograph which I hadn't even *noticed* all these days!'

'I didn't nose about,' she protests, stung. 'It *fell* out.'

'I didn't see certain things before,' he continues, not listening to her. 'But you *made* me see them – and now I can't unsee them!'

He whirls to look at her, and his eyes are so hurt and confused that her heart turns over.

'I'm sorry,' she says brokenly. 'Look, I don't want to fight – you're hurt and weak...'

Shaanu retreats towards the door.

'You've made everything complicated when it's actually so simple! They're our enemy and we're their enemy and we fight each other till somebody wins!'

But this is too much for Tinka. She scrambles to her feet, clutching her bedsheet around her.

'Nobody wins,' she says passionately. 'That's the point. Everybody loses!'

They're standing only a few feet apart, but to Shaanu, at that moment, the distance between them seems unbridgeable. He backs away from her, towards the door, the Kota-grey eyes storming.

'You're going to hate me now,' he says hopelessly. 'I know it. You're that sort of person. Every time you look at me, you'll be thinking...' He pauses, then spits out the word with mocking, melodramatic venom. '*Murderer!*'

'I can never hate you.'

Something in the tone of her voice makes him flinch. He throws up his hands. 'You'd dislike me then! Or pity me. Which is worse!'

'Don't be silly.'

But her voice is unconvincing.

'I'm going,' he says. But he doesn't move an inch.

Standing by the bed, she holds out a hand to him, then slowly lets it drop. They stand without speaking, silhouettes in the moonlight.

And then a hail of bullets shatters the silence, unnaturally loud in the still of the night. The heavy teak door of the hotel room lunges forward, blown off its hinges, and a posse of armed soldiers stands framed where it stood.

'Down, down, down!'

'Surrender or we shoot!'

'Abhi! *Turannt!*'

Ishaan whirls around, his face contorted in a snarl of rage, and stands in front of Tinka...

The soldiers step over the fallen door and thunder into the room.

Ignoring her protests, Shaanu pushes her further back and faces them, fists clenched, eyes blazing...

And then, with the impact of a killer shark breaking through the ocean's surface, the tail of a helicopter shatters through the glass window, drowning the sound of gunfire with the khata-khata-khata roar of rotor blades.

Slivers of glass shower Shaanu, Tinka and the soldiers alike.

As they cough and blink and cower, the tail lashes and reverses out, and a massive, bulbous chopper fills the shattered window, hovering like a gigantic, illuminated bee in the moonlight.

A hoarse, triumphant voice roars over the rotors and the sound of still shattering glass.

'*Dogggfightttt!*'

Ishaan, holding Tinka's hand fast in his own, responds to this greeting with a yell of unbridled glee.

'Wooooohoooo! Ekdum Baaz-ke-maaphik, Maddy!'

Maddy, hunkered down in the pilot's seat, peers out at them through the wildly sliding door, sweaty and dishevelled.

'What would your grandfather say now, bastard?' he crows. 'Big guy, big cock! Now get into the goddamn chopper!'

FIFTEEN

The muezzin's cry rings out with its usual vim and vigour on English Road the next morning, causing the pigeons roosting on the dome of the mosque to flutter away and resettle in a disgruntled mob on the peepal tree beyond. The sky behind them is milky blue, with an edge as red as ox's blood.

The street itself lies uneasily calm after last night's excesses, the only movement the slow sweep of the safai karamchari's broom along the road, gathering up the usual sordid pile of debris – leaf plates, glass bottles, wilted flowers and used condoms.

In the tiny room on the terrace of Harry Rose's narrow white house, Maddy yawns luxuriously, then rolls over to look at Shaanu who is lying with eyes tight shut, mouth slightly open, trying to hold onto sleep.

'Baaz,' he whispers. 'Hey, Baaz.'

'Hmmm.'

'Gimme the *juice*.'

Shaanu groans and covers his head with his pillow.

'What the fuck, man?'

Maddy scrambles closer.

'Did anything *happen* last night?'

'Matlab?' Shaanu voice is muffled, the pillow is still covering his head. 'You were there, you know what happened. We were trapped and you saved us, and then we ran out of fuel and almost crashed, and all the villagers freaked out, and we had to find our way home in a bullock cart.'

Maddy waves away these irrelevancies. 'No, no, what happened *before*. When you were in the bedroom with Tinka.'

Shaanu whips away the pillow and meets his friend's sheepishly eager gaze. 'You tharki bastard. Go back to sleep.'

'You owe me,' Maddy insists. 'I saved your goddamn *life*. Make me a detailed report.'

Shaanu's eyes grow dreamy. He hugs his pillow, looking sleepy and happy and heart-breakingly handsome. 'Fuck off.'

The muezzin hits a high note. They both wince.

Maddy edges closer.

'So, what, you *love* her now?'

Ishaan flops back in the bed.

'Yes,' he says to the unplastered ceiling. 'I love her.'

Maddy's face appears above his.

'And something happened or not? In that fancy hotel bedroom, I mean. *Dishoom*?'

There is a long silence. Then Shaanu grins.

'Dishoom. Dishoom. And dishooooooooom.'

'Yessssss!' Electrified with delight, Maddy slaps his hands upon his thighs and capers wildly about the room. 'Wah, mere sher, mere tiger! I'm proud of you!'

'Yeaahhhhh.' Shaanu's reply is a deeply felt, deeply

drawn-out sigh. 'I'm not giving you any more details, you horny bastard.'

'Okay, man, okay.' Maddy backs away. 'But like, what's the plan, going forward? Love, marriage, babies?'

This makes Shaanu sit up. His smiling face grows sober.

'Yes,' he says strongly. 'Yes, all of that! That's what I want – that's what I want to spend my life doing! Whatever she wants, whatever it takes.'

'Who?'

They look around to see Tinka standing in the doorway. Bundled into the chopper in nothing but a white bedsheet yesterday, she is now dressed in one of Harry Rose's kaftans. It's too long and too loose, so she has had to yank it up and belt it around her waist. She looks vaguely like a samurai dressed for battle.

'Nobody,' Ishaan says quickly, his ears bright red. 'Uh, good morning.'

'Good morning,' she replies composedly, leaning back against the doorjamb and looking much less bashful than him.

Maddy looks at his friend's incandescent face and smothers a smile. A besotted Baaz is going to be pretty entertaining to have around, he realizes.

'Wh-where's everybody?' Ishaan asks next. He's just noticed that her mouth looks a little swollen, a little bruised. My doing, he thinks with exultant possessiveness as his eyes drop to the pillow in his hands.

'Listening to the radio chatter,' she replies, rolling her eyes. 'It's been going on practically non-stop since we tuned in.'

Maddy looks up, surprised. 'The mechanic came? I'd given up on that joker.'

'Oh no,' Tinka replies. 'I had a look at it and it turned out to be exactly the same wireless radio Jimmy used to have. He taught me how it worked. So I fixed it.'

'You fixed the *radio*?' the boys speak in unison, clearly impressed.

She grins and shrugs. 'Yeah.'

'How are you with watches?' Maddy asks. "Coz I broke mine when we bailed out of the Caribou. I've got all the bits, I think. Can you fix it?'

Tinka laughs. 'I can try!'

'Excellent,' Maddy says briskly and heads out of the room.

Alone, Ishaan and Tinka look at each other for a long, crackling moment. Then in two quick strides, he is beside her, his hand wrapping around her wrist, jerking her to his chest. He speaks against her cheek, 'I won't fly any more if that's what you want.'

'*What?*' She laughs as her hand comes up to caress his face. 'I don't want you to stop flying. It's what you do.'

'I can do other things,' he asserts unhesitatingly. 'Really well. Lots of things.'

'Name one.'

'I can box. Drive a tractor. Make love – I make love well, right?'

He looks at her for confirmation, his gaze only slightly anxious.

And now Tinka does blush. An undeniable, beautiful blush. 'Right.'

Shaanu grins.

'And I can knit.'

She tilts her head.

'You know how to *knit*?'

'Then what? Nothing fancy, but I could make you a muffler! My sisters taught me – you think only your brother taught you things?'

She lays her head against his chest.

'Ishaan…'

'Hmmm?'

'Come down and listen to the chatter. Nikka Khan and the rest of the army top brass have been summoned to Governor House by the Governor – the UN contingent has been invited too – I think he wants to surrender.'

• • •

Bloody, hand-to-hand combat has broken out in the streets of Dacca. One by one, every building and every house is being entered, fought over and won. The port towns of Chalna and Khulna have been captured, with not a whimper out of the US's Seventh Fleet stationed right there in the Bay of Bengal. The IAF have been merciless. MiGs and Hunters have been pounding down on the Bangladesh borders ever since the four-hour ceasefire ended.

As Pakistan reels from this relentless attack, they also have to deal with Field Marshal Sam Manekshaw addressing their troops in the eastern theatre directly on the radio, telling them that they are surrounded and appealing to them to use their brains, save their lives and surrender to India.

Crouched over his freshly repaired illegal radio, Macho da cackles with delight as he eavesdrops on General Nikka Khan's increasingly frantic attempts to bypass the petrified Governor and get through to President Yahya Khan and the other high-ups holed up cosily in Lahore.

'The man's been abandoned,' he gloats, his exquisitely embroidered prayer cap set at a rakish angle on his head. 'Hung out to dry! Well, it's only what he deserves. He deserves worse, actually! He should be *lynched* in *public* for what he's done to my land and my people! Mark my words, he will be!'

'What about Macho's secret mission?' Shaanu whispers to Maddy as he slides in to sit next to him in the radio room. 'Why don't you ask him about it?'

'*You* ask him,' Maddy growls back. 'He was in a foul mood because of your stunt last night – thank God Tinka repaired his radio!'

'*My* stunt or *your* st—' Shaanu starts to say hotly, then stops. 'Okay.'

Raising his voice, he addresses the Mukti. 'Sir, if the Governor is indeed planning to surrender, how will that impact our mission?'

'And what *is* the mission, anyway?' Maddy chimes in.

Macho da's eyes skitter away, and land on Front Room, who is standing in the doorway, his expression as serenely unflappable as ever.

'Are we ready?' Macho da asks.

Front Room smiles. For the first time ever, Shaanu and Maddy hear him speak. His voice is soft and rustling. 'We will be.'

The Mukti's eyes turn back to them.

'Yes, well, it's all a little fluid at the moment.'

Maddy and Shaanu exchange looks.

'I'll brief you as and when the time comes.'

Harry Rose, who has been sitting quietly till now, gets to her feet.

'We need to brief India about this high-level meeting at Governor House,' she declares. 'It is vital information – they could use it to precipitate something.'

'India!' The Mukti's dark eyes flash as he curls his lip

contemptuously. 'But they're so untrusting, so holier-than-thou! Why do we have to share information with *them*?'

But when she walks up to the radio, sits down and starts to work the controls, he doesn't object, choosing to just glower behind her sullenly.

'Hello, Gori Kalaiyaan, come in, Gori Kalaiyaan...' Harry Rose speaks into the receiver. 'This is Mukti four trying to re-establish contact. This is Mukti four...'

Lots of static and crackle, some of it loud enough to make them all wince.

'We used to speak to your guys regularly before our radio packed up,' Harry Rose tells Maddy and Shaanu. 'This used to be their frequency. Maybe they've given up on us – we've had no contact with them for over ten days...'

And then a familiar irascible voice crackles through the line.

'Gori Kalaiyaan to Mukti four. Gori Kalaiyaan to Mukti four.'

Maddy and Shaanu look at each other, stupefied.

Then they leap to their feet and yell as one into the receiver: 'Sir! Sir! It's us, sir!'

'Who's us?' Wing Commander Hosannah Carvalho's voice demands grumpily. 'Identify yourselves.'

But the two boys are too elated to be coherent. They just shout hoarsely that it is them.

Kuch Bhi's voice crackles through again, charged with emotion.

'Subbiah! And Chakkahera! That you, ain't it, Chakkahera? Should've known it would take more than three Sabres to quash your Jat ass!'

'Yes, sir!'

'It's us, sir!'

Is their senior officer's voice trembling? Surely not – he isn't a damsel with fair, dainty wrists, as his call sign suggests. He is the Chief Operations Officer of that most feared and revered of bases, AFS Kalaiganga. The tremble must be the static on the freshly repaired wireless.

'The ladies have been missing your piano playing, Subbiah. I'll give them all a kiss from you!'

'Yes, sir!' Maddy shouts back. 'I mean, please don't, sir!'

'All this is very moving, I'm sure,' Macho da says sourly from his place in the corner. 'But we actually contacted you to give you some vital information.'

'Of course.' Old Kuch Bhi's voice grows attentive instantly. 'Update me, please, Mukti four.'

Harry Rose leans in.

'We have information of a high-level party,' she says. 'At Governor House. They're talking surrender.'

'Time?' Carvalho's voice is crisp.

'10.30 a.m. Today.'

'That gives us half-an-hour. Appreciate the tip, Mukti four. Take good care of our boys. Lads, we'll be seeing you soon.'

• • •

'Gentlemen, we have information that the Pakistani top brass are meeting shortly to discuss surrendering. We expect Nikka Khan to be vehemently opposed to this. He may even convince the Governor to hold out and fight, leading to more killing, more carnage and the prolonging of civilian agony.'

The briefing room, packed with MiGGies, drinks this in.

Carvalho leans forward, breathing hard.

'And so, we plan to, uh, *drop in uninvited* at this party and gently nudge them towards surrender.'

He proceeds to brief them on their mission, an audacious

sortie right over Dacca, with the Governor House itself as target. The psychological impact of this, Carvalho feels, will be huge. It will seem that the Indians are everywhere and know everything and that resistance is futile. The MiGGies drink it in, fully enthused ... until the map of the city is handed around.

There is gobsmacked silence, and then J-man and Chatty look up at their briefing officer in disbelief. 'That's it? We're supposed to identify the target on the basis of just *this*?'

Old Kuch Bhi Carvalho looks down at the paper – a small, crumpled childishly drawn map of Dacca, with a waving Mickey Mouse cartoon and a cheerful *Go Well Go Shell* printed at the bottom right – and nods.

'Yeah.'

The MiGGies exchange glances.

'Uh, but sir, why don't we have a decent aerial map of Dacca?'

'We never thought we'd be bombing Dacca, that's why,' Carvalho says tersely. 'And nobody else in the world thought they'd be bombing Dacca either! Who even *wants* Dacca? Anyway, look.'

He moves closer to the Shell map.

'That thing with the little rocking horse cartoon next to it is the Ramanna Race Course – and the big white house with the cartoon of a queen's crown next to it is—'

'Governor House,' J-man says in a small stunned voice. 'Our target.' He looks up at his senior officer. 'Are you *serious*?'

Carvalho beams. 'Yes!'

Chatty studies the small, happy scrap of paper dubiously. 'Is this thing even to scale?'

'Don't quibble, Chatrath!' Old Kuch Bhi roars, his

patience eroded. 'Just get up there, swoop down on the first big, expensive-looking damn white building you see, ekdum Baaz-ke-maaphik, and whip that fucker Nikka into cowering submission!'

Thus whipped into cowering submission themselves, Chatty and J-man stride down dazedly to their MiGs, which the airmen have been fitting with heavy duty T-10 rockets, capable of penetrating armour and concrete.

'What the hell are we going to do?' Chatty asks.

J-man shrugs. 'Didn't you hear the man? Look for a low white building surrounded by gardens. Bomb it to pulp.'

• • •

Nikka Khan, unused to being summoned so summarily by the man he considers a weak-kneed figurehead, is sprawled low in his seat at one end of the Governor's long, glass-topped conference table. Along the length of the table sit officials and advisors, both international and local, and at the other end, the twitching, sleep-deprived gaunt-faced Governor.

'They never stop…' he moans. 'Night and day, from the air, and from the water, on every front! It's a constant invasion – I'm sick of it. We need to make it stop.'

Nikka leans forward. 'Excellency, the Americans and the Chinese will be with us soon … we can hold out…'

The Governor's bloodshot eyes bug out of their sockets.

'Shut up, you fool! Nobody's coming to our aid, don't you get it?'

There is a stunned silence round the table. The Governor has never lashed out at his Defence Services counterpart so openly.

'General,' the head of Pakistani Administrative Services for East Pakistan speaks up in his soft, cultured voice. 'Won't you consider the suggestion? We should concede surrender, or we will be locked into a deadly battle of attrition against the attacking Indian and Mukti Bahini forces. That will be both expensive and pointless, and precious lives will be lost on both sides.'

Nikka snorts. 'What are a few dead Indians and Bengalis? And as for our men, they will be *proud* to lay down their lives for Pak sarzameen.'

'Would you just *listen* to me?' The Governor rolls his eyes. Sweat is rolling down his sagging cheeks. 'I am your leader.'

Nikka draws himself up. 'President Yahya Khan is my leader.'

'He isn't taking your calls, janab!' the Governor snaps, now breathing hard. He stumbles to his feet even as the roar of jets streaking overhead fills the air. Everybody looks at each other, fear rampant on their faces.

'Tumansky engines,' breathes the head of the PAF. 'Those are MiGs. But … they've never dropped bombs on the city before.'

'You think they know we're discussing this?' the Administrative Services head whispers.

'They're coming, you fool!' The Governor turns back to Nikka, his eyes wild, his voice rising to a shriek to make himself heard over the approaching jets. 'What are we trying to prove here, exactly? Your loyalty to the Qaumi Tarana? Your manhood? That your lund is the longest on the subcontinent?'

The last words are practically a scream. They merge with the sound of the MiG engines, now dangerously close.

Nikka licks his lips.

Sshviccck!

And then the beautiful, colonial-era glass windows lining

the conference room, through which the morning sun has been pouring onto the red-and-blue Persian carpet, shatter as one. Glass rains into the room.

Everybody ducks.

For the next four minutes, the mighty building is pounded by what the Indian newspapers report the next day to be a full load of 192 rockets.

'Why are the Indians doing this to me?' moans the Governor ten minutes later, as he cowers in the trenches outside.

'The worst is over, sir,' his ADCs assure him as they lift him out. 'All should be well now…'

But they have spoken too soon. A pair of Hawker Hunters swoop in at that very moment and pump a consignment of 30mm cannon shells into the now easily recognizable target.

When the dust finally settles, the beleaguered Governor has had enough. He signs his resignation with shaking hands and rushes for refuge in the Intercontinental Hotel along with the other foreign nationals, thus bringing an end to the civilian leadership of East Pakistan.

• • •

'Nikka Khan is going to give us the slip!' Macho da's hands are shaking with impotent fury. 'The civilian leadership has already collapsed, and if Nikka Khan surrenders on behalf of the Pakistan Army today, he too will fly home safely to Lahore. I can't let that happen, I want that man *lynched*, hanged, *dead and twitching* at the end of a rope!'

The Mukti is pacing up and down in the little radio room on English Road, clenching and unclenching his hands in frustration. The carefully cultivated Sufi ascetic cover is blown, he is dressed in camouflage fatigues, and his eyes are so bloodshot he looks like he's had a relapse of conjunctivitis.

'I thought you wanted freedom for Bangladesh,' Tinka says mildly.

He glares at her. She is lounging comfortably against Ishaan in the back of the room, her tousled head resting on his chest. Her eyes are soft, his arm is around her, her chin is resting on his hand. The two of them seem to shine with happiness.

'Our lovebirds,' the Mukti says sourly to the others in the room. '*They're* happy, so now they think *everybody* is happy. But nobody is! All around you two, people are still *suffering* and demanding *justice*!'

His voice, thick with fury, reverberates in the tiny room.

Shaanu sits up straighter.

'But Tinka's right, sir,' he says, a little apologetically. 'I mean, we've already broken Nikka's back, an independent Bangladesh is on the verge of being born – let the bugger sign the surrender documents and scurry off home.'

Macho da shakes his head, his pale brown eyes flashing with fervour.

'You don't understand, that man is a monster! He must be made to pay for his sins – brutally and swiftly and *permanently* – or people will think they can get away with such behaviour! A thousand new Nikkas will raise their heads, here and across the border! And don't talk back to me, I'm your superior officer.'

'Actually, you're not.' Shaanu's voice is still pleasant, but there's an edge to it. 'Now that we're back in contact with them, I report only to my senior officers from the IAF.'

The Mukti's smile grows nastier.

'I'll cut you some slack today because you're flying high, Flying Officer. And why wouldn't you, with such a,' he sketches an ironic bow at Tinka, 'lovely lady by your side!

But believe me, vermin like Nikka Khan don't deserve to live.'

'Why don't we let the war tribunal decide that?' says Maddy, who is sitting next to Shaanu and Tinka. 'They're sure to appoint one, and then—'

But Harry Rose interrupts him.

'Nikka must die.' Her voice is deep and cold and pitiless. 'The blood of thousands of innocents rises from this scorched earth and demands his bali – his blood sacrifice.'

Maddy's jaw drops. He stares up at Harry Rose like he is seeing her for the first time.

There is a rustling in the doorway. The boys turn and see Front Room standing there, his kurta flapping around his bare legs, his expression unflappable.

'Oh yes,' he murmurs softly, matter-of-factly, his eyes fixed on Harry.

'Nothing less than his flesh and blood will satisfy the souls of his victims,' she declares next, her hands clenching and unclenching like claws.

Maddy gulps.

'Aur karle je ne sais quoi,' Shaanu mutters from beside him. 'Dekh chhori kitni bloodthirsty nikli.'

'Fuck!' Maddy says faintly.

'You know what I think?' Shaanu continues softly, eyeing the trio of blood-lusting Muktis. 'I think their great, so-called mission is bumping off Nikka. *Just* that. That's all there is to it.'

'Shit,' says Tinka, stunned. 'You're right.'

'Yeah,' Maddy agrees, still gulping like a fish. 'We need to get the hell out of here.'

An irascible voice sounds in the tiny room.

'Gori Kalaiyaan to Mukti four, Gori Kalaiyaan to Mukti four – come in Mukti four…'

Tinka jumps up and runs to the wireless controls.

'We're here, Gori Kalaiyaan!'

'Who's this, now?' Kuch Bhi Carvalho's voice sounds bemused.

Maddy and Shaanu push forward eagerly.

'It's us, sir!'

'There you are, Chakkahera! Okay, our GOC is flying into Dacca in a bit. Nikka Khan is going to surrender to him today.'

Tinka and the two young men look at each other in delight.

'That's tremendous news, sir!'

'Yes, indeed.' Carvalho sounds exhausted but happy. 'The tip-off about the meeting at Governor House helped tremendously, otherwise the bugger could have dithered for days! You saved a lot of lives, well done! Now, the reason why I wanted to speak to you ... we've received confirmation reports from the villagers around the area you went down in, Chakkahera – you did indeed down three Sabres.'

Ishaan snaps to attention.

'Yes, sir!'

Kuch Bhi's voice grows indulgent, more indulgent than they have ever heard it sound.

'You need to get to Delhi ASAP – Air Headquarters will conduct a full psychological check-up to make sure you're fit to fly ... you've been through a lot...'

Ishaan's eyes go to Tinka's. She smiles. He smiles back.

'I'm just *fine*, sir!'

'Let me finish.' Carvalho's voice is severe. 'And on 26 January, you will be awarded an MVC, maybe even a PVC. If that happens, you'll be the first IAF recipient to get it while still alive.'

Speech deserts Ishaan. Tears rush, hot and strong, to his eyes. He dashes them away, hugging first Maddy and then Tinka.

Kuch Bhi winds up, sounding positively fatherly now, 'Also, I don't want to get your hopes up too much, but the doctors seem more positive about young Raka's condition – we may all yet be eating Aggarwal Sweets for Christmas.'

• • •

The meeting between the Indian and Pakistani generals is short and distinctly unsweet. General Nikka Khan is handled politely but firmly by his Indian counterpart, the General-Officer-Commanding of the Eastern Command, a tall, smiling Sikh who tells the Butcher of Bengal in no uncertain terms that his little dream of calling for a ceasefire and then having the UN come in and order the supposed aggressor India to withdraw from all Pakistani territory is just that, a dream.

'Be realistic, General,' he tells him, not unsympathetically. 'You're in a bad position here. Our armies have breached every bastion and are in firm possession of the city. If you try to hold out for anything more than an unconditional surrender, India will simply withdraw and leave you at the mercy of the Muktis. That won't go very well, I'm afraid.'

'I want more time to think,' Nikka says hoarsely.

'By all means.' The Sikh shrugs. 'Here is the surrender document, all typed out and ready to sign. Think over it for half-an-hour.'

He and his men withdraw to the verandah outside, ask for a phone call to be put through to the prime minister's office in New Delhi and settle down to snacks and tea.

After a hearty meal of luchi, mutton cutlets, aloo posto and mishti doi, the call comes through. The GOC gets to his feet and reports that he has left Nikka alone with the document in his office.

'To let him stew over it, ma'am,' he explains. 'I'm very hopeful he'll sign without a fuss.'

'Just make sure he doesn't kill himself in there or something,' replies the prime minister tersely. 'If he does, his officers will immediately cry foul, and fighting will break out in the streets again, and hundreds more will die. Please don't underestimate the intensity of these people's hatred for each other. We're balancing on the edge of a knife here. It's a delicate situation, General.'

'Yes, ma'am!' says the GOC and hangs up hastily.

Rushing back into Nikka's room, he breathes a sigh of relief. The Butcher is still staring down at the document with unseeing eyes.

'Just sign it, General Khan,' the GOC says softly.

Nikka picks up the pen with shaking hands, scrawls across the paper and sits back with a shudder.

'I want the surrender ceremony to happen here,' he whispers. 'Quietly.'

'Oh, no,' says the smiling Sikh firmly. 'It will happen where everybody can see – at the Ramanna Race Course. The cars are waiting. Come, let's go.'

• • •

'It's like a dream,' Tinka says softly. 'Everything's working out so well – Raks on the mend, the war over in just sixteen days, I just wish I didn't have to leave you.'

They are sitting on the sunny, cemented stairs that lead down to the much pitted and cratered Tezgaon runway, watching the IAF pilots run around the place. Maddy has rushed off with a group of other excited Fighters to finally have a look at AFS Tezgaon from ground level. They're busy taking photographs and collecting trophies – a little ghoulishly, according to Tinka, but she's in too good a mood to give them a lecture.

She has been granted permission to fly all the way to Islamabad on Nikka's plane – along with his top aides and a smattering of international journalists. Nikka is to arrive any minute – the surrender ceremony has just been concluded at the Race Course. Neither Tinka nor Shaanu had been interested enough to go. I don't want to see anybody's nose being ground into the mud, she had said – and he had just wanted to be with her.

Now Ishaan glances down at her, his eyes teasing. 'Bullshit, you're dying to see Islamabad.'

She wrinkles her forehead. 'Sort of,' she admits. 'But actually, I just want to go home.'

Make your home with me.

He feels the words so intensely that for a moment he thinks he's said them aloud. Worried, he scans her face, but she is just staring out at the runway, her expression pensive.

'If killing Bilawal Hussain wins me a PVC, it can't be a bad thing, right?' The words are torn out of him.

Tinka squeezes his hand. 'I spoke to his wife on the phone, a while ago. She wants to meet me. She's driving up to Islamabad. She said she has no personal animosity against you and the girls would want to know how their father died.'

He stares down at her, confused. Then his grey eyes flood with gratitude. His hands grip hers with painful intensity.

'*Thank* you.'

She hugs him. 'I'm so proud of you.'

He pulls away, a little uncertain. 'What's ani-mos, though? That word you said?'

Tinka hugs him again. It's dangerously addictive, she has realized, hugging him. Every time she does, she feels like she's received energy enough to power an airbase.

'Oi, get a room, will you?' The old wheezing voice makes them jump apart. They turn, not very sheepishly, to discover Julian Arnott and Leo Stepanov, weighed down with travelling bags, smiling down at them benignly.

'Hullo children,' Leo says in a very fatherly tone.

Tinka springs to her feet and hugs them both.

'I *knew* that dress would get you into trouble,' Julian says to her severely, as Ishaan comes forward to shake hands with them, the tips of his ears bright red. 'It was just too seductive.'

'When's the wedding?' Leo grins.

'Soon,' Ishaan assures him, without missing a beat. 'Very soon.'

'Ishaan!' Tinka's face is incandescent.

'What?' He turns to look at her, very casual.

'You *can't just*—'

Ishaan smiles and turns back to Leo.

'You must come,' he says. 'We'll need a photographer.'

'What are you *talking* ab—'

'Oh shut up, wench.' Julian squeezes her arm. 'Let the lad be masterful! He's a decorated hero, or will be soon enough – ah, here comes your admirer!'

Sure enough, Nikka's motorcade has arrived. As it zooms past them to the IAF de Havilland Dove parked a distance away, Tinka turns to Ishaan.

'So, I'll see you, then,' she says lightly.

He nods. 'Yes. You'll…' He pauses, his eyes raking her face. 'You'll come to Delhi? From Islamabad? Not run off to America or something?'

She laughs. 'Yes! I mean no, I mean I'll come straight to Delhi.'

'Good. I'll come see your father.'

She frowns. 'Shaanu, no—'

'Hello hello, is this the Gnattie from Kalaiganga?'

The deep jovial voice makes them both turn around. A well-fed-looking man with a ruddy, weathered face and a walrus moustache is looking at Ishaan quizzically. He is dressed for flying, his uniform bears the stripes of a Squadron Leader, and his nametag proclaims him to be Deepak Jolly.

'You Faujdaar?'

Ishaan snaps to attention. 'Yes, sir!'

Jolly puts out his hand. 'I'm flying this baby to Isloo. We've heard a lot about you at Hashimara, young man. Did you really take three Sabres out of the sky? Confirmed kills?'

'Yes, sir!'

'Excellent! Recommended for a PVC, eh?'

'My CO said so, sir.'

'And dating a supermodel.' Jolly looks at Tinka with open admiration. 'Bhai wah! Yaaaaar, you're a *star*.'

Shaanu grins. 'Yes, sir!'

Jolly chuckles. 'Superb! Tell me all about it on the flight!'

Ishaan and Tinka look at him, confused.

'I'm not on this flight, sir,' Ishaan says regretfully.

'Nonsense!' declares Jolly. 'I've got an empty seat – and I demand you take it!'

'But, sir, my orders are to stay put and proceed to Delhi tomorrow…'

'I'll get you back before midnight!' Jolly says. 'C'mon!'

Shaanu turns to look at Tinka.

'Come,' she says softly.

Ishaan turns backs to Jolly.

'It would be an honour, sir.'

• • •

'So there we were, cornered in the bedroom...' Shaanu pauses, worried about how this may sound, then carefully clarifies, 'Not that there was any *hanky-panky* going on, of course, nothing like that, she was just trying to protect me – when *suddenly*, there was a knock on the door! Pakistanis!'

He stops – this is a major point in the story – and he's a little hassled that Jolly's only reaction to it is a small, muffled grunt. He had been so gung-ho during take-off, selecting Baaz as his call sign with a wink at Shaanu, but since then he's grown quieter and quieter. Ishaan shoots him an irritated look, then continues.

'And *then* this huge chopper tail rammed through the glass window like something out of a James Bond movie! All the glass shattered – of course we were shocked – but our shock was nothing compared to what the Pakistani buggers went through!'

Again, no reaction from Jolly. Not only is he not hanging on to every word that Ishaan is speaking, but humiliatingly, even his eyes seem to be drooping. Slightly concerned now, Ishaan reaches out and touches his shoulder.

'Sir?'

Deepak Jolly slumps over his seatbelt, his eyelids fluttering back to reveal eyes that have rolled back into his head.

'Sir!'

Ishaan lunges forward, grabs Jolly's clammy fist and finds a thread of a pulse. Cursing, he flips on the R/T.

'Baaz to Base,' he says, praying he's still in range of Tezgaon ATR. 'Emergency – our pilot's ill!'

There is an agonizingly long pause.

'Baaz to Base? *Baaz to Base!*'

Finally, a voice comes crackling over the airwaves.

'How very unfortunate.' It is Bangla-accented and vaguely familiar. 'What appears to have happened to him?'

'Unconscious. Pulse weak, skin clammy, whites of his eyes showing,' Shaanu rattles off the symptoms impatiently. 'What do you advise?'

'Sounds like he's a goner.' The voice tut-tuts chattily. 'Poor Squadron Leader Jolly.'

Ishaan stares at the R/T in confused frustration. 'What?'

'So how are you still flying?' Smoothly, the voice becomes business-like.

'Good question!' Shaanu scans the controls. 'We're on autopilot, I think – but that's okay. I can fly this plane if I have to. If you help me.'

'You're a pilot?' the voice asks, then grows sharper. 'I thought there were no other pilots on the flight!'

'Flying Officer Ishaan Faujdaar, IAF,' Ishaan replies crisply. 'Who is this, please?'

'Baazzzz!' For some reason the voice makes the hair at the back of Shaanu's neck stand up on end. 'You shouldn't be on that plane, bugger.'

A cold finger of premonition runs down Shaanu's spine. He knows this voice.

'Macho da?'

There is a small pause and then a cold, creepy and very drunk chuckle fills the small cockpit. 'Yes. It is I – Major General Maqhtoom Khan.'

Consternation floods Ishaan. 'What are you doing in the Tezgaon ATR tower? And how did you go from major to major general?'

The Mukti chuckles. 'I gave *myself* a promotion in anticipation of what I'm going to do next.'

'Oh yeah?' Shaanu rears up to his feet inside the cramped cockpit. 'And *what* is that, maadarchod?'

'I drugged your pilot.' The Mukti giggles. 'Or, to be more exact – Harry did. They had a glass of fresh coconut water together before take-off...'

Ishaan slams down both palms on the control panel. 'But why?'

'Because Nikka must die.' As Macho da's voice grows dreamy and sing-song, the sense of being trapped in a nightmare grows even strongly on Ishaan. 'So we nobbled his pilot – and we jammed a massive firecracker up the arse of his little plane. Something Front Room has been working on for several months. It should blow up in...' he pauses, checking something, 'twenty-seven minutes exactly.'

Fuck.

Ishaan curls and uncurls his fists helplessly, staring at the laboriously breathing Jolly and, with a sickening feeling, at the ocean appearing below them. Jolly had taken off in a southerly direction and should have turned his nose westwards towards Islamabad a few minutes after take-off. Already woozy from whatever fiendish drug Harry Rose had plied him with, he hadn't done this. They are now flying over the Bay of Bengal.

'I like you, Baaz,' Macho da says, his voice growing fainter as the signal weakens. 'You're a good soldier. And your girl's a pretty thing. Ah well, can't be helped. Collateral damage and all that. Khuda Hafiz.'

SIXTEEN

I am a warrior, fighting is my Dharma,
I will train my mind, body and spirit to fight,
I will excel in all devices and weapons of war –
present and future, I will always protect the weak,
I will be truthful to bluntness,
I will be humane, cultured and compassionate,
I will fight and embrace the consequences,
God, give me strength that I ask nothing of you.

(Code of the Warrior,
National Defence Academy, Khadakwasla)

SEVENTEEN

Staring broodingly out of his window, General Nikka Khan notices that the plane is flying over water. Too sunk in sullen despair to comment, he listens with dim detachment as the pilot's vibrant voice speaks through the speakers.

'Ladies and gentlemen, there's been a slight glitch – this aircraft needs to be landed immediately. Please put on your seatbelts and assume the brace position.'

Even as Nikka feels about for his seatbelt, a female figure runs past him into the cockpit and slams the door shut behind her.

'What's wrong with the plane?'

Ishaan looks around. His grey eyes are shining with a queer, pulsing gleam that Tinka's never seen before. She stares at him, then notices Jolly, slumped over behind him, and sucks in her breath hard.

'Ah, you're here,' Shaanu says, in an oddly calm voice. 'I was going to announce for you to come to me.'

'Ishaan, what's wrong?'

'Nothing much,' he says unhurriedly. 'Jolly's unwell.'

'What!' She lays her hand on the pilot's clammy forehead. *'How?'*

Ishaan doesn't reply.

Tinka stares at him. There's more to the situation, she can tell.

'And?' she demands.

He shrugs, fiddling with the R/T.

'And there's a bomb on the plane.'

She slumps against the plastic bulkhead.

'No!'

'Yes.' Ishaan nods grimly. 'Macho da's little mission is finally unfolding. We just spoke. He says we have twenty-seven minutes before this thing blows.' He glances down at his watch. 'Make that twenty-four.'

'Shit.' She stares down at the laboriously breathing Jolly for a moment, then turns to Ishaan. 'Shaanu, we *have* to save Nikka. If he blows up now, in an *Indian* plane, the fighting will break out again. Thousands will die.'

He stares at her, the queer glow in his eyes growing tender. 'You are so … predictable.'

She pushes her hair off her face, her palms are clammy. 'Can you land this thing?'

He grins. She gets the oddest feeling that he's enjoying himself. 'Oh, yes. But I've got to do it quick.'

She balls her hands into sweaty fists.

'But where will you land it?'

'I've radioed a general request for emergency landing,' he says, his eyes back on the controls. 'There are at least two aircraft carriers and a helicopter carrier bobbing about in the Bay right now. It's a regular party – somebody's got to have a runway we can use, especially with Nikka, so many Americans and even a Russian on board. They should be getting back to me, any moment.'

Tinka's face lightens. 'Brilliant!'

The R/T squawks to life. A young American drawl fills the cabin.

'This is the *USS Enterprise* calling Baaz. Come in, Baaz.'

Ishaan leans in.

'Baaz to *Enterprise*. Give me some good news, man!'

'Baaz,' the young voice drawls. 'I am the LSO aboard the *USS Enterprise*...'

'Lasso?' Shaanu says lightly.

'Landing Signals Officer. We have been granted permission to land you.'

Shaanu throws up his hands in relief.

'Yessss!'

'Have you ever landed a plane on an aircraft carrier before?'

'No,' Shaanu admits. 'But I hear there's not much to it!'

'Typical Air Force talk,' says the voice reprovingly. 'Landing on a carrier is a specialized, hazardous business, requiring very specific training—'

'Typical Navy speak,' Shaanu retorts immediately. Then he sobers. 'I know it's tricky, brother – I'm counting on you to bring me home.'

'I'll do my damnedest to help. What aircraft are you flying?'

'De Havilland Dove.'

'That's good. The Dove has short-field landing capability, but we'll still need to do a barricade landing – d'you know how that works?'

But before Ishaan can reply, the R/T squawks again and a gravelly, guttural voice fills the cockpit.

'*Novorossiysk* to Baaz. Come in, Baaz. Come in, please.'

'What the hell?' Shaanu stares down at the R/T blankly. 'Novo ... uh ... russi? Yeah, this is Baaz. Tell me!'

'Baaz...' the Russian voice crackles. 'You have on board the Pakistani general?'

'Yes!' Shaanu replies, but before he can say anything else, the American voice comes back on the R/T.

'Repeat – do you know how a barricade landing works?'

Shaanu nods. 'Yes, if it's the same as our barrier engagement process, but talk me through your on-board procedure.'

'Okay. Basically, when you approach the stern of the ship, you'll see something like a large tennis net stretched out across the flight deck. That's the barricade – it's to help you decelerate. It's about twenty feet high, and the webbing's reinforced with steel. Just slam right into the thing.'

'Like a lousy tennis shot.'

Shaanu's voice is so flippant that Tinka looks at him worriedly. Isn't he taking all this too lightly? Then she looks down at his hands. They're rock-steady.

'Your Dove is lighter than our C-2 Greyhounds, so we're confident we can catch you. As soon as you know you're engaging, chop your throttles and stand on your brakes. But if you feel you're not stopping, keep speeding and go round again for a second try.'

But that's so confusing! Tinka thinks, feeling sick to the stomach. Should he focus on slowing down, or on taking off again? How will he decide? Don't they need special training to *do* all this?

Ishaan just nods. 'Okay.'

'O-kei.'

Shaanu and Tinka stare at each other in dismay. The guttural Russian voice is back! Comprehensively drowning out the American, it says, 'The *Novorossiysk* is an atomic submarine, part of the 10th Operative Battle Group, Pacific Fleet, deployed out of Vladivostok with the express purpose of preventing American and British ships from getting closer to Indian military objects. We possess a good number of nuclear-armed ships and atomic submarines, but our missile range is 300km or less. How can we help you, Baaz?'

'If you're a submarine, you can't,' Shaanu says brutally.

Tinka shoots him a reproachful look.

'What?' he demands, indicating the R/T helplessly. 'Is this a war-zone or a free-for-all party? Where did Lasso go?'

Right on cue, the American's voice fills the cockpit again.

'Of course, there *is* a chance that the explosive device on your plane may go off on impact...'

Oh *wow!* thinks Tinka, quite at the end of her tether. What a little ray of sunshine he is.

'So it's imperative that you land very very softly. That's tough because you've never done this before and may misjudge the distance. It takes a pilot about twenty landings to get it right – but that's a chance we're all gonna have to take.'

She throws up her hands at this, but Ishaan just nods coolly. 'Okay.'

'That's it. We're waiting for you. There's a bomb-defusing squad on standby and a helo for General Khan.'

And with that, the R/T goes quiet.

Ishaan turns to look at Tinka and smiles encouragingly.

'I'll get you down safe, don't worry.'

She shakes her head.

'I'm not worried. Except...' She looks down at the sweating Jolly. 'Is this poor man going to die?'

'Nobody's going to die,' Ishaan replies, his eyes back on the controls. Then he jerks his head towards the rear of the plane. 'How are things back there?'

She shrugs.

'Sweaty and silent. They've guessed something is hideously wrong, I think. How much time do we have?'

'Twenty-seven minus...' Shaanu glances at the dials. 'Ten. So that's seventeen more minutes to go – unless Front Room messed up somehow.'

'Could Macho da be bluffing?' she says suddenly. 'Oh, God, please let him be bluffing!'

'It's possible,' Shaanu admits, frowning 'He's such a dark, twisted fucker, I wouldn't put it past him. Well, we'll know soon enough.'

He leans forward and speaks into the R/T.

'Baaz to *Enterprise*, circling overhead. Come in *Enterprise*.'

The LSO's voice replies comfortingly, 'Right below you, Baaz, baby. Come to mommy.'

I should be afraid, Tinka thinks as she looks below and sees the warship – 75,000 tonnes of reinforced metal, stubby, grey and curiously flat-headed – like an ugly piece of disembodied tarmac cutting through the churning waters below. I should be absolutely petrified. Why aren't I afraid?

She knows the answer, of course. She's not afraid because she's with Ishaan. And Ishaan, clearly, is on top of this.

He's speaking into the PA now.

'Okay, ladies and gentlemen, as you can probably see, we're flying right over the pride of America's Seventh Fleet, the nuclear-powered aircraft carrier *USS Enterprise*! Touchdown in ten seconds ... hold on tight now. Ten ... nine ... eight...'

The ship is too close too quick, Tinka thinks as the plane drops sickeningly, he's going to overshoot it.

'And ... *one* more time!' Shaanu's voice is cheerful and unperturbed. He noses the plane up and circles over the *Enterprise* again, which from this distance seems way too small and is moving far too much on the heaving seas.

In the front row of the tiny cabin, Nikka Khan starts to mutter some long-forgotten suras from the Holy Quran.

The plane descends again. People moan with their heads between their thighs, a shriek emerges from Nikka Khan's throat, Tinka shuts her eyes tight...

They hit the ship with a deafening, bone-rattling thud and career madly down the deck at full speed. The steel reinforced net slaps onto the snout of the plane, darkening the cockpit and obscuring Shaanu and Tinka's vision. She clutches him, shaken and disoriented, feeling like she's plummeting down a tunnel into total oblivion.

'Slow down!' Nikka shouts thinly, his eyes bulging. 'We're going too fast – who's the fool in command?'

The barricade won't hold us, Tinka thinks, nauseated. We're going to pitch into the water at the other end, explode...

She stares up at the cockpit's perspex, waiting hypnotized for the net to rip ... she can see the fibres tearing ... parting...

And then there is a tremendous backward jerk as the barricade finally manages to constrain the plane. Everybody screams.

With a slow, horribly grating moan, the Dove slithers sideways, slows down and shudders to a stop.

There is a moment of complete, shell-shocked silence.

Then, as whooping and applause break out in the cabin, Tinka gets to her feet and tries to hug Shaanu, but he pushes her away.

'Get out, Tinka.' His voice is sharp. 'Get out and *run.*'

'Shut up,' she whispers firmly, locking her arms around his waist and kissing him hard.

Wordlessly, he hugs her back. His hands are shaking.

Behind them, there is a mad scramble for the door. Nikka

and his officers exit in unseemly haste, tripping a little over the shredded barricade. The journalists follow. As soon as the doorway is clear, uniformed men enter the cockpit, lift the still-breathing Jolly and bear him away. Tinka and Shaanu come out behind him, and are greeted by a tall, young man the colour of dark chocolate.

'Nicely done, Baaz,' he says, showing very white teeth.

'Lasso!' Ishaan exclaims. 'Good directions, boss!'

'Good flying,' replies the LSO. Then adds patronizingly, 'For an Air Force booter.'

They clasp hands, grinning.

'The bomb squad's going in,' the LSO continues, nodding at the scene unfolding behind them. 'That area's being evacuated – come away please – what *the* – excuse me, sir, step away from the 'craft please, *what do you think you're doing?*'

Because a lanky figure has clambered on to the wing of the Dove and is busily snapping photographs of the bomb squad at work.

Tinka gives a little gurgle of laughter. 'It's Leo,' she says. 'Getting a scoop. Oh, typical!'

The LSO hurries away towards the intently clicking photographer, gesticulating furiously. As Tinka and Shaanu turn to each other, laughing, Julian Arnott comes stumping up.

'I *like* this young man,' he declares. 'Tinka, if you don't marry him, *I* will!'

'Hands off my man, Julian,' she says, her voice trembling just a little, as she takes in how fragile the old man looks. 'Thank *God* you're safe!'

'Well, of course, I'm safe!' he replies. Then he points towards the front of the ship, where a chopper is being readied for take-off. 'The fool's missing the best photograph, as usual – of that dastard Nikka fleeing the scene, his tail between his legs.'

He stumps away to get Leo, and Tinka and Shaanu turn to look at the chopper. Nikka is standing outside it, mopping his forehead with a large white handkerchief and asking querulously about the estimated time of departure. Tinka stares up at him indignantly.

'Did he even *thank* you?' she asks Shaanu.

He laughs. 'No!'

Her eyes kindle.

'The dog! But he *will*,' she says determinedly. 'I'll write a story, *now, tonight* – people must know how brave you were!'

He rocks on his heels, grinning.

'You do realize that everybody will say you're biased?'

'Why?' she demands.

'Because I'm your...' He stops, his forehead wrinkling, and cocks one eyebrow. 'Hmm, what am I of yours exactly?'

Her cheeks go hot, but she pulls his ear with remarkable aplomb.

'Slave,' she suggests. 'Sex Toy. Puppy.'

He laughs and pulls her to him.

'You mean hero,' he whispers into her ear. 'Saviour. Husband.'

Tinka is laughing, but at this, she goes still. She pulls back a little, shaking her hair out of her eyes and looking up at him wonderingly.

'Seriously?'

'Uh huh.' He nods, grey eyes sparkling. 'Come live with me in my two-room quarter and do private dances for me under my shower every night.'

Her lashes flutter down to her cheeks, but she raises her chin gamely.

'Jat.'

'That's not an answer.'

She wrinkles her forehead. 'Will I get to see bare-chested boxing practice?'

'Arrey!' His arms tighten about her. 'What a question! Promise! Every *single nigh—*'

A cheer goes up behind them. Ishaan looks up, grinning.

'I think they've managed to defuse the bomb. Hey, Lasso!'

The LSO is hurrying past them, but he stops.

'Defusing proved impossible,' he reports crisply. 'The damn thing's unnecessarily, obscenely potent and the circuitry's super-complex. Whoever designed it is a monster – and also, fiendishly clever!'

Shaanu thinks back to Front Room, his shuffling gait, his blank, saintly eyes, that kurta flapping over bare, defenceless-looking thighs, and for once, is at an absolute loss for words.

'But we did manage to tinker with it enough to delay the explosion for a further ten minutes. So now we can chuck it in the drink and sail a long, *safe* distance away before it blows.'

'That's good!' Shaanu nods, fervently. 'Well done, USA!'

But the LSO is looking behind him, smirking. 'And here comes the USSR. We did consider the possibility, given Maqhtoom Khan's background, that the bomb could have a Soviet-style fuse. We knew the *Novorossiysk* was nosing about in the vicinity, of course, though we were pretending we didn't, so we contacted them. Here they are, now...' He grins. 'Lemme go rub in the fact that we don't need their help.'

He lopes ahead, rubbing his hands together gleefully,

to where the Soviet squad, a dour, stocky, ruddy-cheeked crew, is already examining the canister containing the bomb, talking to each other in guttural, animated Russian, shaking their heads and pulling long faces.

'Thanks for dropping by, gentlemen,' the LSO says condescendingly. 'We won't be needing your assistance howev—'

'Glupyy,' says one Russian, interrupting him rudely.

'Idiyot,' says a second, in execrable English.

'Gandu,' chimes in a third, making the conversation very global indeed.

The LSO blinks. 'Excuse me?'

The first Russian speaks up again, very slowly, like he is talking to a moron.

'This ... bomb ... have waterr-trirggerred fuse. If you thrrrow in the waterr, it blow at *once*. Vairry big kaboom.'

• • •

'Gentlemen, the only way to get this damn thing off our boat is to stick it into a C-2 and cat-shoot it outta here. The pilot will take it up, reach an altitude from which he can abandon the aircraft safely, then para-jump using a static line.'

Smoothly, the crew of the *Enterprise* sets the plan into motion. The Grumman C-2 Greyhound, a small Carrier Onboard Delivery 'craft with multi-engine turboprops, is wheeled to catapult station number 1 and rigged up swiftly and smoothly.

'That seems like the Avro 748s I flew in Kanpur,' Ishaan says interestedly, as the pilot, a youngish boy with short, sandy hair comes striding up, popping a stick of gum into his mouth.

'All the best, buddy.' Ishaan puts out a hand.

The pilot smiles briefly but doesn't take his hand, walking

up to the C-2 and getting into the cockpit. The bomb squad moves in to secure the canister into the belly of the C-2, and then suddenly, their leader gives a sudden cry.

'The delay didn't work!' he shouts hoarsely. 'The circuit's reconfigured itself! This thing will blow in one hundred and eighty seconds!'

Tinka always remembers everything that happens after that in stark, slow motion.

The four propeller blades of the C-2 start to whirl.

The pilot bursts out of the cockpit and staggers to the ground, his face ashen.

'I can't,' he pants. 'It's suicide.'

Everybody stares at everybody else, slack-jawed in horror, and then, as one, they start to run as far away as possible from the doomed plane.

As people stream past him, taking cover from the coming explosion, Ishaan Faujdaar starts to walk towards the rigged and ready plane.

She clutches at his shirt.

'Where are you going?' She means to say it in a normal voice, but it comes out like a scream. 'Ishaan, don't ... *please...*'

He turns.

'But then all these people will die.'

Tears roll down her cheeks.

'They're Americans. And Pakistanis, not *your* people.'

He cocks his head to one side and smiles whimsically. 'People are just people.'

She's sobbing now.

'*Don't...*'

But he is already looking beyond her at the doomed C-2.

'*Doggggfighhht,*' he mutters lightly, squaring his shoulders.

'Shaanu...'

He turns.

'Oh, listen, make sure Sneha does a B.Ed., okay?'

Then he puts her aside and runs lightly to the plane.

The fleeing crew watches him pass in stunned disbelief, then stumble and almost fall as Tinka barrels through them, screaming.

'No, Shaanu, *no ... Wait for me!*'

He swings into the plane and stops at the door to watch her run to him.

Tinka runs faster than she has ever run in her life. She feels every muscle straining as her feet push down upon the metal deck, then rise up again to move forward, step after massive step. Her hair gets in her eyes, her mouth opens, her hands reach out...

Ishaan holds out his hand to her.

She smiles up at him, relieved, a happy implet with darling dimplets. It's going to be okay – he's waiting for her, they'll go out together! She reaches out for him with both hands, he bends forward...

And then his right hand smacks full into her chest, between her breasts, sending her spinning backwards.

She looks down and blinks, reeling with disbelief and betrayal, as she falls back onto the ground in an awkward spill.

The deck is cold and hard. She gasps, winded, and looks up, her vision blurring from the tears welling from her eyes, and sees the beloved grey eyes staring down at her, sparkling with regret and apology and love.

And then he's gone.

A second later, the steam cat shoots the C-2 straight into the brilliant blue sky.

The deck combusts into spontaneous, heartfelt applause; Americans, Russians and Pakistanis raise their arms in a farewell salute.

Freed from the catapult, the C-2 climbs till it vanishes, all sight and sound of it gone, and there is nothing to see but empty sky and nothing to hear but a surprised seagull or two and the lazy slap of water against the flanks of the *USS Enterprise*.

Tinka hugs her knees, her entire body wracked with sobs, then tilts back her head and says goodbye.

Above the brilliantly blue Bay of Bengal, Ishaan's plane soars like a bird of prey. It is a bulky, weighty thing, but it proceeds to do a series of improbable zoom climbs – first one, tentatively, then two, then several in a row. It weaves crazily through the air, and if you were up there, at that altitude, you would have heard the pilot whooping with the sheer joy of being alive.

Sunshine catches the strengthened perspex of its cockpit, glittering like a benediction, the slanting rays reminiscent of the bhavishyavanis depicted in the Amar Chitra Katha comics that have taken the nation by storm. Then there is a blinding burst of orange flame and the plane is gone.

EPILOGUE

The golden jubilee reunion of the class of '68 takes place on a sultry June afternoon at the IAF Officers' Institute in Jodhpur. Old men in sharp suits, jaunty ties and dashing berets (so useful for hiding thinning hair) trickle in on unsteady feet, dragging along wives, children and grandchildren, eager excitement in their rheumy old eyes. What had been a batch of fifty has dwindled to thirty-seven – crashes, conflicts and illnesses have claimed the rest. One officer is in a wheelchair, another is having chemotherapy, several are divorced, one is dressed in a jaunty red T-shirt emblazoned with the legend IAF – *Insane As Fuck*. They stand around in little knots on the lush-green lawn, whooping, back-slapping, talking over each other, while their children and grandchildren sit on the chairs that ring the edge of the lawn, marvelling at their grandfathers behaving as boisterously as schoolboys.

'Thata's in really good form, huh!' whispers one jean-clad little girl to her mother in a distinctly Californian accent.

'He's so happy… It's kinda cute, actually.'

'Your father says he used to be this very dashing pilot,

once,' her mother replies in a slightly bored voice. 'He won a big gallantry medal for crashing a helicopter into a building.'

The girl's eyes widen. 'You mean like *nine-eleven*?'

'Oh, I don't think it was quite like *that*...' Her mother clarifies, her voice sounding a little harassed. 'Go fix your hair in the bathroom, honey, it's gotten all untidy.'

The little girl leaps up and makes her way across the lawn, her shaggy black ponytail swinging. About halfway across, she is yanked to a halt by Air Commodore Madan Subbiah.

Maddy is seventy years old now – his family recently celebrated the big birthday with a cruise through the Mediterranean countries. He has lost some hair and some height, but he is still an imposing man. Kainaz Dadyseth's prophecy has come true, however – his high cheekbones *have* packed on the fat, and he has begun to faintly resemble a chipmunk.

Now he hooks his granddaughter by the loop of her jeans and spins her around.

'Say hello to my friends Group Captain Aggarwal and Mrs Aggarwal. You can call them Raka uncle and Juhi auntie. Esha is visiting India for the first time, folks.'

Juhi auntie, plump and pretty, smiles down at the little girl.

'Here, let me fix your hair, beta,' she says, extracting a hairbrush from a capacious bag and suiting her actions to her words. Esha winces but submits. When it comes to desi people intruding on your personal space, she has realized, resistance is futile.

Raka uncle, a fat, smiling man with a very black moustache, leans on his gold-topped walking stick and enquires if she would like to see the swimming pool.

Esha sniffs, unimpressed.

'What's so great about a pool?' she asks, with a toss of her re-tied ponytail. 'We hardly use ours. It costs a thousand dollars to clean every summer, so many leaves and snakes get into it! Mum's planning to turn it into a lily pond.'

'Ah, but this is a *special* pool,' says Raka uncle persuasively, nudging her away from his wife and down the garden path. 'This used to be our Flying College, you know. It got converted into an Officers' Institute only recently.'

They round the corner, her grandfather close behind, and it comes to them, the slap of water against cement and the sharp reek of chlorine. Esha tilts up her chin, rocks back on her heels and lets out a low, impressed whistle.

'That's quite a diving board.'

The old men stand next to her and gaze up at the monstrous metal spider squatting over the pool with dreamy eyes.

'Yeahhh.'

Esha squints up at the thing.

'Did you jump off the very top of it when you were young?'

She says this like she's talking of the age when dinosaurs still walked the earth.

'Yes,' Thata replies. 'The very top.' After a pause, he confesses, 'It was scary, but I could do it 'coz my friends did it.'

Esha tilts her head to one side quizzically.

'If your friends jumped off a cliff, would you jump too?'

'Without a second thought,' Madan Subbiah replies unhesitatingly.

Meanwhile, Group Captain Aggarwal is leaning on his walking stick and gazing up at the diving board, his thoughts clearly far away. 'Woh bhi kya din thhey,' he sighs heavily. 'Hum kitne thin thhey. Hey, I've got to have a prostrate operation next week, Maddy. Have you had one?'

'Not yet.' Subbiah grimaces. 'I'm still intact. But it'll come to that, sooner or later. Come, baby girl, let's head back – the speeches are starting.'

And indeed, they can hear the sound of the mic being tapped and tuned. The two old men walk slowly – partly because they're old and partly because they want to linger – and enter the hall, where chairs have been set up in rows in front of a screen.

An audio-visual plays footage of their passing-out ceremony mixed with black-and-white photographs sourced by the organizing committee headed by Wing Commander Gonsalves. This committee has been very busy mailing, nagging and badgering people and their families for months to ensure that no batchmate has been missed out or forgotten. All the pictures draw murmurs, sighs, oohs and aahs, but the loudest whoops are reserved for one particular individual. Esha, staring up at the screen, decides she likes him – he has a young, laughing face, sparkling grey eyes and the kind of clothes she likes – bright and tight.

'Have your parents told you who that is?' Thata nods to the figure on the screen.

Esha shakes her head.

'He's a big hero,' her grandfather continues. 'If you went to school in India instead of in stupid America, you would've read about him in your textbooks. There's even a road named after him! It links Delhi to Haryana.'

The film ends with a smiling close-up of the nice young man's face. Under the picture are the words:

Pride of the batch of '68

Flying Officer Baaz Faujdaar
Param Vir Chakra
Nishaan-e-Azmat
Bir Putro
Medal of Valour
Lion of the Soviet Union

Esha doesn't understand what most of these mean, but she does know what a medal of valour is. Thata isn't exaggerating – this dude had been hot stuff.

Then an old gent with a hearing aid and a big paunch, whom everybody has been calling Gunner, begins to speak.

'Ladies and gentlemen, it's so good to see all of you! As always, we'd like to close the function with our combined donation cheque to the Baaz Foundation, which provides free schooling, health and housing to children all over rural India. Thank you very much for your generous contribution.'

'Is the foundation run by Baaz's family?' Esha asks.

'Yes,' Thata replies. 'The main school campus is on a fifteen-acre plot the government bequeathed Baaz for being so brave.'

Esha doesn't know what *beqweed* is, nor what an acre is, so she just nods.

Gunner continues to speak, wheezing a little.

'We now request the trustees of the Foundation, Mrs Sneha Singh, chairperson of the renowned chain of Chakkahera Public Schools, and Mrs Tehmina Dadyseth-Khan, Director, Amnesty International, South East Asia and the Pacific, to please accept the cheque.'

Two elderly ladies enter the room now. One is placid and clad in a yellow sari, while the other is more eye-catchingly dressed in a deep-green tunic. She has grey hair, bright red lipstick and a flower in her hair.

'You speak.' Her voice is assured and determinedly cheerful.

'You speak, Sneha! You do all the work anyway – I travel so much I'm hardly of any use to you!'

Saying which, she hugs the other woman and walks to the back of the room, her eyes searching the gathering eagerly.

'Over here!' Juhi auntie throws up one hand and waves animatedly. 'Over here, Tinka!'

Tinka's eyes light up when she sees Juhi. She rushes over, laughing, and everybody scooches up and lets her sit. She's a hugger, Esha realizes, hugging Thata and Raka uncle and Juhi auntie at least three times each.

Meanwhile, the other lady has started to make a speech. She talks of how providing quality education to village children had always been her dream, one that her brother had funded, and how many awards CPS has won, and other blah things like that. She has one of those soothing, rhythmic voices that always cause Esha's attention to wander.

She smothers a yawn, her eyes wandering back to the young man frozen on the screen. He looks like he would've found the speech boring too.

Esha tucks her arm into Thata's.

'He's cute,' she declares.

Her grandfather chuckles.

'All the girls thought so, too. Especially Tinka auntie – she was his girlfriend.'

Esha's head swivels around to the grey-haired lady sitting behind them. She frowns. 'Really?'

He chuckles again. 'Oh, she may not look like much now, but when she was young, she had a certain...'

'... *je ne sais quoi*,' Esha says knowledgeably.

'Exactly! Don't take my word for it. Just go on YouTube and search for the Freesia ad, original. It has more than eight million ticks.'

'You mean hits. But he looks more like he's my age than your age, no offence.'

'None taken. And you know what, you're right. Me and Raka and all of us, we're a bunch of old farts – but you and Baaz, you're young.' He lets out a gusty sigh. 'Heck, he's young forever.'

'How old was he when he died?'

'Twenty-four.'

She considers this for a moment, her brows furrowed.

'That's a bit young to die,' she says finally. 'I want to die when I'm *really* old, like thirty.'

Raka uncle, who's been listening carefully, sitting on the other side of her, winces at this. 'Ouch, how old are you now?'

A defensive look crosses her face. 'Ten,' she mutters. 'I don't look it, I know. All the kids in my class are like four times my size.'

'Oh, size is nothing!' he assures her. 'In fact, I can tell you a secret that'll ensure you never feel bad about being short again!'

Her eyes light up.

'What?'

Raka bends lower. 'Baaz wasn't too tall, you know. And here's what he taught us – it's one of the scientific principles on which the world is built! Look!' He holds out his hand, thumb extended. 'Big guy, small—'

Then he comes to an abrupt halt.

Esha stares at him wide-eyed.

'Big?' she prompts enquiringly.

'Haan, haan, *tell* her, na,' Juhi auntie entreats from beside him, her black eyes dancing. 'Cut off our noses in front of Maddy's snooty American family! Why did you stop, Raks?'

'Never mind,' says Raka, straightening up, looking rather red-faced.

'Tell me!' Esha demands, dismayed.

'No no...' Raka mops his forehead.

Paunchy Gunner hollers from the front, 'Oi, MiGGie, pipe down! You bloody backbenchers haven't changed a bit!'

Everybody starts to laugh, including the lady who's holding the mic. Esha swivels her eyes to stare gleefully at her grandfather.

'You were a *backbencher*?'

'Shush!' he growls hastily. 'Settle down now!'

Esha hunches, crossing her arms over her chest.

'But I want to know what Baaz taught you!'

The lady who likes to hug people leans in and hugs Esha now. She smells really nice. Like a border of springtime flowers.

'He taught us that size doesn't matter, darling,' she whispers.

The little girl, who has been squirming in her seat, stills at this.

'It doesn't?'

Tinka shakes her head firmly.

'Nope. It doesn't matter how short you are, or how short your lifetime is. Why, I'm sixty-seven years old now, and I *still* haven't done half as much as Baaz managed to do in just twenty-four!'

Something in the lady's voice makes Esha hug her back hard.

'Do you miss him?' she asks in a whisper.

Tinka sighs.

'Every day.'

A NOTE ON HISTORICAL ACCURACY

Kalaiganga is a fictitious Air Force station, based on the real-life Kalaikunda. Kalaikunda did not get bombed on the infamous night of 3 December 1971, Kalaiganga did. The pilots in this novel speak a little more on the R/T than pilots do in real life and, occasionally, fly solo on planes that would require two pilots. The character of Nikka Khan is completely fictitious, loosely based on General Niazi and General Tikka Khan. Sarhind Club does not exist. 34 Squadron-The Streaks does not exist and is loosely based on 22 Squadron-The Swifts. The Battle of Boyra is real, and happened pretty much as described in the book. The cratering of Tezgaon is loosely accurate too, and was carried out mostly by the MiGs of 4 and 28 Squadron. All IAF pilots in this story are entirely fictitious. Deeds done by them were actually done by real soldiers, with real names, of whom the author and the nation are very proud. The climax is entirely imagined, but does exist in the delicious realm of 'could have been'.

Anuja Chauhan
March 2017

ACKNOWLEDGEMENTS

I was born a year before the events described in this book. Seven men from my family were serving officers during the '71 war. War talk dominated our dining table. But in a very casual, matter-of-fact way. The way business people would discuss year-ending taxes or festival-time rush. In fact, till I was thirteen, I thought the world was neatly divided into Defence folk and civilians (who, of course, were lesser beings). In fact, I still think so.

Dhaula Kuan, S.P. Marg, Pratap Chowk, Dinjan, Burdong, Chandimandir – these places were gated communities before India discovered gated communities, with flowering trees, well-brushed dogs, swimming pools and May Queen balls. It was a beautiful world – and the shiniest, most glamorous things there were the handsome, good-natured, fit young officers. They fascinated me.

And so this book, born out of my love for all things fauji.

It couldn't have been written without those initial, weekend-long briefings from the Fighters in my family – my much-larger-than-life uncle Wing Commander Rajendra Singh Rajput, the hero of every child in our family, who motored up from Meerut himself at the ripe old age of eighty-six to meet me, and my dashing light-eyed cousin Group Captain Ashok Kumar Singh, VrC, still so fit at seventy-six. Thank you so much, Rajjan Mama. Thank you so much, Ashok Bhaisaab.

My nephew Wing Commander Naman Singh Bundela and his friend Squadron Leader Kartikeya Singh. Thank you, guys!

The very dapper and suave Wing Commander Jaggi Naath, MVC and bar, for giving me whiskey-paani and perspective at his lovely home in Juhu. Thank you, sir.

I gleaned information in large quantities from *Eagles over Bangladesh* by P.V.S. Jagan and Samir Chopra. And *India's Wars: A Military History* by Arjun Subramaniam. Thank you, gentlemen, it was a pleasure reading (and sourcing shamelessly) from your work.

I also trawled YouTube diligently and found a priceless recording of the real heroes of Boyra being feted by their juniors at what was clearly a rocking party.

But my most important source of all, my personal military Wikipedia, was K. Sree Kumar, who gave me all the technical terms and phrases and handheld me through the dogfights, quietly appalled at my ignorance, but always conspiring to keep it a secret from the rest of the world. Thanks a million, Sree. I owe you so much.

All mistakes made are mine alone. My source material was excellent.

Fully charged by the sources listed above, I started off with much vim and vigour and hammered out forty thousand words in four months. My mother was visiting from Australia for the summer, and we spent many lovely monsoon days drinking tea and gardening, discussing her fauji days and playing kot-piece with the children. She provided invaluable information on how life was for the ladies back then. She also bought me a garden swing. Thank you, Mummy.

And then she went back, randomly caught pneumonia and died.

It was horrifically sudden.

Her worst nightmare was that she would linger (khichdo was the word she used with a fastidious little shudder) and suffer and make her family suffer too. (As if!)

Well, that didn't happen. She departed all self-sufficient and dignified, her girlish good looks intact, with Papa, Mini, Ruhi and Nandu by her side and Anuja bawling her eyes out on FaceTime, with her son-in-laws licked into shape, and her ten grandchildren both devastated and inspired, musing that Nani knew how to live, of course – she was full of josh and joy always and made a gift of her full attention to anybody who wanted a chat – but also how, like Ma Baker, to die.

After she passed, I found I couldn't write.

And that's when my Ruhi didi tucked me into the guestroom bed in her lovely home in Osna, Queensland, fed me trifle pudding and 'superfood' juices and sarson ka saag and let me snivel and snot into her gorgeous bed linen and got me back into writing mode again. So thank you very especially, Ruhi didi.

The writing went steadily for a while and then, when I was almost done, my father, Lt Col. Revti Raman, got chikungunya and gave us all a horrible scare. He bounced back pretty soon but, robbed off his Global Gypsy status for a while, was confined to my home for almost two months, hence becoming a source I could draw upon freely. Thank you, Papa.

To my chacha Dr Rajendra Chauhan and my cousin Rishi Pratap Chauhan for their help with the Haryanvi.

To Ishan Roy, my son's kindergarten bestie, for letting me steal some of his awesome persona for Shaanu.

To V.K. Karthika for being her magical self. To Neelini Sarkar for her usual, obsessively meticulous editing. To Shantanu Ray Chaudhuri for *his* meticulous editing. And Joseph Antony for his painstaking work on the proofs. And to Ananth Padmanabhan, Amrita Talwar and Bonita Shimray of HarperCollins India for getting this book out so well.

Anupama Ramaswamy for another round of kick-ass covers to choose from. Sudip Bhattacharya for the photography and my gorgeous cover boy for being gorgeous.

To Choku, Nika, Tara and Daivik who put up with me on a daily basis as I slob about the house in my pyjamas, cranky and scummy eyed, grumbling that the piano's too loud, the dogs are barking too much and that the pressure cooker seeti is driving me crazy...

Thank you for patiently reading, feed-backing and keeping track of all the various drafts of the book ('Who is Raka now, I thought his name was Racy?' 'Huh, when did you move to Kalaikunda, this book was set in Pathankot!' 'Mamma, man, please don't write *randi randi randi*, what will my school friends say?')

And again to Choku, very especially, for magically resurrecting my MacBook after it got drenched in a freak accident, with the only file of *Baaz* lodged inside its sopping innards. Thank you, baby.

To you, dear reader, please do keep buying and reading, you keep me going.

And finally to the Holy Spirit. And Jesus Christ. And to God the Father Almighty, the creator of Heaven and Earth, the finest creative director of all – love and praise and gratitude.